CW00829505

CENTURY OF SONG

101 SONGS THAT SHAPED AMERICAN MUSIC

by

NOAH LEFEVRE

creator of **POLYPHONIC**

PAGE STREET
PUBLISHING CO.

PAGE STREET
PUBLISHING CO.

Copyright © 2024 Noah Lefevre

First published in 2024 by
Page Street Publishing Co.
27 Congress Street, Suite 1511
Salem, MA 01970
www.pagestreetpublishing.com

All rights reserved. No part of this book may be reproduced or used, in any form or by any means, electronic or mechanical, without prior permission in writing from the publisher.

Distributed by Macmillan, sales in Canada by The Canadian Manda Group.

28 27 26 25 24   1   2   3   4   5

ISBN-13: 979-8-89003-123-5

Library of Congress Control Number: 2023949678

Edited by Alexandra Murphy
Book design by Vienna Mercedes Gambol for Page Street Publishing Co.
Chapter artwork and cover by Noah Lefevre
To see the full list of photographer contributions, see pages 340-342
Sensitivity review by Renee Harleston

Printed and bound in China

Page Street Publishing protects our planet by donating to nonprofits like The Trustees, which focuses on local land conservation.

For my family, who inspired my love of music on long car rides; for my friends who nurtured it through late night conversations over too many beers; and for my wife, who helped it flourish from passion into profession.

CONTENTS

1950–1959

1960–1969

2000–2009

2010–2019

2020–2023

Introduction

I didn't set out to write a history of American music. In its earliest iteration, this book was little more than a thought experiment. I wanted to see if I could come up with one song that captured the aesthetic, political and historical spirit of a century of music. I decided that to allow the most voices to be represented, I would limit each artist to one song. When I started to get my hands dirty on the project, I realized that a story was emerging. It was the story of a musical tradition wrought in a complex history of triumph and trauma. It was a story of race relations, technological innovation and the enduring force of the human will. It was the story of America, as told through the myriad geniuses who combined to create its greatest cultural output.

Of course, this story is longer and more complex than I could possibly tell in 101 songs. So, what you're getting is just a small slice of the history of American pop music. It should be noted here that "pop" music is an ever-shifting thing, so when it is used, I am referring to music designed for commercial or popular consumption—which is to say most of the music created since the birth of the music industry. In the early years, that was a relatively homogenous music. But as the industry grew and new genres branched out, American music became as complex and diverse as its people. As a result,

> **The scale of music today is bigger than ever, but the human stories at its center remain eternal.**

there are countless scenes that I was barely able to touch upon in this book. Don't take this as a comprehensive look, but rather as an introductory glance.

If it sparks your interest, I implore you to dig deeper. My research for this project has enriched my own experience of music listening more than I ever imagined. For all the change and progress, the reality is that the elaborate pop and hip-hop of the modern age are only a few steps removed from a jazz and blues tradition that crawled out of the Mississippi Delta a century ago. The scale of music today is bigger than ever, but the human stories at its center remain eternal. In the pages that follow, you'll get a glimpse at some of those stories. You'll get to know many of the colorful characters who shaped popular music, and you'll (hopefully) leave with a better understanding of the complex systems of power that are intrinsically tied to the music we love.

I hope that this book helps you situate yourself and the music you love within history. I hope that it shows you new songs to obsess over, and I hope it deepens your relationship with songs you already love. Above all else, I hope that this book and the stories within can remind you of the power and capability that humankind has to forge the world in our own image, and to create a better place for one another.

An Industry Is Born

1923–29

What did music sound like a century ago? For the most part, that's a question that we don't really have a clear answer to. Recording technology first emerged in the mid- to late 1800s, but at the time, it was rudimentary and expensive, meaning only a small slice of the music being made was being recorded. As the century turned, sound got better and phonographs slowly became more affordable. Through the 1910s, more households got their hands on phonographs. At the same time, radio was starting to catch on, creating an early rivalry that would come to birth the record industry as we know it today.

By the 1920s, the fledgling industry was starting to boom. The biggest stars in early Broadway theater found themselves in recording booths and cut songs that in turn found their way into homes across the country. A nation that had once been defined by local folk scenes or touring vaudeville acts started to slowly creep toward a shared musical culture.

The first darling of the upstart recording industry was Al Jolson, whose dramatic belting and saccharine love ballads established the first wave of American popular music. He sang his way into the hearts of white America, but he did so by

1923

1924

1925

1926

building on a legacy of racist minstrel performances. Like many of his early pop contemporaries, Jolson was best known for blackface performance. Blackface was a style of minstrel performance that had gained popularity among white populations in the mid-1800s, thanks to a tradition of touring entertainers. The entire practice was built around white performers embodying deeply racist caricatures of Black people while covering their face with greasepaint or shoe polish.

One might be tempted to look back at Jolson and his ilk and dismiss them as a forgotten relic of a backward time, but the reality is not so simple. Racist performances created much of the model for a century of pop music stardom. You cannot have a true accounting of American musical history without discussing the racist traditions that birthed the music industry. The early pop stars were gifted and charismatic performers, but a very real aspect of their success was the fact that white audiences loved to watch them ridicule Black communities.

Even as racist performers were forming the foundation of the industry, new forms of Black American folk music were leaping forth from the Mississippi Delta, poised to conquer the musical world. The decade was still young when an explosion of blues records seized the industry, soon to be followed by seminal early recordings in country and folk. The roots of American popular music were starting to take hold across the country, delivered to Americans of all walks of life through radio and phonograph.

But there was one musical movement that reigned supreme through this exciting era of early American popular music: jazz.

As the American economy boomed, jazz erupted from the New Orleans bayou to stake its claim as the great American art form. Jazz seized the attention of Black and white audiences alike, putting early dents in America's long-standing racial barrier. By the end of the decade, jazz had nearly subsumed the entire recording industry and become the undisputed soundtrack to one of the most exciting eras in American history.

For all of the innovation that happened throughout the '20s, the decade will forever be seared into many people's hearts as the "Jazz Age."

1927

1928

1929

1923

"Downhearted Blues"

Bessie Smith

American popular music is a vast river that stretches out across time and space, branching into near-infinite diversions. Some of its tributaries are thin and winding, others are vast and churning, but each and every branch flows back to the same headwater: the blues.

Born from combining traditional West African folk music with work songs and spirituals, the blues began to take shape around the turn of the century. The blues spent its infancy growing up along the Mississippi Delta, serving as a voice for the everyday life of the Black diaspora. It wasn't until 1920 that blues truly started to explode. That year, singer Mamie Smith recorded a song called "Crazy Blues" for Okeh Records. That song sold over 100,000 copies and kicked off a nationwide blues craze. Performers from across the South saw an opportunity and started to head northward to seek their fame and fortune. One of these performers was Bessie Smith, who would soon be crowned "Empress of the Blues."

You don't get to lay claim to such an auspicious title without fighting a few battles. Luckily, Bessie Smith knew how

Her music was a clear celebration of her own Blackness and bisexuality.

to fight. As a queer Black woman living in the Jim Crow South, Smith had to spend much of her life fighting to justify her very existence. No story better exemplifies this than her run-in with the Ku Klux Klan in the summer of 1927. Smith was performing in North Carolina when she got word that a group of Klansmen were coming to try to shut her show down. Rather than pack up and run, Smith stormed out of the circus tent she was performing in and confronted the Klansmen. She dressed down the racists and chased them off before returning to the tent to finish her set. Nobody was going to stop Bessie Smith from doing what Bessie Smith did best.

That defiant attitude came from an upbringing of struggle in near-absolute poverty. Born in Chattanooga, Tennessee, Smith was an orphan by the age of nine. With no education to speak of, she spent her childhood busking on street corners to help feed her siblings. In 1912, when she was 17, her brother got her a role in a traveling vaudeville show as a dancer. These shows were one of the hottest forms of entertainment of the day. They delivered spectacle, sexuality and comedy to rural communities across the South and helped incubate the sounds that would come to define American music.

Smith quickly rose from dancer to singer, thanks to her full, powerful wail. She sang with an impeccable timing that set a standard for blues greats to follow. Under the tutelage of fellow blues great Ma Rainey, Smith developed a stage persona and grew into a beloved sensation. Her music was a clear celebration of her own Blackness and bisexuality. It was always rooted in her working-class background, a defiant statement that working-class women were just as capable of creating incredible art as anyone else at the time.

She had already been well established in the vaudeville scene when Mamie Smith (no relation) scored her own blues hit and kicked the door open for a torrent of blues recordings. Bessie Smith saw an opportunity and tried for a recording contract, joining thousands of Black people in the Great Migration. Unfortunately, colorism was still rampant, and she was dark skinned. She auditioned for both Okeh Records and the Black-owned Black Swan in 1921 and was turned down by both. It wasn't until 1923 that her imperious voice was finally put on wax.

"Downhearted Blues" is about as perfect a blues song as was ever recorded. Smith sings the tale of heartbreak from deep within the soul. Her only accompaniment in the song is a sleazy piano line laid down by Clarence Williams. That simple arrangement allows Smith to shine front and center with an intimate portrayal of a woman's pain. In addition to being performed by a woman, "Downhearted Blues" was written by a pair of Black women, Alberta Hunter and Lovie Austin.

When "Downhearted Blues" released, the entire country became enamored with Bessie Smith. The record sold 780,000 copies in its first six months and catapulted Smith to stardom. Columbia Records billed her as "Queen of the Blues" and a zealous music press decided to upgrade her to "Empress of the Blues." With her newfound regal title, Smith became the highest-paid Black performer in the country and adopted a life of glamour. As the Jazz Age flourished, she toured the country in a custom-built railcar, drinking and partying to excess. She began to have overt extramarital affairs with both men and women.

In the years that followed Smith, both blues and jazz would go on to become male-dominated fields, but "Downhearted Blues" forever serves as a reminder that it was women like Bessie Smith who trail blazed the genre and became its first stars.

1924

"Rhapsody in Blue"

George Gershwin and Paul Whiteman

From the moment jazz sprang forth from the Louisiana bayou, it was destined to hop the racial line and become America's great art form. Its rhythms were too powerful, its melodies too hot and its ethos too ambitious to ever be denied. It was just a matter of when, where and how. As it would turn out, the when was the 1920s. The where was, of course, New York City. And the how? There are myriad factors that played into the explosion of jazz, but the biggest might just be Prohibition. The exuberance and hedonism of jazz proved a perfect fit for backroom speakeasies. In those underground clubs, jazz dance caught on like wildfire, and soon enough a generation of wealthy young white people began to adopt jazz as the sound of their generation. Before long, the era was dubbed the "Jazz Age."

One of the defining moments in this new age came on February 12, 1924. Music elites from across New York City piled into Midtown's Aeolian Hall to witness a concert called "An Experiment in Modern Music." The concert was put on by Paul Whiteman, a white bandleader who was becoming one of the best-selling musicians of the day. His music was an orchestrated version of jazz, stripping the gritty spontaneity from the genre in exchange for something more ornate. The news media would come to declare Whiteman "King of Jazz," even though his take was a watered-down version of the genre's Black originators. For his part, Whiteman had a genuine appreciation of the jazz tradition. He tried to hire Black musicians, but the segregationist laws and commercial realities of the time stifled these efforts. Still, he worked with Black arrangers behind the scenes and evangelized the beauty of jazz to white audiences.

The centerpiece of Whiteman's Aeolian Hall performance was "Rhapsody in Blue," a marvelous concerto composed by the great George Gershwin. Like Whiteman, Gershwin was an early appreciator of jazz. He got his start in

> The news media would come to declare Whiteman "King of Jazz," even though his take was a watered-down version of the genre's Black originators.

Tin Pan Alley and rose to fame when Al Jolson recorded his song "Swanee" in 1919. Although "Rhapsody in Blue" would become one of the defining works of his career, he almost didn't write it. There are differing stories as to the exact circumstances of the piece's creation. Some have Whiteman trying to commission Gershwin and getting turned down until there was word that Whiteman reached out to a rival; others have Gershwin accepting the commission and then forgetting he had done so. Either way, he only clued into the fact that he was writing the piece when his brother showed him a newspaper article claiming the collaboration was imminent. This left him with just five weeks to write the concerto.

Inspiration for the last-minute piece struck Gershwin while riding on a train from New York to Boston. He began to take note of the constant rhythms of the train's movement, and the piece emerged throughout the ride. By the time he arrived in Boston, he had an outline of the song in mind.

It's fitting that "Rhapsody in Blue" was conceived on a train, because the entire piece plays out like an ode to the noise and speed of modernity and urbanity. Gershwin imagined it as a celebration of America's diversity, represented by a daring collision of classical and jazz elements. The song flows between sleazy, languid woodwinds and bombastic horns, creating a sound palette that has come to be forever associated with New York City.

Gershwin wrote the entire piece in just a few weeks before handing it off to Ferde Grofé to orchestrate. The final orchestration of the piece wasn't ready until a week before the concert. Nevertheless, "Rhapsody in Blue" was met with thunderous applause upon its debut. Neither Gershwin's nor Whiteman's career would ever be the same. Within months, Whiteman scored a hit record with an abridged recording, and "Rhapsody in Blue" quickly became the defining work of the American classical canon. Meanwhile, Gershwin leaped from being a pop songwriter to becoming one of the greatest American composers, single-handedly elevating America's cultural clout on a global scale.

"Rhapsody in Blue" is not really a jazz song, nor is it a classical concerto. It's the sort of collision of cultures and ideas that could have only happened in New York City. It's a wholly unique piece of music that perfectly captured the spirit of the Jazz Age, and to this very day, it remains one of the most iconic pieces of American music ever made.

"See See Rider Blues"

Ma Rainey

Gertrude "Ma" Rainey was already pushing 40 by the time she started her recording career. Up to that point, she'd spent most of her life as a touring vaudeville singer. It was on one of these tours that she had her first encounter with the blues, picking up a song from a sorrowful, young girl in Missouri. The song spoke to Rainey and she began to incorporate it in her set. Before long, she was singing more blues and writing her own songs. Her originals were raunchy pieces filled with raw portrayals of real working-class pains. As a veteran on the touring scene, Rainey bumped elbows with many of the best musicians in the country, and mentored younger artists, such as Bessie Smith. Like Smith, she was openly bisexual, and even sang about romantic affairs with women in her songs.

When blues records started to explode in the 1920s, music executives began searching around for the next big star. It was a Black producer at Chicago's Paramount Records who "discovered" Rainey in 1923 and put her behind a microphone. She was a natural in the studio. Her powerful voice captivated audiences, and Paramount started to bill her as "Mother of the Blues." As her musical career progressed, she made her way to New York, where the record industry was just starting to spring forth. It was in New York that Ma Rainey recorded her immortal "See See Rider Blues."

Like so many blues songs of the era "See See Rider Blues" has no known songwriter. Instead, it was passed down orally from singer to singer. Its lyrics are an archetypal murder ballad. Rainey opens the song by wailing out the sorrow brought on by an unfaithful lover, but by the fourth verse, that sorrow has turned into anger and a thirst for vengeance. As is often tradition in this style of blues, the final verse of the song delivers a heavy punchline: "I'm gonna buy me a pistol just as long as I am tall / Gonna kill my man and catch the Cannonball / If he don't have me, he don't have no gal at all."

Rainey sings her pains out over a slow, lilting rhythm. This rhythmic pattern is just a few generations removed from a West African folk tradition that was brought to the Americas with the

> "See See Rider Blues" has no known songwriter. Instead, it was passed down orally from singer to singer.

slave trade. After marinating in the Caribbean, that folk music spread out across the Mississippi, stretching deep into the heart of America. The West African rhythms mixed with traditional European songs sung by rural Appalachian folk and solidified into the earliest blues song. The piece was already firmly planted into the blues canon by the time that Rainey sang it, but her version was spiced with her distinctive personality and paired with instrumentals by some of the greatest musicians in the country. Rainey recorded "See See Rider Blues" with an orchestra led by Fletcher Henderson. His band professionalized Louisiana jazz music and brought it north while retaining its soul and fiery spirit. The shining star of Henderson's orchestra in the mid-'20s was a singular instrumental talent named Louis Armstrong.

Armstrong's effortless horn lines were a perfect match for the raw charisma of Ma Rainey. His syncopated trumpet blasts weave in and out behind her low, husky voice. They twin Rainey's sorrow but add a lighthearted tinge that offers hope and catharsis. When she delivers the final heavy line of the song and fades out, Armstrong pipes up with a short solo to punctuate the end of the song.

Ma Rainey's music is an eternal artifact of a rich cultural exchange that stretched all across the Atlantic seaboard. She was able to carry the torch of the nameless blues singers who first inspired her, while also putting her own mark on the industry. When she teamed up with the finest musicians New York had to offer, the result was one of the most beloved songs in the entire blues tradition.

1926

"Heebie Jeebies"

Louis Armstrong

It would not be an exaggeration to call Louis Armstrong the single most important musician in American history. At the very least, he's the most important figure in jazz history, and jazz is the primordial ooze from which the modern music industry sprung.

It wasn't that Armstrong was one of the inventors of jazz. The genre that would come to redefine American music had been brewing in New Orleans since around the time of his birth in 1901. Armstrong himself was mentored by one of the movement's early greats, Joe "King" Oliver. And yet, there would be no jazz without Louis Armstrong. Or at least, there would be no jazz as we know it today. He plucked the fledgling genre from the cradle and molded it with his own virtuosic hands, bringing it to the masses and becoming the first true jazz star.

Today, most people remember Armstrong best for the gravelly croon of his later days, and smooth songs like "What a Wonderful World." As brilliant and calming as that later era is, Armstrong in his prime blew the loudest, highest horn of the era. He played with a fire and energy that drove dance halls wild and earned him a rabid following. His 1926 recording "Heebie Jeebies" is a perfect representation of the hot jazz that made him a national sensation.

"Heebie Jeebies" was one of the first recordings he made as a bandleader. After moving to Chicago with Oliver, Armstrong had quickly started to shine in the city's burgeoning jazz scene. He played his horn so loudly that Oliver had to set him up apart from the rest of the band when recording so that he didn't overpower them. Before long, Armstrong was starting to outshine even Oliver. He could have set out on his own, but he remained loyal to his mentor and bandleader. Still, those around him recognized his talent. Armstrong's wife, Lil Hardin Armstrong, pushed for him to become first trumpet rather than playing second to Oliver. At the urging of his wife, Armstrong left Oliver's band and moved to New York for a time, where he shined in Fletcher Henderson's orchestra. When he returned to Chicago, he became the leader of his own band, the Hot Five.

The Hot Five consisted of Armstrong, along with Hardin on piano, and musicians who had played with Armstrong back in New Orleans. The Hot Five were an instant hit in the Chicago scene. Over the course of two years, they cut 30-odd tunes that would signal a seismic shift in the jazz world. The music was a style known as Dixieland jazz, born from the cultural melting pot that is New Orleans. It was a combination of blues music, Caribbean rhythms, marching songs and a half dozen other sounds. This entire mélange was held together by a rich syncopation and a constant improvisation. The Hot Five made infectious music that stirred the body into movement. But for all the talent that Armstrong's band had, its members all stood in the shadow of Armstrong himself.

His playing was like nothing the world had seen. Armstrong was a melodist extraordinaire, wringing profound meaning out of every line he played. He stole the spotlight and elevated the art of the jazz solo, transforming the genre from a communal improvisation to a music that shed the spotlight on incredible feats of individual talent. Armstrong's music was a perfect expression of the spirit of Black America in the '20s. It was full of joy, whimsy and resilience, but even the brightest songs contained a deep, lingering pain at their core, reflections of the racist systems so deeply entrenched in American culture.

Armstrong was most famous for his horn, but his vocal talents are nothing to scoff at, either. In a time when most recorded voices were sweet and clean, like Al Jolson's, Armstrong sang with a raspy growl that oozed charisma. "Heebie Jeebies" is a particularly shining spotlight in his early vocal career, thanks to a serendipitous accident during the recording session. As the legend goes, the Hot Five were in the middle of cutting the song when Armstrong's lyric sheet fell off his music stand. A lesser musician might have stopped the recording session there, but Armstrong was undeterred. Thinking back to his boyhood vocal group on the streets of New Orleans, he began to improvise a vocal melody, replacing the words with playful gibberish. This wasn't the first time that scat singing had been put to record, but it was a landmark moment in the art form, inventing modern scat.

"Heebie Jeebies" was an enormous success. It became one of Armstrong's first hits as a bandleader and made scat an essential part of the jazz vocabulary. For many artists, a recording like "Heebie Jeebies" would be a career-defining accomplishment. For Louis Armstrong, it was an early step in a career that spanned half a century breaking color barriers, defining a new sort of stardom and changing American music in ways that are still felt to this very day.

1927

"Dark Was the Night, Cold Was the Ground"

Blind Willie Johnson

Blind Willie Johnson likely lived his entire life in poverty. Owing to this fact, the details of his biography are spotty at best. There's only one known photograph of Johnson, and the only record of his entire life's work is a collection of 30 songs recorded between 1927 and 1930. Yet, Johnson was the recipient of one of the rarest honors in music history— an honor granted to only a scant few other musicians, such as Stravinsky, Mozart and Chuck Berry. You see, at this very moment, one of Johnson's songs is hurtling through the depths of space on a golden record encased within NASA's Voyager probes.

The Voyager Golden Record is a collection of data meant to encapsulate the human experience as well as it can be encapsulated within such small confines. In addition to 90 minutes of music, the probe also contains photographs and data telling the story of humankind. These documents were carefully assembled by a team of NASA astronomers, including one Timothy Ferris. It was Ferris who selected "Dark Was the Night, Cold Was the Ground" for the record.

Ferris chose the haunting song because he felt it captured a reality that humans have been experiencing since the beginning of time—facing nightfall without a place to sleep. And the song is indeed a representation of that. It's a simple song, just a pained wordless moan by Johnson twinned by his ethereal slide guitar. The song has a deep universality in its simplicity, hitting straight to the core of what makes us human. But universal as it may be, "Dark Was the Night, Cold Was the Ground" was also very rooted within a specific moment for the artist who made it.

In the penthouses and speakeasies of the cities, 1927 was the peak of the hedonistic Jazz Age, a raging boom of wealth and glamour. The same could not be said for many who lived in rural America, especially people of color. The pain present in "Dark Was the Night, Cold Was the Ground" was felt throughout southern Black communities, even before the Great Depression hit.

> The song has a deep universality in its simplicity, hitting straight to the core of what makes us human.

Blind Willie Johnson was born into a sharecropping family. As best as biographers have been able to tell, he likely lost his sight when his stepmother splashed lye into his eyes after a violent confrontation with his father. Like so many at the time, Johnson found hope and escape from his traumas in the promises of the church. He became a gospel singer, gaining notice for his precise slide guitar techniques.

Nearly every one of the 30 songs that Johnson recorded in his career were religious in nature, and that includes "Dark Was the Night, Cold Was the Ground." While the song has no true lyrics to speak of, its title is a reference to "Gesthemane," a hymn that had become popular in the American South. That hymn depicts Jesus in a moment of agony as he considers his own final sacrifice.

The Bible was the lens through which Johnson was able to understand his own world, and for him it provided hope for a better one. He was not alone in this reality. The roots of blues are inextricably tied to southern gospel music. For many, that music was the language of their community and the soundtrack to their struggle.

By including a gospel blues song on the Voyager Golden Record, NASA did more than just depict one of the universal pains of humanity. They tied science and faith together in an act that transcended a single moment in history, and granted Blind Willie Johnson an exalted place in the story of humankind.

"Blue Yodel No. 1"

Jimmie Rodgers

Throughout the 1920s, it was the children of the blues that came to form the foundations of American music. The star was, of course, jazz, but while speakeasies were taking the country by storm, another one of blues' progeny was taking its first steps in the late 1920s. In its day, this new music was called "hillbilly," but it wouldn't be long before it got a new name: country music. In 1928, this burgeoning movement got its first icon in a former rail worker named Jimmie Rodgers.

Like so many of the early blues greats, Rodgers' life was one of struggle and poverty. His mother died when he was young, and Rodgers spent most of his life skipping school to sneak into vaudeville shows and soak in the sorts of proto-blues songs that Ma Rainey and Bessie Smith made their fame on. Rodgers dreamed of one day being an entertainer himself and ran away to pursue those dreams at the age of 13. He joined a traveling medicine show, performing as entertainment to lure in customers for snake oil salesmen who would hawk their wares to rural townsfolk. But this life didn't last long. Rodgers' father caught up to the young boy and brought him home, putting him to work as a waterboy for the rail lines.

Rodgers would spend the next decade traveling around and working jobs on the rails. The whole time, he never gave up his passion for music. He practiced his banjo, guitar and singing, picking up songs and hollers from the Black railmen who worked alongside him. In 1924, he was diagnosed with tuberculosis and forced to give up rail work. With nowhere else to turn, he went back to music to try to make a living and support his young family. Rodgers got his break in 1927, when he was found by Ralph Peer from the Victor Talking Machine Company. Peer recorded a handful of songs in his first sessions with him. A month later, Rodgers hadn't heard back from Peer, so he packed up and made his way to New York, where he convinced Peer to record more songs in person.

It's in that second batch of recordings that Jimmie Rodgers cut "Blue Yodel No. 1." The song was one that Rodgers pieced together himself, a simple twelve-bar with lyrics full of the blues tropes of heartbreak and murder. The defining feature of the piece is the titular yodel, a

> This new music was called "hillbilly," but it wouldn't be long before it got a new name: country music.

howling vocal trick that Rodgers had been developing for years. Yodeling originally came to America by way of immigration, with Swiss migrants settling in the Appalachian Mountains. Once there, it became adopted by the traveling minstrel shows that Rodgers grew up watching. He combined this more traditional yodeling style with the blues hollers he learned on the rails, creating the "blue yodel" and kick-starting a legendary career.

In the months following his second recording session, Rodgers rose to become one of Victor's biggest stars. "Blue Yodel" would eventually sell more than a million copies and would spawn a whole series of "Blue Yodel" songs, including one that featured Louis Armstrong on trumpet.

Even as Rodgers' career took off, his railway roots were ever-present in his music. He billed himself as the "Singing Brakeman," and created songs about the woes of the rambling life. This helped create an archetype that persists in country music to this day. And that wasn't the only country trope that Rodgers popularized. A few years later, he moved to Texas and performed as a singing cowboy, once again setting the stage for generations of country singers. By the time tuberculosis claimed his life at 33 years of age, Rodgers had established himself as the "Father of Country Music," and changed America's musical landscape forever.

By combining traditional folksong and yodeling with blues structures, Jimmie Rodgers helped create an all-new sort of music. By singing for an underclass of poor Americans, he contributed to one of the country's most enduring musical traditions.

"Ain't Misbehavin'"

Fats Waller

By 1929, the Jazz Age was in full swing. Record sales were booming, speakeasies were packed to the brim and folks everywhere were dancing with wild abandon. In this moment of joyous excess, a joyous and excessive pianist named Fats Waller recorded the biggest hit of his career, "Ain't Misbehavin'."

Waller was truly a man of his times. His appetite for food, gin and sex was nearly insatiable. Even the music he played was indulgent. He was one of the foremost pianists in a style known as "stride." Stride was an evolution of ragtime music, named for the way that the left hand strode up and down octaves, creating a pulsing, rhythmic core. Meanwhile, the right hand filled the song with ever-shifting melodies and embellishments.

Like Waller himself, stride rose up from the bumping streets of New York's Harlem. There, pianists were known to face off in competitive "cutting contests" dueling each other in front of large audiences for piano supremacy. Stride was deeply influential in the progression of jazz piano, and its exuberant, upbeat sound helped pave the way for the swing movement of the 1930s.

One of the things that separated stride from ragtime was its willingness to use pop forms, and "Ain't Misbehavin'" is a pop song through and through. Waller wrote it for *Connie's Hot Chocolates*, a comedic music revue that ran in the Hudson Theatre for most of 1929. Louis Armstrong made his Broadway debut as part of that show's pit orchestra, being taught the song by Waller himself. Future great Cab Calloway also had one of his earliest successes as part of the cast for *Connie's Hot Chocolates*, where he was noted for his performances of "Ain't Misbehavin'."

The lyrics are cheeky. They're framed around a singer promising to stay faithful while his love is out. One can read the lyrics as sweet and romantic if they wish, but the swinging music seems to be undercutting the message, giving the audience a sly little wink. This is especially true in the bridge, where the careful arrangement gives way to a chaotic swinging jazz band, complete with booming

> Pianists were known to face off in competitive "cutting contests," dueling each other in front of large audiences for piano supremacy.

drums, wailing horns and a dancing piano solo. This musical interlude seems to be a depiction of the wild partying life of the so-called Roaring '20s. It's a bumping speakeasy hidden in the back of a sentimental love song.

"Ain't Misbehavin'" was the beginning of a celebrated career for Fats Waller, but it was also one of the last great songs of the Roaring '20s. This decade full of optimism and hedonism came crashing down with the stock market in October 1929. In the years to come, the music industry would be pushed to the brink. Although it would eventually recover, things would never truly be the same. "Ain't Misbehavin'" will forever stand as a living document for the last moments of a glorious era that was about to come to a sudden and brutal end.

DUST & DREAMS

1930–39

The 1930s are a decade defined by contrast. Contrast between rich and poor, urban and rural, Black and white. These divisions have always existed in American society, but they were made wider and deeper by the dire conditions of the Great Depression, which spanned nearly the entire decade and touched every aspect of American life.

The most direct impact that the Depression had on the music industry was record sales. At the end of the '20s, the young music industry was booming, selling more than 100 million records a year. By 1932, that number plummeted to just 6 million. Only a handful of record labels were big enough to survive this hit, leading to a consolidation of power that continues to define the music industry to this very day. Countless musicians lost work as people could no longer afford the luxuries of entertainment. Musical movements that were ready to explode in the late '20s began to fizzle and disappear.

Amid all of this poverty and loss, music still found ways to grow and persevere. The disappearance of corporate interests meant that rural music like the blues and country had chances to solidify and define themselves separate from financial interests. In urban centers, new technologies, including sound on film, helped breathe new life into music. People would pinch pennies

and flock to theaters to escape their dreary times, slipping into dreams created by a generation of visionary jazz and popular musicians. This yearning for joy and escapism would eventually birth swing, an enormous movement that redefined people's relationship to popular music and even helped lift the music industry out of the Depression.

But the most important shift to come out of the 1930s was the birth of music's political consciousness. Before the Depression, most of the music being made in America was about either love, heartbreak or God. Once the harsh economic realities of the '30s began to set in, people started to see new purposes for music.

In mining towns across the country, folk musicians used music to organize people, writing radical union songs that proved invaluable weapons in a series of brutal labor wars. Meanwhile, New York's predominantly Black neighborhood of Harlem had become a hub of culture and entertainment, thanks to its cultural renaissance in the 1920s. Even as this renaissance waned in the Depression, the art coming from Harlem was so rich that it began to demand recognition and appreciation from the dominant white culture. In doing so, it sowed the seeds for what would become the greatest social and cultural shift in American history: the civil rights movement.

1935

1936

1937

1938

1939

1930

"Mood Indigo"

Duke Ellington

Throughout much of the 1920s, the radio industry had fallen slightly behind the recording industry. That started to change at the end of the decade. New radio technologies allowed for further broadcast distances and then simultaneous broadcast. This meant that, for the first time in history, entire nations were able to listen to the same things that were broadcast at the same time. When the Depression seized America, the prospect of free radio broadcasts became much more attractive than spending hard-earned cash on records. By 1930, the golden age of radio was in full swing. One of the first to truly take advantage of this new era was Duke Ellington.

Ellington was a singular compositional genius. He rose to fame when his orchestra became the house band at Harlem's Cotton Club, one of the most popular nightclubs in New York City. The Cotton Club was a segregated venue filled with racist imagery of the Jim Crow South. Although Ellington and his band of Black musicians became its marquee attraction, they could not have attended the whites-only club as patrons.

He challenged the racism of his time through his artistic mastery. Even in his early days, Ellington was orchestrating jazz in ways that his peers could hardly dream of. He brought a level of elegance to the music, envisioning it as a high art in a way that few in the music industry

dared. His songs were immaculate constructions, weaving rich harmony together with an unparalleled swing. He made full use of every piece of his big band orchestra, using them to create songs that could cover the entire spectrum of human emotion. All of this was tied together by his virtuoso piano talents.

Ellington wrote "Mood Indigo" for a radio broadcast in October 1930. As he tells it, he wrote the entire piece in just 15 minutes while he was waiting for his mother to finish cooking dinner. The original genesis for the piece was a melody that clarinetist Barney Bigard had picked up from his clarinet teacher, Lorenzo Tio. Tio had referred to this languid melody as "Mexican blues." With Bigard's permission, Ellington orchestrated around this blues. He brought power and form to it, turning the song into a beautiful, dreamy tale of sorrow. Careful punctuations from the rhythm section underscore the rich melody of Bigard's clarinet line, teasing out a playful edge as the melody passes around the instrumentals.

"Mood Indigo" displays more than just a musical vision. It's an example of Ellington's technological prowess as well. He used the song's arrangement to exploit the quirks of electrical microphones. He swapped around the typical big band arrangement, voicing his trombones at the top of their instrument's range, and his clarinets at the bottom. When recorded through an electric microphone, this created a resonance between the two instruments. The sympathetic vibrations created by this resonance create a phantom instrumental sound, filling out the tone with something that's not there. This ghost in the machine is key to the rounded sound of "Mood Indigo," and would become a favorite technique of Ellington throughout the rest of his career.

Before it ever had lyrics, Ellington had his own vision for the story of "Mood Indigo." In his mind, it told the tale of young unrequited love between two children. The music reflects this story by contrasting the joyful innocence of Bigard's clarinet line with the aching wail of the horn sections. It's the entire depth of human experience wrapped up in three tight minutes of music.

When "Mood Indigo" made its broadcast debut, it touched Ellington's fans deeply. Perhaps it was because people across the country were feeling the first shock waves of the Great Depression, and the song captured a rare sort of sorrow. Perhaps it was the technological magic of the mike tone. Or perhaps it was simply that Ellington knew how to pen a pop tune like no other. Whatever the cause, fans flooded the bandleader with adoring mail once the broadcast had finished. Seeing this response, he realized the song could be a hit record, even as sales were declining nationally. Ellington cut two original recordings of the song almost immediately, and would go on to cut the song many more times throughout his career.

Eventually, he even commissioned some lyrics to the song. The official credit to those lyrics goes to his manager, Irving Mills, but the Tin Pan Alley lyricist Mitchell Parish has also laid claim to

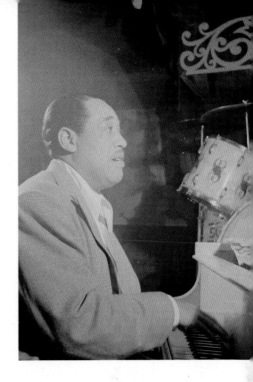

them. Rather than outright describing Ellington's vision of young love, these lyrics rely on the older tropes of Broadway and the blues. They paint a moody picture of Ellington's sorrow, pairing neatly with the ethereal arrangement.

"Mood Indigo" was the perfect way to call in a decade full of change and sorrow. Whether for love or for money, many Americans would find themselves relating to the song's blues as the '30s went on. In the decades since, "Mood Indigo" continues to live a rich life as a jazz standard. Such artists as Frank Sinatra, Nina Simone and Thelonious Monk have used the song as an outlet for the pains in their own life. Even Duke Ellington himself returned to the song throughout his career, with each new recording more astounding than the last. By the time he passed in 1974, the music world had recognized Ellington as one of the most singular minds in music history, and had recognized "Mood Indigo" as a perfect example of the magic of jazz.

1931

"Which Side Are You On?"

Florence Reece

In the decades before and between the World Wars, there were battles of another sort raging within the borders of America. These were not conflicts between nations or empires, but rather battles of class. Industrial workers across the country began to unionize in droves. They were met with intense violence and pushback from the wealthy owning class who ran the mines, the mills and the factories. These strikes came to redefine the ways the American economy functioned and spawned some of the earliest examples of a true political consciousness in American folk music. One of the great enduring songs from this early era of political action was "Which Side Are You On?"

"Which Side Are You On?" wasn't written by some musician seeking fame or fortune, nor by some traveling minstrel or vaudeville performer. It was written by a working-class woman named Florence Reece. Reece's husband, Sam, was one of the labor organizers for the United Mine Workers in Harlan County, Kentucky.

Harlan was a county dotted with mining towns, built to extract coal from the fertile Kentucky Appalachians. Coal mining was dangerous and difficult work that took its toll on the bodies and spirits of its workers. Conditions were poor enough already, but when the Depression hit and the owners sought to squeeze more life from their workers, tensions boiled to a fever. In February 1931, the Harlan County Coal Operators' Association announced that they would be cutting miners' wages by 10 percent.

It was the last straw.

The United Mine Workers of America came in and attempted to unionize Harlan's workers. They were met with fierce resistance from the mine operators, who were backed by J. H. Blair, the local sheriff. This resistance came down on Florence Reece one night, when Blair and his men came into her house looking to intimidate her husband into giving up his organization attempts. Sam got word they were coming and was able to duck away, but the sheriff and his men ransacked the house, terrifying Florence and her children. The men didn't leave until the next morning, standing watch in case Sam came back.

When Blair's men finally left, Reece tore a calendar off the wall and wrote the song that would put her into history books. "Which Side Are You On?" is a simple song, borrowing its melody from an old Baptist hymn. It consists of four short verses detailing the story of the Harlan County War, each punctuated by the titular chorus. These verses are made of simple rhyming couplets, telling an expansive story in just a few words. Writing this song was Florence's way of adding her voice to the union fight. She helped spread the pro-union message across the country while also giving the workers a song of resilience to inspire them in their darkest moments.

The Harlan County War would rage on for nearly a decade. It saw frequent fights, five deaths and national troops being called in before it finally ended in 1939. Florence Reece's song was indubitably sung countless times throughout that struggle, but it was never recorded. The song wouldn't truly make its way out of Harlan County until a wandering musician and activist named Pete Seeger got his hands on it.

Seeger made a lifetime of collecting songs from the labor wars and putting them into his own musical repertoire. In doing so, he hoped to spread a wider message across the country. Seeger and his group the Almanac Singers recorded a version of "What Side Are You On?" in 1941, bringing Reece's words to whole new audiences.

With Seeger's help, the song became a labor anthem. It forever preserved the silenced voices of Harlan County and helped inspire new generations of radical activist folk musicians who would go on to make seismic shifts to American culture in the 1960s.

Florence helped spread the pro-union message across the country while also giving the workers a song of resilience to inspire them in their darkest moments.

1932

"Minnie the Moocher"

Cab Calloway

Music and animation have always had a close relationship. From the early days of Mickey Mouse and Looney Tunes through the Beatles' "Yellow Submarine," all the way to the Disney renaissance of the '90s, the two industries have combined to create some of the most beloved pieces of art of the modern era. The art forms flirted since sound entered cinema in the mid-1920s, but in 1932, their relationship truly started to leap forward thanks in no small part to Cab Calloway.

Calloway was a vocalist and bandleader in the emergent swing movement. He ran his orchestra as a tight ship, hiring many of the finest musicians of the time and driving them to excellence. In 1930, he was brought in to replace Duke Ellington at the Cotton Club while Ellington's band was touring.

But for all the talents Calloway had as a musician and bandleader, his true gift was showmanship. He followed in the footsteps of his older sister Blanche, who was a renowned bandleader, and learned scat under the mentorship of Louis Armstrong. Calloway had a truly singular onstage charisma, drawing audiences in with comedic banter, call-and-response scatting and dance moves that were eons ahead of their time. He was even known to perform an early version of the "moonwalk," though he called it "the buzz" at the time.

This sort of electric performance made Cab Calloway a natural target for the film industry, which was in the middle of a revolution, thanks to the invention of "talking pictures." Throughout the '30s, he and his orchestra became the most frequently filmed act in all of jazz. They appeared first in a number of short films, and even in a feature film, alongside Al Jolson. But the most important films that Calloway took part in barely had him on-screen at all.

In 1932, Calloway teamed up with the animators at Fleischer Studios for a wholly unique sort of film. The animators at Fleischer had developed a technique for creating more fluid animations. They would film real people moving in front of a white sheet, and then use those images as references, to draw more realistic character movements over them. At first this technique was known as the "Fleischer Process," but it later came to be known as Rotoscoping. After seeing Calloway perform in the Cotton Club, Max Fleischer realized that his eccentric dance style would be a perfect subject for Rotoscoped animation.

At the time, Fleischer Studios' most popular character was the twee flapper Betty Boop. Director Dave Fleischer developed a Betty Boop cartoon around Cab Calloway's 1931 hit "Minnie the Moocher" with Calloway himself

Rotoscoped in as a ghostly dancing walrus. The cartoon was a huge success and led to two more collaborations between Fleischer and Calloway in the years to come.

As for the song itself, "Minnie the Moocher" is not exactly what you might think of when you think of a cartoon soundtrack. The lyrics of the song tell the story of an exotic dancer stumbling into an opium den and slipping into fantastical dreams. Typically, such a song wouldn't be able to bypass censors in the era, but Calloway's story is all told in a particular kind of Black Harlem slang known as "jive talk." Calloway was one of the originators of a lot of jive talk and even wrote a dictionary of it in 1938. By couching his lyrics in jive talk, he was able to slip an explicit story by an unknowing white audience and all over the airwaves.

The success of "Minnie the Moocher" was bolstered by an explosive musical arrangement. Tense horn blasts underline the tale of desperation and debauchery, with growling trumpets depicting the sleazy corners of town that Minnie likes to hang out in. The most famous aspect of the song comes in its call-and-response chorus, where Calloway breaks out scat phrases borrowed from his sister. These "hi-de-ho"s were so beloved that Calloway started to bill himself as the "Hi-De-Ho Man."

In an age when cinema was taking off and music on film was one of the hottest trends, nobody made as good use of the medium as Cab Calloway. "Minnie the Moocher" stands as both a song and a cartoon with no equal, and marked a turning point for the medium of the animated musical.

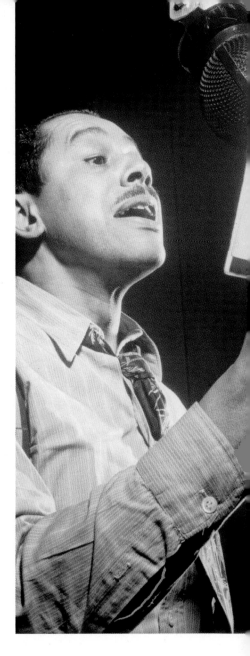

1933

"Stormy Weather"

Ethel Waters

Ethel Waters was, in her own words, in a private hell when she recorded "Stormy Weather" in 1933. Waters was going through a breakup at the time, but the pain ran deeper than that. All the trauma of Waters's 37 years of life were weighing on her soul, threatening to crush it entirely. Her mother had been a teenage rape victim, and Waters herself had been married off to an abusive husband at just 13 years old. She found escape from this cycle of abuse in show business, starting a career on the same vaudeville circuit that birthed Ma Rainey and Bessie Smith.

Through the mid- to late 1920s, record labels started to publish more and more records by black artists. These so-called "race records" quickly grew into a craze that took over the nation. This craze helped launch Waters's career to unimagined heights. Waters could sing the blues as well as anyone, but her career ended up veering more toward show tunes. She recorded with Fletcher Henderson's orchestra and became one of the biggest stars in the country by the 1930s.

Music had bought Waters' way out of poverty, but it couldn't erase the fact that she was a Black woman living in a

> She sang it as a lament for a lost love, but also as a heartfelt expression of Black pain.

white man's world. Many of her performances were for segregated audiences, such as that of Harlem's whites-only Cotton Club. All around the club, Harlem was in the midst of its renaissance, driven by Black creatives and intellectuals. But the Cotton Club served as a reminder of the harsh racist realities that still plagued America. The club's name was a reference to the antebellum South. Its interior was full of art depicting racist caricatures, and it billed itself as a venue for "jungle music."

That said, the Cotton Club consistently hired some of the best Black musicians of the day. Such names as Duke Ellington, Louis Armstrong and Cab Calloway regularly graced its marquee.

In fact, songwriter Harold Arlen actually wrote "Stormy Weather" with Calloway in mind, intended for a 1933 revue to be hosted at the venue. Arlen had seen Calloway perform at the venue before and wrote a melody that moved around and stretched out its vowels, leaving plenty room for his scat acrobatics. But when the time came for the revue, Calloway was no longer with the Cotton Club. So, Arlen and lyricist Ted Koehler met with Waters and agreed to let her perform the song with Duke Ellington's orchestra.

Arlen's mournful melody and Koehler's timeless lyrics resonated with Waters in a way they probably never would have with Calloway. They gave Waters a conduit through which to channel the pain that threatened to swallow her whole. When Ethel Waters sang "Stormy Weather," she sang it as a lament for a lost love, but also as a heartfelt expression of Black pain. Her voice tinges with righteous anger, opening from tension into sheer sorrow in the chorus. She made every use of the song's vocal runs, squeezing each note for all the emotion she could find in it.

"Stormy Weather" is a perfect mourning song. Arlen's melody is the sort that one doesn't easily forget, and Koehler's use of metaphor allows the lyrics to resonate with a sadness of any sort. The pain that Waters' version puts into it hit home with an audience who were going through no shortage of pain themselves as the Great Depression tightened its grip around America's neck. It was an authentic expression for a terrifying time. Her performance stunned the Cotton Club crowd. Before the year was out, Waters recorded the song, bringing her sorrow to an even wider audience.

The success of "Stormy Weather" lifted Waters from her despair and helped revitalize her career. In the years that came, she broke into the film and television industry. She trail blazed as the first African American ever to star in their own TV show and would spend the rest of her life shattering racial barriers, establishing herself as one of the finest voices of her era.

Arlen's melody is the sort that one doesn't easily forget, and Koehler's use of metaphor allows the lyrics to resonate with a sadness of any sort.

1934

"Midnight Special"

Lead Belly

The race records boom of the 1920s brought blues from the rural banks of the Mississippi Delta to booming urban centers like New York. It began to shift the music and blend it with show tunes and jazz. While all this change was happening, the poor rural folks who invented country and the blues were continuing to do what they had been for generations, and when the Depression hit and the music industry crashed, it fell once more on the working class to maintain the art form and its traditions.

One of the shepherds of this '30s country blues tradition was Huddie Ledbetter, a middle-aged guitarist who had been singing the blues since the turn of the century. Ledbetter spent much of his life in and out of prison, where he earned the nickname "Lead Belly." Today, Lead Belly is one of the most celebrated folk musicians in all of American history, having been praised by everyone from George Harrison and Bob Dylan to Kurt Cobain. But none of Lead Belly's work, nor the works of many of his rural blues contemporaries, would have been preserved were it not for a father-son team of folklorists named John and Alan Lomax.

The duo visited prisons across the South... recording the songs the inmates would sing to pass time while working.

John Lomax was a cofounder of the Texas Folklore Society, and one of the first white people in American history to truly take an academic appreciation of and interest in Black American folklore. In 1933, funded by a grant from the American Council of Learned Societies, John took to the road with a truck full of recording equipment and his 18-year-old son, Alan, behind the wheel. The duo visited prisons across the South, speaking with prisoners and recording the songs the inmates would sing to pass time while working. These recordings weren't made with profit in mind, but rather as an attempt to document a rich American cultural history that was fast changing in an era of new technology.

This project brought them to the Louisiana State Penitentiary, where Lead Belly was serving time for stabbing a man in a fight. They spoke with him and made a few early field recordings of his performance. By then, Lead Belly had gained some acclaim within his prison, and was allowed to play the guitar to entertain his fellow inmates. The Lomaxes were astounded by Lead Belly's fingerpicked guitar technique, which relied on drop tunings to help his lower strings imitate a bass. After making recordings with Lead Belly in 1933, they returned a year later with better equipment and recorded as many of his songs as he was willing to play.

The most celebrated recording from those 1934 sessions was "Midnight Special." The Lomaxes believed the song to be one of Lead Belly's own creations, but it actually dated back some 30-odd years. Like any great blues song, the origins of "Midnight Special" aren't exactly known. It had been passed on through generations orally, taking on new lyrics and iterations in the process. Lead Belly likely learned the song during his time at Texas' Sugar Land Prison. A late-night train used to run past that prison, shining its light in on the prisoners. In Lead Belly's version, the train light represents the hope of freedom, and a life outside of prison.

Not long after recording with the Lomaxes, Lead Belly was released from prison on good behavior. With no prospects for work, he turned to the Lomaxes, who took him on as a driver. Through the Lomaxes, he was introduced to audiences across the country. Although it would take another decade and another prison stint for the world to properly celebrate Lead Belly, he finally got his due, thanks to a number of recording sessions throughout the 1940s.

"Midnight Special" is an essential country blues recording. Lead Belly's authentic sound rings out truer and purer than the generations that would follow in his footsteps. His relationship with the Lomaxes is a unique story of racial unity and collaboration in a time that rejected such ideas. The Lomax recordings are not filled with the exploitative othering of the music industry, but rather folklorists realizing

the importance that Black folk music had to the fabric of American history. Lead Belly's music gives a peek into the world and sound of so many unknown musicians who were working through the Depression. These artists created a cultural foundation that generations of music would flourish on, but many died in obscurity without a single recording to their name. Although the Lomaxes helped shine the spotlight on Lead Belly and enshrine him in the annals of history, his breed of folk music wouldn't be long for this world. Before long, the country blues that he pioneered found another life in commercial circles, and true folk music began to evaporate from America's musical consciousness.

1935

"Can the Circle Be Unbroken (By and By)"

Carter Family

Music is a sleazy business full of exploitation, but the industry is also capable of performing true miracles. One such miracle is transforming artists from destitution and poverty into genuine cultural royalty. When talent scout Ralph Peer first recorded the Carter Family in 1927, they were living in a simple mountain home in a region of Virginia so impoverished that it was called "Poor Valley." By the time the '30s came around, the family was selling hundreds of thousands of records, making appearances on radio shows and buying motorcycles with their newfound wealth. In 1928, guitarist Maybelle Carter spent a portion of their earnings on the finest guitar money could buy, a Gibson L-5 archtop. As the decade came to a close, the family was cutting hit after hit and defining what would come to be known as country music in the process.

But the nature of fame is fickle. As the Depression hit and record sales plummeted, the Carter Family's fortunes fell with it. A. P. and Sara Carter, the husband-and-wife duo that made up two-thirds of the band, fell into a messy separation and stopped speaking to each other. For a moment, it seemed that the First Family of Country might fall apart before it ever had a chance to become a dynasty. In the mid-'30s, as the record industry started to limp back to life, Maybelle reached out to her cousin Sara and convinced her to record with the group again. When Sara tentatively agreed to cut some new recordings, Ralph Peer convinced the group to shift record labels, and almost immediately the Carter Family recorded one of the most enduring songs of their entire career, "Can the Circle Be Unbroken (By and By)."

Like almost the entirety of the Carter Family's catalog, "Can the Circle Be Unbroken" was adapted from a traditional piece of Appalachian folk music. In this case, it was a 1907 Christian hymn. The original hymn is an uplifting piece, reminding of the promises of a Christian heaven. A. P. Carter's take on the tune was decidedly darker, perhaps in reflection of the emotional tumult that the family were going through at the time. In his version, the narrator sings the song as he watches an undertaker come to take his mother's body away. But amid this tragic backdrop, the song's chorus provides a religious message of hope, ensuring that everything that happens is part of the circle of life and that the family will be reunited in heaven.

Musically, "Can the Circle Be Unbroken" is a perfect example of what would raise the Carter Family toward country music royalty. The song is anchored by Maybelle's unique brand of fingerstyle guitar, which she learned under the tutelage of the Black musician Leslie Riddle. Rather than playing melody with the higher strings on the guitar, Maybelle played the melody on the lower strings, strumming the upper ones with one finger for the rhythm in a style more akin to banjo playing. This unique guitar style would come to be known as "Carter scratch," and would form the basis of generations of country guitar. Atop the "Carter scratch" is A. P. Carter's eerie vocal holler in the verses, and a beautiful three-part harmony in the choruses. The end result is something that sounds primal, lifted from deep within the hills of Poor Valley and transported into houses across America through the magic of recording technology.

The success of "Can the Circle Be Unbroken" was enough to buy the Carter Family a few more years together, but it was not enough to repair the bridges that had been burned between its members. In 1936, A. P. and Sara officially divorced. The Carter Family would continue to play together until they disbanded in 1944, but by that time, a second generation of Carters was already well on their way to music stardom.

Over the ensuing decades, countless country artists would take their own spin on the song. One of the most famous of these was the Nitty Gritty Dirt Band who, in 1971, brought together some of the biggest musicians in country music to record a take on the song. Among those musicians was 62-year-old Maybelle Carter, who played the song on the very same Gibson L-5 she bought in 1928, when the Carter Family took their first steps toward their eventual immortality. By that moment, the evolution of country had come full circle, sprawling out from backwater poverty to become one of the most beloved and lucrative industries in the country. None of this would have happened had the Carters not reunited to cut "Can the Circle Be Unbroken."

1936

"The Way You Look Tonight"

Fred Astaire

The '30s were an era where the foundations of America's greatest art forms were being laid. Jazz, blues, country and swing all saw landmark recordings that would go on to define their genres. Each of these art forms had its own devoted followers, but on a day-to-day basis, the most popular songs in America were still coming out of the Broadway show tune tradition. Many of these show tunes still displayed the genre's ugly minstrel roots, but others were beginning to refine the Broadway tradition into something cleaner and easier to sell. A professional class of songwriters were working out of a row of buildings in Manhattan's Flower District. These buildings were so full of clanking pianos that the area became known as "Tin Pan Alley."

The songwriters and song pluggers in Tin Pan Alley started a tradition of popular songwriting that still lives on through pop songwriters today. Tin Pan Alley songs were huge through the 1920s, but in the '30s they got a jump start, thanks to a different industry on the opposite side of the country. In the late '20s, Hollywood started to experiment with technology that could add sound to film. Before long, talking pictures had become the country's latest fad. Many of these talking pictures were modeled after the revues and musicals of Broadway. They had simple scripts to showcase the songs and bring them to life with singers and dancers. These talking pictures spawned an entire culture of Hollywood stars, but none was as big as Fred Astaire.

Astaire was a bright spot amid the darkness of the Great Depression. Together with his screen partner Ginger Rogers, he provided much-needed hope and escapism for a suffering nation. Their natural on-screen chemistry warmed the hearts of a weary nation, and their marvelous dancing skills enchanted all who went to the pictures. Those dancing skills were what Astaire was best known for, and what he took most pride in, but he was just as popular in his day for singing. His singing voice didn't have the power of Al Jolson and he couldn't croon like his contemporary Bing Crosby, but Astaire sang with a gentle voice and perfect diction. He could transform even the sappiest ballad into something real and human. One of the most beloved songs of his singing career was "The Way You Look Tonight."

Composed by Jerome Kern with lyrics by Dorothy Fields, "The Way You Look Tonight" was originally featured in the 1936 film *Swing Time*. The song's simple sentimentality was a soothing balm in a world becoming more complex by the minute. It won Best Original Song at the Academy Awards, and a recorded version of it sold like hotcakes even as the industry was floundering.

It's a song that thrives on Astaire's simple sentimentality. He's not trying to perform vocal acrobatics or make triumphant declarations; he's simply singing a sweet melody of love. The song is tinged with a nostalgia for lighter times before, but also carries with it a sort of resilience. It's a sign that, even in the darkest of times, one can always find hope in love.

The songs that Fred Astaire and his ilk sang would live on far beyond the '30s. As talking pictures and Broadway shows brought them into the cultural consciousness, it became the norm for other pop musicians to take on their own renditions. One by one, these pop musicians following in Astaire's footsteps started to create a musical canon dubbed the "Great American Songbook." This would form the basis of songs for the next 30 years of jazz and pop music and still stands as one of the richest, most extensive collections of pop songs in the history of music. There were dozens of artists who contributed to the Great American Songbook, but in the consciousness of Depression-era Americans, none was more important than Fred Astaire.

1937

"Cross Road Blues"

Robert Johnson

If rock music has a creation myth, it goes something like this:

One dark night in Mississippi, a man named Robert Johnson met with the Devil at the crossroads. Johnson wanted to become the greatest guitarist ever to walk the earth. The Devil wanted Johnson's soul. The two parties struck a bargain, and music was forever changed. From that day on, Johnson was gifted with ungodly talents on the six-string. But only a few short years later, the devil returned for Johnson's soul, ending his life at just 27 years of age.

So many of the tropes that would become rock staples are baked into this myth: the satanic connections, the larger-than-life guitar talent, the curse of the "27 Club." The power of this myth is aided by the fact that Robert Johnson was a truly singular guitarist. He could strum melody and rhythm simultaneously, creating the feel of multiple guitars playing at once. He had a mastery of tone, using slide guitar to echo the pained wails of his blues.

"Cross Road Blues" is a masterclass in blues guitar. Johnson puts every ounce of himself into the jangly rhythm that propels the song forward. In between this trainlike momentum, Johnson is filling space with flourishes. His slides and bends in this song would inspire such future guitar gods as Jimmy Page, Eric Clapton and Jimi Hendrix.

This guitar is paired with a raw vocal performance, singing lyrics written by Johnson himself. If the legends are to be believed, "Cross Road Blues" is a retelling of Johnson's fateful deal with the devil. But when you look more closely at the lyrics of "Cross Road Blues," they tell a different story. Nowhere in its five verses does the song mention any sort of Faustian bargain. Instead, a close reading reveals a darker and more real story that's baked into the Delta blues. "Cross Road Blues" is a song with a heavy subtext of segregation and racial violence.

The lyrics of "Cross Road Blues" depict a traveling blues man who is in a moment of despair. He has lost his love and can't flag a ride, and the sun is falling behind the horizon. The threat of night has demonic associations, but when put in the context of the Jim Crow South, the sun's going down means something else entirely. When Robert Johnson was traveling the Mississippi Delta in the 1930s, many of the towns he'd have to go through were so-called sundown towns. These towns were full of white supremacists who did not want Black people in their town. They would put up signs threatening Black people away and implement discriminatory policies. Among these policies were threats of violence, or even lynching, if Black people were seen in the town after dark.

The blues is a music rooted in the lived experience of Black communities in a segregated America. This reality cannot be extricated from its music, and it can't be extricated from "Cross Road Blues." Robert Johnson's harrowing portrayal in this song hinted at the true dangers that a Black artist might face traveling through the Jim Crow South.

The song likely got its demonic associations years after Johnson died. In 1961, Columbia Records released a compilation of Robert Johnson's music called *King of the Delta Blues Singers*. This release came at the beginning of a folk music revival, when musicians in America and the United Kingdom were yearning to get their hands on authentic American folksongs. Johnson and many of his Delta blues contemporaries saw explosions in popularity as young musicians began to incorporate his style of blues into their generation's rock n' roll music. During this blues revival, it seems that Robert Johnson's story got confused with that of Tommy Johnson. Tommy, who bore no relation to Robert, was a blues singer who was known for playing up demonic myths about himself. He was likely the one that created the story of a Faustian bargain at the crossroads, and his story was transferred to Robert Johnson by young blues enthusiasts eager to sink their teeth into blues mythology.

The more fantastical aspects of Robert Johnson's story are likely fable, but the truth of Robert Johnson is that he does, in many ways, represent the birth of rock n' roll. He was one of the finest in a generation of Delta blues singers, and he set the stage for rock n' roll to take over. "Cross Road Blues" will forever live on as a larger-than-life myth, but the reality of it also paints a picture of the pain and terror experienced by Black Americans throughout the 1930s.

1938

"Sing Sing Sing (With a Swing!)"

Benny Goodman

It might seem like a paradox that one of the darkest chapters in American history spawned one of the most joyful, exuberant movements in all of music. But really, it was inevitable. The human spirit is a resilient thing. When pushed to the brink, it will often respond with defiance and celebration. That's what swing music was: an exuberant celebration of all of the joys of human life, forged in an era when so many people had so few joys to look forward to.

Swing was an extension of the jazz music that flourished in the 1920s, thanks to such artists as Louis Armstrong and Duke Ellington. In a time of scarcity, swing was a music of excess. The bands were big, the arrangements were loud and the accompanying dances consisted of elaborate feats of coordination and aesthetics. The most famous of these dances was the Lindy Hop, an acrobatic style of dance that came up in the ballrooms of Harlem alongside swing itself. Both started in predominantly Black communities in the late 1920s, but by the mid-'30s, both had crossed over into mainstream America. Throughout the Jazz Age, jazz had approached the boundaries of popular music time and time again, but had never fully crossed over. As is too often

the case, it took a musician who wasn't from the Black communities that originated swing to cross it over to white America. The man who accomplished that feat was named Benny Goodman, and in his day, he was known as the King of Swing.

Goodman was the ninth child born to Russian Jewish immigrants in Chicago. He grew up in abject poverty in a tenement. He found an escape from his bleak situation by throwing himself into the jazz scene that was exploding in Chicago at the time. Goodman quickly developed a knack for the clarinet. He found work as a sideman while still a teenager, and by the time he was 20, he was leading his own band. In 1935, at the age of 26, Goodman's orchestra scored their first major hit with a Fletcher Henderson arrangement of the jazz standard "King Porter Stomp." That record kicked the burgeoning swing era into high gear and lifted Goodman to levels of fame and fortune that few musicians before him had ever seen.

Radio performances and shows at all-ages venues had endeared Goodman to a generation of younger, teenage fans looking for hope and escape in a world that seemingly had no future. They showed up in droves, plastering posters on their walls and chasing after auto-graphs from Goodman and his swing contemporaries. It was the first time in American history that popular music had truly been a youth movement, led by teenagers. It wouldn't be the last.

In fact, Benny Goodman and the entire swing movement was the birth of so many aspects of pop music that we now take for granted. Because of the tight economic situation, the swing bands were some of the first to embark on the sort of grueling cross-country tours that are the norm in music today. Swing was also one of the first popular music movements to spawn moral panics and culture wars between the younger generation and their parents, a pattern that plays out again and again for each subsequent generation. These panics couldn't slow the meteoric rise of the Benny Goodman Orchestra. As the swing era picked up, his band recorded hit after hit, almost single-handedly jolting the dormant record industry back to life.

In 1937, Goodman and his orchestra released the original recording of "Sing Sing Sing (With a Swing)." The arrangement of this song, done by Jimmy Mundy, took it miles away from Louis Prima's 1936 original version. It wails and roars with wild energy and nonstop rhythm, stretching the song across both sides of a 78 RPM record. The song showed off Goodman's wild clarinet chops. Atop Gene Krupa's legendary rumbling drumline, horn lines come in and out, serving as exclamatory punctuations of pleasure and joy. The song features one of the most famous drum breaks in jazz history and some of the catchiest melodies of the era. It quickly became the band's biggest song and added another feather to Good-man's cap.

By the end of 1937, the momentum of swing was unstoppable. The Benny Goodman Orchestra had become famous for their swinging performances in ballrooms and dancehalls across the country, but publicist Wynn Nathanson had bigger ambitions. He booked the Benny Goodman Orchestra to play the famed Carnegie Hall on January 16, 1938. It was the first time a jazz artist would play such an auspicious venue. In an echo of Paul Whiteman's famous "Experiment in Modern Music," Benny Goodman's Carnegie Hall show was attended by many of the most celebrated names in music at the time. It was a collision of the old classical establishment and a new jazz youth movement. It was the first time that jazz was truly taken seriously as an art form by those outside the movement.

Goodman's orchestra were tentative to start this historic show, but by the end of the first song, they'd shaken off nerves and remembered how to swing. They played a raucous set that included a brief history of jazz and featured guest appearances from members of Duke Ellington's and Count Basie's bands. By the end of the night, Goodman's orchestra had fans old and young alike standing up and dancing in the aisles of Carnegie Hall. They closed the night on a 13-minute version of "Sing Sing Sing," complete with a spontaneous Jess Stacy piano solo that added a touch of elegance to a piece full of vigor and bombast.

The recordings of this Carnegie Hall show wouldn't be released until 1950, but listening to them now, we can understand what it might have been like seeing Benny Goodman in his prime. The Carnegie Hall concert was a landmark moment in jazz and marked a high point in Goodman's career. That concert, like much of his career, is a sheer triumph. It's a celebration of instrumental talent and emotional release, created by a Jewish man who raised himself up from nothing in a burgeoning age of antisemitism.

And yet, Benny Goodman's career comes with complex baggage behind it as well. Like Paul Whiteman before him, he never pretended to own jazz or swing music. Goodman paid deep respect to the Black musicians who pioneered the genre and tried to platform them when he could. But the fact that he was able to find levels of commercial success far beyond that of Black con-

temporaries like Basie or Ellington is an indication of the pervasive racism of the times he lived in. Stating this reality is not a diminishment of his legacy. In fact, Goodman probably helped tear down those very racial barriers by bringing swing into the mainstream. But it also marks the beginning of yet another pattern that would repeat across music history—art forms created by Black communities becoming legitimized in the mainstream only when performed by artists who aren't part of those communities themselves.

The human spirit is a resilient thing. When pushed to the brink, it will often respond with defiance and celebration. That's what swing music was: an exuberant celebration of all of the joys of human life, forged in an era when so many people had so few joys to look forward to.

1939

"Strange Fruit"

Billie Holiday

When Billie Holiday debuted the most important song of her career, she was met with a piercing silence. Not a soul among the audience knew how to react. People seldom know how to react when they witness history being made. After a long moment, one audience member began to clap, and the room broke into a roar of applause. The patrons of Greenwich Village's Café Society nightclub had just witnessed the debut of a song that would not just define Holiday's career, but that would begin seismic shifts in the very fabric of American society.

"Strange Fruit," the song that Billie Holiday debuted that fateful night in Greenwich Village, was a far cry from the music that she'd become famous for singing. Throughout the 1930s, Holiday rose to prominence with sweet love songs and aching blues ballads. She gained renown as a vocal genius for her singular voice, shaping her words so that she sounded like an instrument and pouring every ounce of herself into her songs. She became a staple of Harlem's nightclub scene and played with such celebrated bandleaders as Count Basie and Artie Shaw. Had she never decided to sing "Strange Fruit," Billie Holiday would still be celebrated as one of the most

It was not meant to soothe or entertain. It was meant to educate.

beloved vocalists in the entirety of music history. But her decision to put life and limb at risk by singing a gruesome protest song lifted her into a truly rarified air. With "Strange Fruit," Holiday accomplished the dream of so many musicians—she made real, tangible social change with her art.

Abel Meeropol, the writer of "Strange Fruit," was not a Tin Pan Alley song plugger nor was he a jazz virtuoso. He was a high school teacher and a unionist. He wrote the song after seeing a grisly 1930 photograph of two Black men who were lynched in Indiana. The violence of the photo shocked Meeropol so deeply that he turned to poetry to process it. The result was a three-verse poem using visceral, graphic imagery to depict the horror of lynching, creating ironic contrast with romantic images of the American South. Meeropol was not Black himself, but was no stranger to racial prejudice. As a Jewish person, no doubt he was well aware of what was happening in Europe when he wrote the poem in 1937. Seeing the rise of Nazism in Germany, Meeropol tried to do his part to combat the exact same sort of racial violence happening in his own country.

Meeropol published his poem, then called "Bitter Fruit," in a Teachers Union paper. Following that publication, he put music to the song and found musicians to perform it at union meetings. When Meeropol met Billie Holiday at Café Society and showed her his song, she was moved by the piece. It reminded her of her own father, who had just recently died. Clarence Holiday was a jazz musician who had served abroad in World War I, where he developed chronic lung problems from inhaling mustard gas. While touring in Texas in 1937, he caught a chest cold. The only hospitals nearby were segregated and refused to serve him. By the time he was able to get to a veterans' hospital in Dallas, the cold had turned to pneumonia, and it was too late for the elder Holiday. It was not exactly a lynching, but it might as well have been.

Over the course of a week, Holiday worked with pianist Sonny White and arranger Danny Mendelsohn to create a version of the piece that she could sing. Although she was just 24 years old, she knew the sort of impact that a song like "Strange Fruit" could have if done well.

It was only natural to debut the song at Café Society, not just because that was where Holiday had discovered the song, but also because Café Society was the first integrated nightclub in America. If the audience there wasn't receptive to "Strange Fruit," then nobody would be.

After their initial shock, the audience of Café Society realized the masterpiece that "Strange Fruit" was. Not just that night, but night after night. "Strange Fruit" became an essential part of Holiday's set, first in the Café Society and then in nightclubs around the city and across the country. She started to close every set with it, having waiters stop their serving and the lights dim before she sang it each time. She wanted to draw every audience's full attention to the piece. It was not meant to soothe or entertain. It was meant to educate, to force people to confront the twisted realities of their own country.

On April 20, 1939, Holiday recorded "Strange Fruit." In the sparse arrangement populated by somber piano and a haunting trumpet line, her words ache with the pain of a woman who knew racial prejudice as well as any, despite her being just 24 years old. That recording sent waves across America. It stirred national conversation about the grisly practice of lynching, and it helped feed the intellectual and artistic energy that would eventually culminate in the civil rights movement.

"Strange Fruit" gave Holiday an outsized cultural impact. But in doing so, it also drew the attention of a racist society that wasn't ready to confront the ghosts

in its own closet. Holiday was targeted and harassed by the DEA and the FBI for her protests. She continued to face the same racial prejudices she'd felt all her life on a day-to-day basis. "Strange Fruit" could not provide her with escape from the terrible realities of a segregated America. And yet it was able to do so much more. It was able to give voice to countless victims of American racism. It was able to push a country toward a long-overdue shift. It was able to inspire new generations of musicians to push protest music into more direct, more radical directions. Even today, "Strange Fruit" remains an eternal reminder of the sins of America's not-too-distant past.

Simply put, "Strange Fruit" is one of the single most important pieces of music ever recorded.

A WORLD IN FLUX

1940-49

The Second World War brought with it some of the most dramatic changes in human history. It shook the world to its core and set the stage for the modern era. These tendrils of war stretched far beyond the battlefield. It opened opportunities for women and marginalized populations to fight for the rights they deserved. The war even reached into dance halls and recording studios, into theaters and onto airwaves. It fanned the growing flames of mass media and accelerated the march of technology. The result of all of this was an era of change.

The social and cultural ideals of the interwar years fell apart when forced to bear witness to the atrocities of World War II. All that seemed true and certain was thrown into question, and it was reflected in the arts. Brilliant auteurs seized the tumultuous moment and used it to express their pain, their sorrows. In New York, a new style of theater was born, and a generation of jazz musicians started to redefine what music was capable of. Meanwhile, country music became a mass phenomenon, thanks to the advance of radio technology. The youth culture that had

1940

1941

1942

1943

1944

started with swing grew and expanded, as teenagers started to assert themselves as not just members of society but as defining drivers of culture.

Amid all this breakneck change, a new style of music was starting to take root. The great American art forms of jazz, blues, gospel and country all started to meld together in southern churches and northern nightclubs. A rough beast that would come to be called "rock n' roll" was slouching toward Memphis to be born.

1945
1946
1947
1948
1949

1940

"I Ain't Got No Home in This World Anymore"

Woody Guthrie

In the middle to late 1930s, a series of successive droughts and dust storms washed across America's prairies, leaving devastation and desolation in their wake. For many families already living on the verge, thanks to the economic impacts of the Great Depression, the so-called Dust Bowl was the last straw. Half a million people were left homeless, and 3.5 million people began a great westward migration in search of work. One of these migrants was a traveling musician who would forever change the fabric of American folk music.

Woody Guthrie was born to a middle-class Oklahoma family, but by the time the Dust Bowl hit, he was living in Texas. Passionate about music from a young age, he spent most of his high school years skipping class to learn tunes from the local street musicians. This passion for music developed into a profession for Guthrie when he took up with the migration of Okies headed westward to California.

The road exposed him to a wealth of songs—traditional pieces and old blues tunes from all across the prairies. Guthrie was happy to pick up as many folk songs as he could, and he began to write his own tunes, too. He also started to inject his own unique voice into his singing, filling both his guitar and vocals with a distinct rural twang. By the time he arrived in California, he had been given the nickname the "Dust Bowl Troubadour." He found work at a radio station in Los Angeles and earned enough money to move his family out with him.

While in California, Guthrie developed a political consciousness. He started a column for a communist paper and began to realize the potential that music had to spread political messages. But when the Second World War broke out and the Soviet Union allied with Nazi Germany, Guthrie's station fired him for his communist beliefs. So, he took to the road once more, traveling across the country to New York City, the center of the musical universe at the time.

Guthrie rode rails along the way and refined his songwriting. His works alternated between lighthearted satire and a journalistic sort of human storytelling, documenting the lives of the millions impacted by the Depression, the Dust Bowl and the Labor Wars. On his way to New York, he stopped in Washington, D.C., and cut a number of recordings with Alan Lomax for the Library of Congress. That was the first time Guthrie's music had ever been put to wax, but it wouldn't be long before he recorded again.

In the spring of 1940, Guthrie sat down with Victor Records and recorded 11 original songs that he'd written during his travels. That summer, those songs were released across six 78 RPM records under the name *Dust Bowl Ballads*. Those records are some of the most important in folk history. They're sometimes called the first concept album, even though they predate the modern conception of albums as a medium by about a decade. *Dust Bowl Ballads* also helped introduce a new journalistic conception of folk music. Rather than simply singing old hymns and blues songs, Guthrie took these melodies and adapted them to his times, telling human stories of struggle and spreading his political messages. This process is clear on "I Ain't Got No Home in This World Anymore."

The second-to-last song on *Dust Bowl Ballads*, "I Ain't Got No Home" is a response to "Can't Feel at Home," a gospel song that Guthrie heard migrants singing during his travels. That song is an expression of the pain of losing one's home, but it offers promise of a better home in heaven. Guthrie disliked this idea of coping with poverty by hoping for spiritual salvation. The way he saw it, many of the conditions of this poverty were created by a society that hoarded wealth and abandoned the poor. In "I Ain't Got No Home," he reframes the

hymn to point the finger at police, bankers and those in society who hoarded wealth even as millions in their country were starving. He sings these lines with his signature drawl, coloring the song with a chugging harmonica. Guthrie's sound straddled folk and country music and made him a key early figure in both movements.

Woody Guthrie gave voice to the voiceless with his unique style of folk music. *Dust Bowl Ballads* is not just a fantastic collection of music, it's an archive documenting the stories and struggles of poor folk in America's most desperate hour. With "I Ain't Got No Home," he channels this desperation into rage and offers solutions for how to fix his broken country.

1941

"Chattanooga Choo Choo"

Glenn Miller

Some of the most iconic images of success in the modern music industry are the gold and platinum records. These sales awards presented by the Recording Industry Association of America are highlights of countless musicians' trophy rooms—physical signifiers of their commercial success and symbols of how beloved they were for a moment in time. The first artist ever to receive such an award was a celebrated trombonist and bandleader named Glenn Miller. The golden record itself was a copy of his 1941 megahit "Chattanooga Choo Choo."

Miller's orchestra was one of the single most successful bands of the swing era, even outselling Benny Goodman in the early 1940s. While there were a number of talented instrumentalists in Miller's orchestra, the band truly cut their checks on tight arrangement and brilliant orchestration. Miller's music was clean and structured. Whereas other bandleaders let their soloists go wild, he preferred to have his soloists hold back. Their role was to provide small moments of punctuation within a larger ensemble. This is clear in "Chattanooga Choo Choo," a song propelled by a crisp rhythm and clean melodies. Pulsing horns emulate the titular train leaving the station while clarinet flourishes glisten and dance.

Like much of Miller's music, "Chattanooga Choo Choo" was a vocal piece. After one instrumental verse, singer Tex Beneke offers a crisp, casual vocal delivery in call and response with a chorus of backing singers. The lyrics are simple and lighthearted, tapping into the long history of train songs and describing a journey from New York to Chattanooga. This sort of smooth vocal arrangement and lighthearted lyricism helped give Miller's music a broader appeal, including a more conservative audience that might have been put off by the wilder sounds of the Benny Goodman Orchestra. In doing so, Miller truly carried swing music into the mainstream and set established big band vocal jazz as the sound of the '40s.

"Chattanooga Choo Choo" had a lengthy chart run that saw it sell more than 1.2 million copies in its first year. Its success was a sign that the recording industry was well and truly back, following the Great Depression. Miller's label, RCA Victor, saw fit to celebrate this feat. In early 1942, they presented Miller with a solid gold record that actually had "Chattanooga Choo Choo" cut on it. It was the first time such an award would be given out. That award was the inspiration for the RIAA's golden certification practice, which started a generation later in 1958.

The joy and success of "Chattanooga Choo Choo" came against a backdrop of uncertain times. While the song was on its historic chart run, the Imperial Japanese Navy Air Service bombed Pearl Harbor and pulled the United States into World War II. Despite the fact that Miller was at the peak of his recording career and already in his late 30s, he chose to enlist in the armed forces. He boosted troop morale leading the U.S. Armed Air Forces Training Command Orchestra and was an active participant in counterpropaganda operations. On December 15, 1944, Miller boarded a small military plane flying from London to Paris. Somewhere over the English Channel, his plane disappeared. He was never seen again.

To this day, Glenn Miller and His Orchestra live on as one of the finest and most beloved swing bands ever to play. "Chattanooga Choo Choo" is a perfect example of the sort of rollicking, joyful music that got America out of its seats and onto the dance floor even as the specter of a world war loomed over the country.

"White Christmas"

Bing Crosby

On Christmas Day 1941, just eighteen days after the bombing of Pearl Harbor, Bing Crosby sat down for his beloved radio show, *Kraft Music Hall*, and serenaded his country with a new song called "White Christmas." It was a melancholy song filled with nostalgia for happier times, a fitting choice for a somber moment. Crosby was a fitting performer as well, having spent the '30s singing his way into America's heart with his signature crooning style.

Before Crosby came around, the limitations of recording technology meant that singers needed to project their voice to avoid being drowned out by their band. But that shifted with the invention of electronic microphones, which picked up a broader sound spectrum. These revolutions were happening just as Crosby was coming of age, and he was one of the first to truly realize the potential of this emergent microphone technology. He realized that by singing close to the microphone, he could create a warm, intimate singing sound. This technique came to be known as "crooning," and thanks to Crosby, it would become the dominant singing technique for a generation of musicians.

On top of his smooth croon, Crosby's singing borrowed from the jazz and blues traditions. In particular, he was influenced by Louis Armstrong and another jazz singer named Mildred Bai-

ley. The jazz affectations that Crosby adopted gave a little bit of pizzazz to his vocals and helped set him apart from the other white singers of the day. Like so many from his era, he had a complex relationship with race. He had a deep respect for Black musicians, and worked to ensure they were properly compensated and given the spotlight they deserved, but he also performed in blackface, continuing the racist minstrel traditions of American popular music.

Through the '30s, Crosby became one of the most beloved singers in America. As was the norm for the time, this also meant he had a lucrative film career. By the time he recorded "White Christmas" in 1942, other songs of his had garnered four nominations for Best Original Song at the Academy Awards, including one win in 1937. In 1943, "White Christmas" would add another Best Original Song win to his tally when it was featured in the 1942 film *Holiday Inn*.

The song was written by one of America's most influential and beloved songwriters, Irving Berlin. By the time he wrote "White Christmas," Berlin had been writing hits for more than three decades. He was a master of songcraft, and when it comes to songwriting, Berlin is likely the single most prolific contributor to the Great American Songbook. When working with Paramount

Pictures, he was asked to write songs for each major American holiday. This was a difficult task for him because he didn't personally celebrate most of those holidays.

Berlin was a Jewish immigrant from Russia, so he didn't participate in the holiday of Christmas. For him, it was a day of mourning, as his infant son had died on Christmas Day in 1928. Both of these factors surely played into his writing such a melancholic Christmas song. "White Christmas" was thoroughly unique in its day not just because of this melancholy, but also because it is a purely secular Christmas song. The song features no references to any of the Christian aspects of the holiday, but is a nostalgic dream of winter and snow. It's a magnificent sleight of hand by Berlin that helped turn Christmas into a cultural holiday that could be celebrated by all.

Berlin knew that "White Christmas" would be one of his finest works immediately upon writing it. It took the rest of the world a while to catch on. The first recorded version of "White Christmas" came out in July 1942, before *Holiday Inn* hit theaters in August. Originally, "White Christmas" was overshadowed by other songs from the film. But as the holiday season crept closer, it started to gain some momentum. The dark realities of a wartime Christmas made people gravitate toward Berlin's sorrowful tune. It was topping charts by the end of October. Soldiers abroad were just as taken with the song as were the families they'd left behind. It was one of the most requested songs on military radio stations as young men dreamed of better times back home.

By the end of 1942, "White Christmas" was the biggest song of the year and well on its way to becoming an integral part of the American Christmas canon. It proved that a secular Christmas song could perform commercially, and it became a crowning achievement for both Crosby and Berlin. According to Guinness World Records, Crosby's recording of "White Christmas" is the single best-selling record in music history, selling more than 50 million copies worldwide. When you take into account the dozens of other artists who have recorded their own take on that song, those sales numbers surely double.

"White Christmas" is a Christmas song that's not really about the holiday, written by somebody who didn't truly celebrate it. It completely eschews the joy typically associated with the season and opts instead for a more subtle cocktail of sorrow and nostalgia. It's a piece that tugs directly at the soul and embodies all of the complexities of the human experience.

"Oklahoma"

Richard Rodgers, Oscar Hammerstein II and Original Broadway Cast

Musical theater was deep in a slump in the early 1940s. The medium had once been one of the most celebrated and beloved art forms in the country. From the turn of the century through the end of the '20s, Broadway was the origin point of much of American popular music. In those days, most shows staged were lighthearted musical comedy revues. They were built around showcasing star talents and catchy songs. For most early musicals, story was an afterthought, if it was even there at all. This format worked for a time but, as with so many things, it started to shift during the Depression. With less disposable income, people went to the theater less, and thus the theaters had to cut production values. The result was a stale industry, devoid of innovation. To make matters worse, sound on film had led to a golden age of cinema, with movie musicals stealing audiences away from the theater. In such times, few could have predicted that musical theater was about to launch into its own golden age.

That golden age came courtesy of a new collaboration between Richard Rodgers and Oscar Hammerstein II. Both men were already veterans of the Broadway scene in 1943. Rodgers spent the Roaring '20s writing hit Broadway shows alongside his lyricist and writing partner Lorenz Hart. When the Depression hit and success dried up, they moved across the country and tried to break into Hollywood. But Hart suffered from mental illness and dealt with the trauma of being a gay man in a homophobic society. In the early '40s, he slipped into alcoholism. Rodgers and Hart broke up their writing partnership in 1943, and a few months later, Hart died at age 48.

In need of a new writing partner, Rodgers reached out to Hammerstein. The two had worked together when they were students at Columbia University in 1920, but hadn't collaborated since. Hammerstein had spent the '20s carving his own legacy as a lyricist. His most successful piece of work from that time was *Show Boat*, a musical that he created with Jerome Kern. Unlike most of the other musicals, *Show Boat* had a cohesive narrative woven through its songs. This sort of story-driven musical was something Hammerstein was keen to experiment more with, and he got that chance when Rodgers asked him to collaborate.

The first piece that Rodgers and Hammerstein wrote together was a musical adaptation of the stage play *Green Grow the Lilacs*. Written by Lynn Riggs

in 1930, that play depicts a human drama. It tells a pastoral story of two young lovers in the former Indian Territory at the turn of the century. The original play featured a number of traditional folk songs, which Rodgers and Hammerstein replaced with original pieces. These new pieces were written with Hammerstein's more comprehensive narrative vision. Song and dance are used to express the characters' deepest joys, pains and desires. They are underscored by Rodgers' marvelous orchestration and flesh out the emotional beats of the story in a way that no dialogue could. This kind of storytelling is called a "book musical" and is standard now, but it was wildly inventive in its time.

Rodgers and Hammerstein named their musical *Oklahoma!* and brought it to Broadway in the spring of 1943. It was an immediate sensation. Audiences connected with the folksy Americana nostalgia and fell in love with the young lead characters. The listeners had never before encountered such a cohesive collision of music and storytelling. It was such a success that its Broadway run lasted five years.

The title song—"Oklahoma"—comes toward the end of the musical. It's a spectacular group number, with witty lyrics written in an Oklahoman dialect. The music is sweeping and grand, embodying the landscape that serves as the setting for the story. Immaculate vocal arrangements match form to content, blowing in like the wind coming sweeping across the plain. Gorgeous harmonies back up the show's leads as they sing the joy of their wedding day. This celebratory moment is placed against the backdrop of Oklahoma's impending statehood. All signs are pointing to a bright new future.

Oklahoma! itself provided that bright future for musical theater. Rodgers and Hammerstein continued to collaborate until Hammerstein's death in 1960. They wrote such beloved works as *The King and I* and *The Sound of Music*, and inspired everyone from Andrew Lloyd Webber and Stephen Sondheim to Lin Manuel Miranda. With *Oklahoma!*, Rodgers and Hammerstein completely transformed musical theater from a stale form struggling to compete with cinema into one of the most unique, enduring forms of American art.

"You'll Never Know"

Frank Sinatra

Just after midnight on October 12, 1944, a small crowd of teenage girls started to form outside of New York's Paramount Theatre. By the time dawn broke, that number had ballooned to the hundreds. Before the day was out, that crowd would turn into a near stampede of 30,000 teenage girls, all clad in bobby sox, penny loafers and poodle skirts. Every single one of them was there for the same reason: They'd all come down with a bout of Sinatramania.

Frank Sinatra's rise to fame was nothing short of meteoric. After spending his teenage years and early 20s in smaller vocal groups, he got his first big break in 1940 as the lead singer for Tommy Dorsey's big band. He cut a hit with Dorsey, and by '41, music magazines were declaring him the most beloved male singer. By the autumn of '42, it had become clear that Sinatra could make it as a solo act. He broke from Tommy Dorsey, and at the end of that year, debuted his solo career with a Paramount show that drew an enormous audience of teen girls. Fan clubs began popping up around the country as Sinatra gained the nickname "The Voice." In 1943, he made his first solo recordings, "You'll Never Know" among them.

"You'll Never Know" is exactly the sort of sweet love song that drove a generation of teenagers wild. Sinatra built on Bing Crosby's intimate croon. He knew how to inject his baritone with saccharine sentimentality. Every flourish and quiver make the listener feel as though the dreamy Sinatra were singing directly to them. For the young women of the time, he could represent their fathers, brothers, friends and lovers who had been sent off across the ocean to fight in the war. His ability to enchant was aided by his sharp jawline and piercing blue eyes.

On the day that 30,000 bobby soxers came out to steal a glimpse at those eyes, Sinatra was due to play several sets at the Paramount. When he finished the first show, fans refused to leave, creating a backup of people waiting to get in. Eventually this growing crowd stirred into a frenzy and marched into Times Square in a moment that became known as the "Columbus Day Riot."

As is often the case when teenagers latch onto some cultural object, Frank Sinatra soon became a target of controversy and moral panic. Parents began to think he had corrupted their children and stirred them into frenzies. "Sinatramania" was a target of derision in the press until it subsided in the postwar years. What was really happening was not some intellectual contagion, but rather a generation of young women truly expressing themselves for the first time. A month before the Columbus Day Riots, *Seventeen* magazine had

debuted, acknowledging teenage girls as both creators and consumers of culture.

When it came to the brilliance of Sinatra, the teenage girls were right, as they often are. Although his career would go through a slump, Sinatra bounced back and continued recording hits well into the '60s. He became a master of the Great American Songbook and one of the most beloved icons in the country's history. This pattern of teenage tastemakers that started with Benny Goodman and Frank Sinatra would continue on, as successive generations of teenage girls became the first to embrace such acts as Elvis Presley and the Beatles. The Columbus Day Riots of 1944 were a harbinger of things to come. The sorts of youth movements that started with Benny Goodman were picking up steam with Sinatra. It wouldn't be long before teenagers became the definitive tastemakers of modern music.

"Strange Things Happening Every Day"

Sister Rosetta Tharpe

In the first half of the twentieth century, millions of southern Black families packed up their lives and moved northward and westward to search for jobs and escape the brutal realities of the Jim Crow South. This Great Migration brought on a cultural collision of enormous proportions. In the South, jazz had been the urban music of New Orleans, while blues dominated the rural reaches of the Mississippi Delta. As more and more rural southern folk started to chase work and opportunity in the urban centers of Chicago and New York, those two worlds began to mingle and mix. The result was a new sort of music that people would eventually call "rhythm and blues." This new music combined the swinging rhythms of jazz with the raw, guitar-led grooves of blues. It started to pop up in the 1940s, and one of its earliest pioneers was a queer gospel singer named Sister Rosetta Tharpe.

Tharpe was a musical prodigy. Both her parents were musicians and she learned to play the guitar at just four years old. By age six, she was already performing alongside her mother. Like so many blues greats, Tharpe cut her teeth in traveling shows that toured across the South. But unlike the bawdy vaudeville shows of Ma Rainey, Tharpe and her mother were part of an evangelical group who would spread the word of their God to churches across the region. Eventually, the two landed in Chicago, where a new jazz scene was flourishing. Tharpe recorded her first songs in the 1930s with a jazz orchestra backing her. When she made another move, from Chicago to New York, her career really began to soar. She played the Cotton Club and became one of the first gospel singers to truly find success in secular audiences.

Tharpe was on the forefront of the developing rhythm and blues sound. Having spent her childhood in the South and her adolescence in the North, she was a living example of the cultural cross-pollination brought on by the Great Migration. Her music swung like jazz but highlighted her powerful gospel voice and her effortless guitar playing. This sound truly

> This Great Migration brought on a cultural collision of enormous proportions.

coalesced in her 1945 hit "Strange Things Happening Every Day."

Tharpe's guitar boogies and woogies its way through that entire song. It supports her dramatic, evangelist vocal performance. The highlight is an invigorating guitar solo midway through the song. It's a shamelessly showy piece of music that flaunts Tharpe's extraordinary talent at the instrument.

Lyrically, the song captures the surreal existence that was life in the '40s. Technologies were evolving at a breakneck pace. The world just witnessed a war unlike anything seen before or since, a war that ended with the introduction of nuclear arms. Meanwhile, the cultural fabric of America was in the process of reweaving itself. The war caused changes that shifted the roles of women in society, redefined the political landscape and completely transformed the country's economy. In its own way, "Strange Things Happening Every Day" is a song expressing the uncertain feeling of the era. But its influence stretches far beyond that era.

Much of Tharpe's work can accurately be called "rhythm and blues," but there's another term that some have applied to "Strange Things Happening Every Day." That term is "rock n' roll."

Tharpe is the godmother of the musical movement that would turn the entire world on its head. Her up-tempo gospel/blues sound blasted out on airwaves across the country and into the homes of young aspiring musicians with such names as Little Richard, Elvis Presley and Johnny Cash. Those musicians would soon rise to knock Tharpe out of the spotlight, but by then she was already sending shock waves through another generation. Throughout the '50s and '60s, she would go on tours throughout Europe; her performances

in the United Kingdom inspired the British blues revival of the '60s.

Sister Rosetta Tharpe seamlessly amalgamated three of America's greatest musical traditions. In doing so, she helped spawn a new tradition that would come to overshadow the music she grew up with and become the single most impactful cultural export in her country's history.

1946

"Ko-Ko"

Charlie Parker

The New York jazz scene was sitting on an enormous secret in the early 1940s. While big band mania had swept across the country and packed ballrooms full of eager young dancers, a new culture of renegade jazz musicians was forming in the underground. Unimpressed by the rigid musical structures and blatant corporate interests of swing, these musicians gathered in small clubs for all-night jam sessions. They wanted to bring innovation and improvisation back to jazz, and they were going to do it by pushing the genre to its musical limits. The de facto leader of this movement was not a musician from New York at all, but rather a saxophonist from Kansas City named Charlie Parker.

Parker had spent his teenage years dedicated to the saxophone. He landed a job in Jay McShann's band, where he earned his nickname "Bird" after McShann's tour bus ran over a chicken on the road. Parker told the bus to stop, picked up the chicken, plucked it and served it for dinner that night. When not performing with McShann, he was practicing playing solos at double their speed. He started to obsess over jazz standards, studying their chord changes closely as he searched for new ways to improvise.

In late 1939, he moved to New York, where he would have his great revelation. One day, while playing around with Ray Noble's jazz standard "Cherokee," Parker began to realize that if he played his solo over the chords of the song, rather than over the melody, he could open up a new kind of space in the song, leaving it ripe to be filled with new feelings and improvisational flourishes. This sort of musical acrobatics, combined with lightning-quick tempos and key changes, became the basis of a new style of jazz known as bebop.

Through the early '40s, Parker teamed up with others in this emergent scene, such as Dizzy Gillespie and Max Roach. Together, they pushed jazz into spaces that it had never been before. But nobody outside of the underground club scene knew what was happening. From 1942 until 1944, the American Federation of Musicians went on strike over disagreements on royalty payments. This strike prevented all new instrumental recordings. So, bebop continued to develop in secret until the strike finally ended.

On November 26, 1945, Charlie Parker sat down for a recording with the label Savoy. Those sessions might contain one of the greatest accumulations of musical talent ever to sit in on a session together. He played alongside Dizzy Gillespie, who had been his partner in crime when it came to inventing bebop. The manic drums were laid down by the inimitable Max

Roach, and Curley Russell was on the bass. Also in on these sessions was a young trumpeter named Miles Davis, who would go on to reach the same levels of influence and excellence as Parker himself.

The highlight of these sessions was a song called "Ko-Ko" that featured Parker on sax and Gillespie on trumpet. The song itself was based on the changes of "Cherokee." But any of the smooth comfort of Ray Noble's original piece is gone in "Ko-Ko." Max Roach propels the song forward at a torrid 300 beats per minute. After a 32-bar intro in which Parker and Gillespie play in union and exchange brief solos, Parker breaks into a 64-bar solo the likes of which jazz had never seen before. His improvisations feel nearly effortless, even as they're pushing up against the bounds of what people thought was humanly possible. He soars and dives, able to find points of melody even amid the song's breakneck speed.

The wild virtuosity of "Ko-Ko" was a perfect soundtrack to a world turned upside down by the war. The speed of playing seemed to match the rate of change around the world brought on by mechanization and mass media. The fearless experimentation and dauntless individualism were signals of a new sort of attitude for postwar America. "Ko-Ko" was postmodernism brought to life in jazz form: a rejection of the old forms that beboppers saw as stale, and an embracing of a new style for a new world.

"Ko-Ko" wasn't a commercial success by any means, but it was never meant to be. It was music for musicians. When it released in January 1946, it sent shock waves through the jazz world. For the next decade and a half, many of the most brilliant musicians on earth would be drawn to bebop, and would build on Parker's innovations to create some of the most seminal records in jazz history.

1947

"Move On Up a Little Higher"

Mahalia Jackson

Between the end of 1941 and the summer of 1945, more than one million Black soldiers crossed the seas to fight for the United States in World War II. Many of them did so because they hoped to earn the equality they'd been denied for generations. When they came home after having gone through hell, these soldiers were treated not as heroes but as second-class citizens. The war had changed nearly everything in America, but it had done little to dismantle the country's cultural and political institutions of racism. So, they decided to take matters into their own hands.

A new wave of Black social movements was born in the postwar years, building on the momentum that had started in the '30s with the Harlem Renaissance. This movement was centered on community organization and upward mobility. It got its first great anthem in 1947 when Mahalia Jackson released her surprise hit "Move On Up a Little Higher."

By the time Jackson released the song, she had already tried and failed to crack the music industry. She was an unquestionably talented vocalist, with an enormous voice and a talent for slip-

> When they came home after having gone through hell, these soldiers were treated not as heroes . . .

ping blues phrasing into her gospel songs. Jackson was beloved in Black churches across the country, but much of her audience could not afford to buy records. She could have undoubtedly had crossover success if she were willing to record secular jazz or blues songs, but she was committed to her spirituality. For most of her 20s and half of her 30s, Jackson paid the bills by working odd jobs while she continued to pursue a career as a singer.

She got another chance at stardom when a scout for Apollo Records spotted her at a Harlem show. Apollo signed her and recorded a handful of gospel songs that failed, all the while trying to push her into secular music. But Jackson never gave in, and she finally got her break when she cut "Move On Up a Little Higher."

While the song was ostensibly a gospel piece, it had a clear political undertone. The Reverend W. Herbert Brewster wrote the song in hopes of inspiring Black communities to aspire for a better world. Its repeated titular cry was a call for upward mobility. And its message of empowerment and achievement in the face of violence and segregation was clearly understood by African American listeners.

Brother John Sellers recorded the first version of the song in 1946, but Mahalia Jackson's take was the recording that really took off. The song proved a perfect vehicle for Jackson's commanding voice. The song rolls forward with a slow, but unflappable tempo, building and building with each successive verse.

Not long after its release, "Move On Up a Little Higher" found its way into the hands of a famous Chicago DJ called Studs Terkel. Terkel was entranced by Jackson's voice and spun the song over and over again on his show. This launched the single to success in Chicago first, and then across the country. Shelves started to empty as white and Black audiences alike discovered the power of Jackson. "Move On Up a Little Higher" sold more than two million copies and climbed its way up to number two on Billboard's charts. It was a feat that nobody thought a gospel record was capable of before, and it launched Mahalia Jackson into the spotlight.

Jackson made the most of her fame. She was a powerful critic of segregation, and her politically minded gospel songs fed the fuel of this growing movement. Jackson would be an active participant in the civil rights movement for the rest of her life. She'd sing for civil rights events free of charge, and would use the wealth gained from her recording success to fund civil rights initiatives. Through these initiatives, she became close friends with Martin Luther King Jr.

Mahalia Jackson did more than just call for upward mobility. She was an enormous cultural and economic force for change in the world. By the time she passed in 1971, she would be remem-

bered as one of the key figures of the civil rights movements, and "Move On Up a Little Higher" would be known as one of the most beloved gospel songs ever recorded.

1948

"Nature Boy"

Nat King Cole

One of the most unlikely collaborations in music history has to be Nat King Cole singing eden ahbez's "Nature Boy." Cole was one of the most elegant singers of his day, a consummate gentleman who had found pop success with smooth, easy-listening music carried by a soothing tenor voice. Meanwhile, eden ahbez was an esoteric proto-hippie with long hair and a wild beard who ate only fresh fruit and vegetables, and made his home camping out beneath one of the Ls in the HOLLYWOOD sign. He had been born "George Alexander McGraw," but changed his name as part of his countercultural practice. Throughout his life he'd adopt several spellings of his name, most of them without capitalization.

The story of how "Nature Boy" came to be is just as odd as you might expect. Ahbez had gotten word that Cole accepted unsolicited pitches from songwriters. Eager to take advantage of this, he followed Cole around L.A. for a few weeks before approaching the singer's manager backstage after a show at the Lincoln Theater. He tried to get the manager to give Cole a shabby handwritten lyric sheet, but was turned away. As the legend goes, ahbez settled with giving the lyrics to Cole's valet, who in turn handed them to Cole.

Cole started to incorporate the song into his live set, until one day it caught the attention of Irving Berlin, who wanted to buy it off Cole. Cole declined and decided to record the song himself. His people were able to track down ahbez, who had left no contact information, and in 1948, Cole recorded "Nature Boy." The odd song captured audiences quickly and rode to number one on Billboard's charts as part of a 15-week run.

The appeal of "Nature Boy" is obvious. It's got that strange sort of mystical energy that makes it feel as if it were never written by anybody but rather pulled from the ether or the collective unconscious. Cole's recording underscores the otherworldly nature of the song with ominous orchestral arrangements and twinkling flutes. The whole piece lives in dissonance, creating a slight unease that contradicts the friendly warmth of Cole's vocals.

Lyrically, it's clear that ahbez pulled much of "Nature Boy" from his own odd lifestyle. Throughout the '40s, he was part of a loose countercultural group that called themselves the Nature Boys. They lived outside and foraged for their food, spending their days writing songs and poetry. The Nature Boys were interested in mysticism, and influenced by turn-of-the-century German movements that protested against industrialism. Ahbez had learned about these philosophies from

a man named Bill Pester, who was another point of inspiration for "Nature Boy."

Amid the esotericism and enchantment of "Nature Boy," the song ends on a simple yet profound message about love. This message was in line with new sorts of philosophies that were rising following the horror of World War II. Ahbez was on the forefront of a cultural movement that swelled in the '50s with the Beats, and then exploded in the '60s with the hippies. By that time, ahbez had become somewhat of a cult figure. He was known to hang out with Brian Wilson, and memorialized by Paul McCartney in "Mother Nature's Son."

"Nature Boy" is a song that sits at a cultural crossroads. Nat King Cole was one of the finest pop stars of the '40s and '50s. He was a boundary breaker as the first Black musician ever to have his own radio show, but he also represented an older sort of music: traditional pop and vocal jazz. His songs were lifted by lush arrangements and beautiful vocals. Meanwhile, eden ahbez was ahead of his time. His lifestyle and lyricism are clear influences on the countercultural movements that would spawn in the baby boomer generation. When smashed together, these two worlds ended up creating a song quite unlike anything else recorded before or since.

1949

"I'm So Lonesome I Could Cry"

Hank Williams

There might be no better example of a perfect country song than "I'm So Lonesome I Could Cry." In just 16 lines of lyrics, Hank Williams captured a sorrow so raw, so pure, that songwriters are still chasing it today.

The writing of Williams was always ruthlessly efficient. He could say in four words what it would take other artists an entire career to say. "I'm So Lonesome I Could Cry" is an observational piece, written from the perspective of a quiet night wanderer. Despite the peace and beauty around him, all he can see is woe. The singing whip-poor-will becomes lonesome, and the moon disappears behind clouds to cry; even a shooting star brings with it no magic or joy, just a reminder of distance and loneliness.

Each word is carefully placed, lilting up and down with a simple melody brought to life by Williams' strained yodel. One could be excused for thinking this piece was chiseled from rough drafts into a finely polished diamond. But in reality, Williams had a rare gift for songcraft and was known to pen country classics in 15 minutes with barely a second effort.

Williams himself often attributed his writing to God speaking through him. In reality, his gift for writing pain and despair probably had more to do with how intimately he'd become acquainted with those particular emotions. He came up poor in the Great Depression and started drinking when he was still a child. He was plagued by chronic back pain due to spina bifida, and his marriage to Audrey Sheppard was toxic and volatile. He'd often pull from his spats with Sheppard as inspiration for his music.

He was a complex man with a difficult legacy. When things were good, Williams was known to be friendly and charismatic. When they were bad, he would drink himself into a stupor onstage and fly into a rage at imagined offenses. His struggles with alcoholism led him to an early grave at the age of 29, but not before he'd established himself as one of the most beloved faces in the country music pantheon.

In just 16 lines of lyrics, Hank Williams captured a sorrow so raw, so pure, that songwriters are still chasing it today.

For three years, Williams was the biggest star of the *Grand Ole Opry*, a Nashville radio show that broadcast into radios across the country. His raw storytelling enraptured a generation who were struggling with their own demons. The audience listening to Williams were survivors of the Depression and one, or sometimes two, world wars. They had lost loved ones, seen family members die, known the pain of going to sleep hungry. They were people who had gone through hell but had to hide their scars and put on a straight face. But when Hank Williams came on, they could find kinship in sorrow and be uplifted by his mirth.

Sad songs like "I'm So Lonesome I Could Cry" represent much of Williams' catalog, but he also knew how to let loose and have fun. Many of his more upbeat songs joined Sister Rosetta Tharpe's music in laying a foundation for rock n' roll. The poetry of his writing came to shape future generations as well. He was one of the first true singer-songwriters. Nearly every one of the great songwriters of the '60s, country or otherwise, would name him in their influences. He was a particular favorite of Elvis Presley, the Beatles and Bob Dylan.

Like so many country greats who followed in his footsteps, Williams was a storyteller. His songs were a document of the postwar era, a window into the soul of a generation who had come up through hell and were trying to understand their place in the world. The beauty of "I'm So Lonesome I Could Cry" transcends country music. It's a piece that should be read as literature, and considered among the finest documents of human emotion ever created.

JUKEBOX NATION

The postwar years brought America into a new era of prosperity as the nation rose to become one of the world's greatest economic powers. The shift to a wartime economy had kicked the manufacturing sector into gear. When peace fell on Europe, that manufacturing sector turned its eyes to the home front and started to create all sorts of new technological miracles. Washing machines and vacuum cleaners revolutionized home labor, televisions brought the evening news into living rooms across the country and slick cars brought freedom of movement to a generation of teenagers. Personal turntables got cheaper, and a new method of pressing records emerged. This technique traded the traditions of shellac in for a new kind of plastic called polyvinyl chloride. These so-called vinyl records were cheaper to make and sturdier than the shellac records of old. These shifts in manufacturing facilitated an enormous wave of change across the music industry.

Up until the '50s, households tended to listen to the same music on a shared player. Now, teenagers could get their own cheap turntables and mail-order their own records. They could pile into their cars and drive into diners where they'd spin

1950 1951 1952 1953 1954

the hottest hits from dreamy new artists aimed at this new teen market. The youth has always controlled music culture to some degree, but the generation who came of age in the '50s seized the culture like none before. With entire industries bending over backward to service them, this new generation turned their eyes away from America's historical capital of New York and toward two cities in Tennessee.

In Nashville, the country music that had been the soundtrack to rural America took on an urban tilt. The city turned into a veritable hit factory, churning out smooth, clean superstars who helped create a wholesome culture of Americana. Meanwhile, 200 miles away, a collection of Black and white musicians started to evolve rhythm and blues into a raw, sexual music called rock n' roll. Across the decade, rock n' roll would explode out of Memphis and seize the hearts of a generation of teens. Rock n' roll would become a phenomenon unlike anything the American music industry had ever seen. It spurred moral panics across the country and crowned the kings of a new era. It became a death knell for an era of crooners that had enraptured the previous generation of teens, pushing even Frank Sinatra out of the spotlight. It also pushed jazz out of the mainstream at the very moment that some of the most brilliant jazz players were taking the genre to bold new territory. When rock n' roll arrived on the scene, it kicked off an entirely new era of popular music dominance that would last nearly half a century and reverberate on even further from there.

1955

1956

1957

1958

1959

1950

"Rollin' Stone"

Muddy Waters

Musical change is indelibly tied to technological progress. In the first half of the twentieth century, the invention of recording and broadcasting technologies brought the music industry to life and helped inspire the foundations of modern music. These technologies were based around the premise of capturing sound through a microphone and then transforming that sound into an electronic signal. But sometime in the late '30s, engineers began to experiment with an even more novel idea—cutting the microphone out of the equation and transforming the vibrations coming directly from the instruments themselves. These experiments led to the creation of the earliest electric guitars in the late '30s. Electric guitar technology progressed with the invention of the solid-body electric guitar and advances in electric amplifiers.

By the early '40s, electric guitar technology was ready and ripe for the plucking. Its first adopters were jazz musicians, finding that the amplifiers helped them be heard over the horns in their band. But the guitar was a rhythm instrument in jazz, and it was seldom given a chance to shine. A few blues players made early strides with the electric guitar, but the instrument wouldn't truly get to show the world what it was capable of until a man called Muddy Waters hit the scene.

Muddy Waters was as authentic a bluesman as there ever was. Born in rural Mississippi, he grew up watching the Delta blues greats Son House and Robert Johnson. In 1941, when he was 28 years old, Alan Lomax came through his county, recording blues singers for the Library of Congress. When Waters heard his own recorded singing played back to him for the first time, it was a revelation. He realized that he was every bit as talented as the blues singers whose records he'd been collecting. Two years later, he became one of many great Black musicians moving North as he headed to Chicago to chase a recording career.

Once he got there, Waters found that the city's bustling nightclubs drowned out the sound of his acoustic guitar, so he saved up for an electric guitar and an amplifier. That's when Muddy Waters truly began to shape history. Aided by the exciting new sound of the electric guitar, he and other urban

> He saved up for an electric guitar and an amplifier. That's when Muddy Waters truly began to shape history.

bluesmen started to develop a sound that would be known as "Chicago blues." This style took the original Delta blues and pumped it up with noise and swagger. The grimy sounds of the electric guitar gave the music a raw sort of sexuality, and the bustling sounds of a booming metropolis brought tempo and jump. One of the seminal pieces of Chicago blues was "Rollin' Stone."

"Rollin' Stone" was an adaptation of "Catfish Blues," an old tune that Waters likely had learned when he was still living on the Delta. From the moment he played it on an electric guitar, the tune was forever changed. He transformed it from a jangly Delta blues to a heavy, virile piece of music. His thick guitar tones drench the song in grease, while he moans lyrics full of magic and charisma. Sex had always been a part of the blues, but Waters was one of the first to truly establish himself as a national sex symbol with his playing.

In doing so, he was also setting the standard for the lead guitarist as a sex symbol. The playing of Waters was a seminal influence on Jimi Hendrix and the rest of the '60s generation of guitar gods. "Rollin' Stone" even became the namesake for the Rolling Stones, who would build on Waters' Chicago blues as the vanguard of the British blues revival.

Waters' electric blues didn't catch on immediately. "Rollin' Stone" only came about after several years of blues recordings, and even then it wasn't a smash hit.

What "Rollin' Stone" did do was draw a first wave of attention to Waters. It sold around 70,000 copies for the newly founded Chess Records. This was enough that he could quit his day job and pursue music full-time. He started to tour, spreading his Chicago blues first across the country and then overseas. All the while he continued to push the technology, experimenting with tone and creating the basis for the modern guitar solo.

The electric guitar might have existed for more than a decade before Muddy Waters, but on "Rollin' Stone," the instrument truly began to shake the world.

Honorable Mention

"Foggy Mountain Breakdown" by Flatt & Scruggs and the Foggy Mountain Boys: Lester Flatt and Earl Scruggs were some of the most talented musicians in country music history. They helped create the genre of bluegrass by combining country folk songs with Irish dances and the musical acrobatics of jazz. In 1950, they released one of the all-time classic bluegrass tunes with the searing hot "Foggy Mountain Breakdown."

1951

"Rocket 88"

Jackie Brenston & His Delta Cats

One of the foundational legends of rock n' roll happened on the famed Highway 61, somewhere between Mississippi and Memphis. Ike Turner and His Kings of Rhythm left Mississippi and headed for Memphis, where they were going to cut a few records with Sam Phillips. Somewhere along the way, guitarist Willie Kizart's amplifier got damaged. The stories as to how exactly the damage happened vary—some have the amp falling out of the trunk; others, that it was dropped when the band had to stop to change a flat. Whatever the truth is, one thing is clear: When they got to the studio, Kizart's amp had burst and the cone was hanging loose.

In a serendipitous act of jury-rigging, Phillips stuffed the amplifier with wads of newspaper to hold the cone in place. This fix put the amp in decent enough shape that they could record a song called "Rocket 88," but the loose cone and vibrating newspaper changed Kizart's guitar tone. They gave it a low, buzzing distortion that came out prominently in the mix. Another producer might have scrapped the take and tried to find a better amp for Kizart, but Sam Phillips loved it. He was always searching for strange sounds that he hadn't heard before, figuring that anything novel could set the record apart.

Phillips licensed "Rocket 88" to Chess Records, who released it not under the name Ike Turner and His Kings of Rhythm, but as Jackie Brenston & His Delta Cats, as saxophonist Jackie Brenston provided the lead vocals. The song was an instant hit. It was a new take on the rhythm and blues, and the fuzzy guitar tone gave listeners something they'd never heard before. Phillips encouraged a radio DJ named Dewey Phillips (no relation) to play "Rocket 88" on white radio stations. This helped put another dent in the racial barrier and proved that rhythm and blues music could be commercially viable to a white audience.

Lyrically, "Rocket 88" was a reflection of a new car culture that was starting to emerge across the country. Advances in technology and postwar prosperity brought about beautiful new lines of vehicles. These were designed for both style and power, machines meant to be living embodiments of an era of prosperity. The Oldsmobile Rocket 88 was one such machine, a streamlined space-age car with a powerful V8 engine. It was one of the precursors to the era of muscle cars, and for Ike Turner and Jackie Brenston, the car became a symbol of power and virility.

Between the upbeat boogie rhythm, Kizart's distorted amp and the lyrical

celebration of car culture, "Rocket 88" represented the final steps toward rock n' roll. In fact, there are some who call it the first rock n' roll song. Turner himself disagreed with this assessment, but one way or another, "Rocket 88" was on the verge of something big. It helped launch Turner's career and got Sam Phillips interested in the rhythm and blues market. Within a few years, Turner would be one of the leaders of the rock n' roll revolution. Meanwhile, two years after "Rocket 88," Phillips would strike gold when he recorded the first records of a handsome young gentleman by the name of Elvis Presley.

Phillips encouraged a radio DJ . . . to play "Rocket 88" on white radio stations. This helped . . . prove that rhythm and blues music could be commercially viable to a white audience.

Honorable Mention

"3 O'Clock Blues" by B.B. King: The future King of Electric Blues launched himself onto the national stage with a slow-moving, greasy blues jam. "3 O'Clock Blues" shows off B.B. King's unique style of emotional blues, filled with dramatic bends and emotive picking. This style would turn King into one of the most important electric guitarists ever to live when the generation that followed built on his style to lead a revolution of hard rock and psychedelic blues.

1952

"Singin' in the Rain"

Gene Kelly

In 1929, just as talking pictures were being born, Metro-Goldwyn-Mayer released a musical film called *The Hollywood Revue of 1929*. Inspired by the musical comedy revues that were popular on Broadway at the time, that film was a collection of comedy skits and song-and-dance numbers consisting of traditional songs and original works. One of those original songs was "Singin' in the Rain," written by Arthur Freed and Nacio Herb Brown.

The Hollywood Revue of 1929 was a successful film in its day, but its real cultural impact came more than twenty years after it was released. By 1952, Freed had grown from a young studio songwriter into one of the most celebrated producers in Hollywood's golden age. He was overseeing a new generation of film stars who were taking the baton from Fred Astaire but continuing his style of light, song-and-dance romantic comedies. Many of these films were written around their musical numbers. It was common practice to pluck a piece of music from the Great American Songbook and build a film around that. Freed wanted to create a film written around the songs from his own back catalog, so he hired Adolph Green and Betty Comden to write a film titled *Singin' in the Rain*.

The result was nothing short of cinematic perfection. Green and Comden wrote a piece about the era when "Singin' in the Rain" was first written, as Hollywood was transitioning to sound on film. It was a witty, metafictional film about a silent film star trying to adapt to the changing times. To direct and star, they were able to lure in one of the finest talents of the day: Gene Kelly.

Kelly was, in many ways, the direct successor to Fred Astaire. He was an exceptionally athletic dancer with a million-dollar smile and a genial singing voice. Kelly codirected the film and choreographed all of its numbers, including the immortal sequence to "Singin' in the Rain." That scene, which featured Kelly tap dancing in a torrential downpour, required so much water that the water pressure throughout Los Angeles was impacted by the film. The entire production was fraught with difficulties that included costar Debbie Reynolds doing so many dance takes her feet bled, and Donald O'Connor having to be hospitalized after an elaborate dance number.

None of these tribulations came through in the final product. *Singin' in the Rain* is a delightful film full of heart and charm. It was moderately successful in its day but has since come to be recognized as one of the pinnacles of Hollywood's golden age. For many in

What a Glorious Feeling

SINGIN' IN THE RAIN

MGM's COLOR BY TECHNICOLOR MUSICAL TREASURE!

Starring

GENE KELLY
DONALD O'CONNOR
DEBBIE REYNOLDS

WITH
JEAN HAGEN · MILLARD MITCHELL AND CYD CHARISSE

Story and Screen Play by BETTY COMDEN AND ADOLPH GREEN Suggested by the Song 'SINGIN' IN THE RAIN'

Lyrics by ARTHUR FREED · Music by NACIO HERB BROWN · Directed by GENE KELLY AND STANLEY DONEN · Produced by ARTHUR FREED · AN M-G-M PICTURE

younger generations, the titular dance is practically synonymous with the era, having been homaged and referenced in countless pieces of media over the years. With it, Gene Kelly cemented his immortality in America's cultural history.

"Singin' in the Rain" was one of the finest songs in a tradition that spanned back to the Broadway shows of the turn of the century and created some of America's greatest pieces of art. In the years that followed the release of *Singin' in the Rain*, the movie musical would begin to decline in popularity. Both the film and music industries would start to diverge as New Hollywood and rock n' roll captured the imaginations of the baby boomer generation. The film and music industries that had been so closely entwined since inception began to venture their own separate ways. As all things must, the golden age of Hollywood passed, and many of Kelly's late career movies were flops. But with "Singin' in the Rain," Gene Kelly, Arthur Freed and Nacio Herb Brown came together to create a piece of music and film that can truly be considered eternal.

That scene, which featured Kelly tap dancing in a torrential downpour, required so much water that the water pressure throughout Los Angeles was impacted by the film.

 # Honorable Mention

"Blue Moon" by Billie Holiday: By the start of the '50s, addiction and mental illness were causing Billie Holiday's life to crumble before her eyes. She poured every ounce of this pain into her art, continuing a career of heart-wrenching beauty with a take on a classic ballad written by Rodgers and Hart.

1953

"Hound Dog"

Big Mama Thornton

One can imagine how nervous Jerry Leiber and Mike Stoller were when they first sat down to meet with Big Mama Thornton. The two songwriters were just 19 years old, coming off of writing one of their first hits, Charles Brown's "Hard Times." Big Mama Thornton, on the other hand, was a six-foot-tall, scar-faced blueswoman who carried a pistol in her purse and refused to take guff from anyone.

Although she was just 27 at the time, Thornton was already well acquainted with hard times, having left home at 13 years old and working in a divey tavern while honing her talents as a blues singer. She got her singing break when she convinced the owner of the tavern to let her sing while the usual singer was out. From there, Thornton joined a traveling revue and eventually scored herself a recording deal. But her biggest break came in 1952, after she stole a show at New York's Apollo The-atre and earned her nickname "Big Mama." One of the other musicians on that bill was the bandleader and pro-ducer Johnny Otis, who connected Thornton with Leiber and Stoller.

The two young songwriters were astounded by Thornton's presence and by the power of her voice. They set out to write a song that would be suited to her unapologetic energy. The result was "Hound Dog," a 12-bar blues that had

Thornton reaming out an imagined deadbeat partner. The song resonated with her, so she went into the studio with Otis to record it, with Leiber and Stoller tagging along for the session.

According to Stoller, Thornton orig-inally sang the song in a moaning blues style, but Leiber and Stoller imagined it with more grit. She pushed back on their directions at first, but eventually gave in and sang it as a raw shout. Thornton and Otis have also both claimed to have been responsible for adjustments and rewrites to the song in session. Whatever the actual process was, the results are hard to argue with. Like any great blues singer, Thornton channeled all the pain of her life into the vocal performance of "Hound Dog," and the result was a searing piece of music. Otis played drums on the ses-sion, while the session musician Pete Lewis laid down a grimy blues guitar.

Lewis' guitar was a central feature of the song. He even got a chance to perform a solo punctuated with lively ad-libs by Thornton. The fact that Lewis' frisky guitar was featured so heavily was an oddity at the time, though it wouldn't be for long. "Hound Dog" is among the many songs that can truly contend for the title of "First Rock n' Roll Song." Its case is also helped by the fact that Elvis Presley released his own take on the song in 1956.

risqué piece full of sexuality into a literal song about a dog. Although Thornton's version was a huge success on the rhythm and blues charts, and sold more than half a million copies, it would live in the shadow of Presley's version for white audiences, many of whom didn't even know about Thornton.

Despite giving an all-time blues vocal performance and recording one of rock n' roll's foundational songs, the rest of Thornton's career was plagued with ups and downs. Neither Thornton nor Leiber and Stoller would receive royalties from the song at first. When Presley made it a smash hit, Leiber and Stoller cashed in, but Thornton continued to go uncompensated. Despite the fact that she sang one of the most important songs in rock history, Thornton's total earnings from "Hound Dog" amounted to $500.

Presley's version launched him into superstardom, and it became one of his signature songs, as well as one of the earliest rock megahits. It was based on a take by Freddie Bell and the Bellboys, which modified the lyrics to shift it from a

Big Mama Thornton and her music helped break down racial boundaries in the '50s, but as it happened with so many Black artists, and Black women especially, America denied her the fame and fortune that she was owed.

Honorable Mentions

"(How Much Is) That Doggie in the Window?" by Patti Page: As the new world of rock n' roll was appearing on the horizon, the traditional pop singer Patti Page scored a hit with a quaint novelty song that carries the dubious honor of being one of the last pop hits of a culture that was about to come crashing down.

1954

"That's All Right"

Elvis Presley

There are certain cultural figures with such an outsized impact that history seems to bend around them. A thousand roads lead toward them and a thousand roads branch out from them into the great yawning future. Elvis Presley is one such figure. When a young Presley hit the scene as a handsome, young white boy singing music pulled from the Black rhythm and blues tradition, it was a cultural collision a generation in the making. His natural charm and swagger gave a generation their first love and inspired countless future greats to pick up a guitar and try their hand at music. His coming was the harbinger of a musical shift not seen in America since Louis Armstrong walked on up out of the streets of New Orleans.

And yet, it almost didn't happen.

It's easy to imagine a young Presley strutting his way into Sam Phillips' Sun Records studio, tearing out a couple records and walking out as "The King." The reality isn't so simple. The song that would blow Presley up, "That's All Right," was actually recorded a year after he had his first encounter with Phillips.

The first record Presley ever cut was in 1955, when he was just 18 years old. At the time, Sun Records would cut private records for a price, so he cut a recording of "Happy Birthday" and "That's When Your Heartaches Begin"

as a gift for his mother. His performance on these was good enough that Phillips' business partner Marion Keisker took down his name and number. When Keisker asked Elvis what sort of music he sang, he told her, "I sing all kinds," and added, "I don't sound like nobody."

Presley left enough of a mark on Keisker that she brought him up in 1954, when Phillips was looking for new talent. Having recorded a number of seminal rhythm and blues records, including "Rocket 88," Phillips had dreamed up what he thought could be good business: a white singer who could sing Black songs. Thinking that this potentially could be Presley, Phillips brought him in for a session with Sonny Moore on guitar and Bill Black on bass. The trio gathered on July 5, 1954 and spent the better part of a day recording. By the time evening was falling, they were tired, bored and had little to show for it.

Both Phillips and Presley were unclear as to what his sound should be. They tried out all sorts of different songs, including recording a pair of lilting love ballads, "Harbor Lights" and "I Love You Because." The results were nothing to write home about. Presley could croon nicely enough, but the songs were lacking any energy and passion. The 19-year-old sounded awkward and nervous, and the session was start-

the original tempo and started jumping around the studio while singing. Phillips heard this sound and leaped back to the control board. It was everything he'd dreamed of. They started rolling on a recording live in studio, rather than tracking the instruments separately. Before the night was through, everyone in that studio had made history.

Sam Phillips gave the record to the disc jockey Dewey Phillips, who first aired it on July 7, 1954. The response was immediate. Dewey Phillips got more than 40 phone calls about the song and ended up playing it 14 times that night. Elvis' career took off. By the end of the month, he was debuting his signature dance moves to an outdoor Memphis audience, and before the year was out, he was a regional star. We all know the rest of the story.

Rock n' roll had been brewing in the rhythm and blues scenes ever since Sister Rosetta Tharpe created her novel take on gospel music. There's a number of songs you could argue are rock n' roll before "That's All Right," but once Elvis Presley hit the scene, there was no argument: Rock was here to stay. He combined the worlds of gospel, country and rhythm and blues, and wrapped them all in a youthful shell that oozed sex appeal. He became a beloved icon for a teenage demographic that was gaining more social and economic power, and his fast, energetic music brought Black innovations to an eager audience of white youth.

Presley, himself, was little more than a kid and couldn't have possibly imagined what his music would do to the world. The realities of his legacy would play out in complex ways. Arthur Crudup had to spend much of his life fighting for royalties for the song. He reached an agreement for $60,000 in royalties, but the payments never materialized. Crudup

ing to look like a bust. Phillips called for a break, and Presley decided to relax and shake out his jitters by playing an old blues song he loved.

That song was Arthur "Big Boy" Crudup's "That's Alright," a piece first recorded in 1946. Crudup's song was an upbeat piece of Chicago blues driven by a jangly guitar and a jumpy walking bassline. It was one of the many songs contributing to the early rock n' roll sound, complete with a guitar break and an irresistible groove. When Presley first played it, he let loose like the kid he was. He played the song at nearly twice

died in poverty despite writing one of the songs that birthed rock n' roll. Crudup is far from the only example. Much of Presley's career was built on the work of Black musicians, many of whom got little or no credit during their own lifetimes. And yet, his success transformed the music industry. After he'd made it clear that white audiences would buy Black music, the industry started to shake off its segregationist practices. Black musicians began to find crossover success, and the industry would never be the same. Little Richard, who had much of his style plundered by Presley, went on to praise him for helping to open pathways for Black music.

The cultural reach of Presley spans far beyond the racial conversation. He created the archetype for the first generation of rock stars. He made Bob Dylan want to perform, John Lennon want to pick up a guitar and Freddie Mercury want to sing. Presley hit American culture like a comet and set a fire that still blazes to this day. The world as we know it does not exist without Elvis Presley. So, it's a good thing that Sam Phillips called for a break on that fateful July evening.

 # Honorable Mentions

"Rock Around the Clock" by Bill Haley & His Comets: As rock n' roll was spilling out from its Black origins into white America, Bill Haley & His Comets released one of the genre's seminal early hits. Haley's song rollicks with upbeat energy and features one of the early great electric guitar solos performed by Danny Cedrone. "Rock Around the Clock" was nothing short of a phenomenon, topping charts on both sides of the Atlantic and helping to launch rock n' roll into the mainstream.

"My Funny Valentine" by Frank Sinatra: After going through a deep career slump plagued by personal and financial problems, Frank Sinatra found new life in 1954 by signing with Capitol Records and Nelson Riddle. Together, they released a string of early concept albums that display Sinatra's mastery of the Great American Songbook, leading to one of the greatest second acts in music history.

1955

"Tutti Frutti"

Little Richard

Elvis Presley may have been responsible for bringing rock n' roll to the masses, but if anybody can truly get credit for inventing the genre, it has to be Little Richard. Although his first mainstream hits wouldn't come until after Presley broke through the mainstream, his influence on Presley and the other early rock n' rollers is undeniable. In many ways, Little Richard is the yin to Presley's yang. Presley was straight, white and conventionally attractive. He provided enough edge to anger the older generation and entice the younger, but at the end of the day, he represented much of what mainstream American society valued. Little Richard, on the other hand, was queer and Black. He was rough around the edges, a true rebel who pushed up against the norms of white society on every front and defied the conservative times with every breath he took.

The story of Little Richard's signature song, "Tutti Frutti," even bears an uncanny resemblance to the story of Presley's "That's All Right." Little Richard had been cutting a number of blues songs with the producer Bumps Blackwell, and they weren't landing, so Blackwell took a break and brought him to a local tavern. The tavern had a piano in it; Little Richard went up and ripped out a song that he'd been playing in his live repertoire for years, "Tutti Frutti." In this more casual environment, his true self came out, and Blackwell was floored. They went back to the studio, cut the song, and Little Richard had his first hit.

"Tutti Frutti" is the platonic ideal of the rock n' roll song. Starting with the iconic opening wail of "a wop bop a loo bop a wop bam boom," the song is two minutes of nonstop passion and energy. The microphones can barely contain Little Richard's raspy shouts, and his piano-slamming rhythm practically calls you out of your seat. Most of the early precursors to rock n' roll were rooted in boogie-woogie and shuffle rhythms, but Little Richard played fast, straight, driving chords to fuel the song.

He had been playing "Tutti Frutti" for years before he recorded it as he bounced around on the edge of poverty trying to break into the music industry. In those days, the song had a much raunchier subject matter. It was an ode to anal sex, with a chorus of "Tutti Frutti, good booty." This early version is a

> It sold 200,000 copies within a week and a half and became the flagship record for the rock n' roll movement.

reflection of a queerness that Little Richard had a complicated relationship with throughout his life. Before he broke through as a singer, Little Richard had performed in drag under the name Princess Lavonne. At varying points in his life, he referred to himself as either gay or bisexual, but he grew up in a strict church community and also denounced homosexuality as a sin on several occasions. Blackwell knew the explicitly queer nature of "Tutti Frutti" wouldn't fly on the radio, so he brought in Dorothy LaBostrie to rewrite the song into something more acceptable for radio.

"Tutti Frutti" dropped like a bolt of lightning. It sold 200,000 copies within a week and a half and became the flagship record for the rock n' roll movement. After years of struggling to make it in the industry, Little Richard became an icon nearly overnight. His pompadour haircut soon adorned the heads of teens across the country, and his flamboyant performance style inspired such future icons as Mick Jagger and David Bowie.

But for a Black man in America, cultural success always came with caveats. Thousands of white teens became fans of Little Richard, much to the ire of their parents. Racist groups picketed his concerts, and an entire moral panic began to arise around Little Richard. He adopted more androgynous looks so as not to appear a sexual threat to white America. As "Tutti Frutti" was still on its chart run, a toned-down cover version by the white Pat Boone became a bigger hit. At the time, record companies were also not in the habit of properly compensating Black musicians, so Little Richard didn't receive nearly the financial windfall he deserved.

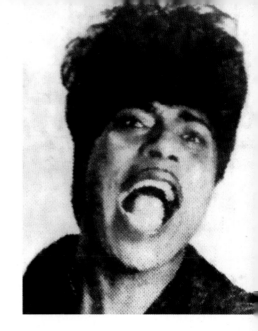

Within a few years of "Tutti Frutti," the backlash drove Little Richard away from the spotlight and back to the church. He left secular music and started to travel as a preacher. But the movement that he'd started had too much momentum to stop. Rock n' roll took on new life as his disciples began to follow in his footsteps. The man, himself, would eventually return to secular music. He came back a king, playing performances with the Beatles and the Rolling Stones, and began to get the credit he was due as a legend.

The rock n' roll music that he helped invent was an enormous force in the movement toward desegregation. The mirrored pair of Little Richard and Presley brought white and Black America together in a way that few other things could. Rock music was the culmination of generations of momentum, but if a single breaking point exists, it might just be the opening wail of "Tutti Frutti."

Honorable Mentions

"Lullaby of Birdland" by Ella Fitzgerald: By 1954, Ella Fitzgerald had already established herself as one of the finest ever to sing jazz. Her greatest innovation was bringing vocal jazz into the bebop world with an incredible improvised scat technique. But she could also croon with the best of them, as she proved on 1954's "Lullaby of Birdland," which would become one of her signature songs as she progressed from hot new talent into jazz's elder stateswoman.

"Maybellene" by Chuck Berry: As rock n' roll's momentum was building, one of its biggest stars hit the scene for the first time. When Chuck Berry first showed up at Chess Records, he intended to record folk songs, but producer Leonard Chess was more interested in Berry's taking on "Maybellene," an adaptation of a western swing song called "Ida Red." "Maybellene" is an embodiment of everything people wanted in rock n' roll, with a big beat, a fast groove and lyrics about young love and fast cars.

1956

"I Walk the Line"

Johnny Cash

One morning in 1954, Sam Phillips showed up at Sun Records to find a wiry young man with a piercing gaze waiting outside the studio for him. The man declared that he wanted an audition. Fresh off the success of Elvis Presley, Phillips let the young singer in. He introduced himself as J. R. Cash and proceeded to play a handful of gospel songs. Phillips was struck by the man's baritone voice but saw no money in gospel, so he told Cash to come back when he had secular music to play.

Cash came back in 1955 with a band consisting of Luther Perkins on guitar and Marshall Grant on bass. They called themselves "The Tennessee Three" and played a handful of songs that Cash had written himself. These songs were a mixture of country and rhythm and blues with an upbeat tempo, no doubt influenced by "That's All Right," which had been making the rounds on local radio. Phillips was impressed. All three musicians were relatively new to their practice, and as a result, they played with a stark, bare-bones sort of minimalism. This sound struck Phillips. He suggested that the group bill themselves as "Johnny

Cash and the Tennessee Two" and cut some records. Just like that, Sun Records had its second golden goose.

Cash's early songs were a hit on local radio, and Phillips started sending him out with Presley on promotional tours around the state. The pair made an odd couple, with Elvis' chaotic energy and Cash's stolid intensity, but their music shared a common sound, driven by their love of rhythm and blues and gospel. This sound was soon dubbed "rockabilly" and became the toast of the American South.

By 1956, Cash was a rising star. He'd quit his job as a door-to-door salesman and started work as a musician full-time, bringing in the funds to support his young family. In August 1954, Cash had married a woman named Vivian Liberto, and in 1955, they had their first daughter, Roseanne. Cash's own upbringing had been fraught with strife and trauma. He'd grown up in absolute poverty with a verbally abusive father, and his older brother had died as a child. Cash wanted to create the stability for his own family that he missed in his upbringing. But life on the road as a young musician is fraught with tempta-

> Despite best intentions, Cash was not able to walk the line. As his profile rose . . . he fell into alcoholism and amphetamine addiction.

tion. Cash was on the forefront of a youth movement that was taking over the nation. He was a tall, handsome man with a cagey sort of charisma, and no doubt had countless young women taking interest in him backstage. One night, after a show in Gladewater, Texas, he decided to stave off these temptations by doing what he did best: writing a song.

Cash penned "I Walk the Line" both as a reassurance to his wife and as a reminder to himself. The song is written in his typical sparse lyricism, no doubt inspired by the poetry of Hank Williams and the clean family image of the Carter Family. Cash had originally imagined his pledge of devotion as a slower ballad, but Phillips encouraged him to speed it up. Cash recorded a take with an upbeat, bluesy rhythm that imitated a freight train. One of the most distinct aspects of "I Walk the Line" is the vocal performance. Cash hums in a crescendo before each verse, sounding like the buzz of rail lines as a train draws near. This hum wasn't an aesthetic choice but rather a necessity: Cash had trouble singing the changing keys of the song, so he hummed to ensure he was on pitch before each verse. Nevertheless, the hum helps to underline the song's rhythmic train imagery.

The image that Cash creates is one that pulls on a long blues tradition of rambling bluesmen riding rails. He had learned the blues playing with Gus Cannon, a veteran Memphis banjo player who had once toured with a jug band. By combining this rambling blues tradition with a more conservative, family-focused country influence, Cash was helping to put yet another crack in the fast-crumbling color line.

JOHNNY CASH

ANOTHER TWO-SIDER
BY ONE OF THE
TRULY GREAT
TALENT FINDS

•

I WALK
THE LINE

b/w

GET RHYTHM

SUN RECORD 241

EXCLUSIVE MANAGEMENT:
BOB NEAL
MANAGER
★ STARS INCORPORATED ★
Suite 1916, Sterick Bldg., Memphis, Tenn.

SUN RECORD
COMPANY, INC.
706 Union Ave.   Memphis, Tenn.

The simple, romantic message of "I Walk the Line" resonated with country audiences. After its May 1956 release, the song shot to the top of the Billboard country charts, and it even crossed over to break into the Top 20 pop charts. This success was enough to earn Cash an invitation to the celebrated Grand Ole Opry and marked the first step toward his country music canonization. But backstage at the Grand Ole Opry, after performing a song about his devo-

tion to Vivian Liberto, he met a young woman who was already a country legend in her own right: June Carter, the daughter of the Carter Family's Mother Maybelle. A few years later, as he was becoming the biggest name in country music, the two would start an affair that eventually led to Cash and Liberto's divorce.

Despite best intentions, Cash was not able to walk the line. As his profile rose in the country world, he fell into alcoholism and amphetamine addiction. The traumas of his childhood and the pressures of fame weighed heavy and tormented him throughout his life. In this way, he was representative of many in his generation. The generational trauma created by the Great Depression and World War II left them fundamentally unprepared to deal with the idyllic family visions expected by postwar America. Countless men would fall down Cash's path, and fail to walk the line, leaving countless women to try to pick up the pieces.

Johnny Cash paved his way to stardom with the wholesome romanticism of "I Walk the Line." In the years that followed, he would give voice to his struggles and discontent and turn his energy outward. His career would see him advocate for prison reform, fight for Indigenous rights and become an icon for a generation that was determined to remake the postwar world. By the time it was done, he would hold a hallowed place in the annals of country history, shared only by a select few greats like Jimmie Rodgers, Hank Williams and the Carter Family.

 # Honorable Mention

"Cheek to Cheek" by Ella Fitzgerald & Louis Armstrong: Louis Armstrong's prolific career stretched onward even well into his middle age. In 1956, he teamed up with Ella Fitzgerald for a legendary collaboration. Together, they created some of the best vocal jazz ever made with stunning, heartfelt renditions of Great American Songbook duets.

1957

"Walkin' After Midnight"

Patsy Cline

When Patsy Cline first got a look at the song that would change her life, she refused to record it. A hard-headed, honky-tonk singer who was drawn to music with an edge, she had no interest in recording a soft, slow pop song like "Walkin' After Midnight." But songwriter Don Hecht knew it would be perfect for her rich voice. Hecht, along with Alan Block, had originally written the song for a pop singer called Kay Starr, but that collaboration had never materialized. Hecht believed in his song and did everything that he could to get it into the hands of Cline. In the end, she only agreed to do the song when the label's owner, Bill McCall, said that if she recorded "Walkin' After Midnight," she could also record another song she liked more for the B-side.

Once Cline had relented, she cut the song at the Quonset Hut Studio in Nashville. At the time, Nashville was starting to boom as a music town. Memphis was exploding with the rough-edged rockabilly music of Sun Records, but a group of producers in Nashville had a different idea for how country music could sound. Owen Bradley, co-owner of Quonset Hut Studio, had been dreaming of a slicker, smoother country music. Recording technology was improving in leaps and bounds, and Bradley realized that he could sand some of the rural Appalachian edges off of country music. Together with a handful of other producers, Bradley spent the late '50s realizing the sound that would come to be known as "countrypolitan," or simply the "Nashville sound."

The Nashville sound traded out harsher banjos for smoother slide guitars, and relied on a smoother vocal styling rather than the nasal Appalachian sound that had dominated country music. As it would turn out, Cline's voice was perfect for this sound. She had been noted for the power and depth in her voice from a young age, but she had preferred to sing in a louder, more raucous style. Even after recording "Walkin' After Midnight," Cline wasn't sold on the song. She didn't like her vocal performance, but Bradley and his co-owner, Paul Cohen, loved it.

Cline's emotional delivery captures the sorrow of Hecht's lyrics. She sings with a clean pop croon, but her natural twang spices the song up just enough to keep it country. Her voice threatens to crack as she sings of forlorn love. By the end of the song, she adds a touch of grit, hinting at what she's capable of, but never truly letting loose. Cline's performance nestles beautifully on an instrumental bed laid down by some of the finest session musicians the country had to offer.

"Walkin' After Midnight" was one of the first true realizations of the Nashville sound, and the world took note. Cline's song hit number two on the country charts, and crossed over to number 12 on the pop charts. It was part of an increasing trend of country musicians crossing over, and it launched the career of one of country's most distinctive voices.

Tragically, the world never got to see everything Cline could have been. In 1963, she died in a plane crash at 30 years of age. But in the few years of recording that she had, she was a complete trailblazer. She became one of the preeminent voices in the Nashville sound. Her heartfelt delivery and devil-may-care attitude inspired the women of her generation. In a country world dominated by male voices, Patsy Cline made an indelible mark. Her career was short, but as one of the flag-bearers of the Nashville sound, her legacy still rings loud in Music City to this day.

Honorable Mentions

"That'll Be the Day" by Buddy Holly: In 1957, Buddy Holly, a lanky Texan with a boyish charm, joined the first wave of rock superstars, scoring a number one hit with "That'll Be the Day." The song was an enormous hit both at home in America and across the Atlantic. There, it captured the attention of a young John Lennon, who cut it for his first recording with the Quarrymen, a band that would soon evolve into the Beatles.

"Brilliant Corners" by Thelonious Monk: Eccentric jazz pianist Thelonious Monk revolutionized bebop, a distinct style of stilted playing, heavy with dissonance and abnormal chord phrasing. His 1957 recording "Brilliant Corners" debuts many of his own compositions, songs that would become essential to a growing movement of avant-garde jazz.

1958

"Milestones"

Miles Davis

Rock music hit the '50s like a tidal wave. By the end of the decade, it had summarily displaced jazz as the music of the youth. The genre's popularity would never again reach the heights of the Jazz Age. But this shift hardly concerned the greatest jazz musicians of the day. Charlie Parker and Dizzy Gillespie's innovations in the '40s had paved the way for a new sort of approach to jazz. Freed from the constraints of commercial viability, jazz became a genre driven by radical virtuosos who sought to evolve the genre through incredible feats of musicianship. The genius at the forefront of this movement was Miles Davis.

Davis was a cocksure trumpeter who knew exactly how talented he was. He was a man of fiery passions, with unmatched style and a wicked temper. But the music he played couldn't have been smoother. He could blow a divine sort of calm loneliness. He could round the sharp edges of any trumpet, turning it from a harsh blaring instrument into the gentlest timbre you'll ever hear. More than that, he was able to make complicated musical acts seem easy and effortless. Listening to Davis' music feels as natural as breathing, even as he was performing feats that few of his peers could come close to.

With "Milestones," Davis set out to chart a new future for jazz. He was wildly successful.

In his early days, Davis played with Parker and Gillespie, but he struck out on his own in the '50s. In the early part of the decade, he developed and kicked a nasty heroin addiction, all while helping advance bebop into a more demanding subgenre called hard bop. This new music pulled from the exploding rhythm and blues scene. It pushed the acrobatics of bebop to the next level, with increasingly difficult tempos and chord changes. It was a competitive sort of music, with each musician wishing to outplay their peers and establish themselves as the most singular talent in the scene.

In 1955, having quit heroin and discovering a new purpose, Davis assembled a collection of those who had proved themselves in the scene and formed the Miles Davis Quintet. In its first iteration, this quintet consisted of Davis on trumpet, John Coltrane on saxophone, Red Garland on piano, Paul Chambers on bass and Philly Joe Jones on drums. Known as Davis' "First Great Quintet," this could well be the most talented group of musicians ever to record together for an extended period. Together, they released a seminal run of genre-defining records. But that wasn't enough for Davis.

By the end of the decade, he believed that bebop had been pushed as far as it could go. In the constant quest for the most tongue-twisting, mind-bending solo, Davis saw that melody was being lost. So, he started to look for the next step in jazz's ongoing transformation. He found it in a school of thought called "modal jazz." Rather than focusing on chord changes as bebop had, modal jazz built its sound around modes—specific types of scales created by shifting the root note. Building songs around modes allowed for new sorts of sounds in jazz, scales that worked outside of the major/minor dichotomy. The result was a more open, melodic sort of improvisational framework.

Davis debuted this new style of modal jazz on an album called *Milestones*. The title track of that album is one of the first great pieces of modal jazz. The song is structured around a repeating pattern of the G Dorian and A Aeolian modes. These modes add a strange tension to the music. They bring the listener to the edge of the seat as a series of solos allows the musicians to flex.

First is Cannonball Adderley, who joined Davis' band on alto sax and expanded the quintet into a sextet. He dances and flutters, quoting Stravinsky and Gershwin, and coloring his notes with immaculate bends before handing off to Davis. Davis' solo is effortless and smooth. His tone is mellow and calm, even as Philly Joe Jones drums away at a fast-paced rhythm. Finally, Davis passes off to perhaps the only instrumentalist that was his equal at the time, John Coltrane. Coltrane took quickly to modal jazz and would go on to create some of the most seminal records of the movement. On his solo in "Milestones," we can see why. Coltrane flutters in wild runs and punctuates with poignant gaps.

With "Milestones," Davis set out to chart a new future for jazz. He was wildly successful. "Milestones" was a proof-of-concept that he would refine a year later with *Kind of Blue*, which would become the best-selling album in jazz history. Each of the members of his band would continue on to prolific recording careers, and John Coltrane would prove to be one of the greatest minds jazz would ever see. As for Davis, his innovations wouldn't stop. *Milestones* was just an early release in an imperial phase that would see him record at least a half dozen more of the most beloved albums in jazz.

Honorable Mentions

"Johnny B. Goode" by Chuck Berry: The rise of rock n' roll had been raising the profile of the electric guitar, but it was Chuck Berry's playing that turned the instrument into the epitome of cool. "Johnny B. Goode" is an autobiographical song about Berry. It rips with riotous exuberance and shows off a solo that guitarists would be teaching themselves to play for decades to come.

"Blue Train" by John Coltrane: Right as Miles Davis' modal jazz innovations were ushering in a new era in jazz, John Coltrane released the perfect hard bop album. *Blue Train* is 42 minutes of immaculate jazz, highlighted by the title track, which sees Coltrane casually showing off extreme runs that would tongue-tie many of his contemporaries.

1959

"Lonely Woman"

Ornette Coleman

Every generation or so, the stars align for a perfect year of music. New talents hit the scene just as old greats refine their sound. Genius talents collide and collaborate. Entire genres turn upside down in a matter of months. In the jazz world, no year exemplifies this sort of serendipitous occurrence more than 1959. It was a year that saw the release of some of the greatest albums the genre would ever experience. Miles Davis perfected his modal jazz experiments with *Kind of Blue*, Dave Brubeck brought shifting time signatures into jazz with *Time Out* and Charles Mingus laid stake to his claim as one of jazz's all-time great composers with *Mingus Ah Um*. Amid this nonstop parade of genre-changing albums, a new face exploded onto the music scene with a sound so radical that it threatened to tear the jazz world in two.

Ornette Coleman is what you might call a musical anarchist. From a young age, he actively defied each and every musical rule or hierarchy that someone tried to impose on him. As a teen, he was kicked out of a school marching band for deigning to improvise during a march. In his early career he was beaten

> . . . a new face exploded onto the music scene with a sound so radical that it threatened to tear the jazz world in two.

up and thrown out of a jazz club for his wild playing style. But he persisted, continuing to push his music to stranger, more experimental places. In 1959, that persistence manifested into one of the single most important jazz albums ever recorded, *The Shape of Jazz to Come*.

When you release an album with such an audacious name, you'd better be damn sure that you make a splash with the first song. And "Lonely Woman" is a splash if ever there was one. The song opens on an ominous bending bass line played by Charlie Haden over a manic cymbal beat laid down by Billy Higgins. Before you even have a moment to orient yourself in this strange rhythm, Coleman's squeaky saxophone wails in perfect disharmony with Don Cherry's pocket cornet. Together, both musicians play a haunting melody out of tune with each other. If you're not ready for it, the sound is strange and jarring. It offends the trained ear. But that's exactly what it's meant to do.

Coleman thought that the typical melodic and harmonic structures of music limited the ability of what the art could truly be. He even described these systems as a "caste system." At the time,

seen, so he turned to music to interpret it. His open dissonance proved the perfect vessel with which to transmit that feeling. There are plenty of wonderful songs about loneliness, but most of them are dreary and sad. Coleman's approach is something else entirely. Listening to "Lonely Woman" makes you physically uncomfortable. It makes you want to squirm around and cry out for someone to touch you, to comfort you.

That's the power of Coleman's music. By removing himself from the theoretical rules of music, he was able to deliver an aesthetic perspective that simply would not exist otherwise.

But many people find comfort in rules and structure. As such, the response to *The Shape of Jazz to Come* was mixed, even amid musicians who were themselves trying to meld the jazz scene. Miles Davis was unimpressed with the album, but his rival and collaborator John Coltrane loved it and began to embrace this new style of jazz that came to be known as "free jazz." Over the next decade, Coleman and his collaborators would continue to push the boundaries of jazz, releasing music that got even stranger, even wilder and even more boundary-breaking.

In 1959, amid a scene of radical experimentalists, Ornette Coleman proved himself the most radical and the most experimental. "Lonely Woman" stands as a testament to the power of rule breaking, and generations on, *The Shape of Jazz to Come* would be a prophetic album name.

many of his contemporaries were trying to push jazz forward by approaching it like mathematicians, finding intricate patterns and exploring ways to exploit them. Coleman came at the problem more like a manic six-year-old—through raw emotion.

As the title would suggest, the emotion present in "Lonely Woman" is loneliness. The song was specifically inspired by a painting that Coleman once encountered, depicting a rich white woman with everything she could desire in life but an expression of sheer desolation on her face. It was one of the most striking images Coleman had ever

Honorable Mentions

"Blue in Green" by Miles Davis: Miles Davis and John Coltrane perfected the modal jazz sound that they created in "Milestones." "Blue in Green" is a smooth and cool song, in which Coltrane lays down one of the greatest solos ever played on any instrument. It's a standout track on *Kind of Blue*, an album that perfects modal jazz and goes on to become the best-selling jazz album in history.

"Take Five" by the Dave Brubeck Quintet: America's West Coast offered up its response to New York's thriving jazz scene in the form of an ambitious album by Dave Brubeck called *Time Out*. That album brought new time signatures into jazz and displayed some of the smoothest playing ever recorded. "Take Five" would go on to become a jazz standard, helping invent smooth jazz.

WOMEN DEMAND EQUALITY

ARCH WITH
LMA!

REVOLUTION

1960–69

In the 1960s, musicians across America collectively came upon a revelation: The reach of popular music could span further than anyone ever thought. Nobody had ever doubted music's ability to shape hearts and minds, but in the '60s, people began to realize that music actually had the power to reshape the world. The emergence of mass media gave musicians a wider platform than ever, and a new culture of progressivism inspired musicians to use that platform. As a series of historic social movements gripped America, popular music became the cultural fuel to an era of change and revolution.

In the first half of the decade, this change was driven by a civil rights movement that was writing a new chapter in the long fight for racial equality. As civil rights leaders faced off against violent terrorists, racist police and powerful institutions, a new style of music combined jazz, gospel and rhythm and blues to provide a soundtrack to resistance. Soul music was forged in the fires of collective action, and many of the

genre's greatest stars marched hand in hand with Martin Luther King Jr. Meanwhile, a growing culture of progressive whites were finding their own avenues of protest music. A folk scene grew out of New York City, standing in solidarity with the civil rights movement and speaking loudly against an imperialistic war that was heating up in Vietnam.

Midway through the decade, something would hit that would turn this boiling pot of protest into a veritable supernova of radical collective action: LSD. When LSD hit the West Coast in the mid-'60s, it brought with it an era of radical experimentation, both politically and creatively. Rock musicians sought to elevate their art form into something beyond simple two-minute songs, and realized the power that music could have to organize people and spread messages. Musicians from all walks of life began to challenge the straight white male hegemony, releasing songs of feminism, LGBTQ+ rights and Black Power.

It was a sort of progressive momentum the country had never seen before, and it brought with it all new levels of tumult. Some protestors clashed with cops in the streets, while others dropped out entirely to form their own imagined utopias. All throughout, young men were being drafted into a war in Vietnam that became increasingly unpopular by the minute. It seemed that America was on the verge of a true revolution as half a million people gathered near Woodstock, New York, for an enormous free music festival while the world watched on in awe.

And yet, the seeds of this counterculture were already falling apart by the end of the decade. The dreams of a utopian America were giving way to a new reality as the systems of power figured out how to get a hold on the new era. Many of the gains made by the counterculture fell away, but some were here to stay. Among those eternal influences from the '60s was an entirely new vision of what music could sound like and of the incredible things it could accomplish.

1960

"Georgia On My Mind"

Ray Charles

In 1960, Ray Charles was putting together a concept album. *The Genius Hits the Road* was a collection of songs written about specific parts of the United States. It included such songs as "Chattanooga Choo Choo," "Basin Street Blues" and "Blue Hawaii." Charles needed a couple of songs to fill out the track list, so he decided to take a crack at an old American standard that his driver was fond of whistling. That song was a piece by the great Hoagy Carmichael, called "Georgia On My Mind."

Although nobody expected the song to be a hit, Charles' take on "Georgia On My Mind" proved to be his signature song. It was a perfect vehicle for the sound he had spent the 1950s developing. This sound was a mixture of the traditional croons of artists like Nat King Cole, the rhythm and blues scenes growing around Charles, the jazz stylings of Louis Jordan and the gospel music from the Black churches of Charles' youth. It was called "soul music," and Charles was one of the best ever to sing it.

He was already a child prodigy when he lost his sight at seven years old. He learned to play piano using braille music and developed a deep love of jazz music. In his early days, he played stride piano, but with the rhythm and blues scene exploding around him in his early 20s, Charles' music began to shift. He focused in on the blues and started to pour his soul into deeply melodic piano lines. It was this love of melody that drew him to "Georgia On My Mind." Despite the fact that he was born in Georgia, he wasn't drawn to the song for its lyrical content. When he played the song, he found himself getting lost in Carmichael's sorrowful melody.

It's no surprise that a Hoagy Carmichael melody sounds so perfect with Ray Charles singing it. Carmichael was one of the most celebrated writers of the Tin Pan Alley scene. He wrote some of the most beautiful jazz standards ever, including "Stardust" and "Heart and Soul." These sorts of songs were pieces that Charles would have heard on the radio growing up, sung by a generation of debonair musicians, such as Nat King Cole, who oozed style. Charles' own style was an update on these classic looks. His sunglasses and tuxedo became the epitome of "cool" as soul music

> Although nobody expected the song to be a hit, Charles' take on "Georgia On My Mind" proved to be his signature song.

started to gain momentum. That generation of musicians was happy to pass the torch on to Charles. Frank Sinatra once called Charles "the only true genius in show business."

That genius is apparent on "Georgia On My Mind." Charles' vocal performance is enough to warm even the coldest heart. He sings a patient lull with a full voice, hanging on each phrase to let the emotions stew. Behind, a bluesy set of backing vocals underline the longing. It was a new style of crooning pop star for a new generation. Charles had been a rising star when he released "Georgia On My Mind," and that song put him over the top. It was his first number one hit, and it cemented soul's place as the sound of the upcoming '60s.

This emergence of soul couldn't have happened at a better time. In 1960, the civil rights movement that had started in the postwar period was gaining more and more steam by the day. For any social movement to thrive, it needs a corresponding cultural movement. Soul music was that movement. It was a combination of the greatest Black art forms in jazz and the blues, and its gospel influence fit in with the church communities that were the driving force behind civil rights. The music itself could be somber for moments of sobriety, but also had a profound uplifting power.

Although Charles was rarely political in his music, he played his own part in the push toward desegregation. In 1961, he refused to play in front of a whites-only theater, making him one of the first popular musicians of the era to make such a statement. After this radical action, he wouldn't play in Georgia again for years. The racist history of Georgia as a state adds another level to his performance of "Georgia On My

Mind." One can read his heartfelt performance as an expression of sorrow for the hatred that still ran thick in the state of his birth.

Before Charles' career was over, the segregationist walls of Georgia would fall. By giving birth to soul music, he helped provide spiritual fuel for the civil rights movement. In 1979, the State of Georgia formally apologized to Ray Charles after he had refused to play at a segregated club years earlier. To underline just how important he and his music were to the state, "Georgia On My Mind" was then declared the official state song.

Honorable Mentions

"The Twist" by Chubby Checker: In 1960, famed television host Dick Clark brought an upstart pop rocker named Chubby Checker onto his nationally broadcast *American Bandstand*. Checker's performance of "The Twist" ignited one of the wildest dance crazes in American history. As people across the country started swiveling their hips to "The Twist," an old guard that was afraid of rock n' roll started to see the fun of it, and the mainstream fully embraced the music that defined it for the next half century.

"Giant Steps" by John Coltrane: John Coltrane capped off the bebop era with the logical conclusion to the drive for technical complexity. One part athletic exercise, one part mathematical treatise and one part spiritual deliverance, "Giant Steps" is as perfect a jazz song as ever was written. The song sees Coltrane and his band rip through a gauntlet of complex chord changes at a breakneck pace. Today, learning to navigate Coltrane's complex chord structures is a rite of passage for any aspiring jazz musician.

1961

"Please Mr. Postman"

The Marvelettes

In 1955, a 26-year-old Michigander named Berry Gordy took a job on the assembly line at Detroit's Lincoln-Mercury factory. It was far from a dream job for Gordy, who wanted to be a songwriter, but it made enough money to support his young family, and gave him time to write songs in his off hours. He soon came to appreciate the genius efficiency of the assembly line, seeing a new potential for this sort of organization that nobody had dreamed of before. Assembly lines were commonplace in the manufacturing sectors, but it took Gordy's visionary mind to realize that the very same principles could be applied to the creative industry.

Within a few years, Gordy had scraped together enough money and contacts to open his own record label. On June 7, 1958, he founded Tamla Records. Two years later, he incorporated the company under the name "Motown Records." He bought his own studio, dubbed Hitsville U.S.A., and began to churn out songs.

The entire operation at Motown was designed to run with factory efficiency.

> It was the first Motown record ever to sell a million copies, and it became a harbinger for the oncoming era of Motown chart dominance.

Rather than bringing in bands or contracting out session musicians, Gordy assembled an in-house band. The studio would be open nearly every hour of the day. He would cycle through performers, bringing them in to cut an album's worth of records with his band in a few hours, and then sending them out on tour to do promotion. Motown even had a "quality control" meeting at the end of each week, where they would play the week's recordings side by side with the biggest pop hits of the day, and ensure that they would fit well in a radio run. Gordy had complete control over this factory, and final veto power on every song.

By 1961, Motown had a handful of hits, courtesy of one of their first groups, the Miracles. But they were constantly in search of new talent. They found the group that would get them their first number one in an unlikely place. The Marvelettes were high school girls, discovered after performing at a high school talent contest. Gordy let them audition and liked their sound, but told them to come back with an original song. They returned with an

unfinished blues song written by one of their friends, "Please Mr. Postman."

Gordy brought in the songwriting team of Brian Holland and Robert Bateman to rework the tune. Motown had the song ready to record within weeks, and it would release to massive acclaim in the summer of 1961. "Please Mr. Postman" had a 26-week run in the Top 100, including a claim to the top spot in December. It was the first Motown record ever to sell a million copies, and it became a harbinger for the oncoming era of Motown chart dominance.

"Please Mr. Postman" embodies the distinct pop sound that would come to define Motown. It combined the call-and-response singing of gospel churches with an emergent soul sound, and tied it all together with a busy backbeat. The musicians that made up many of Motown's hits represent some of the finest session musicians ever to play. Among them are bassist James Jamerson and guitarist Eddie Wills, who both played on "Please Mr. Postman." On the drums was Marvin Gaye, who was about to emerge as Motown's biggest star.

The Marvelettes would go on to score two more Top 10 hits, but they'd never reach the heights of their debut single. Nevertheless, "Please Mr. Postman" proved the viability of girl groups in the Motown system. The sound and success of this song became a blueprint for the Supremes, who would become some of Motown's biggest darlings. Cowriter Brian Holland became part of Motown's in-house writing team, Holland-Dozier-Holland, and ended up writing some of the most successful hits of the era.

"Please Mr. Postman" helped raise Motown Records' profile internationally as well. In December 1961, an up-and-coming group of mop-top boys from Liverpool started incorporating the song into their playlist, enthralling a British audience that hadn't heard it on the radio. Two years later, they'd record a cover on their second U.K. album, *Meet the Beatles*.

The sprightly voices of the Marvelettes, combined with Berry Gordy's business acumen, helped launch Motown into unprecedented levels of success. Motown's style of soul became some of the defining popular music of the 1960s, and birthed such artists as Stevie Wonder, Marvin Gaye and Michael Jackson. Between 1961 and 1971, Motown Records would have an astounding 110 different songs crack the U.S. Top 10. Their assembly line approach to hit-making completely transformed the music industry, and marked the true birth of a girl group and boy band culture that persists in pop to this day. And you can trace it all back to a make-ends-meet job on an assembly line and a high school talent contest.

> Their assembly line approach to hit-making completely transformed the music industry. . . . And you can trace it all back to a make-ends-meet job . . . and a high school talent contest.

Honorable Mention

"Crazy" by Patsy Cline: One of country's most promising songwriters in the early '60s was Willie Nelson. Nelson's lyrics were minimal and humanistic, speaking profound human truths in simple words. One of the finest songs he ever wrote was a forlorn love song called "Crazy." In 1961, Patsy Cline brought the song and Nelson himself into the public consciousness with a lush, aching performance.

1962

"Love Me Do"

The Beatles

American music has always been able to find audiences in Europe. Jazz caught on in the interwar cabarets of Paris and Berlin, while the Broadway tradition was a huge influence on seminal European composers, such as Kurt Weill. But American music really started to catch on in Europe in the years following World War II. Blues and country landed on the other side of the Atlantic with the American armed forces during the war. As the world order was being reshaped, and a new closeness developed between America and Britain, more and more American music found its way into British record stores. Gospel and blues artists, such as Sister Rosetta Tharpe, Big Bill Broonzy and Muddy Waters, embarked on a number of European tours throughout the 1950s. In doing so, they sowed the seeds for a cultural exchange unlike any the world had ever seen before.

As Britain's baby boom generation came of age, they became obsessed first with the blues and then with the rock n' roll sounds that were spreading like wildfire in America. British labels started to press their own versions of the great rock records, and teenagers would

> It's impossible to overstate the importance of "Love Me Do," as it's the song that introduced the world to the Beatles.

flock to the shops in droves to get a chance to listen to this American music. Inevitably, many of these teens started to develop their own takes on American songs.

In the mid-'50s, a Scottish musician named Lonnie Donegan became a star playing "skiffle," a combination of New Orleans jug band music, country and rock n' roll. Donegan's skiffle music started a craze across the United Kingdom, inspiring all sorts of teens to form their own skiffle groups. Two of those teens were named John Lennon and Paul McCartney. In 1956, Lennon formed a band called the Quarrymen. McCartney joined a year later, and in '58, they recruited a talented young guitarist named George Harrison. By 1960, the Quarrymen had changed their name to the Beatles in homage to Buddy Holly's band, the Crickets. They were already well on their way to making history.

One of the first songs that Lennon and McCartney ever wrote together, long before the Quarrymen changed their name, was a piece called "Love Me Do." The song was a true Lennon-McCartney composition: McCartney wrote the orig-

inal lyrics for a high school girlfriend, and Lennon helped him develop a harmonic framework. Lennon also contributed the song's iconic harmonica line, emulating the sorts of American blues artists that he'd come to love. "Love Me Do" is nothing short of a perfect pop song. The Beatles' beautiful vocal harmonies are the stuff of legend; the band's upbeat energy still grooves like hell.

In those early days, most of the Beatles' repertoire consisted of covers of songs by such American rock artists as Little Richard, the Crickets and Elvis Presley. That wouldn't last long. "Love Me Do" marked the beginning of one of the most prolific songwriting partnerships in music history.

In the years following, the Beatles would take up residency in Hamburg, cutting their teeth playing all-night sets for a ravenous German crowd. By playing hour after hour, day after day, they came to understand the contours of rock music like few before them had, and their profile started to rise both in

Germany and in their hometown of Liverpool. After finishing a residency and returning to Liverpool, the Beatles met Brian Epstein, who saw their potential and became their manager. Epstein freed them from contractual obligations and got them a deal with the label Epiphone.

In the summer of 1962, the Beatles sat down for their first recording session and recorded an early take on "Love Me Do" with their original drummer, Pete Best, on drums. Before their second session in September, they had replaced Best with Ringo Starr. They recorded a new version of "Love Me Do," as well as a number of tracks that would become their debut album, *Please Please Me*. The single for "Love Me Do" was released in October 1962, and *Please Please Me* would drop in the new year.

It's impossible to overstate the importance of "Love Me Do," as it's the song that introduced the world to the Beatles. It would, however, be another two years before the song got an official

U.S. release. By that time, Beatlemania was sweeping the world, marking the proper beginnings of '60s culture.

Before the Beatles, most rock n' roll groups consisted of a front man and a backing band. They often had saxophones and backup singers, and rarely wrote their own songs. The Beatles were something different: four personalities, each visibly adding his own spice to the group, writing original songs and playing his own instruments. The Beatles weren't the first band to have such a lineup, but they were the biggest. They codified the modern rock band, down to the four-piece instrumentation set with drums, lead guitar, rhythm guitar and bass. They established a new style of songwriting, rooted in American blues and rock, but flavored with a distinct sort of British schoolboy charm and wit.

By combining their own British culture with American rock n' roll and blues, the Beatles were continuing in the long tradition of cultural collision that brought rock about in the first place. They'd spend the rest of their career deepening that practice, bringing influences from country music, classical music, Indian music and more into their sound. They would capture teenagers and once again prove the immaculate musical taste of young girls. It can be hard to grasp just how fast things moved for the Beatles. Within four years of the original release of "Love Me Do," they would be redefining music again and becoming countercultural icons with the psychedelic revolution.

The 1960s are the most significant decade in the history of popular music, and the Beatles were the most significant band of the '60s. Sixty years later, their early music still feels as fresh and profound as the day it was first released.

Honorable Mention

"Misirlou" by Dick Dale: On the sunny beaches of California, the early '60s birthed a new spin-off of rock n' roll. Surf Rock sought to emulate the roar of the sea and the rush of catching a wave with loud, fast guitar sounds. The loudest and fastest of the entire scene was Dick Dale, who adapted a Mediterranean folk song into a riveting rock n' roll jam. His tremolo picking on "Misirlou" makes it one of the earliest influences on heavy metal guitar.

1963

"Alabama"

John Coltrane

On September 15, 1963, America bore witness to one of the most heinous acts of malice the country had ever seen. Martin Luther King Jr.'s Southern Christian Leadership Conference had spent the year bringing attention to the most segregated city in the United States: Birmingham, Alabama. Black organizers targeted the city with boycotts, protests and sit-ins. In response to this growing tide toward desegregation, a group of Ku Klux Klansmen planted dynamite in the 16th Street Baptist Church and detonated it on a Sunday morning. The explosion injured nearly two dozen, and killed four girls, the youngest of whom was just 11 years old.

It was not the first such bombing in Birmingham. In fact, there had been so many white nationalist bombings in the city over the course of the civil rights movement that the town had garnered the grim nickname "Bombingham." These bombings served as a constant reminder that many in white America were willing to do just about anything to deny Black communities their basic human rights. But this act of hatred did nothing to deter the civil rights move-

Coltrane wrote the song as a tribute . . . and a meditation on the pains and traumas that victimized Black communities.

ment; it only underlined the necessity of its cause. On September 18, a funeral for three of the bombing victims was held at the church. More than 3,000 mourners, Black and white, showed up in a powerful moment of solemnity and unity. Among them was Martin Luther King Jr., who gave a stirring speech encouraging faith and resilience in the face of this tragedy. Two months later, John Coltrane would turn that speech into one of the most powerful pieces of jazz ever recorded: "Alabama."

By 1963, Coltrane had already established himself as one of the most brilliant minds that jazz had ever seen. While playing with Miles Davis and Thelonious Monk, he'd perfected a style of bebop that came to be known as "sheets of sound," defined by virtuosic runs of cascading arpeggios. In 1960, he had released "Giant Steps," a mathematical treatise in jazz form relying on a complex set of chord changes that are now known as simply the "Coltrane changes." And when modal jazz took over, he was among its finest proponents. His playing was a highlight on Davis' album *Kind of Blue*, and his own *My Favorite*

Things applied modal jazz to the Great American Songbook and made him one of the most popular jazz musicians of the era.

With "Alabama," Coltrane tread once more into new territory. Coltrane wrote the song as a tribute to the victims of the 16th Street Baptist Church bombing, and as a meditation on the pains and traumas that victimized Black communities in the long fight for justice and equality. These emotions are conveyed through his tormented playing. The song doesn't have a single lyric, and yet it is populated with words. Coltrane shaped his saxophone line on "Alabama" around the cadences spoken by Martin Luther King Jr. in his speech at the Birmingham funeral. That speech was broadcast on the radio and printed in a number of newspapers at the time. Using these, he was able to emulate King's celebrated oration patterns. In doing so, Coltrane added his voice to the cries of outrage and despondence following the attack.

He recorded "Alabama" on November 18, 1963, without telling his bandmates the name of the piece or its message. This was typical for Coltrane, who preferred to let his music speak for itself. The simple title of "Alabama" and the context of its release matched with his playing to carry more political weight than any words he might have spoken. He's backed in his message by his so-called Classic Quartet, consisting of McCoy Tyner on piano, Jimmy Garrison on bass and Elvin Jones on drums. This quartet performed the song in a powerful television performance on December 7, 1963, and then released a live recording of it on *Live at Birdland* the next year.

With his interpretation of King's words, and the raw, moving power of the song, Coltrane stepped into his era of spiritual jazz. His faith had been deepening ever since he recovered from a heroin addiction. He believed that music was a way to reach divinity. "Alabama" did that by channeling the words and cadences of one of the greatest preachers ever to live. A year later, Coltrane would refine the concept that began with "Alabama" into *A Love Supreme*, a transcendent album of spiritual music, shaped around saxophone recitations that emulated religious psalms.

The sorrow of Coltrane and the rest of Black America following the 16th Street Baptist Church bombing wouldn't be in vain. The attack proved to be a turning point in the civil rights movement. Thanks in no small part to the attention of artists like Coltrane, it became a touchstone for people to rally around. Less than a year later, Lyndon B. Johnson signed the Civil Rights Act into law. One of America's darkest moments, memorialized by some of America's most brilliant minds, brought on a new era of hope and optimism for a long-suffering people.

Honorable Mention

"Blowin' in the Wind" by Bob Dylan: At just 21 years old, Bob Dylan penned a protest song that shook the nation. "Blowin' in the Wind" was inspired by the academic and political pursuits of the Greenwich Village folk scene, pulling the melody from an old African American spiritual and combining it with abstract, philosophical poetics. Dylan's lyrics reached out to a civil rights movement at its zenith and an anti-war movement that was just sparking. In uniting these movements, he helped start an enormous countercultural movement that would define the '60s.

1964

"A Change Is Gonna Come"

Sam Cooke

For most of Sam Cooke's career, his music was apolitical. It wasn't that he didn't care about the civil rights struggle raging around him. In fact, he was a proud supporter of the civil rights movement and was friends with the likes of Malcolm X and Muhammad Ali. But Cooke had accomplished a rare feat for a Black man in the 1960s—he'd captured the hearts of white America. At the time, it was nearly unheard of for Black artists to cross over onto the pop charts. Cooke was only a generation removed from Billboard having a chart category called "race records," and the legacy of that little piece of segregation still hung heavy on pop music. Just existing as a Black pop artist was a radical action. Cooke was worried that if he brought too much of his politics into his music, he would alienate his white audiences and undo all of the hard work he'd done breaking into the mainstream.

The events of 1963 changed all that. It was a moment of monumental change in America, marked by Martin Luther King Jr.'s March on Washington for Jobs and Freedom. There, King delivered his famous "I Have a Dream" speech, inspiring a nation in the process.

One of the guests on that march was a young white musician named Bob Dylan, who had been creating a stir in the music world with his original songs supporting the civil rights movement. Cooke was a fan of Dylan's, and was particularly stricken the first time he heard his simple, profound "Blowin' in the Wind." Cooke felt ashamed that someone who was not Black had written such a powerful song about the state of America, while he, himself, was avoiding the topic in his art. Cooke loved the song so much that he started incorporating it in his set list.

Still, he needed one last push to convince him to write his own civil rights song. That push came on October 8, 1963. Cooke and his band were traveling to a show in Shreveport, Louisiana. Cooke called a Holiday Inn just outside the city and made a reservation for the night, hoping to get a good night's sleep before the next day's performance. But when Cooke

> Cooke felt ashamed that someone who was not Black had written such a powerful song about the state of America, while he, himself, was avoiding the topic in his art.

arrived at the hotel, the desk clerk told him there were no vacancies. The segregationist hotel was turning him away because of the color of his skin.

Cooke had an early version of "A Change Is Gonna Come" ready by Christmas that year.

His defining civil rights song is a far cry from the Dylan song that helped inspire it. Whereas Dylan is poetic and philosophical, Cooke is raw and spiritual. His words seem pulled from a long line of great Black writers and orators. The song opens on a statement that calls to mind Langston Hughes' seminal poem "The Negro Speaks of Rivers." The chorus echoes Martin Luther King's sentiment that "The arc of the moral universe is long, but it bends toward justice." But for all of its influences, "A Change Is Gonna Come" is Sam Cooke through and through. It's born from his own personal struggles, and sung with the smooth, soulful vigor that made him one of America's most beloved performers.

Above all, "A Change Is Gonna Come" is a song about hope and resilience. It's Cooke comforting his long-suffering community with a promise of change.

Cooke recorded the song in early 1964. He trusted René Hall with the arrangement, and Hall took the job seriously. He brought in an entire orchestra to give the song both a lush, cinematic treatment and the severity it deserved. Just a week after that recording, Cooke performed the song live on *The Tonight Show*. That was the only time he would ever perform the song live.

Some of that change would come sooner than Cooke knew. In 1964, the civil rights movement was fast gaining public and political support. That came to a head on July 2, 1964, when U.S. president Lyndon B. Johnson signed the Civil Rights Act into law. It was a monumental victory for the movement, but far from the end of the fight.

Cooke gave the movement an anthem to continue to motivate that fight. "A Change Is Gonna Come" got a single release on December 22, 1964, and was immediately adopted by the movement.

But he wouldn't live to see this.

On December 11, 1964, Sam Cooke was shot in the heart. He died at just 33 years of age. The circumstances around his death are complicated and contentious. The woman who shot him said she did so in self-defense, and courts ruled in her favor. The public wasn't as convinced. More than 200,000 fans lined up to see Sam Cooke at his funeral, still coping with the news of his death. Almost immediately, conspiracy talk around his death started and much of that continues to this day.

"A Change Is Gonna Come" became an untimely swan song for Sam Cooke, and one of the most widely celebrated protest songs ever made.

"A Change Is Gonna Come" became an untimely swan song for Sam Cooke, and one of the most widely celebrated protest songs ever made. It stands as a representation of the resilient spirit that drove the civil rights movement. That spirit, like Cooke's song, has been passed down through generations of activism. It still lives on today in each new generation of marginalized activists and artists who know that the world can, and will, change for the better.

Honorable Mentions

"Mississippi Goddam" by Nina Simone: Nina Simone was a classical piano virtuoso with a rich tenor voice and fierce politicism. In 1964, she debuted her own protest song in response to the Baptist Street bombing and the racist backlash of the era. Unlike the stalwart optimism of Sam Cooke, her protest song is a paranoid piece full of grim gallows humor and simmering resentment. It speaks to the more revolutionary side of the civil rights movement, and embodies Black America's desperate desire for the equality they deserve.

"You've Lost That Lovin' Feeling" by the Righteous Brothers: A maverick producer named Phil Spector perfected his production technique known as the "Wall of Sound," which used the recording studio itself as an instrument, filling every inch of his recording with instrumentals and vocals. The result is an awe-inspiring drama never before seen in pop music.

1965

"Like a Rolling Stone"

Bob Dylan

It's hard to imagine the pressure that Bob Dylan must have felt as he entered the 24th year of life. Barely past the threshold of adulthood, he had already been proclaimed the voice of his generation. By mixing the great American traditions of folk and blues with poetic lyrics inspired by the Imagists and the Beats, Dylan had captured the spirit of a revolutionary time and become the de facto leader of the booming Greenwich Village folk scene. His "Blowin' in the Wind" was an anthem of the civil rights movement, and the apocalyptic "A Hard Rain's A-Gonna Fall" was one of the definitive anti-Vietnam songs. He performed at Martin Luther King's March on Washington and developed a rabid following of fans and press who hung on his every word. By the time 1965 came around, Dylan had already cemented his place as one of the greatest musicians ever to live.

The weight of fame began to hang around Dylan's neck. A seven-date British tour in the spring of '65 had left him exhausted almost to the point of delirium. His songwriting drifted away from topical political pieces toward more esoteric pieces of poetry. He even considered taking a break from songwriting altogether to focus on prose. One spring evening, he sat down to write out his feelings. He ended up pouring all of his tension and vitriol into an enormous screed of text that spanned 10 pages, or even 20 pages by some accounts. Dylan didn't even truly know what he was writing; he simply let the words flow through him until he had nothing left to say. Over the next few weeks, he would trim that dense piece of writing down into four verses that represented some of the finest writing of his entire career. It wouldn't be long before that writing was developed into a monumental song called "Like a Rolling Stone."

The lyrics of "Like a Rolling Stone," like most of Dylan's lyrics at the time, are difficult to parse. They're loaded with archetypal imagery and strange turns of phrase. The poetic meter is sophisticated, dense with internal rhyme and packed with evocative metaphor. On its surface, "Like a Rolling Stone" appears to be about a young socialite who likes to slum it in artistic circles. When she is cut off from her wealthy upbringing, the song's "Miss Lonely" is suddenly forced to fend for herself and create a new identity. There are plenty of theories about the song's subject. The most prevalent of these says that she is based on the Warhol superstar Edie Sedgewick, with whom Dylan had a brief affair in '65.

Dylan himself has always pushed against these sorts of interpretations of his lyrics. The press at the time would constantly hound him for the meanings

tion home. For all the tension present in the lyrics of Dylan's opus, the music of "Like a Rolling Stone" is wild with abandon. It freed the listener from the shackles of cold war America, and the song turned from a piece about karmic comeuppance into a piece about self-discovery and actualization.

This arrangement was the culmination of a radical musical experiment Dylan had begun a few months before the writing of "Like a Rolling Stone." He'd gathered a group of blues and rock musicians, and started to record electric songs. At the time, rock music was seen as antithetical to folk. It was loud and passionate, whereas folk was calm and contemplative. Rock bands were dominating the charts, while folk groups had little to no interest in commercial viability, seeing themselves more as political actors and the lifeblood of the counterculture. When Dylan debuted his electric sound on the first side of *Bringing It All Back Home,* many in the folk scene saw it as a betrayal. He was accused of selling out and abandoning the cause. Rather than succumb to the pressures of his scene, Dylan decided to lean in. He assembled a collection of the best blues players he could, highlighted by Mike Bloomfield on lead guitar, and recorded an album that was even louder, and more electric, than *Bringing It All Back Home.*

In July 1965, Dylan took his band with him for his appearance at the Newport Folk Festival. He had been a highlight of the past two festivals, playing quiet acoustic sets alongside Joan Baez. When he took the stage with an electric band for the first time, it shook the music world. His set was loud and plagued with feedback, shocking the folk crowd. Arguments erupted backstage, and Dylan's band left the stage

behind his songs. His responses tended to be sardonic and exasperated. He didn't think of the songs as he was writing them; he just put his fingers on a typewriter and let the muses do the work. In the end, it doesn't matter what Dylan's thought process was, if any existed, when writing "Like a Rolling Stone." What matters is how the world interpreted it.

Although Dylan had tried so hard to shy away from the prophetic labels assigned to him, "Like a Rolling Stone" managed to capture the spirit of the baby boomer generation. A youth movement was breaking free from the conservative generation in power. They were protesting the Vietnam War, joining up with the civil rights movement and experimenting with drugs and sex. Many found themselves cut off from their old lives, left alone with no direc-

after just three songs, one of which was "Like a Rolling Stone."

In subsequent shows, the backlash grew. Fans would accost Dylan and boo him any time he showed up with his electric group, even as "Like a Rolling Stone" was climbing pop charts and transforming the rock scene. He set out on a world tour that was plagued with negativity from fans. At one infamous show in Manchester, an audience member even called him "Judas." This only seemed to encourage Dylan. He responded by sneering, "I don't believe you, you're a liar" into the microphone before turning around to his backing band and instructing them to "play it fucking loud" and erupting into "Like a Rolling Stone."

The harsh words of Dylan's detractors could do nothing to sedate the sleeping giant that he had awoken. "Like a Rolling Stone" was a rock song unlike anything the world had ever seen. It turned the heads of Dylan's contemporaries, and it was a world-changer for such young listeners as Bruce Springsteen, Lou Reed and Jimi Hendrix. Never before had rock music been paired with such ambitious lyricism. It was the first moment that rock truly made its case for being considered "high art." It did so not by bowing to pressures, but by embracing the devil-may-care attitude that was always present in rock's DNA.

As for Dylan, he spent the next year touring and concluding his trilogy of electric albums with the monumental *Blonde on Blonde*. In the summer of 1966, he got into a near-fatal motorcycle accident and disappeared from the spotlight, returning a year later with a strange, understated country album called *John Wesley Harding*. As the counterculture movement reached its pinnacle in the late '60s, Dylan opted out, choosing instead to pursue a quiet life away from the spotlight for a time. But the movement he began had gathered more than enough momentum on its own. "Like a Rolling Stone" proved to be the catalyst for a cultural moment whose aftershocks are still felt to this day.

> Never before had rock music been paired with such ambitious lyricism. It was the first moment that rock truly made its case for being considered "high art."

Honorable Mentions

"People Get Ready" by the Impressions: A year after the signing of the Civil Rights Act, Curtis Mayfield penned another song to be added to the growing list of soul songs fighting for equality. "People Get Ready" takes old sayings Mayfield heard in church and sings them over a warm gospel arrangement. This combination made the song a perfect fit for Martin Luther King Jr. and his followers, who adopted it as their unofficial anthem almost immediately.

"Papa's Got a Brand New Bag" by James Brown: James Brown invented funk by speeding up rhythm and blues and creating arrangements thick with syncopation. With his raspy call, signature dance moves and unending energy, Brown would become one of the most beloved and influential performers of the era.

"California Dreamin'" by the Mamas and the Papas: As a hippie counterculture was emerging in California, driven by radical politics and psychedelic drug use, the Mamas and the Papas recorded the movement's early theme song. The jangly guitar tones, rich flute solo and experimental production perfectly capture the weirdness and optimism of this new California subculture, calling all of America to travel westward and build a new society.

"Good Vibrations"

The Beach Boys

In 1966, Brian Wilson had a song stuck in his head. There was just one problem: That song didn't exist yet. This wasn't exactly a new experience for Wilson. Through most of his life, he was hearing music in his head. Often, his coping mechanism was to make that imaginary music real. Throughout the early '60s, he had established himself as one of the premier songwriters in pop music. In just a two-year span between 1963 and 1965, the Beach Boys released 10 singles that cracked Billboard's Top 10, every one of which was written or cowritten by Wilson. Typically, he was able to write the songs out of his head and move on, but in '66, he began to obsess over a single piece of music unlike anything he'd written before.

This obsession was fueled by enormous changes, both in his personal life and in the broader musical culture. Wilson hated the life of the touring musician. He had horrible stage fright, and the pressures of traveling and performing in front of hordes of young fans stressed and exhausted him. Late in 1964, he had a brutal panic attack while on a plane to Houston for a concert. This led to a complete nervous breakdown that saw Wilson enter a near-catatonic state in the band's dressing room. From that point, he decided he wouldn't tour with the Beach Boys. Instead, he stayed home to write the band's next album while the rest of the group went out on tour.

Left to his own devices, Wilson enjoyed a level of creative freedom he'd never seen before. He used it to make a masterpiece, inspired by the Beatles, who had released the monumental *Rubber Soul* in 1964. *Rubber Soul* was an album with scope and soundscapes that the pop world hadn't seen before. It was a full album where every track had thought and meaning, rather than a collection of singles. It featured novel instrumentation, with George Harrison taking up a sitar on "Norwegian Wood." It was a sign that pop music could be bigger and more ambitious than anyone thought at the time. Wilson didn't just want to emulate *Rubber Soul;* he imagined a project that could exceed the Beatles' triumph. He wrote an album with a cohesive vision that rivalled the Beatles', and filled the instrumentals with dense orchestral arrangements. These arrangements were inspired by the technique called the "Wall of Sound," invented by producer Phil Spector, which envisioned the music studio itself as an instrument and filled each song with a spectacular, dense array of instruments.

Pet Sounds took the "Wall of Sound" to new levels. Wilson brought in the best studio musicians Los Angeles had to offer, a group of musicians known as the "Wrecking Crew," and carefully arranged their every note. The result was a beautiful album that became one of the defining pieces of psychedelic pop music. Although the album didn't sell at first, and was the subject of deep criticism from Wilson's abusive father as well as his bandmate Mike Love, it's now considered one of the greatest albums ever made. But there was one song that Wilson couldn't make work in time for the album, the song that had been stuck in his head all year. That song was called "Good Vibrations."

The writing and recording of "Good Vibrations" was one of the most expensive, painstaking processes in music history. Rather than write the song as a singular piece, Wilson wrote and recorded a number of smaller modular pieces that could be arranged and stuck together for the final product. He recorded the song over dozens of sessions in multiple different studios, something completely unheard of at the time. This sort of multitrack approach to songwriting has since become the norm in nearly all genres of music, but it was completely novel when Wilson was doing it. He experimented with different instrumental takes and different arrangements of his modules, and he brought in new instruments that the pop world had never seen before. All of this tinkering made the studio costs pile up. The final cost of "Good Vibrations" was somewhere between $50,000 and $75,000, about the same amount as the entire *Pet Sounds* album had cost. These costs were exacerbated by Wilson's own erratic behavior. He would often show up at studios and bring all the musicians in, only to decide that the things weren't right and head off without recording a single second of music.

This strange behavior was a reflection of Wilson's growing mental illness, a problem that had been exacerbated when he first tried LSD in 1965. Although it was first synthesized in the 1940s, LSD had remained a research drug for two decades. But in 1963, the patent for LSD expired, and countercultural thought leaders, such as Aldous Huxley and Timothy Leary, began to advocate for its use, hoping it could be used to open minds and help build a better world. For Wilson, acid helped expand his vision and inspire some of the brilliant arrangements on *Pet Sounds* and the song "Good Vibrations." But this creative expansion came at a cost. His mental state began to change and deteriorate after his first acid trip. Already an eccentric man, he became paranoid and obsessive.

Although he only did acid three times in his life, Wilson's music would become the soundtrack to the psychedelic revolution sweeping across the West Coast at the time. The brilliant, dense soundscapes enthralled psychedelic users. His lyrics, written alongside bandmate Mike Love and songwriter Tony Asher, captured the transcendent energy of the flower power revolution.

When "Good Vibrations" was finally finished, it became a living representation of the optimism and ambition of late '60s California. The song was a technical marvel, held together by radical tape splices that connected vastly different pieces of music recorded at different studios. The vocal arrangements are filled with the immaculate harmonies that made the Beach Boys famous, elevated by the careful musicianship of the Wrecking Crew. A Carole Kaye bassline provides a novel countermelody, while Paul Tanner plays an otherworldly line on the Electro-Theremin, an instrument of his own invention. Journalist Derek Taylor dubbed "Good Vibrations" a "pocket symphony," a fitting description that spoke to the ambition of the project.

"Good Vibrations" was an instant hit on release. It topped charts on both sides of the Atlantic and became the biggest hit of the Beach Boys' career to date. It helped inspire countless psychedelic artists at the time, and even challenged the Beatles to push their own psychedelic sounds further on 1967's monumental *Sgt. Pepper's Lonely Hearts Club Band*. But as Wilson was experiencing the greatest triumph of his career, his mental health was crumbling. He would try to follow up "Good Vibrations" with an even more ambitious album, but in chasing perfection, he ended up succumbing to a deep addiction and going through another mental breakdown. The Beach Boys were able to cobble together pieces of that project into more of the finest work of their career, but Wilson was becoming more secluded, and falling further into a cycle of mental illness. This was exacerbated by an abusive therapist who took full control of his life until the 1990s.

The story of "Good Vibrations" is a classic tragedy of a tortured genius. It's a song of love and optimism written by a man in a constant fight with personal demons. But unlike so many of these stories in music, it's not one with a tragic ending. After many dark periods throughout his life, Wilson emerged stable in middle age. Today, he continues his music career and has lived to see himself celebrated as the genius that he is.

Honorable Mentions

"Eight Miles High" by the Byrds: Inspired by John Coltrane's forays into Indian classical music and psychedelic LSD experiences, the Byrds created one of the first and finest songs in the new psychedelic rock movement. "Eight Miles High" experiments with new guitar distortion technologies, creating a loud and chaotic sound filled with all the tension, confusion and euphoric catharsis of a psychedelic experience.

"River Deep Mountain High" by Ike and Tina Turner: Phil Spector teamed up with rock n' roll royalty for the most ambitious take on his "Wall of Sound" yet. Ike and Tina Turner had been cutting rock hits since the '50s, but this collaboration proved that they were ready for a new era. Although it underperformed on the charts, "River Deep Mountain High" is one of the finest songs that '60s rock n' roll had to offer. Over the decades to come, its legacy would be marred as dark truths about Ike Turner's and Phil Spector's abusive personalities came out. Nevertheless, it remained a staple of Tina Turner's catalog as she carried onward into one of pop music's most prolific careers.

1967

"Respect"

Aretha Franklin

In 1967, radical music was flooding recording studios, radio stations and venues across the world. On the West Coast, the "Summer of Love" had taken full hold and brought with it utopian dreams of society and a powerful protest movement against the Vietnam War. In New York City, Andy Warhol's Factory scene was bringing about new takes on gender and sexuality, as well as a wave of extreme auditory experiments. It was the year that it truly felt that rock music could change the world, but the most powerful protest song of the year came from a woman who was about to be crowned the "Queen of Soul."

On Valentine's Day 1967, Aretha Franklin stepped into Atlantic Records' New York City studio and laid down one of the greatest feminist anthems ever put to wax, "Respect." The song was a cover of a piece written and recorded by the great Otis Redding back in 1965. That piece was one of the first crossover hits of Redding's career, and helped establish him as one of the era's rising stars. It was a complex sort of love song, with lyrics influenced by the male chauvinism of his time. It had Redding telling a lover she could do whatever she wanted when he was away on the road, but when he came home, she was to respect him as the breadwinner. It was a song that seemed to acknowledge and accept infidelities, but the whole conceit was still built

around a relationship model that was falling to the wayside with the rise of the sexual revolution and second-wave feminism. When Franklin got her hands on "Respect," she stripped it down to its bones and rebuilt it into a powerful message of feminine empowerment that transcended any single era.

Franklin was no stranger to civil rights activism. Her father was a Baptist minister and a leader in the civil rights movement, a legacy that she would continue throughout her career. But for all of the racial progress that the movement brought on, it was fraught with the misogyny of the time. Despite the fact that women played key roles in the movement, many of the male activists still believed that women should stick to their traditional roles as wives, mothers and homemakers. But Franklin yearned for more than this.

She was impregnated at just 12 years old but wouldn't let that stop a musical career. Franklin spent her early adulthood in the start of the '60s recording a catalog of standards with Columbia Records. She had some early successes, but was never able to break through as she'd hoped. By the time her contract had run out at the end of 1966, Franklin owed the record company money. Meanwhile, her marriage was beginning to disintegrate as her husband abused her at home. In 1967, she signed with

society. It framed Franklin as the bread-winner, a drastic shift from the "woman as housewife" mentality that was prevalent in the '60s.

The Franklin sisters' reworking of "Respect" could not have come at a better time. The second wave of feminism was building across the country, and women everywhere were beginning to demand respect. The message went wider than women, though. The call for "Respect" was also one for Black communities, who were still facing intense backlash following the passage of the Civil Rights Act. It was a call for the youth, who were trying to step out of their parents' shadows and build a better world. At a moment when the world was being turned upside down, "Respect" became an anthem for change.

When Franklin's Atlantic debut, *I've Never Loved a Man the Way I Love You*, came out, it soared to success on the back of "Respect." Atlantic released the song as a single, and it became an international hit for Franklin. She'd finally found the success that had evaded her for years and became one of the defining figures of the late '60s counterculture. Even Otis Redding would acknowledge the power of her cover. In 1967, when performing at the landmark Monterey Pop festival, Redding declared that Franklin had took the song away from him and that it was hers now.

In the modern era, the profile of "Respect" has only grown. The song has piled up praise and accolades, and in 2021, *Rolling Stone* magazine declared it the greatest song of all time. The power of "Respect" comes in its simplicity. Its immortal hook encapsulated all of the social movements happening in its day, and its universal message means it will remain an anthem for generations to come.

Atlantic Records, who encouraged her to move away from the Great American Songbook and toward the genre of soul, which was blowing up at the time.

With a mandate to record soul music, Franklin turned her gaze toward "Respect." She loved the song's groove, but no doubt took issue with some of the chauvinism present in the lyrics. So, she gathered her sisters together to rework the piece into something more befitting of a woman who was starting to carve her own path in a man's world. They switched the lyrics around, making it about a woman demanding respect from her man, and tinkered with the arrangement. Crucially, Franklin and her sisters came up with the idea of a chant of "R-E-S-P-E-C-T" to drive home the message of the song. She delivered these new lyrics with passion and power, channeling the energies of countless women who felt disrespected at home and cut out of participation in

Honorable Mention

"White Rabbit" by Jefferson Airplane: The counter-cultural movement started to peak in 1967 with San Francisco's "Summer of Love." One of the anthems of this summer of hedonism and protest was "White Rabbit," a trippy retelling of *Alice in Wonderland*. Jefferson Airplane's lyrics question the older generation, who scoffed at the hippies for using drugs even while they filled their own lives with alcohol and pharmaceuticals. The song's climactic cry of "feed your head" embodied the era's call for mind expansion.

"All Along the Watchtower"

Jimi Hendrix Experience

The transatlantic cultural exchange between the United States and the United Kingdom shaped the 1960s. It injected new energy and vision to rock and ushered in an era where music began to entwine itself with every aspect of life. At first this exchange consisted of successive cultural volleys across the sea. But in late 1966, a group came together to become the physical embodiment of this cultural conversation. The Jimi Hendrix Experience was born out of an exhilarating London blues revival scene packed with such virtuosic guitar players as Jimmy Page, Peter Green and Eric Clapton. All these men were talented in their own right and helped push blues to new territory, but none had any cultural connection to the blues. That's where Jimi Hendrix came in.

Hendrix was born to a poor Black family in Seattle. He grew up with the generational trauma and pain that informed the invention of the blues, and he was drawn to the music from a young age. He spent his early adulthood gigging as a sideman, playing with a number of groups, including Little Richard's Upsetters. The rhythm and blues scene brought Hendrix to New York City, where he met Chas Chandler, the former bassist of British Invasion superstars the Animals. Chandler was the first to truly spot Hendrix's potential. He convinced the young guitarist to move to London, and set him up with guitarist turned bassist Noel Redding and drum phenom Mitch Mitchell. The result was an explosive psychedelic blues sound that changed the scene forever.

The Jimi Hendrix Experience was the radical visions of their time made manifest. Hendrix played loud, and he played strong. He was fascinated with the new technology of guitar pedals and used them to create thick waves of psychedelic fuzz. The London school of blues consisted of smaller bands with more space for improvisation. This format let Hendrix shine. His solos felt musically effortless, but the performances were pure showmanship. He'd play guitar behind his back, pluck strings with his teeth and even set his guitar on fire. He was a new kind of rock star for a chaotic world being plunged into an age of mass media, social strife and brutal warfare.

One of the many feathers in Hendrix's cap was his incendiary 1968 cover of Bob Dylan's "All Along the Watchtower." Just as Aretha Franklin transformed Otis Redding's "Respect" into something more befitting of her moment, Hendrix turned an understated, cryptic piece of Dylan poetry into a bombastic protest song against the Vietnam War.

By 1968, the Vietnam War had escalated to catastrophic proportions. Ever since Lyndon B. Johnson's escalations in 1964, a protest movement had been growing in America. Musicians like Dylan fueled it, as did an increasing number of media reports showing the death and destruction. Still, much of the propaganda messaging said that America was winning the war, so many had hope. That changed in January 1968, when the Vietcong launched a massive campaign called the Tet Offensive. This included strikes deep into the heart of South Vietnam. A country that had been told it was winning the war was suddenly bombarded by graphic newsreels showing death and destruction in Saigon. A new wave of rage and political action emerged. Meanwhile, the home front saw assassinations of Martin Luther King Jr. and Robert F. Kennedy, two figures who were providing hope for the progressive protest movement. America was beginning to look more and more like a powder keg ready to blow.

The music of Hendrix perfectly captured the tension of the moment. He filled Dylan's song with dissonance and used his guitar as a paintbrush to depict the chaos of war in vivid auditory portraits. Dylan's esoteric lyrics felt more grounded with a Hendrix backdrop, in particular the evocative opening line, "There must be some way out of here." Hendrix's guitar is complemented by a thunderous Mitchell drum line that fires off like artillery in the song's most heated moments. The highlight of the song is, of course, a series of cascading solos, each more intense than the last. Hendrix plays with studio panning and leans heavy on a wah pedal for a guitar solo that still triumphs over anything recorded since.

Hendrix's chaotic sound painting was the latest step in a march toward heavier and heavier music that had begun in the London blues scene. It helped set the stage for the heavy metal explosion that would come out of that scene in the next few years.

When Hendrix left New York for London, he was an unknown, rejected by the music industry and barely hanging on to his career. When he returned to New York to record parts of *Electric Ladyland* just three years later, he was a god. His London-infused psychedelic blues was exactly what America was looking for. It spoke to a moment that was equal parts exciting and terrifying. As it turned out, *Electric Ladyland* would be the last album the Experience recorded together, but Hendrix's legacy was cemented.

A year later, he would take the sound painting of "All Along the Watchtower" to new heights when he played a protest version of "The Star-Spangled Banner" on Woodstock's final morning. Tragically, that would be one of Hendrix's final great moments. On September 17, 1970, he was found dead at the age of 27.

The career of Jimi Hendrix happened in a flash, but it seemed to span an eternity. In just a few short years, he transformed the world's perception of what a rock band could be and how a guitar could be played. He innovated constantly and spoke an abstract truth to power with his music. Never was that truer than on "All Along the Watchtower."

Honorable
Mentions

"Folsom Prison Blues" (Live at Folsom Prison) by Johnny Cash: Johnny Cash revived his career with a landmark recording at California's maximum-security Folsom Prison. The highlight of the show was a song he had written more than a decade earlier about that very same prison. By embracing the marginalized population of American prisoners, Cash threw his hat into the ongoing protest movement, proving that country music could advocate for a better world too.

"(Sittin' on) The Dock of the Bay" by Otis Redding: Just three days before he would die in a helicopter crash at age 26, soul genius Otis Redding recorded the greatest song of his career. "Dock of the Bay" is a sweet, relaxing soul song with a beautiful depiction of the San Francisco Bay. Released after his death, the song became one of the most beloved tunes of the era. It was particularly big with soldiers in Vietnam, soothing their worries with idyllic depictions of home.

1969

"Candy Says"

Velvet Underground

In 1969, it felt like the counterculture was winning. The civil rights movement had made enormous gains, the antiwar movement was growing bigger by the day and hippie culture was pushing up against the mainstream. The summer was dominated by monumental movements both within and outside of the music world. The Woodstock Music and Art Fair drew nearly half a million people to a free concert headlined by some of the biggest names in music. Meanwhile, an ongoing cultural festival in Harlem spotlighted the greatest talents of the Black musical world. Both were turning points in America's cultural history, the culminations of movements that had been growing for more than a decade. Elsewhere in New York, another sort of marginalized community, emboldened by this march of progress, was starting to stand up and fight for their spot in American culture.

For decades, queer Americans had been forced to live in the shadows. Homosexuality was made illegal, and queer communities were denied basic rights, excluded from public life and constantly harassed by the police. All this despite the fact that many of the greatest figures in American culture, from Ma Rainey to Cole Porter, were queer. But in the 1960s, a new scene in New York started to coalesce around the visionary artist Andy Warhol. Warhol embraced the community that America had been rejecting for decades. He assembled a collection of queer and alternative artists in his Factory and turned them into a clique of superstars.

The house band of Warhol's Factory was a group of innovative musicians who called themselves the Velvet Underground. Combining noisy rock n' roll with avant-garde experimental music, the Velvet Underground laid the groundwork for punk and created sound palettes that would influence generations of alternative musicians. The Velvet Underground were some of the first musicians ever to write openly about queer characters and queer relationships. Their front man and songwriter Lou Reed was queer himself and spent much of his life struggling with gender identity and sexuality. This struggle comes through in music across the Velvets' career, but one of the most powerful examples is 1969's "Candy Says."

Inspired by Reed's friendship with the transgender Warhol superstar Candy Darling, "Candy Says" might be the first example of a pop song singing openly about a character struggling with gender identity. The opening line, "Candy says, I've come to hate my body and all that it requires in this world," is a devastating piece of melancholy. Reed creates an empathetic portrait of a

character trying to find joy and self-actualization in a world that systemically oppresses their very existence. It's an emotionally complex song, undeniably sad and yet shrouded in a warm sort of calm. Doug Yule's soft vocals lie on a bed of doo-wop–inspired sound. "Candy Says" is a step away from the noisier proto-punk that the Velvet Underground were known for. It's airy and dreamy, creating a sound that is remarkably ahead of its time, one that feels at home alongside indie rock songs created half a century later. This calming sound transforms Reed's lyrics. Despite the difficult subject matter, the song as a whole proves to be quietly uplifting. The last verse offers up hope of a better future.

The first steps toward that future would come just a few months after "Candy Says" was released. It would begin a mile away from Warhol's Factory, on the edge of New York's West Village, at a gay bar called the Stonewall Inn. On June 28, 1969, the New York Police Department raided the bar. These sorts of raids were commonplace in the era, but this time, the patrons of Stonewall wouldn't take it. They rose up in resistance to the police and started a series of riots and protests that would come to be known as the Stonewall Uprising. This marked the birth of a gay rights movement that would go on to flourish in the '70s, carrying the progressive legacy of the '60s into a new age.

When the Velvet Underground sang openly about queer struggles, they became key players in a cultural and social movement that would define the '70s. Lou Reed went on to become one of the champions of a glam rock scene that gleefully subverted the gender and sexual expectations of mainstream society. Meanwhile, Candy Darling would stand as one of America's earliest trans icons, forever immortalized by the Velvet Underground's song.

Honorable Mentions

"Fortunate Son" by Creedence Clearwater Revival: The swampy sounds of Creedence Clearwater Revival made them a perfect soundtrack for the Vietnam War. To this day, there might be no song as closely associated with Vietnam as "Fortunate Son," a righteous protest song about how America was drafting its poor to die overseas while the rich could draft-dodge and live comfortably at home.

"Everyday People" by Sly and the Family Stone: As an integrated band made up of a multiracial collective of men and women, Sly and the Family Stone truly represented the optimism of the hippie era. They rode to fame on optimistic funk preaching radical messages of acceptance. One of their most essential songs was "Everyday People," a piece that celebrated the rich diversity of human races, cultures and bodies. The importance of Sly and the Family Stone was cemented in the summer of 1969, when they were one of the finest performances at Woodstock, the countercultural movement's zenith.

"Pachuco Cadaver" by Captain Beefheart and His Magic Band: The psychedelic movement brought no shortage of weirdness into American music, but even its most out-there bands paled in comparison to Captain Beefheart. Beefheart's music broke every rule that music had to offer, creating dissonant, off-time soundscapes full of elaborate screeds of near-incomprehensible lyrics. It epitomized the era's experimental drive and became a landmark album for any rule-breaking musician in the future.

The
DECADENCE

1970–79

The hippie dream that had so much promise in the '60s collapsed almost the moment the decade turned, and yet its legacy still rang out across the '70s. Black Americans were not about to stop at the Civil Rights Act. As a new era of policing dawned, the soul artists who shaped the '60s continued to expand soul music with overt messages of political optimism. The second-wave feminist movement that was born out of the '60s sexual revolution carried on as women entered the workforce and started to speak their own truths through music. But the broadest legacy that continued into the '70s was one of excess and hedonism.

The music of this decade grew bigger and more expensive than ever. The experimental rock of the '60s had padded the pockets of music stars and industry executives alike. So, the industry started to fund the creation of more elaborate records. Rock and soul musicians stretched their songs out and filled them with elaborate instrumental arrangements. Orchestras became the norm and state-of-the-art studios allowed for a crisper, cleaner sound than anyone had ever heard before. The scale of everything got larger in the '70s. Artists thought beyond individual songs and started to conceptualize their music in the

1970

1971

1972

1973

1974

terms of albums. Stadium tours popped up across the country, bringing live music to enormous crowds. Even within the limitations of radio, artists who once would have been allowed two minutes were able to stretch their songs beyond five-minute run times.

The wealth and excess gained by musicians created a wider gap than ever for their audience, who were facing the harsh realities of an economic recession. By the mid-'70s, this meant that people couldn't afford to see live music and instead flocked to emergent discotheques, where the greatest musical fad of the decade would flourish. Born out of the Black and queer underground, disco rose to take over the mainstream with a speed and ubiquity that outshone even the rock n' roll revolution. Dance music became the music of the '70s and transcended even the enormous ambition of a golden age of rock stars. But just like the hippie revolution before it, the disco movement came crashing down at the end of the decade, when it was met with a racist and homophobic backlash that culminated in a public demolition of hundreds of disco records.

By the end of the decade, any remnants of the hippie dream had burned themselves out. A new rock n' roll was emerging, as punks threw back to the simplicity of the '50s while chasing noise, speed and righteous anger. And in the poorest neighborhoods of New York City, the next great American music form was already being born out of the ashes of disco and progressive soul.

1975

1976

1977

1978

1979

1970

"Move On Up"

Curtis Mayfield

At the end of the 1960s, the two biggest musical forces pushing for change were soul and rock n' roll. In their own way, both painted visions of better worlds. Along the way they created a canon of some of the greatest protest songs ever recorded. When the 1970s hit, rock music fell off this wagon. As the hippie dropouts tuned back into life, rock music became more abstract and hedonistic. Soul music, on the other hand, only became more radical.

The '70s saw the birth of a new subgenre often called "cinematic soul" or "progressive soul." Building on the advances of the psychedelic revolution, this movement saw musicians create enormous pieces of orchestration that stretched for half of a record side. They populated these psychedelic soundscapes with unapologetically powerful lyrics calling for Black power and political change. Throughout the '70s, such artists as Marvin Gaye, Sly and the Family Stone and Stevie Wonder would release brilliant, socially conscious masterpieces, but the man who really kicked things into gear as the decade opened was Curtis Mayfield.

Mayfield was no stranger to protest songs. In 1965, he wrote "People Get Ready" for his group, the Impressions. Martin Luther King Jr. adopted that song as an anthem in the late stages of the civil rights movement, and the song

has been used as a protest song for many other movements since. Five years later, Mayfield would kick off his solo career with "Move On Up," a musical triumph that deepened the lyrical themes of "People Get Ready" and offered an even more ambitious musical arrangement.

From the joyous blare of its opening horns through to the very final moments of percussionist Henry Gibson's extended conga solo, "Move On Up" is a relentless hurricane of righteous positivity. Rich beds of string entwine with a grooving funk bassline while Mayfield belts in his smooth falsetto. The guitar in "Move On Up" is quiet and subtle, but it nevertheless remains a display of Mayfield's incredible talent at the instrument. His guitar rode on simple syncopated grooves given flavor by jazz voicings. He played his guitar in a unique F tuning, inspired by the black keys on the piano. Although the guitar on "Move On Up" is mixed subtly and sits right in the background, it's an essential part of the piece. Mayfield's rhythmic playing is a sound bed that lets his instrumentalists shine.

"Move On Up" was the execution of a symphonic vision that Mayfield had dreamed of since he was young. He worked with producers Gary Slabo and Riley Hampton to create the symphonic arrangements. The result was something damn near hubristic in scope. But rath-

er than fill the song with ego, Mayfield stepped back and highlighted the music. His 21-man orchestra tossed the song's themes back and forth with one another, never skipping a beat and never breaking the groove. Every inch of the mix is occupied by infectious hooks, and yet the song doesn't have a moment of chaos. Instead, it feels like the living embodiment of the sort of unity that Mayfield had been pushing his entire career: nearly two dozen people coming together and putting aside ego to create a seamless piece of music.

This message of excellence and togetherness is woven through the lyrics, which are made eternal by their simplicity. Having given voice to one generation of Black Americans with the Temptations, Mayfield looked forward to the future, offering up a mandate: "*Take nothing less / Than the supreme best.*" It was a message of defiance for an ailing community. Black America was still reeling from assassinations of such leaders as Martin Luther King Jr. and Fred Hampton. The infrastructure that housed poor Black communities in the inner cities was crumbling, and new drug epidemics were hitting the most vulnerable populations.

Mayfield wasn't turning a blind eye to these issues. In fact, his solo debut album *Curtis* even opened on a darker piece of extended music, a bleak song called "(Don't Worry) If There's a Hell Below, We're All Going to Go." But rather than wallow in the pain, he contrasts that song on the second side with "Move On Up." The two songs are Mayfield's depiction of the world as it was and the world as it could be.

This act of sheer hope is built on a history of gospel songs that found hope from desperation. Mayfield grew up in the same neighborhood as the Staple Singers and was deeply influenced by their socially conscious gospel music.

The lyrical conceit of "Move On Up" is not a novel one, but rather one that builds on a rich gospel history. It calls to mind the postwar call of Mahalia Jackson, and it's a phrase that also appeared in "Keep on Pushing," one of the Impressions' biggest hits. Mayfield also includes that song's title in the lyrics to "Move On Up."

When he released "Move On Up," it wasn't met with the commercial success that it deserved. It became a hit in Britain but failed to chart entirely in the United States. That didn't stop it from being one of the most influential songs of the era. Just a year after "Move On Up," Marvin Gaye released *What's Going On*, a progressive soul album that plays in the same territory both lyrically and musically. By the mid-'70s, the sound palettes and extended drum breaks of "Move On Up" had helped give birth to the disco movement, and a generation later, Mayfield would be an early influence on hip-hop.

Meanwhile, he would go on to spend his 1970s releasing an array of classic progressive soul albums. In 1972, Mayfield would score the film *Super Fly*. When he released that score as an album, it topped Billboard's pop charts and gave Mayfield's solo career the success it deserved. All the while, he remained humble. Even after leaving the Impressions, he continued to write and produce for his old bandmates. For the rest of his career, Mayfield continued to be a symbol of hope and resistance for millions fighting for the rights they deserve.

 # Honorable Mentions

"Truckin'" by the Grateful Dead: The Grateful Dead were one of the most important acts of the psychedelic rock movement, pioneering the jam band song with their legendary live performances. In 1970, their sound had shifted to a more laid-back Americana, exemplified by their road trip classic "Truckin'." While many of the hippies would fade out in the new decade, the Grateful Dead retained a cult following of proud freaks and weirdos, carrying the legacy into a new era.

"Bitches Brew" by Miles Davis: Miles Davis continued his legacy of nonstop innovation with one of the seminal jazz fusion albums. By combining jazz with funk and psychedelic rock, he created a way for jazz to stay fresh and relevant against the backdrop of a fast-changing world.

1971

"It's Too Late"

Carole King

There's a good argument to be made that 1971 is the most important year in popular music history. Following the shocking collapse of the '60s dream, the musicians who helped make it happen suddenly had a blank slate to start anew. This time, they weren't scrappy underdogs, but rather superstars with money, resources and a fan base that was hungry to see what came next. Such groups as Led Zeppelin, the Rolling Stones and Sticky Fingers were extending the psychedelic rock movement into new territory, while soul and funk saw masterpieces like Marvin Gaye's *What's Going On* and *There's a Riot Goin' On*. But the music that most enraptured the American public in 1971 came out of a Hollywood neighborhood called Laurel Canyon.

Laurel Canyon was home to an impressive list of musicians that included Joni Mitchell, Neil Young, Frank Zappa, Jim Morrison and a half dozen more of the most important names in music history. In 1968, a recently divorced songwriter named Carole King moved across the country and landed in Laurel Canyon. In 1970, inspired by other songwriters in the community, such as James Taylor and Joni Mitchell, King released her debut album. Despite the fact that she'd been writing pop hits in New York for nearly a decade, the album failed to capture audiences. A

year later, King took another crack at solo music and released an album called *Tapestry*. This time, she'd found her audience. *Tapestry* was a historic hit record. It captured the imagination of a generation of women and created a soft rock sound that defined the decade. Since its release, the album has sold more than 25 million copies in the United States, making it one of the single best-selling records in music history.

The centerpiece of *Tapestry* is a marvelous breakup song called "It's Too Late," which King wrote alongside the songwriter Toni Stern. Together, they were able to capture the feelings of countless women who were coming into their own and breaking off from toxic relationships following the sexual revolution of the '60s. Stern's lyrics are written from the perspective of a woman telling her partner that their relationship is over, inspired by her own breakup with James Taylor. They reflect a reality that was setting in for plenty of women at the time. These women, like King herself, were often married incredibly young and forced into an isolating life of domesticity. As they entered adulthood and realized that the promises of young romance had faded, many had to look inward and decide what they truly wanted in their life. As states across the United States adopted no-fault divorce laws, the country's

singer at all, but rather as a songwriter in New York's Brill Building system. Starting her career there as a teenager, King and her then-husband Gerry Goffin were the team behind a number of pop hits throughout the 1960s. She brings that sort of professional songwriting attitude to "It's Too Late." It's a song built around a beautiful melody that captures the mixed emotion of breakup more than any words possibly could. The professionality of this songcraft is juxtaposed with the amateur tinge of King's vocals. Her performance is simple and approachable, almost verging on conversational at times. It grounds the song, and brings out the all-too-real emotion.

All of this is brought together by a smooth instrumental arrangement featuring quiet congas and a warm sax line. Lou Adler's production on the record is immaculate. While much of '70s rock was louder and wilder, King and Adler were creating a softer, easy-listening palette. As recording technology improved and stereo systems got better, this immaculate clean sound would catch on.

To say that "It's Too Late" was well received would be an enormous understatement. When it was released as a single in April 1971, it eraptured the music world. It topped Billboard's charts and went on to win a Grammy for Record of the Year. That made King the first solo female act ever to win that award, and it marked the start of a new era in pop music, one in which women's struggles and women's pain could be spoken of openly. The feminism of Carole King is more subdued than the bra-burning of the sexual revolution, but it might be that much more essential for it. By giving voice to their own struggles as women, and doing so in a smooth, approachable shell, King and Stern encouraged millions of women to speak up for themselves and to pursue a better life and a better world.

national rate of divorce spiked, and women set out on their own. As they did so, King's calming voice and Stern's careful words proved a balm for the difficult emotions that came with divorce.

Most breakup songs lean heavily into dramatics, filling lyrics with righteous rage or terrible sorrow. "It's Too Late" has neither. Instead, it brims with a somber sort of resignation. As Stern puts it in the song "something inside has died and I can't hide, and I just can't fake it." There's a freedom to be found in this breakup, but also a deep melancholy.

The messages of Stern's lyrics are underlined by a brilliant vocal performance and subtle instrumental arrangement. King's history was not as a

Honorable Mentions

"What's Going On?" by Marvin Gaye: The 1960s saw Marvin Gaye ride to become one of the nation's biggest pop stars, thanks to Motown Records. But he was under strict orders from Berry Gordy to remain apolitical. When the '70s came round, Gaye could remain silent no more. He risked his career and demanded to write a protest album about the strife and discord he saw around him. The result was one of the most celebrated albums in all of soul. "What's Goin' On?" still stands as a perfect document of America's hurt and confusion in the late Vietnam era.

"Maggot Brain" by Funkadelic: After the death of Jimi Hendrix, a new guitarist rose up to pick up the psychedelic torch. Under the direction of the funk visionary George Clinton, Eddie Hazel played his soul out on one of the greatest guitar solos ever recorded. With brilliant distortion effects and heartfelt playing, "Maggot Brain" stands as a raw lament for the death of the hippie dream.

"Blue" by Joni Mitchell: At the start of a new era, Joni Mitchell made a transition from folksinging hippie dream queen to raw confessional artiste. She opened her soul to the world and poured her heart into one of the saddest albums ever made, highlighted by the crystalline breakup song "Blue." Mitchell's gentle pain opens up America to an honesty it had never seen from its musicians and starts a timeless trend of confessional songwriters.

1972

"Superstition"

Stevie Wonder

Of all the many, many talents to go through Berry Gordy's Motown hit factory, the most important might just be Stevie Wonder. Wonder was just 11 years old when he first auditioned for Motown Records, and in 1963, he scored his first number one hit at age 13 with "Fingertips." While most of his peers were struggling through high school and chasing young loves, Wonder was establishing himself as one of the biggest hitmakers in soul. Before his 20th birthday, he already had eight Top 10 hits.

On Wonder's 21st birthday in May 1971, his contract with Motown expired. Gordy and Motown had given Wonder his career, but they had also exercised total creative control over him and taken a generous portion of his royalties. Now that he was an adult, and quickly maturing into one of the finest songwriters in the world, Wonder held all the cards. He was able to negotiate a deal that gave him a hefty portion of royalties, as well as complete creative control. What followed was a totally unprecedented run of creative and commercial success that saw him release four golden records, five

> Wonder was just 11 years old when he first auditioned for Motown Records, and in 1963, he scored his first number one hit at age 13.

number one singles and win an astonishing 12 Grammys. This run would come to be known as Wonder's "Classic Period."

One of the highlights of the Classic Period, and Wonder's first number one single of his new contract, was 1972's "Superstition." That song is a brilliant display of a new funk sound that was emerging in the early '70s. It's a joyous piece of music driven by thick keyboard grooves and punchy horn lines. As was common during the Classic Period, Wonder played nearly all the instruments on the song. He laid down the funky Clavinet riff, and supported it with a heavy Moog bassline, then tied the thing together with an open, sloshing drumline characterized by his open hi-hat drumming approach.

That driving drumline wasn't actually written by Wonder himself, but rather by guitar great Jeff Beck. Guitar was one of the few instruments that Wonder couldn't play, so he had a habit of bringing in talented guitarists to play with him. In exchange for Beck playing guitar on his album *Talking Book*, Wonder was going to write a song for Beck. One day in the studio, Beck sat down at the drums and started pounding away at a little drumline. Wonder walked into the room and, upon hearing the rhythms, made straight for his keyboard setup. Without a second thought, he then tore out one of the best riffs in funk history. Before long, he'd turned that spontaneous jam into "Superstition."

Wonder gave "Superstition" to Beck, who recorded his own version. Beck's was supposed to release first, but his album got delayed, and Berry Gordy realized the hit potential of "Superstition," so he rushed Wonder's release. By the time Beck was able to drop his version of the song, Stevie Wonder's had already topped the pop charts.

Even as "Superstition" provides an eerie warning against superstitions, the sheer joy that Wonder has in creating music comes through in his vocal performance. It's that joy and passion for music that lifted him to such great heights. His music always kept a persistent happiness and joie de vivre throughout the entire Classic Period. Wonder, himself, was just as positive a figure as his music would sound. This didn't stop him from trying to push for political change. Many of his songs in the Classic Period fought against racism and inequality, but all this messaging was wrapped up in a profound joy and belief in humanity.

The combination of Wonder's virtuosic natural talents and his uplifting attitude made him an easy favorite for a pop audience that was searching for more sophisticated music. He combined jazz scales and voicings with the Motown formula and the progressive soul pioneered by Isaac Hayes, Marvin Gaye and Curtis Mayfield. In doing so, he became the single most successful artist of the 1970s.

Honorable Mentions

"Walk on the Wild Side" by Lou Reed: Lou Reed's sophomore solo album saw him team up with David Bowie to create an American take on British glam. Its standout track is "Walk on the Wild Side," an ode to Andy Warhol's superstars, and a song that challenges a queerphobic culture by celebrating trans icons.

"Heart of Gold" by Neil Young: After a run as one of the loudest psychedelic guitarists of the '60s, Neil Young calmed his sound down in the '70s, writing quiet songs with acoustic guitars and country orchestrations, such as "Heart of Gold." That song would ride to the top of Billboard's chart, becoming the biggest hit of Young's career and setting off a huge movement of country rock that would thrive in the mid-'70s.

1973

"Jolene"

Dolly Parton

One of the most important days in country music history came sometime in 1972, when Dolly Parton sat down for a writing session. That session would churn out not one, but two of the biggest hits of Parton's prolific career, "I Will Always Love You" and "Jolene." Although the former wouldn't be universally known until Whitney Houston's 1992 cover, the latter was almost immediately accepted into the country canon and would soon become Parton's signature song.

The inspirations for "Jolene" were twofold. The name came from a 10-year-old fan that Parton met, named Jolene. Parton thought the name was beautiful and vowed to the girl that she'd write a song using her name. The song's subject matter, on the other hand, came from a much more adult situation. When she was writing the song, Parton's husband had adopted a habit of flirting with a red-headed clerk at their local bank. Parton decided to channel the jealousy she felt witnessing these flirtations into song.

A lesser songwriter might have written "Jolene" as a tirade against an unfaithful husband, or a lashing out against a supposed homewrecker, but Parton writes the song as a conversation between the two women. Her character is frank and honest, pleading, "Please

don't take him even though you can." She acknowledges her own lack of agency in the situation but seeks to resolve the issue through a radical act of feminine solidarity. It's an unexpected, empathetic approach for a new age of feminism that was emerging in the '70s, even in the conservative world of country music.

Parton was a walking image of this new kind of self-determinism. She wrote "Jolene" while in the process of breaking off from her longtime friend and controlling producer, Porter Wagoner. "I Will Always Love You" was written as a breakup song of sorts for him, convincing him to let her go out on her own. When she was able to leave, Parton thrived. "Jolene" and "I Will Always Love You" proved the beginning of a fruitful decade for her, one where she molded her own model of femininity. At a time when many women were trying to downplay their own sexuality, Parton took control of her appearance and became an icon for her over-the-top makeup looks and outfits. In doing so, she also became an idol in the queer community—a role that she embraces openly.

Musically, "Jolene" is built around one of the greatest guitar licks country music has ever seen, a driving riff punctuated by rolling hammer-ons. Parton sings the song in her distinctive Tennes-

There might be no better sign of Parton's cultural permeation than the rich, ever-growing catalog of "Jolene" covers. Since its original 1973 release, it has seen covers by everyone from Olivia Newton-John to Miley Cyrus, from the White Stripes to Lil Nas X. "Jolene" has entered the cultural canon and become a true musical standard in a way that few songs have since the decline of the Great American Songbook.

"Jolene" carries in it decades of country music history. Parton's rural upbringing has ties to the earliest roots of country in the folk music of Appalachia, but her pop-minded approach echoes the countrypolitan sound of Nashville. But above all else, it was a forward-looking song, predictive of the country pop sounds that would go on to spawn such megastars as Garth Brooks and Taylor Swift. To this day, Parton remains a deeply beloved figure both within and outside of the country music scene. She's a brilliant businesswoman who has turned herself into a brand and a tireless philanthropist who has used her platform to build a better world.

see accent, filling each word with passion and desperation. The sounds that she and producer Bob Ferguson created on "Jolene" marked a shift for country music. The fourth generation of country musicians had a vision for the music as something that could once more cross over into the mainstream, appealing to an audience that stretched far beyond the American South. Parton was on the forefront of this country crossover movement. She spent the '70s establishing herself as a superstar and a cultural icon with a broad appeal that few country musicians before her had ever achieved.

A lesser songwriter might have written "Jolene" as a tirade against an unfaithful husband . . . but Parton writes the song as a conversation between the two women.

Honorable Mention

"Search and Destroy" by the Stooges: The Stooges played louder and wilder than anybody else in the era. Their absolute masterpiece was 1973's "Search and Destroy." Iggy Pop's opening sneer is a furious declaration of the oncoming storm. Ron Asheton's red-hot guitar sound and Pop's incredible onstage antics made them harbingers for the punk rock movement that would shock the world at the end of the decade.

"Free Bird" by Lynyrd Skynyrd: Lynyrd Skynyrd released one of the earliest power ballads, a stunning piece of music that sees a slow lament build into a breathtaking four guitar solo. "Free Bird" helped contribute to an opulent era of longer guitar rock jams, proving that America could keep up with the guitar innovations coming out of Britain in that era. Fans demanded to see the song live so much, that the request of "play 'Free Bird'" is still a musical meme today.

1974

"Rock the Boat"

The Hues Corporation

In the early 1970s, there was a quiet revolution happening in the underground of Philadelphia and New York City. Faced with near-constant discrimination in public spaces, the city's queer, Black and Hispanic populations were starting to create their own spaces. They would gather in private house parties and underground clubs to dance away their troubles. It was a revolution of joy, love and sex in the face of an increasingly bleak political reality. Inner-city infrastructure was crumbling, and new drug laws were leading to the rise of the prison industrial complex and more brutal policing. Race riots had erupted around the country, and Watergate had shaken faith in the political system. Faced with a world that hated them, these communities made the radical choice to love each other.

That love took the form of all-night parties filled with drugs and dancing. The hosts of these parties couldn't afford to bring in live bands, as was the standard at the time, so the parties instead gathered around DJs who would curate the soundtrack for the night. These DJs became obsessed with finding the choic-

Upon release, the song failed to chart and had almost no radio play. In any other era, that probably would have spelled the end for "Rock the Boat."

est dance cuts. They'd dig through crate after crate of records, looking for underappreciated songs with solid rhythms and groovy basslines. These discotheque DJs mashed together genre, spinning soul records next to jazz fusion, psychedelic rock next to Latin dance music. As long as the song had boogie, it was fair game. As this underground discotheque movement started to grow, producers across the country began to realize that they could sell more records if they made music that entered circulation in the club scene. The club DJs were unintentionally curating a new genre of music that would soon take over the world: disco.

In '72 and '73, songs popular on the discotheque circuit started to appear in Billboard's mainstream charts. The Love Unlimited Orchestra released "Love's Theme," an instrumental piece defined by lush string arrangements and syncopated guitar lines. "Love's Theme" was the first disco song to top Billboard's charts. Disco was bumping up against the mainstream.

It was on this backdrop that the Hues Corporation released their single, "Rock the Boat," in May 1974. "Rock

the Boat" was a perfect execution of all of the disco sounds that had been coalescing. It was a positive love song, characterized by a syncopated percussive session and warm instrumental arrangements. The song had an easy sort of groove, simple and laid back with just enough build in it and a memorable prechorus switch from the simple 4/4 time to a novel bar of 7/4 time. Horns and strings create texture and depth as the song goes on, with a tempo change building it to a delightful conclusion.

"Rock the Boat" is '70s pop perfection, but at first it was barely recognized. Upon release, the song failed to chart and had almost no radio play. In any other era, that probably would have spelled the end for "Rock the Boat." But sometime in the early summer, the New York discotheque scene picked up on the song and started to spin it. This happened to coincide with a dramatic influx

of club-goers. The previous year had seen a dramatic economic recession hit America after the 1973 Oil Crisis, and the tanking of the U.S. dollar following Watergate. No longer able to afford pricier rock shows, the white middle class began to flock to discotheques in droves. They quickly fell in love with the brilliant sounds curated by queer and Black DJs. Suddenly, disco was mainstream.

"Rock the Boat" was brought back from the fringe. It entered the Top 40 in early summer, and in just its fourth week, hit number one. All of this happened with virtually no radio play. It was a cultural statement by DJs and disco dancers. They were here to stay.

The next week, another disco song topped the charts, and before long, disco was pumping out one-hit-wonder after one-hit-wonder. Up until this point, the music industry had been

> ...the music industry had been built around creating superstars and highlighting personalities. In the disco world, all that mattered was the song.

built around creating superstars and highlighting personalities. In the disco world, all that mattered was the song. Studios scrambled to put together bands, and a simple disco formula began to emerge. By the time the year was out, disco had achieved a near-unprecedented dominance over the American pop scene. It wouldn't be long before it was the definitive cultural movement of the 1970s.

 # Honorable Mention

"Rikki Don't Lose that Number" by Steely Dan: Steely Dan were meticulous champions of '70s studio technology. They used the finest equipment and hired the country's best session musicians to create an easy-listening, immaculate jazz rock sound. One of the biggest hits of their career was 1974's "Rikki Don't Lose That Number," which lays down a Latin groove as a base for Walter Becker and Donald Fagen's sardonic lyrics criticizing the indulgences of the '70s high life.

1975

"Born to Run"

Bruce Springsteen

Ever since it first walked out of the muddy Mississippi and took root in Memphis in the 1950s, rock n' roll music had been growing in scope and scale. Bit by bit, it began to shift, grabbing pieces from other music and birthing a dozen new genres. Such genres as psychedelic rock, prog rock, blues rock and metal started to peel off and overtake good ol' fashioned rock n' roll through the late '60s and early '70s. But the more traditional rock n' roll still had a few loyal proponents. One of these was an angsty New Jersey man named Bruce Springsteen. In 1973, he released his first two albums to little acclaim. It seemed that many in the music world had moved beyond the sort of rock n' roll Springsteen wanted to play.

Columbia Records still had some faith in him, though. They gave him one more chance to try to break through, with a budget and the creative freedom to create the album that he wanted to. Springsteen holed up in the studio for more than a year, banging his head against the wall as he tried to catch the sound he was chasing. Five

> Springsteen holed up in the studio for more than a year, banging his head against the wall as he tried to catch the sound he was chasing.

months of that process was spent on a single piece of music, the eventual title track for Springsteen's third album: *Born to Run*.

Springsteen has described the sound he was looking for on "Born to Run" as "Roy Orbison singing Bob Dylan produced by Phil Spector." It was a lofty ambition, but with the time and money afforded to him by Columbia, he was able to create something that lived up to his dream, and did so much more. "Born to Run" is the triumphant end point of the first wave of rock n' roll music. Whereas most of Springsteen's contemporaries had become smaller bands focused on virtuosic guitar work, his arrangement called back to the genre's originators, such as Little Richard and Elvis Presley.

Springsteen played the part of the charismatic front man and surrounded himself with some of the most talented instrumentalists he could get his hands on. He took the standard rock arrangement and opened it up into something broad and epic. Poetic verses cascade into a series of escalating lyrical and

rock history, Springsteen sings: "In the day we sweat it out on the streets of a runaway American dream / At night we ride through mansions of glory in suicide machines." It's a bleak image of a working-class America that was in the process of being gutted in the name of corporate interests. The muscle cars that had been such a signal of wealth and virility in early rock have been turned into "suicide machines," an adrenaline-fueled escape from the creeping national ennui.

When Springsteen was working on "Born to Run," America finally pulled out of the Vietnam War. It was a brutal, prolonged conflict that proved to all be for naught. In its wake, the country was going through a national crisis of identity. The utopian dreams that he had grown up on all came crashing down just as he was well and truly entering adulthood.

With seemingly no political or economic hope in the future, the song finds its optimism in the eternal search for love. "Born to Run" is written as a plea to a lover named Wendy. Echoing the adolescent search for meaning in Peter Pan, Springsteen muses on the nature and reality of love. His character is pleading to Wendy not to escape the sadness in their heart, but to live with it and overcome it together. Entwined with that is another existential plea—to run away: to hit the highway and flee America's dying heartland headed for any place that was somewhere else.

"Born to Run" is one of the most complex expressions of love and pain that rock music had ever seen. After years of failing commercially, Springsteen had finally found his breakthrough. He released the single "Born to Run" to the radio months before its album was even completed. This helped build a groundswell of hype, such that when he

musical interludes, gaining momentum the entire way until a climactic finale. The instrumentals of the song are relentless, opening on a machine-gun spray of snare hits and riding on the backs of roaring saxophones and growling guitars. It's the musical equivalent of stomping the gas pedal to the floor and flying down an open highway. Springsteen's high romanticism is underlined by Spector's "Wall of Sound" production technique. The layers of horn and guitar are sweetened by twinkling bells and squealing organ lines. It's a careful orchestration that makes the heart want to leap out of the chest, underlining the desperate romanticism of Springsteen's songwriting.

The lyrics of "Born to Run" take imagery from the optimistic Golden Age of Rock n' Roll and twist it to fit with the darker era of the mid-'70s. In some of the greatest opening lines in

finally did finish *Born to Run*, Columbia felt comfortable pushing it with a massive $250,000 promo campaign. Within two weeks, *Born to Run* hit the Top 10 of Billboard's album charts. Springsteen, whose career seemed almost over just 18 months earlier, was being celebrated as the next Bob Dylan.

With "Born to Run," Springsteen resurrected rock n' roll and almost single-handedly invented the next phase of American rock music. His huge sound translated to enormous arena tours and inspired a whole wave of artists to follow in his footsteps. Even more importantly, it turned him into a poet laureate of sorts for the northern working class. Springsteen's narrative songwriting painted vivid pictures of a life that so many could relate to. He gave them an outlet for their angst, a belief that they could find some salvation in love and the ongoing search for human connection.

Honorable Mentions

"Mothership Connection (Star Child)" by Parliament: George Clinton had a vision for a new kind of funk that combined the relentless groove of James Brown with the ambitious psychedelia of the Beatles. He spent the '70s assembling a brilliant collective of musicians to play it, and in 1975 he debuted his masterpiece. "Mothership Connection" is a wild piece of Afrofuturist groove. It helped make Parliament superstars in the '70s, and would go on to become one of the foundational samples of hip-hop in the '90s.

"Gloria" by Patti Smith: Patti Smith was another step in America's acceleration toward punk rock. In "Gloria," she pairs poetic, Dylan-inspired lyrics with a raw, half-spoken delivery and relentless guitar energy by Lenny Kaye. In this opening track to her landmark album *Horses*, Smith delivers an opening line that captures the devil-may-care ethos of her generation of rockers: "Jesus died for somebody's sins, but not mine."

1976

"Blitzkrieg Bop"

The Ramones

On August 16, 1974, four scrawny twenty-somethings in leather jackets took the stage of a dismal East Village bar. Music would never be the same. The scrawny twenty-somethings were a newly formed band called the Ramones, and the dingy bar was a venue called CBGB. Together, the Ramones and CBGB would become the center of a new generation's counter-culture. Two years after that obscure CBGB debut, the Ramones would release their self-titled debut, the first album in punk rock history. The opening song of that earth-shattering record was "Blitzkrieg Bop," a tune that was the perfect distillation of all of the musical and aesthetic goals of the punk rock movement.

The Ramones were made up of four young men from Forest Hills, Queens. Each of them had taken up a stage name to create a mock family band: Joey, Johnny, Dee Dee, and Tommy Ramone. In generous tellings, the Ramones were childhood friends, but the reality is that the members could hardly stand one another. The personalities of Joey and Johnny clashed with each other, and the

In generous tellings, the Ramones were childhood friends, but the reality is that the members could hardly stand one another.

two were constantly getting into political and personal fights. The only thing holding them together was a shared love of loud, fast rock n' roll music. All the members of the Ramones grew up listening to the garage rock legend Iggy Pop and became entranced by the heavy glam rock of the New York Dolls.

The Ramones came up in a time where rock music had become expensive and indulgent. The '60s revolution spun out into a world of expansive psychedelic and prog rock created by such bands as Yes and Pink Floyd. Musicians were constantly trying to outdo one another with extended solos and high-concept pieces that stretched across entire record sides. Much of this music was spectacular, but it was also thoroughly unattainable. Its use of advanced musicianship and expensive studio technology put it far out of reach for the average rock fan. The Ramones decided to revolt against this by stripping rock back to its roots, and then some. They would be the first to admit they could hardly play their instruments, but that didn't matter. The Ramones weren't about virtuosity. It was

about removing everything unnecessary from music to create emotional energy in its most raw form.

"Blitzkrieg Bop" does just that. It's a song made of three identical verses and a simple, shoutable chorus. The guitar strums simple power chords and the bass chugs along on eighth notes. The lyrics are half a celebration of the energy of rock shows and half nonsense. It's everything that makes rock music work distilled down to its finest, loudest form.

For all of Ramones' proto-punk influences, they also had an undeniable pop edge. Dee Dee quotes the British Invasion stars Herman and the Hermits in "Judy Is a Punk," and the chanted chorus of "Blitzkrieg Bop" was partially inspired by the pop rock outfit Bay City Rollers, who had a chant-heavy hit song called "Saturday Night" in 1975. By pulling from these pop sounds, the Ramones were able to pull together the bubbling garage scenes into the singular sound of punk rock.

The same year they released their debut, the Ramones made a visit to London, where a punk scene was just about to boil over. Nearly everyone in the first generation of Britain's punk scene attended those shows, including future members of the Sex Pistols and the Clash. The Ramones encouraged these future punks that they didn't need to be good at their instruments to play. Within a year of the Ramones' first London shows, the British punk scene was just as explosive and vibrant as New York's CBGB scene. This trend continued as the Ramones toured across the states. Like a swarm of leather-clad honeybees, the Ramones pollinated small towns and urban centers across the country and brought on a new age of punk rock.

Many of those bands who picked up cheap guitars after witnessing the Ramones live no doubt learned to play "Blitzkrieg Bop." Its distilled simplicity and perfect gang chorus have made it an early favorite for any aspiring punk. "Blitzkrieg Bop" still gets chanted in arenas across the globe. While that's an earmark of success that any songwriter would yearn for, the greatest success of "Blitzkrieg Bop" comes from the fact that even half a century after it was written, it remains a go-to song for first guitar learners. Even today, chances are that in some dismal bar in some corner of the world, yet another young band is taking the stage and closing out their set with a shouted cover of "Blitzkrieg Bop."

Honorable Mentions

"Sir Duke" by Stevie Wonder: Stevie Wonder's Classic Period culminated in the astounding double album *Songs in the Key of Life*, a masterful work full of constant groove, warm vocal arrangements and the purest keyboard tones you'll ever hear. The album's highlight is "Sir Duke," a loving ode to the power of music, and to Wonder's jazz heroes, who included Duke Ellington, Louis Armstrong and Ella Fitzgerald. With *Songs in the Key of Life*, Wonder definitively proved that his name deserves just as much reverence.

"Hotel California" by the Eagles: The enormous heights reached by '70s rock turned the scene into a world of rampant abuse and excess. In late 1976, the Eagles wrote a cryptic song criticizing the dark underbelly of the California rock star dream. "Hotel California" depicted the industry as a dark, inescapable labyrinth of debauchery and hedonism. Ironically, the song only threw the Eagles further into that world, as it soared to become one of the most beloved hits of the "classic rock" era.

1977

"I Feel Love"

Donna Summer

Disco fever had reached a pitch in 1977. In the spring of that year, a legendary discotheque called Studio 54 opened in midtown Manhattan. Its hedonistic parties were attended by everybody who was anybody in New York, and the stories of the debauchery that took place there made front page news. Studio 54 was the logical conclusion of the early parties that had started in New York's gay underground. It was the ultimate celebration of pleasure and escapism, a scene that discos across the country tried to emulate in their own way. The queen of this scene was Donna Summer.

Summer was a pop diva of the highest caliber. Her mezzo-soprano voice could be breathy and ethereal, or full and inspiring. It mixed seamlessly with the lush string beds and warm wah-wah guitars favored by disco producers. This sound gave Summer a massive hit in 1975 with "Love to Love You," produced by the European duo of Giorgio Moroder and Peter Bellotte. To this day, "Love to Love You" remains one of the quintessential disco songs, a perfect representation of everything that made the genre thrive.

But Moroder and Summer weren't about to call it there. Following the suc-

> Finding that sound meant looking . . . toward a new technology that was beginning to emerge: the synthesizer.

cess of "Love to Love You," Moroder began to envision more conceptual albums for Summer. These albums would push disco into a higher plane of artistic excellence. He debuted his conceptual suites with two albums in 1976, *A Love Trilogy* and *Four Seasons of Love*. Both albums went gold and Summer's star continued to rise. For 1976, Moroder's conceptual vision was an album called *I Remember Yesterday*, which would serve as a walk through the history of pop music. To close out the album, he decided he wanted to write a song with the sound of the future.

Finding that sound meant looking away from the traditional disco sound palettes and toward a new technology that was beginning to emerge: the synthesizer. Moroder got his hands on an enormous Moog synthesizer, and hired a technician to help him work the monstrous instrument. He and Bellotte started to push this novel technology as far as they could. In that day, working synthesizers was a task of electrical engineering. Progress was slow and fraught with errors, but after a time, the team was able to hone a sound unlike anything anyone had ever heard before, a sound that would become the basis for "I Feel

human voices ever put on tape.

Summer's take on "I Feel Love" is nothing short of transcendental. Newly in love with the man she would one day marry, her vocal is a wash of romantic eroticism. She draws out her syllables until the words dissolve atop the mix. With her magic touch, Summer transforms the emotionless sound of the Moog into a piece brimming with the vitality of the human spirit. In colliding these worlds, Summer and Moroder were helping to give birth to a new movement that would one day be called electronic dance music.

Although it would go on to become one of the essential dance floor hits of the late '70s, "I Feel Love" was never expected to be a success. It was more of a passion project for Moroder, who didn't expect that anybody could dance to it. When Casablanca Records first issued "I Feel Love," it was actually as the B-side to "Can We Just Sit Down (And Talk It Over)." That ordering was swapped in a reissue two months later, and "I Feel Love" climbed to number six on Billboard's chart. It would be even more successful abroad, topping charts in seven different countries.

Moroder and Summer's contemporaries took notice. Production genius and synthesizer innovator Brian Eno proclaimed the song the future of pop music when he first heard it, and it convinced the Human League to become a synth-pop band. In the disco world, it proved the viability of the synthesizer as a lead instrument and brought a new fervor to dance floors across the country. To this day, the synthesizer remains an essential piece of any Top 40 pop song.

"I Feel Love" represents a turning point in music history. It is a pop masterpiece of the highest degree, and a crown jewel in the catalog of the Queen of Disco.

Love."

The synthesizer line that drives "I Feel Love" is clinical and robotic. Moroder's team were able to create a perfectly synchronized melodic line, the first time such a feat had ever been accomplished in music history. They filled this line with a series of synth hits that cascade over one another, panning across the mix for a powerful sound that feels like driving through the utopian cover of a golden-age sci-fi novel. Moroder and Bellotte stripped the humanity from their song to imagine a cold, robotic future. Then, they injected the song with one of the warmest, most

Honorable Mentions

"Dreams" by Fleetwood Mac: The British-American group Fleetwood Mac drew all the eyes of the nation with their soft-rock masterpiece *Rumours*. Written as the band's relationships were falling apart, *Rumours* is a document of an era where all the drama of the sex lives of rock stars were starting to play out in public. "Dreams" is rooted in this era, but has a smooth, timeless energy as Stevie Nicks sings of the resigned reality of a breakup. Decades after it first found success, "Dreams" would have a surprise chart comeback, thanks to Tik-Tok, proving just how eternal it is.

"The Expanding Universe" by Laurie Spiegel: Laurie Spiegel used emergent synthesizer technology to create "The Expanding Universe," a daring musical adaptation of a Johannes Kepler astronomical treatise, "Harmony of the World." It serves as the lead track for the Voyager Golden Record launched into space that year, forecasting a future of electronic music and capturing the space-age optimism that had continued on through the '70s.

"Stayin' Alive" by the Bee Gees: As disco rose to unthinkable heights in 1977, *Saturday Night Fever* hit theaters across the country. Powered by nonstop disco from the Bee Gees, that film told the relatable story of an Italian American escaping working-class struggles by heading to the disco each Saturday night. Its standout track was "Stayin' Alive," whose perfect dance groove paired with uneasy lyrics spoke to the masses running from their problems.

1978

"Heart of Glass"

Blondie

You'd have a hard time finding two more disparate music scenes in 1978 than the CBGB crowd and the attendees of Studio 54. One was full of low-down, working-class punks searching for catharsis in simplicity and noise. The other housed millionaire celebrities indulging themselves in musical and spiritual hedonism. Disco's elaborate production techniques and 10-minute grooves were a sharp contrast to punk's lo-fi shrieks and 90-second statements. And yet, in 1978, Blondie were able to seamlessly bridge these two antithetical scenes with "Heart of Glass."

This was a song that had been in Blondie's catalog as far back as 1974, when disco first went mainstream. Back then, the band called the song "Once I Had a Love," or simply "The Disco Song." Those early versions of the song were slower than the final cut, colored by funky chicken-scratch guitar lines by Chris Stein. It was a staple of many of the band's early shows, much to the chagrin of their punk-loving crowd. As one of the earliest bands to find success at CBGB, Blondie had gathered a cult following who yearned for them to be part of the counterculture. The anger that "Once I Had a Love" drew from these fans only encouraged the band, who weren't about to let anybody dictate their sound. Blondie were more than happy to be seen as uncool if it meant playing music they loved and believed in.

Despite this attitude, the band couldn't quite find an arrangement that would work for their song. They tried to slow it down into a ballad, and even tried a reggae version, but nothing worked. In 1978, when they sat down with producer Mike Chapman to start work on their third album, *Parallel Lines*, the band dug the song up again and played it for Chapman. The song itself hadn't changed, but the world around it had. In 1978, Donna Summer's "I Feel Love" was spinning in disco dance floors everywhere. Giorgio Moroder's revolutionary synth sound had proved it was possible to make the synthesizer work in a pop framework. Chapman envisioned doing the song, which had by now taken on its proper name, in the style of Summer. Blondie's front woman Debbie Harry had always been a fan of Donna Summer, and the band would even cover "I Feel Love" at gigs, so she was game.

Chapman brought a synthesizer into the studio and went about the painstaking work of synchronizing it with Blondie's instrumental play. These trying sessions saw drummer Clem Burke having to spend three hours recording just bass drum hits to line up with the synthesizer so that his playing could be

blended with a drum machine. This marked one of the first times that a drum machine had ever been used by a rock band. The result was a doubled drumline that grooved like all hell. On top of this, Blondie wove in soaring lines of Moroder-esque synthesizers with their more traditional rock instrumental setup. Chapman loaded the song's mix and doubled up Debbie Harry's vocal takes. All of these decisions worked in concert to create a song that bridged the gap between rock and pop.

Harry's lyrics for "Heart of Glass" are a subversion of the sorts of lyrics she was hearing in the pop songs of her day. She was sick of seeing female artists sing songs that put them on the wrong side of a breakup. The way she saw it, women were just as often the ones doing the breaking up. So, she wrote a song about

discovering that the man you're in love with might not be that great after all. Originally, the lyrics had gone "Once I had a love and it was a gas / Soon turned out to be a pain in the ass." This line was eventually replaced in all but one verse, but even that verse was changed in the radio release.

The disco sounds of "Heart of Glass" may have alienated some of Blondie's fans, but they brought in a whole host of new ones. "Heart of Glass" became the band's mainstream breakthrough, riding up to the top of the charts and giving Blondie the success that helped them become one of the key groups of the New Wave movement.

Honorable Mentions

"I Will Survive" by Gloria Gaynor: After recovering from a grueling back injury, while still in a back brace, Gloria Gaynor recorded the greatest self-empowerment anthem of the era. "I Will Survive" was a disco anthem with a message that resonated particularly with the queer communities that birthed the genre.

"Eruption" by Eddie Van Halen: The hard rock guitarists of the 1970s waged an ongoing race to see who could play the fastest, most difficult songs. When Eddie Van Halen arrived on the scene and debuted his two-hand tap technique in "Eruption," he blew his contemporaries out of the water. Van Halen would lead hard rock into a new era over the '80s, establishing himself as a true guitar god.

1979

"Rapper's Delight"

The Sugar Hill Gang

When disco swept across the country in the early '70s, DJs took on a new role in the culture. Fewer and fewer venues hired live musicians to play, so DJs started to be the main event. Fierce competition rose as each DJ tried to lure as many partygoers as they could to their parties. At first, this was accomplished by digging through crates of old records to find the rarest cuts, songs that you could only hear from one DJ.

Then, in one of New York's poorest neighborhoods, a generation of young DJs figured out ways to push things even further. These Bronx DJs realized that if they set up a turntable switcher and two copies of the same record, they could switch back and forth between the same instrumental sections to create looping beats that lasted as long as they wanted-ed. Rather than spinning disco records, most of these DJs focused on digging up funk and soul, genres rich with drum breaks. They'd loop these drum breaks back and forth, inserting themselves in between and speaking in small rhyming couplets. At first, these rhymes would be making announcements or hyping up the party. But before long, this kind of rhyming became the centerpiece. In block parties and house shows all across the Bronx, hip-hop was being born.

By the mid-1970s, these early hip-hop artists were gaining a cult following in the underground. It was spreading across New York's Black communities as a generation of youth saw a new way to gain notoriety. But almost none of the first wave of hip-hop legends had been recorded. It was thought that hip-hop was a live-only experience, something that couldn't—or maybe shouldn't—be put to tape. All of that changed in 1979, when a struggling record executive named Sylvia Robinson walked into a Harlem birthday party and witnessed hip-hop for the first time.

Robinson was a music industry veteran. She had a two-decade recording career with only one minor hit to show for it before crossing to the other side of the business and starting a record label. That label, Sugar Hill Records, soon found itself in financial trouble. On the verge of bankruptcy and desperate for a hit, Robinson showed up at that fateful party and witnessed a rapping DJ for the first time. Then and there, she decided that she would record hip-hop.

> But almost none of the first wave of hip-hop legends had been recorded. It was thought that hip-hop was a live-only experience . . .

The only problem was that most of the DJs at the time had little interest in being recorded. The culture was fiercely competitive, and people didn't want their rhymes stolen. So, Robinson set out to find her own rapper. In the end, she found not one but three, working in a Bronx pizza place called Crispy Crust Pizza. These three rappers were named Wonder Mike, Master Gee and Big Bank Hank. Robinson combined them to create the Sugar Hill Gang. Just a few days later, she brought them into the studio and cut one of the first hip-hop songs ever put to wax, "Rapper's Delight."

The basis for "Rapper's Delight" was a song called "Good Times" by the disco visionaries Chic. Robinson brought in a group of young musicians to lay down the "Good Times" instrumental, and the Sugar Hill Gang began to rap. These rhymes were lighthearted and carefree, not truly representative of the more ambitious poeticism that had been happening in the underground. That didn't matter. A mainstream audience that had never heard rapping before was enthralled. The song was a modest chart success in the United States, cracking the Top 40, but it was enormous internationally. After simmering in the underground for most of the '70s, hip-hop had finally arrived in the mainstream.

The arrival of recorded hip-hop brought with it one of the first hip-hop feuds. The first generation of rappers who had pioneered hip-hop in the underground hated "Rapper's Delight." The mainstream began to celebrate the Sugar Hill Gang as the inventors of rap, ignoring the innovations of the underground. To make matters worse, Big Bank Hank's verse was lifted almost verbatim from one of the greats of that first generation, Grandmaster Caz.

This theft was of little concern to the record industry; they only saw a new avenue for hits. Record labels scrambled to sign rappers. Some of these were artists from the underground, but more were from a new generation inspired by the success of the Sugar Hill Gang. Through the start of the '80s, the industry struggled to figure out exactly what hip-hop was, but before long the genre was starting to gain a foothold. Sylvia Robinson's vision helped birth an industry built on self-made hustlers as hip-hop provided a route out of poverty for countless young Black artists. Despite the controversy surrounding its origin, the release of "Rapper's Delight" is undeniably a watershed moment in music history.

The arrival of recorded hip-hop brought with it one of the first hip-hop feuds. The first generation of rappers who had pioneered hip-hop in the underground hated "Rapper's Delight."

 # Honorable Mentions

"I Was Made for Lovin' You" by KISS: Nothing embodies the sheer ubiquity of disco by the end of the '70s more than KISS's foray into disco. "I Was Made for Lovin' You" was a dance song by a hard rock group best known for elaborate glam outfits full of satanic imagery. It was proof that nobody was immune to catching disco fever.

"Don't Stop 'Til You Get Enough" by Michael Jackson: After getting his start as a child star in the '60s, Michael Jackson returned to the spotlight, thanks to a collaboration with producer Quincy Jones. "Don't Stop 'Til You Get Enough" came at the tail end of the disco era, but its brilliant pop arrangement allowed it to persist as a classic even as the world turned away from disco. In the years to come, Jackson would flourish into a pop star the likes of which the world had never seen.

ROYALS & REBELS

1980–89

The 1980s saw America jump head-first into an era of extreme consumerism and unfettered capitalism, and few in the country embraced this new reality with as much zeal as the recording industry. Record executives began to look beyond U.S. borders, realizing the lucrative potential of exporting American music across the world. The suits began to distance themselves from the average music fan, viewing music more as a commodity than art. The result was the birth of a new corporate pop, produced in lavish studios by rich songwriting teams and promoted with enormous marketing budgets. Such technologies as the cassette tape and, later in the decade, the CD ramped up record sales as it became easier than ever for people to listen to music.

There were plenty of artists under this new system who found 15 minutes of fame only to flame out and disappear, but a select few auteurs thrived like never before. Near-limitless resources were afforded to the biggest names in pop. They were given access to cutting-edge

1980

1981

1982

1983

1984

synthesizers and digital recording techniques, and they used them to form the foundations of modern pop music. This new breed of dance-funk influenced pop was born out of the collapse of disco. It was characterized by clean, computerized production sounds and a focus on catchy hooks that could loop on the radio all day.

This cohort of pop auteurs also began to innovate in a new artistic form that was just being born at the time: the music video. When MTV first hit the airwaves in 1981, they barely had enough videos circulating to keep the channel going. By the end of the decade, they were airing enormous visual spectacles directed by A-list directors on multimillion-dollar budgets. Pop music had gone visual, and it was never going back.

While a generation of pop royalty was taking over MTV, dominating radio airplay and selling millions upon millions of records, an entirely different ethos was gripping the underground. The punk rock scene that had been born just a few years earlier was growing angrier, faster and more political. When none of the major labels would sign punk artists, they took to creating their own network of do-it-yourself distribution. These networks allowed punk communities to thrive as an anticorporate antidote to America's "greed is good" era.

Of course, the corporate world still gave options for those who wanted some edge to their music. Rock n' roll grew bigger than ever in the '80s. Hard rockers donned skin-tight pants and teased out their hair, cranking their amps up to 11 and blowing away stadium audiences with enormous sounds. Their under-ground counterparts combined the power of heavy metal with the speed of punk to invent thrash, the first truly American form of metal.

But with all due respect to punk and metal, the biggest sound to come out of the roiling underground of the '80s was born in the streets of New York, where hip-hop first start-ed to take root. Growing from block parties to political blocs, hip-hop developed a social consciousness in the '80s, giving a voice to the Black communities left behind in the era of Reaganomics. As rap spread across the country, it grew harder and angrier. On the West Coast, it became the soundtrack to the gang wars erupting in Los Angeles. This new, violent breed of hip-hop shocked the world. Panicked news reports brought word of so-called gangsta rap into suburban homes across the country, and inadvertent-ly set it on track to cross over into white audiences and take over music entirely.

1985

1986

1987

1988

1989

1980

"Once in a Lifetime"

Talking Heads

Talking Heads were always ahead of their time. Their early records in the late '70s helped pioneer New Wave sound palettes. They were some of the first white American musicians to incorporate African rhythms into their music, and they were early appreciators of hip-hop. They were even among the first musicians to publically recognize that the world's future would be built on the backs of computers. The most prescient moment of Talking Heads' career happened in 1980, when they released "Once in a Lifetime." That song would preemptively capture the spirit of the '80s, tapping into a growing sort of alienation and exploring the ennui of millions of middle-class Americans. It would also bring with it one of the first truly great music videos, setting a high-water mark for the music video era a year before MTV had even made their first broadcast.

The origins of "Once in a Lifetime" are manifold. It was musically birthed from "I Zimbra," a jam on their 1979 album *Fear of Music* that was itself inspired by the Nigerian Afrobeat pioneer Fela Kuti. The production process brought in the brilliant Brian Eno, who experimented with the song's recording and arrangement. Eno and front man David Byrne created an early take on looping and sampling, whereby the

band would jam until they found interesting hooks, then isolate and repeat those hooks over and over. Byrne's vocal delivery on the song was an imitation of the oration style of television preachers, which Byrne found distinctly eerie and inhuman.

The result of this unlikely mélange was a strange sort of robotic funk. Tina Weymouth's bassline gels perfectly with Chris Frantz's drums in an endless loop, colored by keyboardist Jerry Harrison's gurgling synthesizer line. The music pulls the listener into a trance, never looping or resolving, and only changing marginally throughout the song. When paired with Byrne's half-spoken vocals, the result is something strange and isolating. The words wash over the listener with a sort of disjointed inevitability. The repeated call of "Same as it ever was" echoes the song's structure and underlines its lyrical message.

Byrne wrote the song about the ways that people operate on autopilot, sleepwalking their way through a prescribed life path until one day they wake up to discover themselves empty and unfulfilled. He narrates these lyrics in the second person, telling the listeners of their own life: "You may find yourself in a beautiful house, with a beautiful wife," only to wonder how did you get there. As a perennial artist and product of

New York's alternative scene, Byrne had never known or understood this life. "Once in a Lifetime" served as a sort of voyeuristic gaze into the life of the middle-class suburbanite.

When "Once in a Lifetime" came out, the hippie dream was good and dead. The rise of disco and hard rock had brought with it a new wave of consumerism. Ronald Reagan was campaigning for president, and America was gearing up for a hypercapitalistic era of growth and greed. Although Byrne hadn't intended it, "Once in a Lifetime" ended up serving as a cautionary tale for the oncoming generation. In trying to write a song about the unconscious, he had unwittingly written a song about the empty promises of consumer culture. In the song, a "beautiful house," a "beautiful wife" and a "large automobile" bring no joy and no fulfillment, only a creeping ennui. This ennui is represented by the motif of water, made audible by Harrison's keyboard line. The water is the inevitable flow of time and life. It moves beneath the singers' feet, pushing them onward toward an inevitable end even as they seek escape in material pleasures.

Talking Heads paired the complex subtext of "Once in a Lifetime" with an abstract, surreal music video. In that video, the band used new blue screen technology to isolate footage of David Byrne performing an odd dance choreographed by director Toni Basil. Byrne and Harrison poured through videos of folk dances and religious rituals, and used them to create an absurd dance sequence. Multiple iterations of Byrne, sweaty and clad in a drab gray suit, are composited on a white background to underline the monotony of the life he's singing about. Meanwhile, his jittering dance moves look the part of an inhuman ritual.

When "Once in a Lifetime" came out, music videos were just starting to catch on. Most consisted simply of live performances of the band, occasionally with interesting backdrops or novel costumes. This was something else entirely. It was a video with an oblique, artistic message. Rather than serving as a simple accompaniment for the song, the video for "Once in a Lifetime" underlined the lyrical themes and elevated the piece into a larger multimedia work.

Like many artists ahead of their time, Talking Heads didn't get the due they deserved when "Once in a Lifetime" came out. A few critics in the know celebrated the piece, but it failed to have any chart success. As the decade progressed, more and more people would begin to realize the genius of the song. In 1981, MTV went on the air for the first time. As the standout video in a limited field, "Once in a Lifetime" saw tons of early rotation. Meanwhile, the '80s morphed into a decade of consumerist greed, and the song's themes of alienation grew more and more prescient.

In the modern age, the song has only become more relevant as we reap what was sown in the '80s. So many people today find themselves cold and disconnected in a world that promises escape only through an endless cycle of consumption. Same as it ever was.

Honorable Mentions

"California Über Alles" by Dead Kennedys: The Dead Kennedys mixed satire with political outrage to protest the liberal politics of California governor Jerry Brown. The ironic lyricism was paired with ominous instrumentals and a dramatic, louder sound that marked the latest development in a punk rock scene that was on the verge of going hardcore.

"Rapture" by Blondie: Blondie proved their musical vision by being one of the first mainstream artists to embrace hip-hop. Debbie Harry interjected a rap verse into the middle of a spacey new-age disco song. This shone some light on the emergent genre of hip-hop. While the song itself can't truly be considered a hip-hop song, it does hold the distinction of being the first song with rap in it ever to top the Billboard charts.

1981

"Rise Above"

Black Flag

If punk music was born in New York City and raised in London, it came of age in California, when a younger generation of punks started to make their own mark on the scene. At the center of this movement was an infamous group called Black Flag. Formed in 1976 by Greg Ginn and Keith Morris, Black Flag spent the late '70s cycling through band members as they developed a new sound.

Ginn had a vision for a new sound of punk. He took the political ethos that had come out of the London scene and refined it, creating songs that advocated for radical anarchist politics. Meanwhile, he pulled musical influences from the emergent genre of metal and drove his band to play faster and louder than anyone had before. The result was a new subgenre called "hardcore punk."

In its early days, hard-core punk met resistance at every corner. Black Flag's shows frequently turned to riots as police showed up to try to stop the playing. They were the subject of moral panics across Los Angeles, and no record label would sign them. Undeterred, Ginn converted his small electronics

> **They were the subject of moral panics across Los Angeles, and no record label would sign them.**

equipment business into an independent record label, SST. This do-it-yourself attitude became a key part of the hard-core scene, and SST would soon become one of the most important labels in punk.

In January 1979, SST put out the first Black Flag recording, an EP (extended-play record) called *Nervous Breakdown*. That EP was five minutes of pure energetic rage. It soon found its way into the hands of punks across the country, including a Washington, D.C., teenager named Henry Garfield. By that time, a punk scene was beginning to ferment in the nation's capital. That scene included Garfield's band, State of Alert. That band would only ever play nine shows. They broke up in 1981, because Garfield got an invitation to join Black Flag.

The invitation came after a 1980 show in New York. Garfield was working at an ice cream shop and had a shift the next morning, but he loved Black Flag, so he drove out to New York to see them live. During the show, Garfield jumped on the stage, and Black Flag's vocalist Dez Cadena let him sing a tune. Unbeknownst to Garfield, Cadena was

looking to step down from singing and focus on his rhythm guitar role. Garfield's passion and energy were exactly what the band were looking for, so they invited him to be their singer. Garfield quit his job, packed up his bags and went to meet Black Flag on the road. He took up the stage name Henry Rollins and set about becoming an icon.

Late in 1981, with Rollins at the mike, Black Flag were finally able to record their debut studio album, *Damaged*. That album remains one of the greatest punk albums ever recorded. Its opening track, "Rise Above" is a perfect distillation of everything hard-core punk hoped to be. The music rips along at a searing tempo well above 200 beats per minute, while Ginn's lyrics provide an anthemic call to the disaffected youth. Rollins shouts with breathless energy, calling "We are tired of your abuse."

The chorus of "Rise Above" captured the spirit of the band, and of the movement. Despite being harassed by police, stiffed by venues and rejected by the music industry, Black Flag couldn't be stopped. They went on to become one of the central bands in a hard-core punk scene that formed the most cohesive counterculture of the decade. In the hands of Ginn and Rollins, punks grew from a DIY underdog into a persistent cultural force organizing communities against hegemonic power and systemic oppression.

Honorable Mentions

"9 to 5" by Dolly Parton: Dolly Parton crossed over to pop as she kicked off her film career. Written for the workplace comedy of the same name, "9 to 5" was an anthem for the American women who had begun to enter the workforce in full and had to deal with rampant barriers of sexism and misogyny that came with this new reality.

"Don't Stop Believin'" by Journey: At the start of the '80s, the stadium rock sound that had defined the '70s started to sand off its edges. The result was a cleaner pop rock driven by dramatic ballads and enormous vocal performances. The first true classic of '80s pop rock was Journey's "Don't Stop Believin'," an inspirational ballad that builds to one of music's most iconic key changes for a climactic finish.

1982

"The Message"

Grandmaster Flash & the Furious Five

Black communities in New York were going through a creative renaissance in the early 1980s thanks to the birth of hip-hop, but the Black neighborhoods themselves were on the verge of collapse. This was particularly true of the Bronx. The building of the Cross Bronx Expressway had displaced many of the borough's poorest, and the city had no money to repair the crumbling infrastructure. Meanwhile, the crack epidemic was starting to take hold. A violent police force was clashing with street gangs and harassing innocent civilians. A string of arsons swept across the neighborhood, leading to the infamous phrase "The Bronx is burning." Despite all this, the neighborhood's calls for help were falling on deaf ears.

Sylvia Robinson believed that music could help change this. She decided to put together a piece of hip-hop protest music. She called on rapper and songwriter Edward Fletcher, better known as Duke Bootee, to write a hook. He did her one better and wrote two of the most iconic hooks in hip-hop history: "It's like a jungle sometimes / it makes me wonder why I keep from going under" and "Don't push me 'cause I'm close to the edge / I'm trying not to lose my head." He followed this up with a series of observational lyrics about life in the ghetto. Robinson and Fletcher put together a demo of this song and called

it "The Message." Robinson then brought the song to the Sugar Hill Gang, but they refused to do it. So, Robinson took it to a recent signing to her label, Grandmaster Flash and the Furious Five.

Grandmaster Flash had been one of hip-hop's holy trinity in the early days. He was possibly the greatest of the early DJs, and a pioneer of turntablism, inventing or perfecting many turntable techniques that would define the early sounds of hip-hop. Flash's techniques were too intensive for him to rap alongside, so at his parties, he would offer up the microphone to anybody who wanted to come and MC. Through this process, he was able to assemble the Furious Five, consisting of some of the best MCs on the scene. After the Sugar Hill Gang proved rap's commercial viability, Flash and the Five signed with Sugar Hill Records and made a crack at the mainstream.

When Robinson brought "The Message" to Grandmaster Flash, he was incensed. For Flash, and almost everyone else at the time, hip-hop was meant to be an escape from the hard times around them. It was party music, all about having fun and letting loose. Flash didn't want his music to remind people of the very thing they were trying to get away from. He, and most of the Furious Five, refused to be on the

song. Only one member of the five, Melle Mel, agreed to rap on the song. Even then it wasn't because he believed in the song, but rather because he understood Robinson's iron will. Realizing the song would be made one way or another, Melle Mel figured he might as well be on it.

With Mel in, Robertson and Bootee went to work assembling the song. Musician Clifton "Jiggs" Chase put together a slow-moving funk groove influenced by the Zapp Brothers, Tom Tom Club and the works of Brian Eno and David Bowie. They reappropriated a Mel verse from a song called "Superrappin'," and pieced together the first protest song in hip-hop history. The lyrics of "The Message" were raw and observational, an honest look at a city on the brink. Mel's "Superrappin'" verse was particularly poignant, a bleak image of a child, born into a world of strife and poverty, who gets lured into gang violence and ends up committing suicide in prison.

Robinson decided to release "The Message" under the name of Grandmaster Flash & the Furious Five even though most of the group, including Flash himself, had nothing to do with it. She figured his name would lend legitimacy to the song and help it become a hit. She was right. "The Message" became a phenomenon in the rap world and was one of the first hip-hop songs ever to draw critical attention from the white music media.

"The Message" proved for the first time that hip-hop could be about more than just partying. By introducing a political consciousness to hip-hop, Sylvia Robinson was instrumental in kicking off an evolution that would transform hip-hop across the '80s. By the end of the decade, a genre that had once completely rejected all things political was putting out some of the most radical protest music ever made. Artists like Public Enemy, N.W.A. and KRS-One would release songs born out of the same inner-city struggles that were first rapped about on "The Message."

Honorable Mentions

"Billie Jean" by Michael Jackson: Michael Jackson's *Thriller* is the single greatest-selling record in music history. Jackson's incredible ear for pop hooks manifested in unstoppable hits like "Billie Jean." The success of *Thriller* catapulted him and the entire industry into a new era of wealth and record sales, kicking off the golden age of pop.

"1999" by Prince: As the cold war began to heat up again with the United States and the Soviet Union building up nuclear weapons and increasing propaganda pushes, Prince wrote a funk protest album. "1999" ironically embraces nuclear apocalypse, saying that we might as well party if the end is just around the corner. It was a challenge to an era that was trying to distract from real geopolitical problems with a drive for ever-more consumption.

"Planet Rock" by Afrika Bambaataa & the Soulsonic Force: Afrika Bambaataa was one of the greatest DJs that the Bronx had to offer. As hip-hop was finding its footing in 1982, he released the Afrofuturistic "Planet Rock," which sought to unite warring Black communities through music. Bambaataa combined the soul influences of hip-hop with the exciting new synth-pop sounds coming out of Europe. The result was electro, one of the first genres of electronic music.

1983

"Whiplash"

Metallica

When the psychedelic rock scene hit its peak in the 1960s, it began to sprout off into new movements. One of these movements came to be known as "heavy metal." Inspired by the loud, distortion-heavy music of such artists as Jimi Hendrix and Cream, metal started to prioritize noise and speed above all else. In the hands of British pioneers, such as Black Sabbath, Deep Purple and Led Zeppelin, metal music started to establish itself with more ambitious instrumental arrangements and dark lyrics that fixated on occultist imagery, the paranormal and satanism. As the genre progressed through the 1970s, most of its biggest acts remained British. But in the early '80s, a new wave of British metal music that had been pushing for more speed and louder noise began to collide with hard-core punk, an American music pushing for much of the same. The result was thrash, a subgenre that changed the trajectory of metal and birthed the most successful American metal act of all time: Metallica.

Most of Metallica were barely in their 20s when they released their debut album, *Kill 'Em All*, and the band's line-up had only just solidified. If the young musicians felt any uncertainty about the debut, it didn't come through in the music. *Kill 'Em All* is 50 minutes of some of the loudest, hardest music you'll ever hear. Metallica seemed to arrive on the scene fully formed, with a relentless sound that became the standard for much of '80s metal. The best example of this might be the album's lead single, "Whiplash."

Written as an homage to Metallica's head-banging fans in the underground, "Whiplash" is the perfect realization of thrash metal. Lars Ulrich's drums throb with relentless momentum, perfectly in sync with the bassline of Cliff Burton, who had only recently joined the band at the time of recording. This rock-solid rhythm section supports the twinned guitars of founding member James Hetfield and the newly added lead guitarist Kirk Hammett. It's a song that calls audiences to throw themselves around a mosh pit and head-bang until their necks hurt. Midway through the song, Hammet breaks into a face-melting solo, soaring up and down the neck at a breakneck pace with flaming fingers. It's a masterclass in tone and style, the relentless energy of a

> It's a song that calls audiences to throw themselves around a mosh pit and head-bang until their necks hurt.

growing scene of underground metal-heads channeled into a singular instrumental break.

Up until Metallica hit the scene, much of heavy metal was still served with a healthy dose of British influenced camp and glitzy kitsch. Metallica stripped all of this away. Inspired in part by the sincere, DIY aesthetic of the hard-core punk scene, they made their music about earnest and raw emotion. Thrash was angry, youthful music made by and for angry youth. It was a rage against a political and musical establishment that were both progressing toward a corporate sheen. *Kill 'Em All* was brimming with grit. The album was funded by an indie record store owner who created a label for the sole reason of putting Metallica's music out into the world.

With this underground ethos, it's no surprise that *Kill 'Em All* made no real mainstream impact when it was released.

Instead, it began to circulate around in small metal communities. The album's reputation grew through fanzines, tape-trading and word of mouth. In the beginning, the label was limited to pressing 500 copies at a time. Nevertheless, a groundswell of support for the band started to grow. Metal acts across the world took note of the insane energy of these young L.A. kids, and metal began to re-form itself in their image. By 1986, Metallica had broken into the mainstream with their third record, *Master of Puppets*. Their success only grew from there. *Kill 'Em All* would eventually go on to earn a 3x platinum rating in the States, and thrash would seize the attention span of the metal world. Metallica had started in the underground, but before the decade was out, their aggressive sound had cemented them as the biggest metal band ever to come out of the United States.

Honorable Mentions

"Girls Just Wanna Have Fun" by Cyndi Lauper: The movement for women's liberation took on a new tilt in the 1980s. Cyndi Lauper was a step away from the bra burning of the '70s, but was no less a challenge to male hegemony. "Girls Just Wanna Have Fun" is a playful celebration of femininity, with Lauper expressing the desire to break free from the strict gender roles women are assigned by a patriarchal society.

"Pancho & Lefty" by Willie Nelson & Merle Haggard: Two of country's greatest singers teamed up to cover a song by one of the genre's most underappreciated songwriters. Townes Van Zant was a tortured soul whose alternative country music scored him fans within the industry in the '70s. When Nelson and Haggard took on his story song "Pancho & Lefty," it was a display of the rich legacy of country music continuing into a new decade.

"Sucker MC's" by Run-DMC: Run-DMC brought on the next step in hip-hop's evolution with a heavy, raw beat, effortless rhymes and a cool factor that the genre had never seen before. "Sucker MC's" was Run-DMC staking their claim to hip-hop's throne and daring any of their contemporaries to try to compare.

1984

"When Doves Cry"

Prince

For a long time, the meaning of the term "pop music" was in a constant state of flux. At the beginning of the music industry, it referred to the popular show tunes of Tin Pan Alley. Before long, jazz and swing had been adopted into the pop canon. A generation later, jazz fell out favor and "pop" began to refer to rock n' roll music. With the rise of disco in the '70s, "pop" once again took on new meaning. When the '70s ended and disco collapsed, a post-disco synth-funk seized the pop crown. This time, however, it wasn't doomed to be supplanted. This dancy synth-funk sound began to solidify into a pop tradition that continues to dominate Top 40 charts to this day.

This crystallization of pop music happened throughout the early '80s, with such releases as Michael Jackson's *Thriller* and Cyndi Lauper's *She's So Unusual*, but it really took hold in 1984, thanks to a string of releases by the pop auteurs that would define the '80s. Madonna dropped her incendiary *Like a Virgin*, while Bruce Springsteen released the pop-rock *Born to Run*, but the crowning achievement of the greatest year in pop history was Prince's magnum opus, *Purple Rain*, and its revolutionary lead single "When Doves Cry."

Although it would become the most successful single on *Purple Rain*, and perhaps the most beloved song of Prince's

entire career, "When Doves Cry" was actually a late addition to the album. Prince had spent most of 1983 working with director Albert Magnoli to create a semiautobiographical musical film that would pair with the album. The process was an open collaboration, with Magnoli telling Prince scenes that he needed songs for and Prince writing the music. The request for "When Doves Cry" came in early 1984, after the shooting for *Purple Rain* had wrapped. While editing the film, Magnoli realized that he needed one more song to play under a montage of Prince's character losing his love interest to his rival. So, in the spring of 1984, Prince went into the studio to develop some tracks.

The early writing process for "When Doves Cry" took just two days. Prince wrote the song in a night, then spent a day recording all his instrumentals, and another day doing overdubs. This breakneck production pace was normal for him; he had been a prolific writer his entire career. When it came time to mix the song, Prince started to tinker. He had originally recorded an enormous and bombastic piece of music, with a mix loaded with layers of instrumentation. But for some reason, that didn't satisfy him. He decided to pare it down, taking away much of his instrumentation and even deciding to cut the bassline from the song. This was an absolute oddity, given that bass was usually the foundation of the funk music that Prince played. In lesser hands, this process might have torn the song apart. Instead, it transformed "When Doves Cry" into a wholly unique pop song.

The bare arrangement of the song is carried by a brilliant beat on an LM-1 drum machine that Prince programmed. A few synth hits give the song harmonic structure, while Prince's vocals give melody. A few synth and percussion flourishes add color throughout the song. Amazingly, this arrangement doesn't create an absence. Instead, all of the arrangements that had once been in the song are implied. The booming kick drum sound fills the role that a bassline would have, and minimalist synth hits let the listener imagine a broader arrangement.

The profound absence in the song pairs with lyrics that depict the pained absence of love. Prince sings surreal, dreamlike images in the verses before a chorus that questions whether his character is just repeating the same patterns of control and abuse as his parents. It was a perfect fit for the emotional nadir of the *Purple Rain* film, a song full of desperation but lifted by the optimistic subtext of the music. Prince sends this home with the titular image—the bird of peace crying.

To pair with this unique take on dance funk, Prince released a surreal, erotic video in which he crawls nude around a violet room, surrounded by flowers and doves. This video made its debut on MTV, which was transforming into a pop-oriented format and starting to gain a foothold in mainstream culture. The overt sexuality of the video worried record executives, but fans loved it. Prince's ethereal androgyny made him an instant sex symbol. This overt eroticism would help start a trend of more and more explicit music videos that served as

an alternative to the rising tide of conservative Christian culture.

With "When Doves Cry," Prince took the blueprints to funk music, crumpled them into a ball and tossed them out the window. The result was something that became instrumental in a new movement of Top 40 pop songs. Between his drum machine and synthesizers, he made incredible use of the era's advancing technology. His creative vision allowed him to dream of becoming something bigger than simply a pop star. Prince was a fashion icon, an artistic trailblazer and a cultural iconoclast. *Purple Rain* made him the first artist since the Beatles to simultaneously have the top song, top album and top film in America. In the midst of a historic year for pop music, he staked his claim as the movement's foremost auteur with "When Doves Cry."

 # Honorable Mentions

"Born in the U.S.A." by Bruce Springsteen: As Ronald Reagan rode to a landmark second term, Bruce Springsteen released a protest song mocking the blind patriotism of the era. The enormous chorus of "Born in the U.S.A." is such an earworm that many people to this day still misunderstand the lyrics criticizing America's terrible treatment of its Vietnam veterans.

"What's Love Got to Do with It" by Tina Turner: In 1984, Tina Turner was already 44 years old, with a rock n' roll résumé that put even some of the greats to shame. But that didn't stop her from becoming one of the era's greatest pop divas. "What's Love Got to Do with It" made Tina Turner the oldest solo female artist ever to top the Billboard Hot 100 and introduced her singular performing talents to a whole new generation.

1985

"Material Girl"

Madonna

In 1985, America's greed era was in full force. Ronald Reagan had won a landslide reelection on the back of a new model of laissez-faire capitalism. Tax reforms were making America's richest even wealthier, and a new consumerist culture had taken hold of the nation. On this backdrop, Madonna released a single that seemed to capture the ethos of the era, "Material Girl."

"Material Girl" came at a turning point for Madonna's career. It was the second single from her incendiary sophomore album, *Like a Virgin*. That album was unlike anything the pop world had ever seen. It featured a sexually empowered female artist with a distinct voice and a clear vision for her own career. It was an album that challenged religious norms as aggressively as it innovated pop convention.

The lead single, "Like a Virgin," was a masterclass in pop irony. Madonna sang of a hyperbolic virginal image while simultaneously displaying her own liberated sexuality. For the follow-up single, Madonna picked another song that she envisioned as tongue in cheek. "Material Girl" played on the tropes of pop culture femininity at the

> **[*Like a Virgin*] featured a sexually empowered female artist with a distinct voice and a clear vision for her own career.**

time. The lyrics, written by Peter Brown and Robert Rans, play out as a sort of inversion of the Beatles' "Can't Buy Me Love." Madonna sings in an over-the-top voice about her love for men that can buy her things. In the background, a robotic chant of "Living in a material world" seems to be commenting on the dehumanizing effect of consumer culture.

Madonna created the sound of "Material Girl" alongside one of the greatest geniuses in pop. Nile Rodgers had been the creative force behind Chic in the disco era. When disco collapsed, he teamed up with David Bowie and produced his synth-pop smash *Let's Dance*. Madonna had grown up dancing to Chic and had been an avid fan of *Let's Dance*. Rodgers' admiration was mutual. Together, the two were able to craft a funky synth-pop dream. The clean, futuristic sheen of the synthesizers emphasize the message of the lyrics. With layer over layer of synth and vocal takes, "Material Girl" manages to sound expensive enough to sate the character Madonna plays.

The video for "Material Girl" played on some of the greatest iconography of consumer culture. It was framed as an

homage to Marilyn Monroe's "Diamonds Are a Girl's Best Friend" from the 1953 film *Gentlemen Prefer Blondes*. As an outspoken woman well on her way to becoming a beauty icon, Madonna had often drawn comparisons to Monroe. In the early years of her career, she played these down, but for "Material Girl," she seized this narrative and made it her own. It opens with a skit showing a sleazy studio executive watching Madonna on a screen and lusting over her. This shows a clear awareness of the male gaze on her. After the elaborate Monroe-inspired dance piece, Madonna ends the video by driving away with that producer in a beat-up car. It's a subversion of the materialistic imagery of the video, and a statement of Madonna's choosing to seize control of the male gaze. Objectification and sexualization had long been the price of admission for female pop stars. Madonna was one of the first to truly understand that and use it to her advantage.

For as much as "Material Girl" tried to satirize the material world, there was some truth to it. In an '80s culture that was obsessed with money as a means of status and power, Madonna was undoubtedly chasing after fortune and fame. She was constantly in glamorous photoshoots, her style defining much of '80s fashion. Perhaps as criticism, or perhaps as misplaced celebration, people started to dub Madonna the "Material Girl," even as she shunned the nickname. The ironic aspects of her "Material Girl" were overlooked as Madonna's star continued to rise. The song climbed to number two on Billboard's charts, becoming an anthem for the age of Reaganomics.

Whether you choose to read it as ironic or sincere, "Material Girl" captured the spirit of the time. It was the second volley in a barrage of pop hits that would mark Madonna's imperial phase. Over the rest of the decade, nearly every single she released broke into the Top 10. Six of them topped the chart. She was a new kind of pop diva for a new era, a pop auteur with a singular vision and a deep-seated hatred for the glass ceiling. Madonna's contributions to modern pop music are so big that today she is known by the honorific "Queen of Pop." It's a well-deserved title, and one that reflects just how big an impact she had in shaping our material world.

 # Honorable Mentions

"The Greatest Love of All" by Whitney Houston: In 1984, Whitney Houston hit the scene for the first time, displaying one of the most powerful voices ever to hit pop music. Her take on the inspirational ballad "The Greatest Love of All" helped set the stage for a growing movement of pop divas who would shatter sales records across the late '80s and early '90s.

"We Are the World" by U.S.A. For Africa: As an enormous famine tore through Ethiopia, a lineup of many of the greatest stars in America came together for a massive charity single in hopes of raising money to help. The effort raised more than $63 million, but "We Are the World," itself, has a mixed reputation. Nevertheless, its success led to a continuing trend of millionaire musicians stepping out to raise money for charitable causes.

1986

"Walk This Way"

Run-DMC and Aerosmith

In the early days of hip-hop, a favorite record at block parties across Queens was Aerosmith's *Toys in the Attic*. It wasn't that early DJs were particularly fond of rock n' roll, but rather that the 1975 track "Walk This Way" opened on a catchy little drum and guitar hook that was easy to loop and rap over. Two of the MCs that loved to rap over it went by the names DJ Run and DMC. In 1983, they teamed up with the DJ Jam Master Jay and, within a few years, they were hip-hop's biggest stars. Run-DMC's debut album went gold, and their second went platinum at a time when hip-hop was still an underground phenomenon.

For their third record, *Raising Hell*, Run-DMC began to work with a young white kid named Rick Rubin. Rubin had been a rock fan growing up, and he had even played in a punk rock group in the early '80s. But as hip-hop began to rise in New York, Rubin began to gravitate toward it. He learned hip-hop production from the legendary DJ Jazzy Jay, and began to sign rap artists to his label, Def Jam Recordings. Rubin was a living bridge between the disparate worlds of hip-hop and rock. In the past two years, he'd produced the Beastie Boys' "Rock Hard" and LL Cool J's "Rock the Bells," two hip-hop songs built around hard rock samples. With these successes under his belt, Rubin

sought to further his experiments in rap rock. Inspired by conversations with a *Spin* magazine editor Sue Collins and old friend Tim Sommer, Rubin began to come up with a vision for a mainstream rap rock cross-over. All he needed was the right song. He found that song one day when he walked into the studio to find Run-DMC experimenting with a sample of "Walk This Way."

In homage to those early block parties, Run-DMC were going to take that opening beat and write an original set of raps over it. Rubin had a more radical idea. He thought that Run-DMC should cover the song's original lyrics. The band took one look at the lyrics and laughed off the idea. But Rubin was determined. He eventually convinced Run-DMC to do the song, and then turned around and reached out to Aerosmith, hoping to bring them onto the track.

Aerosmith were as enthusiastic about this idea as Run-DMC, but they weren't exactly in a place to be turning down potential publicity. After riding a wave of hard rock success through the 1970s, Aerosmith had fallen from grace. The band were recovering from serious drug addictions, and their 1985 album *Done with Mirrors* was flopping. Meanwhile, Run-DMC's stock was gaining value by the day. Aerosmith decided not to look a gift horse in the mouth. Front man Steven Tyler and guitarist Joe Perry

flew over to New York for an awkward studio session with Run-DMC.

Neither group were excited about the recording, and they barely even knew each other's music. Aerosmith's Tyler was a rap appreciator, but Perry only knew of the music through his teenage son. When DMC first saw Aerosmith in the studio, he thought they were the Rolling Stones. Aerosmith came with their own prejudices, quipping to one another that Run-DMC were probably smoking crack in the corner. There were enormous racial, cultural and generational gaps between the two groups. Had it not been for Rick Rubin's vision, the sessions likely would have fallen apart. Instead, they turned into one of the most legendary moments in early hip-hop.

Aerosmith's original "Walk This Way" had a half-ranted vocal line in a meter that worked perfect for Run-DMC's rap. Despite Run-DMC's balking at the lyrics, calling them "country bumpkin bullshit," they were able to rap them with the sort of energetic bravado that had made them the first true rap stars. For their part, Aerosmith were able to provide a roaring guitar line for the song, and Tyler's raspy delivery on the chorus was a perfect encapsulation of hair-metal rock, a movement that the band were crucial in pioneering.

Even still, Run-DMC were iffy on the song after recording. They didn't think it should be released as a single, but Rubin sent it off to rap and rock stations anyway. To the surprise of nearly everyone involved, the song started to catch on. So, Run-DMC brought a reluctant Aerosmith in again to shoot a video. In that video, the two acts are playing in rooms next to each other, each angering the other with their volume and noise until Tyler tears down the wall with his microphone stand and the two begin to play together. It was a literalization of what the song had accomplished—punching a hole in the wall between two disparate genres. The video became an enormous hit on MTV, sometimes even being played twice an hour at its peak. This helped launch the song into the stratosphere, making it the first hip-hop song ever to crack the Top 10.

On the strength of "Walk This Way,"

Raising Hell became Run-DMC's best-selling record, and one of the best-selling hip-hop albums of the entire era. Meanwhile, the song completely revitalized Aerosmith's career. With hair-metal rock peaking in the mid-'80s, Aerosmith were able to find new life in a scene that they had helped launch. Their next album, *Permanent Vacation*, spawned three huge hits and went quintuple platinum.

When Aerosmith and Run-DMC teamed up for "Walk This Way," they were able to break down a barrier that Rick Rubin had been chipping away at for years. It brought hip-hop to new levels of mainstream success, while opening the door for acts like the Beastie Boys and Rage Against the Machine, and eventually the entire nü-metal movement. After years of flirtation, rap and rock had finally consummated their relationship.

Honorable Mentions

"Nasty" by Janet Jackson: After living in the shadow of her superstar brother, Janet Jackson finally made it big in the mainstream in 1986. "Nasty" was based on her true experiences dealing with abusive men. It established her as an empowered woman who wasn't about to be walked over. When it rose to number three on the Hot 100, it helped Jackson carve her path as a pop genius in her own right.

"Livin' on a Prayer" by Bon Jovi: Bon Jovi continued the progression of '80s stadium rock with an anthemic rock classic. "Livin' on a Prayer" drew on the narrative ballads of Bruce Springsteen, but sang it with the teased-out hair and over-the-top sound of glam metal. "Livin' on a Prayer" became one of the biggest rock hits of the '80s, riding high on the era's overblown aesthetics.

1987

"Bad"

Michael Jackson

There has never been, and will never be, another pop star like Michael Jackson. The King of Pop was already a force in the music industry before his 12th birthday. As the star attraction of the Jackson 5, he sang some of the biggest hits of the '60s with Motown Records. When disco took hold of the pop world, a 21-year-old Jackson seized control of his own career and released one of the finest records of the era, 1979's *Off the Wall*. Three years later, he dropped the most important and best-selling pop album ever made, *Thriller*, thereby achieving a level of success reserved for the likes of Elvis Presley and the Beatles. This level of fame had previously been denied to Black artists in America. It was as much a curse as it was a blessing.

Jackson's life became marred with the incongruity that comes from being the most beloved figure in a nation that was systemically violent toward Black people. He experienced an unprecedented level of press scrutiny, and his family relationships began to crumble. Rumors spread of erratic behavior, and he decided to step away from the spotlight for several years while quietly working on a follow-up to *Thriller*. While his pop contemporaries like Madonna and Prince had prolific runs through the mid-'80s, Jackson was holed up, trying to figure out how to follow up an album that had been certified 20x platinum just two years after its release.

Finally, in 1987, he was ready to debut his new sound to the world. He put together an enormous TV special to drop the album, centered on a 15-minute short film for its title track, "Bad." Jackson tapped the legendary filmmaker Martin Scorsese to direct that film, and produced an elaborate piece of art that drew much of its visual inspiration from *West Side Story*. The film tells the story of an inner-city kid who wins a scholarship at a private school, only to come home and face anger and jealousy from his onetime best friend, played by a young Wesley Snipes. The film begins as a gritty depiction of the inner-city decay happening in poor Black neighborhoods in the States, before transitioning into an elaborate, fantastical dance sequence in an abandoned subway station.

From the beginning, Jackson had been an early adopter of the music video medium. His videos from *Thriller* broke MTV's "color barrier" and became some

> **The King of Pop was already a force in the music industry before his 12th birthday.**

influence from the hard rock and hair metal scenes at the time in an attempt to prove his hardness.

"Bad" was Jackson's way of reshaping a piece of slang used by the youth of the day. With the rise of gang violence, "Bad" was being used to mean "cool." Jackson wanted his video to prove that badness didn't need to come from crime or violence. His version of being bad meant standing up for what was right, even in the face of peer pressure to do otherwise. His lyrics called for unity among Black communities that were tearing each other apart. It was a hopeful message from an artist who had always wanted to change the world with his music.

The sound of "Bad" was a steep progression of the pop that Jackson and Quincy Jones had debuted on *Thriller*. Naturalistic instruments were traded out for layers of funky synthesizer and drum machines. It was a dense, clean mix made with the finest recording technology that the decade had to offer. Jackson threw some grit and edge into his famous falsetto, and supported it with powerful backing vocal arrangements in the chorus. It's a song that moves with an effortless energy from start to finish, culminating in an enormous earworm of a finale punctuated by Jones' trademark blaring horn hits.

This enormous pop scale stretched across the entirety of the *Bad* album, as Jackson created a perfect amalgamation of all the pop sounds in the zeitgeist. Following up *Thriller* had seemed an impossible task, but he had somehow pulled it off. *Bad* sold more than two million copies in its first week. It produced a record-setting five number-one singles, including "Bad." These singles would spawn their own ambitious video projects, most notably the Fred Astaire–inspired "Smooth Criminal."

of the most celebrated videos of the era. With "Bad," he escalated this to an even greater scale. It captured much of the inner-city fashion of the era, and displayed yet another level to his brilliant dance talents. It also marked a shift in Jackson's personal image. With "Bad," he hoped to portray himself as someone harder edged. He clad himself in a strappy leather jacket, and drew musical

If any doubts remained about Jackson's star power by 1987, *Bad* silenced them all. Jackson proved himself to be a sort of all-encompassing pop star that the world hadn't seen in generations. But for all of his success, Jackson was only met with more scrutiny from the press. Following the triumph that was *Bad*, his mental state began to deteriorate as the media fixated on his eccentricities. Just a few years later, allegations of child abuse would emerge, and Jackson's career began the kind of monumental collapse that can only happen when you're the most famous man on earth. Although his legacy is a complicated one, *Bad* remains one of the most important pop albums ever made. It was groundbreaking in its musical and visual ambitions, and it still stands as a defiant statement of a singular sort of Black excellence.

Honorable Mentions

"Sweet Child O' Mine" by Guns N' Roses: As hair metal reached its height, Guns N' Roses hit the scene with a darker, edgier take on the genre. As a romantic love ballad, "Sweet Child O' Mine" is softer than the rest of their catalog, but Slash's opening guitar riff and soaring solo ensured that nobody would doubt their cool.

"I Ain't No Joke" by Eric B. & Rakim: Rakim introduced the concept of "flow" into hip-hop with a song full of bars filled with syncopation and internal rhymes. His distinct style came from listening to John Coltrane records and trying to apply their lessons to rap. His cocky boasts on "I Ain't No Joke" proved true as countless rappers started to find their own flows inspired by Rakim's distinctive style.

1988

"Fuck tha Police"

N.W.A.

In the late 1980s, South Central Los Angeles was at war. Huge shipments of cocaine began to flood the country and landed in the hands of L.A.'s street gangs. Almost overnight, small-time street gangs found themselves moving millions of dollars of product and evolving into full-on cartels. Turf wars broke out across the city, spawning violent clashes and drive-by shootings. This was all exacerbated by a third sort of gang: the police. The LAPD would roam through the streets racially profiling young Black men and seeking any reason to assault or arrest them. This only encouraged the gangs to arm themselves more as neighborhood after neighborhood fell victim to the crack epidemic. As prospects in the city grew bleak, the music of Los Angeles' Black communities began to shift.

Hip-hop was just starting to take hold in L.A., though much of it was still lifting its style from New York's electro scene. In 1986, a rapper named Ice T released "6 'N the Mornin'," an observational rap that described the day-to-day life of someone with gang affiliations. This was a step away from the lighthearted party raps and an embracing of something truer to the experience of South Central. Everyone in L.A. took notice. Though it didn't have a name yet, gangsta rap had been born. The movement would gain steam in the next year,

when a group of aspiring rappers and former electro DJs joined together and dubbed themselves N.W.A. On August 8, 1988, N.W.A. dropped their debut album, *Straight Outta Compton*. It hit the rap scene like a bomb. Producer Dr. Dre's beats banged hard, and the group filled their bars with militant lyrics about gang life. Where the early gangsta rappers had tread cautiously, the second song in *Straight Outta Compton* came out and shouted what almost every Black man in South Central had been thinking for years: "Fuck tha Police."

The main writer behind "Fuck tha Police" was Ice Cube, who came up with the idea of the song after seeing his bandmate Dr. Dre get thrown into jail weekend after weekend for minor offenses, all while violent gang members were turning the neighborhood into a battleground. The lyrics are framed around a courtroom, with N.W.A. turning the tables on the cops and putting them on trial for violence, harassment and racial profiling. For six minutes, N.W.A. take turns railing on the cops. It's a violent wail against a prison-industrial complex that was chewing up Black communities in the name of the ongoing fruitless war on drugs.

The radical lyrics of "Fuck tha Police" are supported by a bombastic beat put together by Dr. Dre. Before N.W.A., Dre was one of the most cele-

brated DJs in L.A.'s electro scene. That scene put the DJs in the forefront, encouraging showy turntablism and ambitious sample flips. Dre brings that attitude to "Fuck tha Police," making rich use of a pair of James Brown samples for the drumbeats and pulling in an assortment of hooks from soul deep cuts. Record scratches serve as punctuation throughout the song while horn and string lines punch in with an eerie precision. While this production still owes a lot to the New York sound, it marked some of the beginnings of the West Coast's developing its own flavor of hip-hop.

N.W.A. expected controversy when they released the song, and they got it in droves. It angered concerned parent groups, received ban orders from radio stations and even attracted a letter of warning from a bureaucrat at the FBI. What they didn't expect was for this gangsta rap sound to catch on among audiences who had never lived through police oppression and harassment. The media storm around the group made them attractive to disaffected suburban

teens looking for any reason to rebel. The overt rebellion of N.W.A. was something nobody had seen before and it spawned a generation of young hip-hop fans. *Straight Outta Compton* went gold within a year of its release. N.W.A. set out on a tour across the country, riling up the police force of every city they landed in.

This came to a head in Detroit in the summer of 1989. When word spread that N.W.A. were coming to town, Detroit police informed the group that they wouldn't be allowed to play the song, for fear that it would start a riot. This only egged them on: In front of an eager crowd who had packed into Joe Louis Arena, N.W.A. defiantly began "Fuck tha Police," only to have the police storm the stage and shut down the show.

This sort of controversy started to follow the group everywhere, which only raised their profile more. N.W.A. only lasted two more years after "Fuck tha Police," but they had already changed the world. They'd given voice to America's underclass and brought hip-hop out from the underground and into living rooms across the country once and for all. Many of the members of N.W.A. would become superstars throughout the '90s, shaping the next generation of rappers. Meanwhile, sadly, the message of "Fuck tha Police" would only grow more relevant as the militarization of America's police force grew and grew. With "Fuck tha Police," N.W.A. shouted out on a racial tension that had been silently boiling in American culture for generations. They captured the rage of their community, giving voice to a sentiment that Black people across the country had thought thousands of times.

Honorable Mentions

"Fast Car" by Tracy Chapman: In an era of over-the-top antics and enormous production sounds, Tracy Chapman swam against the grain with a low-key, narrative folk song. "Fast Car" is beloved for its beautiful storytelling, but the song's genderless lyrics yearning for escape from a bad situation resonated deeply with the lesbian community, who adopted it as one of their anthems.

"Every Rose Has Its Thorn" by Poison: All the melodrama and kitsch of the '80s glam metal movement come to a head in Poison's signature song. "Every Rose Has Its Thorn" is a sappy power ballad inspired by songwriter Bret Michaels' experience with an unfaithful partner. The song topped the Billboard charts and became enshrined as a grunge classic, but it was one of the last hits of an era that would soon be erased entirely by grunge.

"Teen Age Riot" by Sonic Youth: Sonic Youth were key players in an indie rock scene that simmered in the '80s underground, giving an edgier alternative to the era's blown-out stadium rock. Made up of layer upon layer of guitar noise, "Teen Age Riot" calls a new generation to break free from the corporatized era they're living in.

1989

"Fight the Power"

Public Enemy

In the summer of 1988, filmmaker Spike Lee reached out to the rap group Public Enemy and asked them for an anthem. He was working on his seminal film *Do the Right Thing* and wanted a song that could play out of the character Radio Raheem's boom box. Lee envisioned the song as a hip-hop version of the African American spiritual "Lift Every Voice and Sing," but Public Enemy's production team, known as the Bomb Squad, had different ideas. They wanted something more representative of the streets, something that might actually be heard rebounding off of New York's scorching concrete on a summer day. To achieve this, the Bomb Squad pulled together a song that was a living record of generations of Black protest music: "Fight the Power."

> It was one of the most musically dense songs that hip-hop had ever seen, pulling in more than a dozen samples in its first 10 seconds.

Public Enemy front man Chuck D wrote "Fight the Power" in partial homage to the Isley Brothers' 1975 song of the same name, a piece of music that had been part of his political awakening as a young man. The Isleys weren't the only piece of Black protest woven into the song. It also contains samples of James Brown as well as Sly and the Family Stone, and opens on a clip from civil rights leader Thomas "TNT" Todd. It was one of the most musically dense songs that hip-hop had ever seen, pulling in more than a dozen samples in its first 10 seconds. This density created a chaotic cacophony that emulated the energy of the New York City streets. It also reminds listeners of the enormous history of Black protest that Public Enemy were building upon. Chuck D's ferocious lyrics are even populated with references to Malcolm X and turns of phrase inspired by Bob Marley. While creating a musical parade of Black leaders, Chuck D reminds listeners of how many of these figures had been overlooked by white history books.

White audiences were scandalized by Public Enemy's lines such as where Chuck D calls out Elvis Presley and John Wayne, two of white America's most beloved cultural figures. As Chuck D saw it, Presley was disproportionately celebrated over Black rock n' roll innovators like Little Richard. Meanwhile, John Wayne was still being

put on a pedestal as one of America's most venerated actors despite having a long history of overtly racist comments.

"Fight the Power" is a fearless stand against white hegemony. There's no shortage of anger in the song, but by and large, it has the upbeat energy of a block party, or a protest. Spike Lee channeled this energy when directing the music video for "Fight the Power," a returned favor to Public Enemy for writing the song in the first place. Lee organized a march for the video, drawing on the iconography of the Million Man March. A crowd of people walked through Brooklyn behind Chuck D, eventually landing in the Bedford-Stuyvesant neighborhood that was the setting of *Do the Right Thing*. Fans hold placards with the public enemy logo while Black Panthers breakdance in the street. It was an optimistic counterpoint to the heartbreaking finale of *Do the Right Thing*, which shows the police choke out a young Black man leading to a neighborhood riot.

"Fight the Power" was a statement of unity across a Black neighborhood—that New York City, and the wider Black community, could organize together around a celebratory joy and become a powerful political bloc advocating for their own needs. The Bomb Squad's production on the song was some of the most ambitious sampling hip-hop had seen to date. The days of spinning one drum break over and over were long gone, as Public Enemy helped encourage producers to get as dense and radical as they could with layer after layer of sample. Spike Lee had asked Public Enemy for an anthem, and he got exactly that. "Fight the Power" still gets played at rallies to this day, and with good reason. It's a timeless protest song and its 1989 release was a bombastic declaration that the golden age of hip-hop was in full swing.

There's no shortage of anger in the song, but by and large, it has the upbeat energy of a block party, or a protest. Spike Lee channeled this energy when directing the music video . . .

Honorable Mentions

"Here Comes Your Man" by the Pixies: The Pixies were one of the most essential groups of the alternative rock revolution fomenting in the late '80s. "Here Comes Your Man" mixes noisy punk sounds with influences from surf rock and ties it together with an unashamed embracing of pop hooks. Their sound made them a favorite of a young Kurt Cobain, who would use their approach to become the voice of a generation.

"Part of Your World" (from *The Little Mermaid*) by Alan Menken and Howard Ashman: The songwriting duo of Alan Menken and Howard Ashman brought Disney back from the brink with an all-new sort of animated musical. Inspired by Broadway's book musical tradition, *The Little Mermaid* fuses beautiful melody with a raw love story deeply informed by Ashman's own experience as a gay man.

The

ALTERNATIVE

Generation

1990–99

The underground movements born as a response to the extremes of the 1980s burst into the mainstream when the decade turned. Grunge sprang forth from Seattle and wiped away a decade of rock indulgence almost overnight, catapulting punk rock into the mainstream. It enraptured millions of disaffected white Gen-Xers raised on an era of cold war propaganda, giving them a strange cocktail of rage and irony that became their own avenue for resistance. This new movement would burn out halfway through the decade, but its legacy continued as the industry began to realize that it could wrap up anticapitalist resistance into a neat little package and sell it back to the people on its own terms.

The booming record industry also turned its eyes to hip-hop in the '90s. At first, it was family friendly pop rap, but before long all hip-hop was fair game in the mainstream. Rap's second generation innovated new styles of flow and lyricism, solidifying the tropes of the genre and creating some of the finest rap

1990
1991
1992
1993
1994

records in history. But this golden age of hip-hop was tainted by a brutal, violent rivalry between New York and Los Angeles. This war would spawn the worst feud in music history and wind up claiming the lives of the era's two most brilliant minds. As it raged on, a new hip-hop scene erupted out of the South, and an underground white rapper from Detroit was slowly working his way toward a debut album that would change rap forever.

The media landscape of the '90s became obsessed with the high drama playing out in celebrity culture. A wider array of TV channels meant that people could scrutinize celebrity life down to the minute, and the market became flooded with magazines obsessing over pop cultural heroes. The prime targets of this generation of celebrity worship were a movement of boy bands and girl groups who had refined rhythm and blues to clinical efficiency and were becoming the biggest pop fad of the era.

The paparazzi were particularly nasty to the female artists of the '90s who were using their platform to hype up an invigorated women's liberation movement. Born from the rebellious punks of the Riot Grrrl movement, this new girl power crossed over first into rock, and then into mainstream pop. As the boy band/girl group fad started to fade, pop looked forward to a future dominated by empowered divas with a girl power agenda.

As the decade came to a close, people across America were starting to realize that the new millennium was going to bring unprecedented change. Households across the country were connecting to the internet and starting to imagine what the future could be. The digital revolution was just around the corner, and it would soon spell the end of three decades of nonstop growth and pocket padding for the music industry.

1990

"U Can't Touch This"

MC Hammer

When the '80s rolled over to the '90s, hip-hop was already well on its way to becoming the next big musical movement. The genre's second generation was inventing and solidifying hip-hop staples like flow, sample flips and turntablism. What had started in the '80s as a local phenomenon in New York had spread across the country, with new scenes popping up in every major metropolitan area. But one thing was holding the music back from being truly mainstream: White audiences were still afraid of it. Fed on a steady diet of fearmongering news reports and think pieces, much of white America couldn't (or didn't want to) understand the artistic brilliance of hip-hop and continued to view it as only the music of drug dealers and gang violence. For rap to truly go mainstream, white America would need a family-friendly, uncontroversial rapper to latch onto. They found it in 1990 with a rapper named MC Hammer.

Rising out of Oakland's vibrant street dance scene, Hammer self-funded his 1986 debut album, *Feel My Power*. That release was enough of a local success that it convinced Capitol Records to sign Hammer and release his major-label debut, *Let's Get It Started*, in 1988. That release sold well and saw Hammer's profile rise even more, but it failed to reach the pop charts. So, Ham-

mer decided to take a new approach for his third album, *Please Hammer Don't Hurt 'Em*. He stripped away some of the more traditional rap sounds and instead focused more on musicality, creating an album that he could entertain and dance to. He put together songs based on liberal samples of existing funk and soul tracks, pieces that could show off his skills as a dancer and entertainer. One of these was "U Can't Touch This," an upbeat dance song that lifted the bassline from Rick James' 1981 funk hit "Super Freak."

Hammer and his team felt optimistic when they put together "U Can't Touch This," but nobody could have possibly anticipated just how big it would be. Hammer's accessible, funky fresh sound was exactly what white America was hungering for. It let people who otherwise might have been alienated by hip-hop experience the sheer joy of it. "U Can't Touch This" topped charts around the world and hit number eight on Billboard's Hot 100. It made MC Hammer a household name and propelled *Please Hammer Don't Hurt 'Em* to a diamond certification, making it the first rap album ever to achieve such a feat. Along the way, it raked in three Grammy awards and put Hammer on the cover of *Rolling Stone* magazine.

This rocket ride to fame and fortune was aided by an iconic music video.

Hammer always considered himself as an entertainer first. As such, he had a keen eye for aesthetics and understood that a strong video was a key to pop success in the early '90s. He dressed in enormous baggy pants, now known as "Hammerpants," and produced a shiny, bright video loaded with dynamic dance moves. Hammer created a sharp visual image that people could always associate with him and debuted a series of dance moves that kids around America would try to emulate, including the Hammer Dance, where he shuffled from side to side as his pants waved around. He explicitly wanted the video to be fun and silly, something that had audiences smiling the whole way through.

Hammer's vision for an accessible pop rap lifted him to fame and fortune, but they also drew the ire of the hip-hop community. He was accused of selling out the genre's underground ethos. Rappers across the country started to take pot shots at Hammer, but the artist himself insisted he had no beef with underground rap. He was happy to keep letting street rappers continue in the underground while he rode a wave of pop success. In time, however, Hammer's approach would become the norm in hip-hop. Within a decade even many of the hardest street rappers were trying to sell out and turn themselves into business empires.

In the years following "U Can't Touch This," MC Hammer was offered nearly every brand deal imaginable. He got his own Mattel doll and a Saturday morning cartoon called *Hammerman*. Hammermania seized America for a few years, but it wasn't long before audiences were getting sick of seeing him everywhere. The continued hatred shown to him from other rappers started to plague Hammer's career, and he pivoted to a gangsta rap sound in hopes

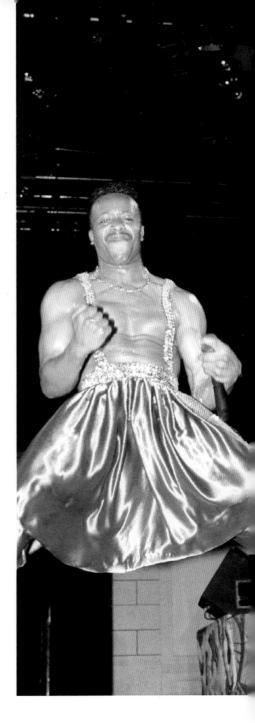

of proving his realness. These efforts were fruitless, and his career collapsed, culminating in a highly publicized declaration of bankruptcy in 1996. Hammer remains a controversial figure to this day, but the fact remains that he was rap's first pop star. "U Can't Touch This" gave millions of Americans something they had been thirsting for in 1990 and marked the beginning of hip-hop as pop music.

Honorable Mentions

"Vogue" by Madonna: When the backlash chased disco into the underground, queer communities reclaimed it and developed it into a new kind of dance music called house. With 1990's "Vogue," Madonna embraced this underground art form, bringing it from Black and Latino ballroom culture into the mainstream and helping to normalize a gay culture that was suffering from stigma and trauma at the height of the AIDS epidemic.

"Can I Kick It?" by A Tribe Called Quest: A Tribe Called Quest hit the scene and added fuel to hip-hop's golden age with a laid-back jazz rap sound and positive, socially conscious lyrics. "Can I Kick It" is a sample-rich piece of psychedelia, pulling from Lou Reed, Ian Dury and the composer Sergei Prokofiev. This brilliant production work is exactly what made hip-hop one of the most exciting music scenes of the new decade.

"Cemetery Gates" by Pantera: As glam metal fell away, more extreme metals began to thrive. Pantera were a distinctly American take on heavy metal, mixing the neoclassical European influences with a heavy, blues-based groove. One of their great triumphs is "Cemetery Gates," a sprawling ballad that climaxes with guitarist Dimebag Darrell tearing out one of the greatest solos ever played.

1991

"Smells Like Teen Spirit"

Nirvana

Few songs have ever captured the spirit and aesthetic of a generation as purely as "Smells Like Teen Spirit." In just five minutes of music, Nirvana managed to give voice to the angst, alienation and reckless abandon of Generation X. Kurt Cobain's raspy shouts and Dave Grohl's thunderous drums hit like a defibrillator, shocking life back into a rock world that was well on its way to flatlining. Overnight, Nirvana went from an underground indie band to a household name and the face of the biggest youth movement since the hippies. They single-handedly shifted the trajectory of rock music in the '90s. And they did it all with nobody, least of all the band, seeing it coming.

In the late '80s, mainstream rock had progressed to a point of self-parody. The skin-tight pants and teased out hair that had once seemed cool and radical were starting to look like exercises in ego and navel-gazing. Huge stadium rock bands were becoming increasingly detached from reality as they traveled on private planes and bought enormous mansions paid for by a booming record industry. The music that had once been synonymous with counterculture had become the epitome of the mainstream industry. But in the underground, a response was starting to simmer. The hard-core punk movement had grown in force throughout the '80s, and a tour

by Black Flag helped inspire new regional scenes across the country. Each of these scenes spun off and developed its own unique voice and character. The most distinct of these came out of Seattle. The Seattle Sound mixed the loud, political energy of punk rock with the slower, doomy aspects of '70s heavy metal. Such bands as the Melvins, Mudhoney and Soundgarden stripped away all sheen from their performance. They created a heavy, dirty sound that was appropriately named "grunge."

Grunge was just starting to rise when Nirvana came into Seattle from nearby Aberdeen and started to make a name for themselves. They could play just as heavy and loud as any of the other grunge bands, but the brilliant songwriting of Kurt Cobain started to give them an edge. Unlike many in the scene, he was a fan of a lot of pop rock. He adored the Beatles in particular, and wrote his songs in the Lennon-McCartney style with simple conceits and approachable, catchy choruses. On their debut album, 1989's *Bleach*, these pop sensibilities were toned down at the suggestion of Nirvana's independent label, Sub Pop. Sub Pop had been trying to keep the label's sound raw and underground, but the lack of pop sensibilities meant that they were in danger of being bought out by 1990. So, the band decided to jump ship and signed with the major label Geffen Records.

With a new record deal under their belt, Nirvana teamed up with producer Butch Vig and started to put together a new album, *Nevermind*. This new album also saw the introduction of drummer Dave Grohl, who was one of the loudest ever to sit behind a kit. Grohl and bassist Krist Novoselic had a perfect chemistry, and with a tighter rhythm section, Cobain's guitar and vocals could shine. Vig's production style kept the noise and rage that was essential to Nirvana, but paired it with a crisper studio sound. At just 24 years old, Cobain was still progressing as a songwriter, and *Nevermind* saw a newfound maturity enter his lyrics and melody. There was a certain optimism around *Nevermind*, as Nirvana's clout in the underground was growing, and alt rock groups like Sonic Youth were starting to gain more momentum across the country. Some thought the album might sell 250,000 copies, while the most liberal estimates had it selling half a million copies in a year.

Nevermind hit that latter number in two months. A little more than a year after its release, the album was platinum, and by the end of the decade it had a diamond certification with over 10 million copies sold in America.

The combination of simple pop melodicism and heavy grunge noise made it a perfect entry point for millions of teens who were curious about the underground. Cobain's lyrics were filled with themes of teenage alienation, antiauthoritarian rage and a deep-seated subtext of mental illness. They spoke to teens raised on cold war fears and Reaganist propaganda, offering a sort of freedom through rebellion. *Nevermind* was loaded with hits but as the opening track, "Smells Like Teen Spirit" was foremost among them.

Cobain wrote the song as a protest against the apathy of his generation. He sings of a hedonistic party culture in a morose, sardonic tone. Cobain's character is too lazy, too disaffected to care about anything. Even the lyrics cease to interest him in the third verse ending with: "Oh well, whatever, nevermind." Cobain felt that many in his generation had been zombified by consumerism. They'd been fed lies for their whole life and found themselves entering adulthood with no true purpose or meaning. His music gave them one potential path to meaning: rebellion against authority.

This message is supported by a video that depicts a cohort of bored high school kids rising up and trashing their school as Nirvana wail on their instruments. The entire video is soaked in a yellow haze and reeks of rage and destruction. It has none of the high budget polish of its contemporaries. Nirvana wear plain shirts and baggy jeans, a grunge fashion trend that would sweep across the nation. The teens Nirvana brought in to shoot the video were genuine fans, and the sheer joy they feel moshing and head-banging comes through. The raw energy of this video made it a favorite on MTV and raised the profile of the song. Before long, MTV was pivoting much of its programming to accommodate the underground alternative rock movement that was crawling out into the sunlight in the wake of Nirvana's success.

"Smells Like Teen Spirit" earned Kurt Cobain the auspicious title of "Voice of a Generation." Like most who are talented enough to receive such a designation, he resented it deeply. For all his pop songwriting, Cobain was ultimately a punk at heart, and a man of the underground. With *Nevermind*, he suddenly found himself charting higher than Michael Jackson, and playing to ravenous audiences of tens of thou-sands. This unprecedented fame brought with it an enormous pressure that exacerbated Cobain's lifelong struggle with mental health and addiction. In the end, it brought on a tragic suicide in 1994, when he was just 27 years old.

In many ways, "Smells Like Teen Spirit" is a cautionary tale about the ways that the music industry commodifies talent and leaves its artists on the wayside in the name of ever more money. But it is also a story of human brilliance and artistic genius—about the ways that some artists can tap into a collective unconscious, give voice to millions and, against all odds, transform the world.

Honorable Mention

"Losing My Religion" by R.E.M.: After enrapturing the underground for much of the '80s, the alt-rock revolution helped R.E.M. rise to the mainstream. Their biggest hit was "Losing My Religion," an understated tune driven by twinkling mandolin and Michael Stipe's famous esoteric lyrics. It's paired with a beautiful music video that helped move the video trend away from performances and toward an era of artistic abstraction.

1992

"Killing in the Name"

Rage Against the Machine

In the spring of 1991, a horrific video started to circulate on news broadcasts across the country. The video depicted four LAPD officers brutalizing a young Black man named Rodney King, who had been pulled over for impaired driving. The video, filmed by an onlooker named George Holliday, was living proof of the sort of police brutality that L.A.'s Black community had been dealing with for years. It divided the country along racial lines and exacerbated the anticop attitudes that had birthed '80s gangsta rap. Soon after, a series of charges including assault with a deadly weapon and excessive use of force were brought against the police officers.

Among the many stirred by the beating of King was a radical songwriter from Long Beach named Zack de la Rocha. De la Rocha was the grandson of a Mexican revolutionary, and the son of a Chicano muralist. He had been steeped in leftist politics from a young age and found his own outlet for his political voice in California's music scenes. At the time, Los Angeles was the home of two of the most politically radical music scenes in America: hard-core punk and West Coast rap. De la Rocha had a vision of combining these two

De la Rocha equates the police to the Ku Klux Klan . . .

sounds. This vision became real when he was teamed up with the metal and rock guitarist Tom Morello, who was himself a descendent of Kenyan revolutionaries. The two were joined by bassist Tim Commerford and guitarist Brad Wilk. Together, they created a revolutionary band with an equally revolutionary name: Rage Against the Machine.

With his band newly formed and Los Angeles careening toward a breaking point, Zach de la Rocha sat down and penned the defining song of his career, "Killing in the Name." His lyrical style tended to be dense and verbose, with his songs reading like political manifestos. For "Killing in the Name," he swapped this out for a simple anthemic approach, with a few key repeated phrases. The first of these phrases drew attention to the racist history of American police, and the LAPD in particular: "Some of those that work forces / Are the same that burn crosses." De la Rocha equates the police to the Ku Klux Klan, an incendiary line that has its roots in history. The explosive chorus builds on this statement, while referencing those who have been killed by police brutality: "Those who died are justified / For wearing the badge, they're the chosen whites." It's a ruthless indictment of institutionalized racism, delivered with unceasing passion and fury.

The music supporting de la Rocha's lyrics is just as tense and angry. Most of the song was written around a heavy drop-D riff that Morello wrote on the spot to demonstrate to a guitar student the power of dropped tunings. Commerford mirrors that line on the bass to create a thick, heavy sound, while Wilk wails on his drum kit. It's a sludgy sound that reflects the evolutions in heavy metal across the '80s, but rides on a syncopated funky groove. Throughout the song, the music and lyrics work together in a slow build toward an explosive coda. There, de la Rocha roars out the most memorable of his repeated slogans: "Fuck you, I won't do what you tell me." It's a simple, in-your-face thesis of punk rock. Anger and defiance dance at a furious volume as de la Rocha calls his generation into action.

With such an overtly radical message, Rage Against the Machine never expected commercial success. But with the growing tide of punk and gangsta rap, record labels started to realize that the public was hungry for political music. Epic Records signed Rage off the strength of a demo tape, and the band went to work turning that demo into a proper album.

While they were in the studio putting together their infamous debut, the Rodney King case went to trial. America watched with bated breath as all four officers were acquitted. That acquittal was a matchstick on a powder keg; Los Angeles erupted into a riot that lasted for a week and burned much of the city to the ground. The riots had died down by the time Rage Against the Machine's

debut dropped in November, but revolutionary energy was still in the air. "Killing in the Name" became an anthem for the radical protests of the '90s, and has continued to be a staple of any countercultural movement since.

Honorable Mentions

"Nothin' But a G Thang" by Dr. Dre (featuring Snoop Dogg): Dr. Dre's acrimonious breakup with N.W.A. brought on his landmark solo debut in 1992. *The Chronic* saw Dre perfect a new hip-hop sound called G-Funk, a slowed down gangsta rap flavored with the laid-back rhythms of George Clinton's P-Funk. "Nothin' But a G Thang" is a perfect example of the G Funk sound, with Dre's fresh beats serving as a perfect vehicle for Snoop Dogg's smooth flow.

"I Will Always Love You" by Whitney Houston: Whitney Houston continued an incredible run with a soul-stirring rendition of a Dolly Parton song. "I Will Always Love You" stands as one of the most incredible vocal performances of Houston's career, and was instrumental in the incredible sales of *The Bodyguard* soundtrack, which would sell an astounding 18 million copies in the United States.

1993

"Rebel Girl"

Bikini Kill

Leftist thought and action have long been the lifeblood of punk rock. From the working-class rage of the Clash to the political satire of the Dead Kennedys to the anticonsumerist ethos of Fugazi, progressivism will be forever tied to punk rock. And yet, for its first two decades, punk remained a deeply sexist scene. Sexual assault was common at punk shows, punk zines would spout sexist phrases and punk's first generations' female-fronted bands never got the credit they were due.

This sexism started in the first wave of punk and continued through the hard-core movement, but by the early '90s, a group of female punk fans decided they'd had enough.

Young women in Washington, D.C. and the Pacific Northwest started to organize their communities. They used homemade zines to spread information to women, created support networks for sexual assault survivors and inclusive spaces for queer women, and they stood up against sexism at shows. Before long, this network of punks had dubbed the movement "Riot Grrrl," and published a manifesto calling for the creation of feminist-focused punk scenes. The author of the Riot Grrrl Manifesto was a punk singer from Portland named

Kathleen Hanna. She first published the manifesto in a zine of her own creation, called *Bikini Kill*.

"Bikini Kill" was more than just a zine, it was also the name of the band that Hanna performed in alongside fellow Riot Grrrls Tobi Vail, Billy Karren and Kathi Wilcox. Bikini Kill first recorded a demo cassette in 1991. They started to tour around the region, distributing their zines at their shows and building momentum for the movement.

By 1993, Riot Grrrls were spawning new chapters in punk communities across the country. That year, Bikini Kill released the signature song of the entire movement, "Rebel Girl."

The sound of "Rebel Girl" is as heavy as any punk song of the era, with a stomping beat by Vail and a chunky guitar line by Karren. Where it differentiates itself is in the carefree, playful vocal delivery by Hanna. This childlike aesthetic was a key cornerstone of the Riot Grrrl movement. Riot Grrrls felt that they had been most liberated when they were children, before they felt the pressures of the male gaze. They called themselves girls as a specific attempt to reclaim that freedom and create joyful spaces free from patriarchal hierarchies.

> For its first two decades, punk remained a deeply sexist scene.

hood. It was a perfect promotion of the sort of girl-girl friendships that Hannah and her ilk hoped to build through their music.

Before the Riot Grrrls hit the scene, most feminist discourse was reserved for the high halls of academia. *Bikini Kill* brought that discourse down to earth, and used it to create the sort of community that so many punk girls had been thirsting for. With "Rebel Girl," Bikini Kill, the band, laid out a blueprint for a sort of woman who would take over in the '90s. They helped kick off third-wave feminism and made sure that women of all sorts would forever be welcome at punk shows across the globe.

This girl aesthetic is key to the lyrical conceit of "Rebel Girl." Hanna opens the song with admiration of another rebellious woman, framed through a youthful lens. It's a deliberate celebration of female solidarity, put in direct contrast to much of the media of the time that sought to pit women against one another. It's also an openly queer song, celebrating lesbian love: "In her kiss, I taste the revolution."

The Riot Grrrls were at the forefront of a radical wave of feminism and queer acceptance that would only gain momentum through the '90s. They never broke through to the mainstream, but their manifesto would turn punk scenes upside down, allowing women to thrive in the decade's later alt rock scenes. "Rebel Girl" is the perfect example of everything that Kathleen Hanna laid out in the Riot Grrrl Manifesto. It's a song full of sheer defiant joy, a pure celebration of the experience of girl-

Honorable Mention

"Protect Ya Neck" by Wu-Tang Clan: One of hip-hop's greatest groups rose from the Staten Island underground in 1992. The genius producer RZA collected the best rappers that borough had to offer and assembled them into a collective the likes of which hip-hop had never seen. "Protect Ya Neck" is a display of the sort of relentless bars that helped Wu-Tang kick off the East Coast renaissance, proving that New York still had plenty to offer even as West Coast rap was taking over.

1994

"Waterfalls"

TLC

Genre categorizations are always ephemeral at best, but none has taken on as many meanings over the years as rhythm and blues. In its conception, rhythm and blues was a rebranding of the segregated "race records" of the early industry. That legacy continued through the decades, as the "rhythm and blues" label was applied to nearly anything created by Black artists that didn't fit neatly into an existing category. As it turns out, that captured a wide spectrum of music, as Black creativity has always been in constant conversation with itself. Rhythm and blues was tied to rock in the '50s and '60s, soul in the '60s and '70s and pop music in the '80s. By 1990, it was taking on yet another new form. This time, it involved blending the pop sounds innovated by such artists as Michael Jackson and Prince with the hip-hop music that was taking the nation by storm. The result was "contemporary R&B," a pop movement that dominated the charts throughout the '90s and spawned a whole generation of hitmakers.

That generation includes some of the biggest names in pop history. Whitney Houston, Mary J. Blige and Janet Jackson all soared to new heights of success, thanks to contemporary R&B, but the biggest cultural impact of the entire scene came at the hands of a girl group called TLC. Made up of Tionne

"T-Boz" Watkins, Lisa "Left-Eye" Lopes and Rozonda "Chilli" Thomas, TLC created a new model for girl groups in the '90s. They smashed sales records and rose to international success while becoming fashion icons and fearlessly shifting their sound throughout the decade. Even more impressive, they did it all as three politically outspoken Black women in America.

This political consciousness was front and center in one of the biggest songs of TLC's career, and one of the defining pop hits of the decade, "Waterfalls." Left-Eye wrote "Waterfalls" alongside Marqueze Etheridge and the legendary Atlanta production team Organized Noize, who helped put Atlanta on the hip-hop map in the '90s. The song is framed as a series of cautionary parables tackling some of the biggest issues of the day. The first verse tells the story of a "lonely mother" who witnesses her son fall into gang life and dies young. The second verse is an empathetic look at a character who gets HIV and then dies of AIDS, made clear by the verse's closing line: "Three letters took him to his final resting place."

By the mid-'90s, the AIDS epidemic had become the leading cause of death for Americans between the ages of 25 and 44. Left deliberately unchecked by the government in the late '80s, it had torn through queer communities before

leaping to the rest of the country, leaving hundreds of thousands of dead in its wake. Despite the stigma around the virus, TLC became champions for HIV awareness. In addition to singing about it on "Waterfalls," they took to pinning condoms to their clothes as a fashion statement to promote safe sex and to make their young fans feel more comfortable talking openly about protection.

TLC's warnings against drugs and unsafe sex are couched in an oblique metaphor: "Don't go chasing waterfalls." The waterfall is a thrilling and beautiful temptation when seen from afar, but the reality is that they are dangerous and getting too close will only bring pain. To send home these darker, cautionary messages, Left-Eye ends the song with a rapped verse about optimism and the joy in life. She wrote the verse after getting out of rehab and realizing the beauty that life had to offer. By ending with such open positivity, she gives the audience a bright hope for the world, even amid the bleak realities of addiction, violence and disease that were gripping the nation.

TLC's uplifting message was paired with a million-dollar music video that saw regular circulation on MTV, helping to make "Waterfalls" a chart topper and an international hit. "Waterfalls" led TLC's sophomore album, *Crazy-SexyCool*, to soar to a diamond certification in the United States, making them the first girl group ever to accomplish such a feat. It was a moment of maturity for a young trio that had risen to fame on carefree fun. With "Waterfalls," TLC were stating that they deserved to be celebrated alongside the likes of Marvin Gaye, Stevie Wonder or Michael Jackson. They also proved the viability of a politically-minded girl group, inspiring such others as the Spice Girls and Destiny's Child, who would dominate the pop world of the late '90s and early 2000s.

"Waterfalls" is one of those truly special pop songs that hit at the exact right time. It spoke to the struggles of the moment while solidifying a new kind of pop sound and capturing the hearts of a generation.

 # Honorable Mentions

"N.Y. State of Mind" by Nas: The East Coast renaissance continued as Nas releases the most impressive debut album in hip-hop history. *Illmatic* is an album full of incredible multisyllabic rhyme schemes and powerful stories about Nas' upbringing in the housing projects of New York. "N.Y. State of Mind" hit with a thunderous New York boom bap, delivering a brilliant autobiographical narrative of street violence and struggle over an ominous, looming bass-and-piano loop.

"Juicy" by The Notorious B.I.G.: Biggie Smalls' debut single displayed his endless cool and laid-back flow to the world. He raps a hopeful rags-to-riches story over a classic funk bassline, celebrating his rise to hip-hop superstardom. Biggie's debut is yet another mark in the oncoming era of New York rap. With his arrival, the stage was set for hip-hop's greatest rivalry, and greatest tragedy.

1995

"You Oughta Know"

Alanis Morissette

In the summer of 1995, a label representative for Madonna's Maverick Records brought a CD into L.A.'s legendary KROQ-FM radio station. Burned onto that CD was one of the purest expressions of jilted rage ever put to tape, Alanis Morissette's "You Oughta Know." The Maverick rep played it for KROQ's music director, Lisa Worden. She was floored. The moment the song ended, she ran the CD over to the broadcast booth and told them to play the song. Four minutes later, the station was flooded with calls from eager listeners, demanding to know more about the song they'd just heard. Overnight, Morissette went from an unknown artist into one of the most celebrated women in the boys' club that is rock n' roll.

To most of the world, the 21-year-old Morissette's jump to stardom seemed completely unheard of, but she herself was already a five-year industry veteran. She'd gotten her start in the industry as a teenager in her native home, Canada, and released a pair of pop records that found success there. But as a teen in the industry, Morissette found herself being controlled and hit on by nearly every man she interacted with. When the labels said she couldn't write her own songs, she decided to drop out of a promising career path and pursue music on her own terms. She moved from Ottawa to Toronto and met producer Glen Ballard. Together, they began work on the album that would become *Jagged Little Pill*.

Jagged Little Pill was the opposite of the corporate-friendly pop that Morissette had cut her teeth on. It was heavy and raw, filled with all the rage and angst that the then teenager could muster. She wrote the album in small, intimate sessions with Ballard, which meant she felt comfortable opening herself up completely. In Morissette and Ballard's most optimistic predictions, they thought the album might sell enough copies to fund a second record. When "You Oughta Know" took off on KROQ, it launched the album to some of the highest record sales in music history. *Jagged Little Pill* went an incredible 16x platinum in the United States, and it has sold more than 25 million copies worldwide. The intimacy of Morissette's

> **In Morissette and Ballard's most optimistic predictions, they thought the album might sell enough copies to fund a second record.**

songwriting was an enormous draw for an alternative generation seeking authenticity in music. It was especially impactful on women, who had seldom seen their pains and struggles depicted so overtly in rock music.

"You Oughta Know" became an anthem for these women, thanks to its candid lyrics and gritty vocal performance. In her young days as a pop star, Morissette had become accustomed to recording dozens of vocal tracks for songs, so when she set out on her own, she decided she would try to cut as few vocal takes as she could. For "You Oughta Know," it only took one. She wailed out her furious vocal performance at 11 p.m. after an entire day in the studio. Her voice is full of emotion, feeling on the verge of cracking at any point, but exploding with power and freedom in the chorus. She rants about an ex-lover, delivering explicit details that made heads turn. The most infamous line is probably "Is she perverted like me? / Would she go down on you in a theater?" But for all the attention that line drew, it's the chorus that really makes the song soar, singing that she's going to remind her ex of the mess that he left. Morissette stands on a rooftop and shouts out the sentiments that everyone keeps inside after breakups.

The music behind Morissette features a vivid bassline played by the Red Hot Chili Peppers' Flea, and rich guitar textures by Dave Navarro. It took the grunge sound that had been exploding out of Seattle, and twisted it up with a spacier industrial sound palette. The result was a perfect realization of the dream of alternative rock.

While *Jagged Little Pill* was tearing

up the airwaves, rock was still a deeply misogynistic field. KROQ-FM had a policy that DJs weren't allowed to play two female-fronted rock songs back to back, and nobody in the industry believed that a woman could truly sell rock records. Morissette proved this entire mentality wrong, as *Jagged Little Pill* spawned hit after hit to become the best-selling rock album of the '90s. Despite this enormity, Morissette's legacy is still underrated decades later. She's often remembered in the context of being a woman in rock, but the reality is that she was one of the most important rock stars of her, or any era, bar none. *Jagged Little Pill* easily outsold even Nirvana's *Nevermind*, putting up numbers comparable to such classic albums as *Led Zeppelin IV*, *Rumours* and even Michael Jackson's *Bad*. With the success afforded to her by these sales, Morissette was able to seize complete control over her career. She spent the rest of the '90s winning awards, astounding critics and selling out arenas around the globe.

Her entire career deserves to be celebrated and remembered, but "You Oughta Know" has a special place in history. It pulled Morissette from relative obscurity and threw her face-first into stardom. It was a passionate and unapologetic piece of music that served up a primal roar loud enough to shatter rock's glass ceiling.

 # Honorable Mentions

"Dear Mama" by 2Pac: 2Pac (a.k.a. Tupac Shakur) showed that for all its rage and bravado, hip-hop can also have a sentimental side. His ode to his mother, legendary activist Afeni Shakur Davis, tugs at the heartstrings and breaks through the toxic masculinity that was so pervasive in hip-hop scenes. It proved that 2Pac was a songwriter truly apart from nearly all of his peers.

"Gangsta's Paradise" by Coolio: The mid-'90s saw hip-hop take over as America's mainstream music. One of the most successful songs of the era was Coolio's "Gangsta's Paradise," which interpolates a Stevie Wonder classic to tell a harrowing tale about the dangers of a gang life that had become glamorized by so many other rappers. It became the best-selling single of the year, and one of the most celebrated rap songs of the entire era.

1996

"Hit 'Em Up"

2Pac

On September 13, 1996, the golden age of hip-hop came to an end with the murder of one of the movement's greatest minds, Tupac Shakur, a.k.a. 2Pac. The story of Shakur and his friend turned rival Biggie Smalls is a tragedy of Shakespearean proportions. It saw communities turn against each other, it saw crucial networks of Black solidarity erode and it culminated in the needless deaths of two of the greatest ever to pick up a mic.

The East-West Coast war that ended up claiming the lives of Shakur and Biggie didn't start with either party. It began with a Bronx rapper named Tim Dog, who released a diss track called "Fuck Compton" in 1991. That song spawned a return volley from Dr. Dre a year later, and rappers on both coasts began to throw their hats into the ring as tensions heated up. In these early days, Shakur was focusing on socially conscious hip-hop, writing verbose raps that drew attention to institutionalized racism, sexism and police brutality. In 1993, he even struck up a friendship with Biggie Smalls, who was a rising star in New York. They performed together onstage, and Biggie asked Shakur to be his manager. This budding friendship could have provided a bridge to unity between the coasts. Instead, it turned sour and escalated the rap wars to a whole new level.

On November 30, 1994, Shakur was in Manhattan, scheduled to record a guest verse with the New York rapper Little Shawn. Shakur and his crew arrived at Manhattan's Quad Studios to record, and members of Biggie's group, Junior M.A.F.I.A., waved down at him from the eighth story of the building. Shakur would never make it up to the studio. When he walked into the ground floor, three men held him up at gunpoint. The robbers stole $35,000 worth of gold from him and shot him five times. Though Tupac survived the shots, he would be forever changed by the incident.

Having seen Junior M.A.F.I.A. in the studio, Shakur believed that Biggie had set him up. Biggie wouldn't get a chance to correct this notion, as Shakur began to serve a prison sentence for sexual assault just two months later. While he was in prison, Biggie released a song called "Who Shot Ya?" Although the song had been recorded before the robbery, Shakur took it as a slight against him. This only increased the paranoia that Shakur had developed from being hounded by police for much of his life.

While he was recovering from his trauma in prison, the East-West rivalry continued to escalate. At the 1995 Source Awards, Suge Knight, the executive behind Compton's Death Row Records, called out New York's Puff

Daddy, and Dr. Dre and Snoop Dogg called out the crowd. A few months later, Knight paid Shakur's $1.4 million bail, and Shakur signed with Death Row. Freshly out of prison, Shakur went on to record the biggest diss track of the entire East-West era, "Hit 'Em Up."

Released on June 4, 1996, "Hit 'Em Up" was a caustic attack on Biggie and the whole East Coast scene. Shakur and his crew spat five minutes of sheer vitriol, calling out Biggie, Lil' Kim, Mobb Deep and more by name, while lacing his bars with violent rhymes. Shakur specifically references his robbery, saying that five shots couldn't bring him down. He goes on to threaten his enemies with an AK and declare himself as a thug that "you love to hate." It was a blatant and outright call to arms; a pivot from Shakur's social conscious music

into the violent gangsta rap of Death Row Records. Shakur paired this attack with a video featuring parodies of Biggie, Lil' Kim and Puff Daddy, the executive behind Biggie's Bad Boy Records.

"Hit 'Em Up" was one of the hardest, most ruthless records in hip-hop history. Shakur pulled no punches, setting a new standard for what hip-hop diss tracks could be. It was deeply personal, with Shakur claiming to have slept with Biggie's wife and issuing direct threats to members of the New York scene. This caught the attention of the East Coast, and spawned responses from Mobb Deep and Lil' Kim. Biggie included an off-handed line taking a shot at Shakur on Jay-Z's "Brooklyn's Finest," but never wrote a full response.

The East-West rivalry might have continued to escalate in the hands of Shakur and Death Row, but three months after Shakur released "Hit 'Em Up," he was killed in a drive-by shooting in Las Vegas: The night of September 7, 1996, he was in a car being driven by Suge Knight, when a shooter pulled up alongside the vehicle and fired a number of shots into the car. Four bullets hit Shakur, including one that punctured his right lung. He was rushed to the hospital, where he was put into a medically induced coma, before dying a week later. To this day, the identity of Shakur's murderer remains the subject of conspiracy theories, with many trying to link Biggie Smalls to the murder. The most probable explanation has nothing to do with the East-West violence, but rather with the gang violence in L.A. That theory states that Shakur's murder was at the hands of the South Side Compton Crips, who'd had a run-in with Shakur earlier that night.

Regardless of who committed the murder, Shakur's death came as a stark wake-up call for the feuding hip-hop scenes. One of the greatest talents in rap history had been stolen from the world at just 25 years of age. Over the course of the East-West war, the rap community watched one of its most sensitive, politically active voices descend into paranoia and ruin, thanks to a volatile territorial beef. Even so, the later output of Shakur's career remains some of the finest rap music ever made. His 1996 album *All Eyes On Me* is one of the most celebrated and best-selling records in hip-hop history.

"Hit 'Em Up" is a song with a difficult legacy that's representative of one of hip-hop's most complicated legacies. On the one hand, it is a lyrical triumph from one of the greatest rappers ever to live. It's the perfect execution of the diss track, a song archetype that is key to the formation of hip-hop. At the same time, it's a turning point in the most tragic chapter of music history. It is a song whose very existence begs the question "Could things have been different?"

Honorable Mentions

"Santeria" by Sublime: Sublime were leaders in a movement combining Jamaican ska with a new pop punk sound in the mid-'90s. One of their greatest outputs was "Santeria," a pure stoner classic with some of the grooviest guitars the '90s had to offer.

"Macarena" (Bayside Boys Remix) by Los del Rio: A new dance craze swept across the nation as Miami's Bayside Boys remixed a Latin pop tune and added English-language lyrics. While "Macarena" is a novelty hit, it marked an example of Latin pop's slow creep toward mainstream acceptance.

1997

"Hypnotize"

Biggie Smalls

Following the death of Tupac Shakur, the Black nationalist and Nation of Islam leader Louis Farrakhan held a peace summit in hopes of reconciling the East-West rivalry and putting an end to the increasing violence in hip-hop. Just a few months later, in February 1997, Snoop Dogg and Puff Daddy held a press conference calling for a public truce to end the violence. Hope seemed on the horizon for a community still in mourning. But less than a month after that public truce, Biggie Smalls was gunned down in a drive-by shooting. All of the calls for peace and friendship were for naught. In the end, the only thing that put a stop to hip-hop's most infamous feud was the death of both of its greatest figureheads.

Just like Shakur, the true circumstances of Biggie's death remain unknown. One theory claims that Suge Knight conspired with corrupt LAPD officers to kill Biggie as revenge, believing that he had played a role in Shakur's murder. Other theories have claimed that record companies conspired to kill Biggie, thinking he was worth more dead than alive. Whatever the case, his death was an enormous loss that still looms over the rap community to this day.

The last song that Biggie released was "Hypnotize," the lead single off his eerily named upcoming album *Life After Death*. "Hypnotize" dropped on March 4, 1997, four days before he was killed. "Hypnotize" is a fitting final testament, as it exemplifies everything his music strove for and displays his unparalleled rhymes and flow. It's not a song playing up any rivalry with the West Coast rappers, but rather a celebration of Biggie's own wealth, style and talent. He specifically raps about his approach to the beef that was plaguing hip-hop: "Poppa been smooth since the days of underoos / Never lose, never choose to, bruise crews who / Do somethin' to us, talk go through us." Biggie is claiming that he wins his feuds by not stooping to diss tracks, and instead just by dropping fire tracks and celebrating the joys in life. He backs up this ethos with some of the most tongue-twisting rhymes of his career, squeezing a half dozen internal rhymes into a scant few bars: "So I just speak my piece / Keep my peace / Cubans with the Jesus piece / With my peeps."

> . . . Snoop Dogg and Puff Daddy held a press conference calling for a public truce to end the violence.

Biggie's laid-back flow bounces over a beat that samples Herb Alpert's 1979 jazz-funk hit "Rise." It's one of the smoothest beats of the era, with a thick, grooving bassline powering through the song. For all the rivalry between the East and West Coasts, "Hypnotize" is living proof of the cross-cultural exchange happening in hip-hop as well. Although few would admit it, the song clearly has influence from the laid-back, California G-Funk sound that Dr. Dre invented in the early '90s. In fact, Alpert's nephew had been approached by both Eazy E and Ice Cube to sample "Rise" before but he turned them down. Of course, the New York rap history still lives on in "Hypnotize," with a chorus interpolating lines from Slick Rick's "La Di Da Di," one of the defining tracks of old-school hip-hop.

By looking past the feuds and combining East and West, Biggie was on the forefront of ushering in the next era of hip-hop. Although he wouldn't live to see it, his influence loomed large over the late '90s and early 2000s, as rap entered its so-called bling era. This period was defined by commercial success, with rap artists taking over the mainstream and riding to new levels of fame and fortune. They did so by eschewing the more violent and less commercial gangsta lyrics, opting to rap about money and fashion. "Hypnotize" is loaded with braggadocious bars about Biggie's own wealth. This celebration of excess is paired with a music video that's equally over-the-top. In it, Biggie and Puff Daddy escape pursuit from the police in a yacht, and then in his convertible BMW M3. In the end, they're able to escape and land at an opulent party.

This aspirational wealth and Biggie's effortless cool propelled "Hypnotize" to the top of Billboard's charts, a feat accomplished by only a handful of rap songs before. In the wake of his murder, *Life After Death* also soared to the top of the Billboard album charts and would go on to sell more than five million copies. Rap music had first crossed over to the mainstream in the early '90s, but thanks to Biggie's influence, it would completely take over by the end of the decade. Puff Daddy, who rose to fame alongside Biggie, became the most successful executive in hip-hop history, and Biggie's friend and collaborator Jay-Z became a household name.

Although Biggie barely took part in the East-West hip-hop feud, he became the face of East Coast hip-hop, and ended up losing his life for it. His legacy will forever be tied to Shakur thanks to their friendship, rivalry and tragically similar fates. Despite dying at just 24 years old and only ever able to release two studio albums, Biggie Smalls left behind a legacy as one of the most important, and greatest, rappers of all time.

Honorable Mentions

"Everybody (Backstreet's Back)" by the Backstreet Boys: The lead single of the Backstreet Boys' sophomore album delivered a perfect dance-pop groove, and the boy-band craze seized the nation's youth.

"On & On" by Erykah Badu: Erykah Badu was on the forefront of the latest progression of soul, a '90s sound that pulls from the classic soul sounds of the '70s, but combines it with a more futuristic sound. Electronic sound palettes and hip-hop beats provided a bed for Badu's mellow voice, tinged with shades of the jazz greats of old.

1998

". . . Baby One More Time"

Britney Spears

On September 28, 1998, Britney Spears gave the world a sneak preview of what pop would look like in the new millennium with her debut single, ". . . Baby One More Time." Pop music was then dominated by girl groups, boy bands and glamorous divas performing vocal acrobatics. In fact, Spears almost joined a girl group called Innosense, who were modeled after 'NSYNC and the Backstreet Boys. But when Spears delivered a vocal demo, Jive Records saw her potential as a solo act. They put her in touch with a vocal coach for a month of vocal development before sending her off to Stockholm to work with Max Martin, a producer and songwriter whose star was rising, thanks to his work with the Backstreet Boys.

Martin wrote the song from the melody out, working with fellow producer Rami Yacoub to create a contemporary R&B sound built around a drum machine rhythm, a groovy slapped bass, and funky wah-wah guitar accents. For the lyrics, Martin put himself into the headspace of a teenage girl. He imagined himself pining after a boy that got away. This leads to the desperate call of the chorus: "Hit me baby one more time."

Martin's intention was to tap into youthful slang with something akin to "hit me up." But the Swedish producer was still working on his English, so he ended up writing something a little off-kilter and strange. American executives tried to convince him to change the lyric, but he wouldn't budge. When he offered the song to TLC, they turned it down because of that chorus. Martin offered it to Robyn, who said no as well, so it wound up in the hands of Spears.

Although she was only 17 at the time, Spears had a clear vision for her interpretation of the song. She wanted her vocals to sound like Soft Cell's 1981 new-wave take on "Tainted Love." To achieve this breathy, worn-out feel, Spears decided to stay up late the night before the recording session. This vocal decision pays dividends in the opening moments of the song, when she moans out a now iconic "Oh baby, baby." Her voice is low and nasal, teetering on the verge of raspy. It's a far cry from the powerful pop divas of the era, but no less impressive. Throughout the rest of the song, she announces herself to the world as a confident pop star with a talent and independence beyond her years.

> Spears almost joined a girl group called Innosense, who were modeled after 'NSYNC and the Backstreet Boys.

Spears' vision extended to the music video for ". . . Baby One More Time." She pitched the high school aesthetic to director Nigel Dick, and even dreamed up the controversial Catholic school girl outfit that she wears in the video. Spears wanted to create something true to her own experience as a teen. She wanted something fun, and a little over the top, and Dick helped her see that vision through. But when ". . . Baby One More Time" started to enter circulation on MTV, it caused a wild stir. Parent groups took issue with the fact that Spears' midriff was shown when she was dancing, fearing that her overt sexuality would corrupt their children. But some saw her sexuality as an empowering one, following in the footsteps of greats like Madonna.

Spears' brand of adolescent empowerment made her a teen icon overnight. ". . . Baby One More Time" raced to the top of the charts and would go on to become one of the best-selling singles of all time. She shattered the pop trends of the era and captured the eyes of a nation—for better and for worse. As she soared to success, Spears became the target of attacks from all angles. Rockers and rappers started to use her as a stand-in for the entire corporate pop world, paparazzi started to flock to her and some conservative conspiracy theorists even claimed that, when played backward, the phrase "sleep with me, I'm not too young" could be heard in the lyrics. Britney Spears represented a kind of empowered sexuality that terrified the old and inspired the young.

Within months of dropping ". . . Baby One More Time," Spears had become the biggest pop star on earth. Over the next few years, she followed it up with hit after hit and became one of the defining cultural figures of her era. Her elaborate, campy music videos set a standard that would be followed by the next wave of pop stars, inspiring acts like Katy Perry, Ariana Grande and Taylor Swift, all of whom would follow in her footsteps and collaborate with Max Martin. A generation after Michael Jackson and Madonna had been

crowned King and Queen of Pop, Spears picked up the torch and earned the title "Princess of Pop." Unfortunately, such titles always come with baggage. The public's treatment of Spears wreaked havoc on her mental health, and eventually led to her being put into an abusive conservatorship. However, she has cemented herself as an empowerment icon once more in recent years, sharing her story and fighting publicly for her own independence.

 # Honorable Mentions

"Doo Wop (That Thing)" by Lauryn Hill: Lauryn Hill's debut album, *The Miseducation of Lauryn Hill*, saw her break off from previous success with Fugees to produce the definitive album of the neo-soul revival. Her rich mélange of hip-hop, rhythm and blues and soul provided a perfect vehicle for messages about equality of the sexes. "Doo Wop" became the first song by a female rapper to top the Hot 100, and it won one of *Miseducation*'s record-setting eight Grammys. It seemed to be an announcement of a new solo star, but Hill's battles with her label ended up collapsing her career before it could take off.

"Hard Knock Life (Ghetto Anthem)" by Jay-Z: As the hip-hop wars came to an end in tragedy, Jay-Z rose up to become the new king of New York rap. "Hard Knock Life" represents a new direction of hip-hop sampling, turning away from soul samples in favor of an unlikely clip from the Broadway musical *Annie*. Jay-Z uses this strange sample to deliver a cocky rap about his own street upbringing.

1999

"My Name Is"

Eminem

The first two decades of rap's recorded history were populated with a smattering of white rappers. Blondie's Debbie Harry rapped on 1981's "Rapture" when the genre was still in its infancy. A few years later, the Beastie Boys brought the worlds of rock and hip-hop together alongside producer Rick Rubin. When rap went pop in the early '90s, one-hit wonders like Vanilla Ice and Snow both scored charting hits. These white rappers saw varying levels of success in the mainstream, but none of them displayed the technical abilities of their Black contemporaries, and few gained any respect in the hip-hop scene. So, when a white rapper calling himself Eminem appeared on Detroit's battle rap scene, people refused to take him seriously.

Even as Eminem's songwriting and rapping skills improved, nobody would give him the time of day. He dropped an independently produced EP, and then an album, to little fanfare, and began to get desperate. By this point, Eminem was approaching his mid-20s and still living with his mother. He could barely put food on the table for his daughter. In a last-ditch effort to try to make something of himself, he decided to switch up his rap style. He started to perform as a twisted alter ego named Slim Shady. This new persona was a reckless and dark id, channeling the most brutal, violent parts of Eminem's

spirit. He rapped overtly about murder, sexism, homophobia and any other urge that had to be hidden from mainstream society. Slim Shady was a strange and pained lash at a world that had beaten Eminem down to a pulp.

In a bizarre turn, that world started to respond.

The Slim Shady character intrigued the Detroit scene, which had never heard such brash and vicious bars. Suddenly, people began to appreciate Eminem's incredible rhyming talent and brilliant delivery. He recorded an EP as Slim Shady, and that cassette tape began to circulate around the underground scene. After an event in Los Angeles, that tape landed in the hands of record executive Jimmy Iovine, who passed it on to Dr. Dre.

Although Dre had firmly established himself as a hip-hop legend by this time, his career faltered in the late '90s. The decline of gangsta rap had left him on the sidelines as hip-hop was taking over the mainstream. When he listened to *The Slim Shady EP*, he heard the future of rap, and realized that Eminem could be his ticket back into relevancy. He brought Eminem into the studio, and the two had instant chemistry. Within their first hour of working together, they cut the song that would introduce the world to Eminem and Slim Shady: "My Name Is."

Eminem's lyrical schemes in "My Name Is" are acrobatic and verbose. From the opening moments, he asks, "Hi kids, do you like violence?" and follows through with vitriolic bars full of homophobia, sexism, references to drugs and basically any other taboo you can think of. It's an expression of the hatred that lingers in the darkest corners of everyone's mind, but also a satire of a post-gangsta rap world that had seen more and more rappers making wild boasts of imagined violent acts. Eminem weaves together surreal verses that jump between raw confession and dark, pop-culture laden humor.

Unsurprisingly, Eminem's lyrics went through several rounds of censorship. First, Labi Siffre, a gay activist and blues guitarist who wrote the main sam-ple used in "My Name Is," requested that homophobic lyrics be changed before he cleared the sample. After that, more extreme lines were changed for a clean version of the song that could get airplay on radio and MTV. Even after censorship, the song remained more extreme than anything most people had ever heard. Naturally, this immediately attracted millions of rebellious teens, and terrified nearly as many parents. "My Name Is" rode a wave of controversy into the mainstream, and even managed to crack Billboard's Top 40.

The success of "My Name Is" launched Eminem into fame, but before long, he began to resent the song. As a piece written in just a few spontaneous minutes, he didn't feel it was representa-tive of the sort of careful songcraft that he was capable of. Many who loved the track seemed to miss the satirical points and sincerely embrace Eminem's alter ego. Before the year was out, he would be openly trying to combat the wild Slim Shady mania that he had inspired.

As the twentieth century drew to a close, Eminem became the herald for a new era of rap. Legions of white fans flocked to him, bleaching their hair to look like him, copying his fashion style and trying their own hand at his fast-paced, rhyme-dense rap style. Few among them would gain much respect in rap's original Black communities, but

Eminem, himself, was welcomed into the fold. His major-label debut, *The Slim Shady LP* proved that he was more than just a gimmick. A year later, he would drop *The Marshall Mathers LP* and display that he truly deserved to be recognized as one of the greats of the genre.

 # Honorable Mentions

"No Scrubs" by TLC: TLC continued their reign as pop queens with one of their most lasting songs. "No Scrubs" inspired their audience of young women to raise their dating standards and ask for more out of their men. It brought the term "scrub" into common usage, and the song lives on to this day as one of the greatest songs of the girl group era.

"Believe" by Cher: Cher became a pioneer in the use of brand-new Auto-Tune technology with an inspirational dance-pop song. "Believe" was an international smash hit, bringing on a career renaissance for an artist who had been going since the 1960s. Its success kicked the pop world into a craze of distorted, Auto-Tune vocals, providing a new computerized sound for the oncoming digital age.

AT ERA'S END

2000–09

For nearly half a century, rock music reigned supreme. After being the voice of the baby boomer generation, it managed to fend off disco, go head to head with the enormity of '80s pop and reinvent itself for Generation X in the '90s. But all empires must fall eventually. By the late '90s, it was clear that the world was tiring of the era's stale, corporate postgrunge. At the same time, visionary producers were taking hip-hop beats beyond the golden age's funk samples, starting to cross over and collaborate with pop artists. Slowly but surely, more rap songs started to appear on the charts. Hip-hop didn't happen at the same torrid pace as original rock n' roll or disco, but by the early 2000s it was clear that rock music had a challenger to its mainstream throne.

The last bastions of rock's mainstream popularity were rooted in punk and metal. A garage rock scene that combined traditional blues and rock n' roll with a punk edge delivered some of the last universal rock anthems. Nü-metal fused rock together with hip-hop to create some of the loudest, oddest music of the era. Pop punk and emo captured

2000

2001

2002

2003

2004

teenage millennials, speaking openly about mental illness and serving as the loudest voices protesting America's war on terror.

This protest movement galvanized some, but for many in America, the trauma of 9/11 brought on a new era of paranoid patriotism. Nashville's song factory fired on all cylinders in support of war, star-spangling their music videos and blacklisting any in their number who disagreed.

The social consciousness of hip-hop continued in the underground, but the mainstream was dominated by an unquenchable thirst for wealth. Hip-hop was finally able to deliver the American Dream of upward mobility to Black communities that had been previously denied wealth for generations. The response was a bling era that celebrated hip-hop's arrival at the top with expensive cars, glamorous jewelry and a celebratory air of opulence. Together with a pop-driven rhythm and blues, the bling era brought Black culture into the spotlight. There was no shortage of white stars operating in these modes, but unlike the history of swing, rock and disco, this time white artists operated next to Black artists. The days of cultural artistic theft were beginning to wane.

As this shift was happening in the mainstream, technology was dismantling the industry's era of financial growth. File-sharing software emerged and brought with it a wave of online piracy that terrified music execs and had millionaire rock stars trying to turn on their fans. Listeners benefited from these new networks of distribution, but artists might have benefited even more. Personal computing allowed people to produce music in their bedroom for the first time. This eroded the power of studios and labels, who had previously owned all of music's means of production. While they were able to adapt and keep hold of their wealth, the record industry would never again reach the heights of power or monetization that it had at the turn of the millennium.

The 2000s were a transitory period in music history. The first half was a continuation of many of the legacies of the '90s, but the second half had yet to solidify into the social-media, tech-driven era of the 2010s. MTV shifted away from music videos and toward reality TV, while *American Idol* delivered a new sort of promise to aspiring musicians across the country. The MP3 was rising to unseat the CD, as the age of the iPod began. Above all else, the era saw the birth of the modern internet, and the world watched in awe as it began to understand the true power of viral media.

2005

2006

2007

2008

2009

2000

"B.O.B."

Outkast

Most of the attention of the '90s hip-hop scene was focused on the rivalry between the East and West Coasts, but the entire time that war was raging, another scene was fermenting in a smoke-filled basement in the South. A loose collective of Atlanta artists known as the Dungeon Family spent the decade establishing their city as a hip-hop hotbed. The most important act to come out of the Dungeon Family were two rappers named Big Boi and André 3000, together known as Outkast. Throughout the mid- to late-'90s, Outkast released a trilogy of albums that could go blow for blow with New York or L.A.'s finest. When the millennium turned, they decided to outdo themselves. On Halloween Night 2000, Outkast dropped *Stankonia*, an album that completely disintegrated the genre boundaries stifling hip-hop. The lead single was "B.O.B.," a frenetic piece of music that captured the terrifying pace of the twenty-first century and proved an eerie predictor of things to come.

Like all of *Stankonia*, "B.O.B." was born out of long hours experimenting in studio. Two years before the album's release, Outkast had bought a studio that once belonged to rhythm and blues great Bobby Brown. No longer needing to worry about renting studio time, Outkast could spend all day tweaking songs and playing around until every-

thing sounded just right. Most of the recording sessions involved their inviting local musicians into the studio to throw around ideas and try new things.

At the time, Outkast were concerned that hip-hop was beginning to go stale. As the genre became commercially viable, the corporate music world was starting to take over. Big Boi and André were getting sick of seeing artists drop uninspired bars followed by easy hooks. They tried to break that trend by making an album that pulled together disparate sounds from across the music world and used them to say something about the times they were living in. In the case of "B.O.B.," that meant throwing a psychedelic organ line over a breakneck drum n' bass drumbeat, and tying it all together with salient lyricism inspired by the punk rap of Rage Against the Machine. On top of that, André and Big Boi rap with an accelerated version of the southern flows that made them famous. Those flows are heavily syncopated, loaded with complex internal rhyme schemes and lyrics that bounce back and forth between a victory lap celebration and an existential reflection on a changing world.

In André's verse, he contrasts the freedom allowed by the new millennium with the heavy consequences hitting marginalized communities, declaring that they are forced to face consequenc-

es just for living. Big Boi spits quick bars about Outkast's rags-to-riches success story, and challenges ghettoized youth to find hope in it, encouraging them to make a business for themselves, and to turn coal into diamonds. Outkast were particularly worried about the patterns of drug abuse and gang violence that they saw taking hold of lower-class youths. The glamorization of the gangsta lifestyle, along with new waves of such street drugs as meth and ecstasy, were continuing to ravage Black communities. In the early days, Big Boi and André had been heavy drug users themselves, but André decided to get sober as Outkast took off, and he found his creativity flourish for it.

The chorus of "B.O.B.," which shouts, "Bombs over Baghdad!" wasn't meant to be political. It was just a phrase André heard on the news one night and liked the sound of. But a few years after the song's release, it would take on a new meaning as America invaded Iraq in a war that would define the decade. Outkast would speak publicly against that war as "B.O.B." became a protest anthem of the era.

"B.O.B." might have predicted the future and explored new territories in rap, but upon release it disappointed. The song's frenzied energy proved a little too much for the mainstream, and the song failed to crack the Top 40. Among hip-hop heads, however, it was a game changer. "B.O.B." encouraged people to break the rules of the genre and displayed a production ethos that would take control of rap in the 2000s.

It wouldn't be long before the commercial success came. Outkast's next single, "Ms. Jackson," hit number one and became one of the most beloved rap songs ever recorded. *Stankonia* soared to a 5x platinum rating, with its diverse mixture of sounds pulling in audiences that might otherwise have ignored hip-hop.

The 2000s were a moment of immense change. The information age was about to launch into full swing, and the world raced forward at a seemingly impossible pace. With "B.O.B.," Outkast were able to capture the exciting uncertainty of the time and ensure that hip-hop would continue to be one of the most dynamic music scenes on earth in the new millennium.

 # Honorable Mentions

"Stan" by Eminem: Eminem's meteoric rise inspired a legion of bleached-blond fans trying to imitate Eminem's look and music. In "Stan," he tells a story that explores the dark side of obsessive music fandom. The song's verses are epistolary, written as letters from a fan named Stan to Eminem as he spirals out and murders his girlfriend, inspired by Eminem's violent lyrics. In the final verse, Eminem writes back as himself, but the letter arrives too late. "Stan" is a harrowing narrative born from Eminem's twisted mind and shows how uncomfortable he was with his enormous fame.

"Bye Bye Bye" by 'NSYNC: 'NSYNC delivered one of the last hits of the boy band era that started in the '90s with "Bye Bye Bye," a futuristic rhythm and blues breakup song, with lyrics that may also serve as a subtle reference to their parting ways with manager Lou Pearlman. It wouldn't be long before 'NSYNC were saying "Bye bye bye" to one another, as the world turned away from boy bands and toward solo pop acts.

2001

"Get Ur Freak On"

Missy Elliott

Rap music has always been a boys' club. It's not that there have been no female MCs—each era of rap history has been dotted with powerful women, but all of them had to break through rampant misogyny on their way to success. Rap lyrics were frequently loaded with sexist turns of phrase and hypermasculine boasts of bravado. Meanwhile, rap videos were famous for only giving women roles as scantily clad dancers. For the few women who were able to break through this deep-seated chauvinism, the price of entry was often an overt self-sexualization. All of that began to change when Missy Elliott hit the scene in the late '90s.

Elliott was already an industry veteran when she hit the scene as a solo act. In her early 20s, she had been part of a girl group that was abandoned by their label and disintegrated. From there, she developed her career on the other side of the booth, working with her friend Timbaland as part of a production-songwriting duo. They wrote hits for the rhythm and blues superstar Aaliyah. These songs often contained backing vocals or rap interludes by Elliott, where she would display her brilliant gift with words. The hype of these tracks convinced Elliott to take another crack at putting herself center stage.

The late '90s were seeing women across the industry prove themselves as critically successful and commercially viable auteurs, but nearly all of them shared something that Elliott didn't: They were skinny. In a world that had a deeply unhealthy fascination with body image, bigger women like Elliott were a rare sight on TV, and an even rarer sight headlining shows and selling records. There was an intense pressure on and scrutiny of women in the industry, telling them to conform to a male gaze and sexualize themselves. Missy Elliott refused to. On her 1997 debut *Supa Dupa Fly*, she sculpted an image of herself free from these demands. Elliott used exaggerated humor, wicked clever bars and an elaborate futuristic style to make her mark. And it worked. Over the course of the '90s, her style made her a queen and role model to the hip-hop world. Her ethos of individualism and self-confidence was still going strong in 2001 when she released one of the defining hits of her career, "Get Ur Freak On."

"Get Ur Freak On" is an anthemic celebration of individuality. Its chorus is a call to oddballs and outcasts of all varieties to step forth and party in their own way. This message is underlined by a truly unique Timbaland beat that pulls

from bhangra, an Indian dance music. While this beat was unlike anything else on the radio, it wasn't out of Timbaland's wheelhouse.

Timbaland was one of the most eclectic producers of his day, and one of the leaders in a new style of beat making. A series of copyright cases had spelled the end of the golden age of sampling in the '90s, but new technologies also meant that producers had more tools than ever to work with. This spawned a new production approach, led by auteurs like Just Blaze, Kanye West, J Dilla and Timbaland. Timbaland's style was a combination of contemporary R&B and hip-hop. He was fond of using strange, electronic sounds and pulling sounds from musical traditions that existed outside of Western pop. As Missy Elliott's star rose, Timbaland got more chances to

display his eclectic beat making. Together, the duo represented a new version of the DJ/MC combo that had existed since the beginning of hip-hop. Their sounds were bizarre but completely accessible, a perfect fit for the new world of pop rap.

Missy Elliott's distinct sounds always paired with visual aesthetics that were just as much of a statement. She was an artist with a clear vision for how her videos should look, and she pursued fruitful collaborations with directors to realize these visions. In the early days, she partnered with Hype Williams to create a series of Afrofuturistic pieces. When she released "Get Ur Freak On," Elliott wanted to change things up, so she partnered with director Dave Meyer for a new style of video. "Get Ur Freak On" is almost postapocalyptic, with Elliott and a crew of dancers busting out moves in strange, overgrown sewers while the video uses digital effects to morph people together. Dancers are painted in sickly grays. They hang from the ceiling and contort their bodies while Elliott and a dance crew break out more typical hip-hop moves. The whole video is a collision of glam and horror. It's surreal, strange and unquestionably freaky.

In an industry dominated by men, Missy Elliott defied everyone to carve her own path. Together with Timbaland, she was able to push an experimental approach to music while still finding chart success. The duo was among the leaders of a new era of hip-hop, one that saw rappers stepping forth to sing, and producers taking advantage of digital technology to sculpt inventive beats. Her brilliant energy and positive lyricism in "Get Ur Freak On" helped inspire a generation of rappers and paved the way for such women as Nicki Minaj, Cardi B and Lizzo to take over hip-hop.

> In a world that had a deeply unhealthy fascination with body image, bigger women like Elliott were . . . an even rarer sight headlining shows and selling records.

 # Honorable Mention

"The Middle" by Jimmy Eat World: Jimmy Eat World scored one of the early hits of an emo-pop movement that would come to be the defining music of millennial adolescence. "The Middle" is an empathetic song, advising their teen audience to ignore peer pressures and live an authentic life. It became a Top 10 pop hit and lives on as a staple of alt-rock radio.

2002

"Cry Me a River"

Justin Timberlake

The 2000s were a golden era for pop music. Two decades after Michael Jackson, Prince and Madonna defined the modern iteration of pop, the genre had grown bigger than ever. Pop had welcomed hip-hop into the fold, injecting a new spirit of experimentation, and the pop stars of the '90s who got their start in the corporate world were setting out on their own with creative freedom and ambitious artistic goals. One of these artists was Justin Timberlake, whose 2002 hit "Cry Me a River" is undoubtedly one of the strangest, most brilliant songs ever to crack the American Top 10.

With the context of Timberlake's career success, "Cry Me a River" seems like a natural hit, but if you take the song in a vacuum, it is exceedingly weird. The beat was created by Timbaland, who dialed up his experimentation after his success with Missy Elliott. It opens with clips of Gregorian chant while he and cowriter Scott Storch drop a dissonant minor melody on layers of synth and keyboard. When the beat hits, we get a beatboxed torrent of mouth clicks that barrage the listener's ears from alternating sides of the stereo

> "Cry Me a River" is undoubtedly one of the strangest, most brilliant songs ever to crack the American Top 10.

mix. As the song progresses, this odd beat builds with dramatic string lines and tiny vocal interjections. The result of this cacophony is something dark and ethereal, a sound that underlines the psychosexual drama of Timberlake's breakup lyrics.

Timberlake wrote "Cry Me a River" after the end of a three-year relationship with Britney Spears, which had been the single most publicized relationship in an era defined by rampant paparazzi and celebrity culture. Spears was the Princess of Pop, and Timberlake was one of the most beloved figures of the boy band craze. His group, 'NSYNC, had seen a run of four consecutive multi-platinum albums between 1997 and 2001. But when Spears found enormous success as a solo act, the writing was on the wall for boy bands and girl groups. In 2002, the band decided to take a hiatus and pursue solo projects. That same year, Timberlake's relationship with Spears came to a messy end, with him levying accusations of infidelity at Spears. Following the breakup, he went to a Spears concert and heard her talking about him onstage. Feeling upset and betrayed, he

called Spears afterward and the two had a heated phone conversation that inspired the lyrics to "Cry Me a River."

Throughout the song, Timberlake spits his accusations at Spears in a vitriolic falsetto, declaring that he already found out about her infidelities from her lover. His own hurt and pain makes it into the song, but it's shrouded in brutal anger. All of these emotions are delivered with some of the catchiest melodic hooks of the era. In the prechorus, Timberlake lands his clearest blow by saying that the bridges are already burned and it's her turn to cry.

Timberlake's song was fodder for a press that fed on drama. Celebrity magazines ate up all the gossip they could find as the breakup dominated the news cycle. He fed this fire when he released the moody video for "Cry Me a River." In it, he breaks into an elaborate mansion, goes through the owner's things and films a sex tape in their bed. Once his lover has left, the homeowner comes home, played by a Britney Spears lookalike. Timberlake stalks behind her and

spies on her as she undresses for a shower, before leaving with the sex tape he shot playing on her TV.

The twisted psychodrama of the "Cry Me a River" video made it the talk of the music world. It won acclaim at the MTV Video Music Awards and drew public comment from Spears, who declared it little more than a publicity stunt. If that was the case, it worked. "Cry Me a River" hit number three on Billboard's charts and proved to the world that Timberlake was a bona fide star on his own. But even more important than that, "Cry Me a River" was a declaration that the pop world was ready to enter an era of dark confessionalism and raw sexuality. Pop stars, who had long been made fun of in the press and had their music dismissed by rock elitists, were ready to step forth and display that their work had just as much depth and vision as any rock song and were just as deserving of the critical and academic lens.

Honorable Mentions

"Courtesy of the Red, White and Blue (The Angry American)" by Toby Keith: After the 9/11 attacks shocked America and mobilized them into war, a wave of patriotic music started to dominate country radio. One of the most jingoistic of these songs is "Courtesy of the Red, White and Blue." Toby Keith's country rock song was a call to war, laden with archetypal images of American patriotism.

"A Moment Like This" by Kelly Clarkson: The first season of *American Idol* was an absolute sensation, helping push America into a new era of reality television. After winning the season, Kelly Clarkson topped charts with her inaugural single, "A Moment Like This," and launched herself into a career as one of the biggest pop divas of the 2000s.

2003

"Seven Nation Army"

The White Stripes

In January 2002, while messing around in a warm-up before a show in Melbourne, an eclectic guitarist named Jack White wrote rock n' roll's last universal anthem. "Seven Nation Army" is undoubtedly the White Stripes' signature song, but it's transcended far beyond that in the two decades since its release. Today, it is one of the most ubiquitous melodies in all of music. It's a stadium anthem sung the world round, and a piece of the collective cultural heritage of the entire planet.

As is often the case with songs that reach such a pinnacle, the people around Jack White thought little of the riff when he first wrote it. He showed it to an employee who shrugged it off as "okay" and went on with his day. In defense of that employee, even White himself failed to see the full potential of his ominous blues riff. In his most optimistic vision, he believed that it could serve well as a James Bond theme if he were ever called upon to write one. He tucked the riff away in his back pocket while he finished off his tour. It resurfaced a few months later, when the White Stripes went into the studio to record their fourth studio album, *Elephant*.

By that point, the riff had evolved into a proper song. White used a pedal effect to drop the riff an octave, making it sound more like a bass. He added on a simple but powerful second phrase, made up of an intense run of ascending power chords. White deliberately wrote the song without a proper chorus, relying on the guitar riff played at a higher pitch to serve in its place. The result is a repetitive song, a hypnotic ongoing build that grows through Meg White's drumbeat. Those drums start with a booming kick drum and grow through tom hits, a crisp snare and crashing cymbals.

Jack White wrote the title of "Seven Nation Army" before he had any lyrics, giving the riff a name so he could easily talk and think about it while developing the song. The phrase "seven nation army" came from his childhood, when he thought that was the name of the Salvation Army. It was a fit for the dark, almost militaristic precision of the riff, underlined by Meg White's wicked snare hits. The phrase might also have been inspired by the fact that the riff consists of a repeating seven-note pattern.

When the White Stripes released *Elephant* in 2003, their star was on the rise. Their third album, 2001's *White Blood Cells*, broke them out of Detroit's underground and introduced them to the mainstream. They became leaders in a new movement of independent garage rock artists erupting across America. This movement was a response to the corporate overproduction that seized

rock music in the late '90s. They emphasized raw, simple sounds, inspired by the original rock n' roll greats of the '50s and the punk music of the '70s and '80s. Its sound was also a throwback—the entirety of *Elephant* was recorded analog at a time when digital technology was taking over the industry.

The minimalist approach of these garage rockers was paired with carefully thought-out aesthetics. In the case of the White Stripes, this manifested through a strict palette of red, white and black that they used in their live performances and videos. This striking color scheme helped the White Stripes stand out in the crowd. Paired with their DIY approach and indie street cred, it gave them a cool factor that simply couldn't be matched.

Few in the garage rock revival scene expected mainstream success. They made music out of sheer passion, imagining it playing in basements and pubs, not on arenas and TV shows. This unexpected success brought scrutiny, as the

media began to peer into Jack White's claims that he and Meg were siblings. They uncovered the truth that Jack and Meg had been married from 1996 until 2000, with Jack taking Meg's maiden name. This sort of press attention bothered both members, but especially Meg, who was a quiet and private person.

The realities of this unexpected fame informed the songwriting of "Seven Nation Army." The song's lyrics don't really play into the title's theme. Instead, they're an abstract bout of paranoia, with Jack singing of a deteriorating mental state that has him talking to himself at night.

As well executed as the lyrics of "Seven Nation Army" are, they take a clear backseat to the singular guitar riff that makes up most of the song's runtime. That riff is emblematic of everything the White Stripes were trying to accomplish with their music. It's an exercise in simplicity, drawing on punk and the blues to create something novel that feels as if it could have existed for decades. The constant repetition of that riff made it an instant earworm and earned it play on mainstream radio. From there, the song began to explode.

In an October 2003 UEFA Champions League soccer game, fans of Belgium's Club Brugge KV started to chant the song in the stadium. The simple approachability of the riff made it easy for thousands to chant together, and its minor tension created a sinister sort of sound. When Club Brugge KV won the game, "Seven Nation Army" entered the canon of stadium chants. Across the 2000s, it would become a sports anthem.

Meanwhile, the song saw continuous play on radio stations that had once thrived on this sort of riff-based rock. Before long, *Elephant* was an international success, giving the White Stripes their first multiplatinum album. The Stripes became bona fide A-listers, and in 2008, Jack White even got his chance to live out his onetime dream for "Seven Nation Army" and write a James Bond theme.

Since its release, "Seven Nation Army" has soared beyond being a simple hit. It is a landmark moment in rock music. It's an instant classic that certified Jack and Meg White's places in the pantheon of rock gods, and announced to the world that indie rock was a force to be reckoned with.

 # Honorable Mentions

"Crazy in Love" by Beyoncé (featuring Jay-Z): Two of the defining artists of twentieth-century music collaborated on a classic pop hip-hop song that helped kick off Beyoncé's legendary solo career. "Crazy in Love" is a celebratory pop song that proved to be prophetic, as Beyoncé and Jay-Z would go on to become pop's most lasting and important power couple.

"Hey Ya!" by Outkast: After establishing himself as one of rap's most eccentric geniuses, André 3000 looked away from hip-hop and toward pop. "Hey Ya!" saw him establish himself as a pop singer, delivering an all-time catchy chorus that distracts from the song's dark lyrics about romance falling apart. While André's crossover to pop faltered after the success of "Hey Ya!" the song remains one of the defining pop tunes of the era.

2004

"American Idiot"

Green Day

On March 20, 2003, the United States of America began an invasion of Iraq. It was the second phase in George W. Bush's war on terror that began as a response to the September 11 attacks two years earlier. The country's line was that this was a campaign to deliver democracy and freedom to the Iraqi people, but detractors both at home and among the international community saw it as an imperialistic war of conquest with shades of Vietnam. And just like during Vietnam, rock musicians rose up in protest. The antiwar movement of the early 2000s had nowhere near the cultural impact of its predecessor in the '60s and '70s, but it did spawn a number of key protest songs calling America into action. Chief among these was Green Day's "American Idiot."

Nobody would have pegged Green Day as the band to write the defining protest song of their era. Their roots were in the politically charged punk rock scene, but through the '90s, they had been on the forefront of a different brand of punk. Their music cut some of the radical edge off hard core and opted for pop melodies and shoutable choruses more in the tradition of the first wave of punks such as the Ramones. Their lyricism was less concerned with tearing down the establishment, and more focused on day-to-day life. They wrote slacker anthems about smoking weed and masturbating and angsty teenage hits about romance and friendship.

This approach turned Green Day into stars in the '90s as the pop punk scene grew, but the novelty had worn off by the new millennium. In 2003, the group found themselves on the wrong side of age 30 with their career on the brink. Their 2000 album *Warning* had flopped, and things turned from bad to worse when the master tapes for their planned follow-up, *Cigarettes and Valentines*, were stolen from the studio. Rather than try to remake that album, Green Day decided to scrap the whole thing and start from scratch.

Wiser by the experience of adulthood and galvanized by the direction his country was headed, Billie Joe Armstrong envisioned an album that would be more ambitious, and more culturally relevant than anything Green Day had done before. *American Idiot* was more than just a protest album. It was a narrative punk rock opera telling the story of a disillusioned suburban teen who sought salvation in the drugs and music and nightlife of the city, only to discover more pain and destruction. It's a story that ends on a bleak anticlimax, with a would-be punk returning home for an office job and a life full of regrets. Green Day told a story that contrasted the fantastical visions of individual success promised by TV and movies. It was a grounded look at a crumbling American dream that had long since washed away, if it had even existed in the first place.

In the context of this rock opera, *American Idiot*'s title track serves as an overture, painting the bleak backdrop on which the story will take place. The song opens on a ferocious, crunchy guitar lick before Armstrong delivers an impassioned opening verse: "Don't wanna be an American idiot / Don't want a nation under the new media." In Armstrong's eyes, post-9/11 America was a nation being kept in perpetual fear by a corporate-controlled media. An Islamophobic hysteria had gripped the nation and was being used to manufacture consent for an unjust war and push people against their own interests. Meanwhile, as he details in the second verse, hatred was running rampant against queer communities. Armstrong cheekily identifies himself with a homophobic slur, before declaring that he's not part of a redneck agenda. Armstrong, himself, is bisexual, and his androgynous presentation no doubt drew hate from a growing tide of conservatives who equated whiteness and straightness to patriotism.

When he wrote "American Idiot," Armstrong intended it as a condemnation of American society broadly, but many took the title to be a specific shot at President Bush. Bush's folksy aphorisms and penchant for public speaking gaffes had made his intelligence—or lack thereof—a frequent talking point among his critics. Green Day's song seemed all too applicable to this image, and the association stuck. But the reality is that Bush was more than just a harmless idiot. His war led to the death of hundreds of American soldiers and hundreds of thousands of Iraqi civilians. His tenure saw the rise of a new breed of

hyperpatriotic American conservatism that would set the stage for the rise of Trumpism a generation later.

These realities are baked into the lyrics of "American Idiot." Green Day's protest song captured the moment of its creation, but it has proved to have a longer tail than the band might have liked. The war on terror sprawled far beyond 2004, weighing over the head of Americans for a decade. The homophobia and racism that Green Day were protesting seemed to improve for a time, but in the late 2010s and early 2020s, it came surging back into the mainstream. There are certainly aspects of America that have changed since Billie Joe Armstrong penned his opus, but for the most part, America remains a land of alienation, "where everything isn't meant to be okay."

By eschewing the formula that had brought them success and calling out the trouble that they saw in America, Green Day reinvigorated their career. They penned one of the country's all-time protest songs and secured their legacy as some of the earliest musical predictors of the decline of the American empire.

Honorable Mentions

"Wake Up" by Arcade Fire: Arcade Fire ushered in a new era of indie rock with their art-school baroque pop classic *Funeral*. The album's climax is the anthemic "Wake Up," which sings open-heartedly about the loss of youth. The song's "woah" chorus started a trend that will flourish in the 2010s to become one of the defining aesthetics of millennial rock.

"Jesus Walks" by Kanye West: Kanye West was one of the most sought-after producers in the early 2000s. With "Jesus Walks," he finally lived his dream and established himself as one of the most exciting rappers of the era. West's Christian hip-hop hit "Jesus Walks" takes a militaristic beat and uses it to embrace his own faith, progressing a career that saw him become the most controversial figure of his era.

"All Caps" by Madvillain: The underground legend MF DOOM never broke through to mainstream success but is forever cemented with the label "your favorite rappers' favorite rapper." His crowning achievement was *Madvillainy*, a collaboration with the psychedelic producer Madlib. "All Caps" shows off DOOM's tongue-twisting lyricism, with the kind of verbose rhyme-dense lyricism that rappers still aspire to today.

2005

"B.Y.O.B."

System of a Down

There has never been another band like System of a Down. Their sound defies any easy categorization, leaping seamlessly between thrash metal, hard-core punk, new wave and pop rock with added dashes of Armenian folk music, opera, reggae and a dozen other esoteric influences. In another time, they might have been an underground band with a cult following, or an obscure critical darling, but in the tumultuous place that was post-9/11 America, they rose to become countercultural heroes and leaders in the anti-Bush protest movement. Their music was able to speak to the disenfranchised masses with an eclectic mixture of righteous rage and surreal humor. As America descended into a world of constant war, System's career took off. They reached their commercial pinnacle in 2005, when their protest song "B.Y.O.B." crossed over to the mainstream and cracked the American Top 40.

True to System of a Down's form, "B.Y.O.B." is a thoroughly unique protest song. It looks at war broadly, and the Iraq war specifically, from a class

> In another time, they might have been an underground band with a cult following ... but ... in post-9/11 America, they rose to become countercultural heroes ...

perspective. This message is underlined in the anthemic repetition of "Why don't presidents fight the war? / Why do they always send the poor?" But that clear messaging is paired with more surreal and abstract lyrics, and a song structure that jumps between brutal thrash riffs and a laid-back chorus groove. That chorus taps into a deeply ironic delivery, describing the war on terror as a party, parodying the propaganda used to stir Americans into a fervor. It calls into question the glamour with which America depicted the war on terror. Violence and death in the desert were wrapped in a sheen of stars and stripes, called freedom and sold to a disenfranchised populace in exchange for promises of college tuition and self-actualization.

In the second verse, vocalist Serj Tankian makes the references to the Iraq war clear. System was particularly fascinated with the engine of American propaganda. It makes its appearances throughout *Hypnotize/Mezmerize*, the double album that spawned "B.Y.O.B." Like Green Day's *American Idiot*, *Hypnotize/ Mezmerize* depicted the mass media as a

propaganda arm of the Bush government, used to stoke fear and hatred. In the bridge, Daron Malakian screeches out an ironic condemnation of Bush's government and the Patriot Act. System backed their political ideas in the video for "B.Y.O.B.," which featured faceless drones marching forward as words like "obey," "buy" and "god" flashed on screens on their faces.

"B.Y.O.B." is a hypermanic protest song. It surges forward at a wicked pace, jumping around in an odd structure, and overwhelming the listener with hook after hook all screamed in defiant rage. Its success made it one of the last gasps of nü-metal, a movement of experimental metal bands that had popped up after Rage Against the Machine's success a decade earlier. While System's sound is radically different than that of Rage, their raw energy and overt political consciousness made them spiritual siblings. Like Rage before

them, they were able to channel the seething discontent of the American populace into unexpected chart success.

As nü-metal declined, so too did the mainstream viability of metal as a whole. The music has continued to have a strong following in the underground with loyal fans and talented musicians breaking heavy music off into a thousand microgenres, but System of a Down represented one of the last times that these outsider scenes could be heard on mainstream radio and seen on MTV. The band themselves would go on an extended hiatus just two years after the release of "B.Y.O.B.," and creative differences have prevented them from releasing a new album since. Nevertheless, the strange and defiant spirit of System of a Down remains a perfect representation of the surreal fear and horror that gripped America during the early years of the war on terror.

Honorable Mentions

"Chicago" by Sufjan Stevens: Sufjan Stevens picked up the legacy of Brian Wilson with *Illinois*, a sprawling opus of an album dedicated to his home state. One of the highlights of the album is "Chicago," a song with soaring strings and triumphant lyrics depicting the idyllic hope of young love, and the brilliant promise represented by the city of Chicago.

"Candy Shop" by 50 Cent: After being mentored and platformed by Dr. Dre, Eminem decided to take on his own rap protégé. 50 Cent's sound combined Dre's G-Funk beats with pop sounds and the bling lyricism of the era, making him one of the most successful rap artists of the mid-2000s. "Candy Shop" is a sleazy sex jam displaying 50 Cent's easy charisma.

2006

"Welcome to the Black Parade"

My Chemical Romance

In 2006, America's generational tide was beginning to turn. Generation X aged out of youth culture and were replaced with a new group of millennial adolescents who would come of age in a new world transformed by digital technology and social media. As it always does, this generational change brought on a new wave of musical movements. One of the first movements to truly sink its teeth into the budding millennial generation was a punk rock subgenre called "emo."

The first wave of emo came in the mid-'90s as an offshoot of Washington, D.C.'s hard-core punk scene, called "emotional hard core." That music was raw and intense, defined by confessional lyricism that opened up about struggles with mental illness. Soon, emotional hard core began to blend with the pop punk that was taking over rock radio in the late '90s and early 2000s. The result was a more pop-friendly take on emo that captured the hearts of angsty millennial teens across the country. This wave of emo pop birthed bands that would dominate the rock scenes of the late 2000s. Such groups as Jimmy Eat World, Fall Out Boy and Panic! At the Disco all came to shake the world in their own way, but the most lasting cultural impact from this scene came from My Chemical

Romance and their signature song, "Welcome to the Black Parade."

To this day, few things will unite a room full of millennials quicker than hearing the echoing piano G note that opens the song. Gerard Way's quivering recall of a father taking a son into the city to see a marching band is one of the most iconic opening couplets in rock history. It's a rousing image, with a gravitas that exceeded anything anyone expected from the emo movement.

My Chemical Romance had risen to fame with songs about the teenage experience. They sang gothic pieces about heartbreak, bullying and mental health, and found a legion of youth who related to them. Their 2004 sophomore album, *Three Cheers for Sweet Revenge*, blasted in the Discmans of teenagers across the country and soared to triple platinum on the backs of songs like "I'm Not Okay (I Promise)." The band could have continued that formula in their follow-up, but instead they decided to chase after a more mature, ambitious sound. Like Green Day before them, My Chemical Romance took on the monumental task of creating a rock opera. They called it *The Black Parade*.

The Black Parade isn't a diversion from the grim subjects that My Chemi-

cal Romance were fond of, but rather an evolution. It tells the story of a character known only as "The Patient" who is forced to confront mortality and reflect on love and life as he dies of cancer in a hospital bed. "Welcome to the Black Parade" is the centerpiece to this story, depicting the moment The Patient dies and transitions into the underworld. He experiences his death as a poignant childhood memory, going to the parade with his father. This is depicted in the video, where My Chemical Romance play the act of musical psychopomps, rocking out on a float of roses as The Patient shambles through the apocalyptic ruins of the underworld.

In a fitting turn of events, the video that marked the shift to the millennial era was directed by Samuel Bayer, who had helped usher in the aesthetics of Generation X by directing the video for "Smells Like Teen Spirit." To match their new sound, My Chemical Romance debuted a new look. Gerard Way bleached their own hair and wore white makeup to give a deathly pallor, and the band donned black and white band jackets in a morbid twist on the Beatles' iconic *Sgt. Pepper's Lonely Hearts Club Band* look.

The classic rock influences on "Welcome to the Black Parade" stretch beyond aesthetics. The song was inspired by the progressive rock of the '70s, in particular Pink Floyd and Queen. This '70s rock nostalgia predicted a generation whose creative output was a constant stream of nostalgic remixes. My Chemical Romance have even called the song their own version of "Bohemian Rhapsody," a designation that fans and the music press have happily agreed with. Just as Queen did, My Chemical Romance open "Welcome to the Black Parade" with a theatrical intro before jumping into a rocking middle section that takes the form of high-energy dance punk. In this song, Way sings of the legacies and memories that will carry on after death, injecting a moment of hope into the morbid material. Throughout their entire career, My Chemical Romance have written about the power that love has to transcend death. The promise of love gives Way the motivation to dance and shout into the void. This applies to The Patient in the story, but it also speaks to the resilience that Way hopes to inspire in their fans as they face the tribulations of life. But the influences stretch beyond classic rock.

The entire *Black Parade* album also pulls heavily from musical theater, and "Welcome to the Black Parade" even has a gang-vocal bridge inspired by the musical *Annie*.

The ultimate message of "Welcome to the Black Parade" is one of hope, perseverance and the search for love and meaning. These themes were key to the entire emo movement, but they were misunderstood by older generations. The macabre fascinations of the emo movement spawned no shortage of backlash from people who claimed the music was pushing teens toward self-harm and suicidal ideation. It got bad enough that My Chemical Romance, and several of their peers, vocally tried to distance themselves from the emo label. In truth, emo was trying to do the opposite. It was trying to help young people who were already struggling with the mental illness and alienation that came from growing up in a world of constant war, mass media and enormous social pressures.

Today, many look back at the emo movement and cringe, dismissing it as little more than a fad born out of teenage angst. And while angst did fuel the movement, the reality is that the emos were some of the first to tap into the cul-

> The ultimate message of "Welcome to the Black Parade" is one of hope, perseverance and the search for love and meaning. These themes were key to the entire emo movement, but they were misunderstood by older generations. The macabre fascinations of the emo movement spawned no shortage of backlash from people who claimed the music was pushing teens toward self-harm and suicidal ideation.

tural identifiers that would define the millennial generation. Emos pushed gender norms with their fashion and advocated for queer rights. Many kids who grew up listening to My Chemical Romance have gone on to become part of an ongoing revolution redefining gender in modern society. In 2015, Gerard Way even opened up and discussed their own feelings of queerness. Meanwhile emo's discussions of mental health that spawned so much backlash helped break down stigmas around depression and suicidality, and helped bring on a world where more and more people are seeking the help that they need.

When My Chemical Romance wrote "Welcome to the Black Parade," they were trying to create an enduring piece of music that would last beyond their own moment. Such a goal might have been hubristic, but the band approached it earnestly. They were rewarded with musical immortality.

 # Honorable Mentions

"Not Ready to Make Nice" by the Chicks: While most of country music supported the war on terror, the Chicks stepped up vocally in protest. In response, the industry blacklisted them, turning them into pariahs and killing off a promising career. In 2006, they addressed the controversy with "Not Ready to Make Nice," a song that doubled down on their stance and raged against the censorship of the country industry.

"I'm N Luv (Wit a Stripper)" by T-Pain: T-Pain brings a heavy Auto-Tune sound into pop rap. While his sound would be the target of derision from many in the industry, his distinct use of Auto-Tune revolutionized pop, showing the potential that the technology had to create unique sound palettes, not just adjust vocals. T-Pain's experiments with Auto-Tune would inspire further advances from such artists as Kanye West and even Bon Iver in the years to come.

"Before He Cheats"

Carrie Underwood

Ever since Dolly Parton crossed over to mainstream success in the '70s and '80s, country and pop music have had flirtations and dalliances every few years. In early '90s, it was Garth Brooks and Shania Twain giving the urban mainstream their dose of rural twang. In the late '90s and early 2000s, the Chicks and Blake Shelton topped the Hot 100 a number of times. In the middle of the decade, that torch was picked up by Carrie Underwood. Underwood's success was the product of a new phenomenon that was gripping the nation—reality TV.

In June 2002, *American Idol* aired its first episode on national TV. It brought with it an enticing promise for the future of music— the chance for everyday people to show off their talents and get a crack at stardom. This promise seemed fulfilled when Kelly Clarkson won the first season and went on to multiplatinum success. But the next few winners didn't have nearly as much luck. Reuben Studdard and Fantasia both had moments in the sun following their wins but had trouble holding on to mainstream success. This issue wouldn't plague Underwood.

> Underwood's success was the product of a new phenomenon that was gripping the nation—reality TV.

In 2005, she released her debut single, "Inside Your Heaven," which debuted on top of the Billboard charts. A few months later, she dropped her first album, *Some Hearts*. The country world fell in love with that album immediately, making Underwood an A-lister. But it took the mainstream a while to notice. The third single from *Some Hearts*, "Before He Cheats" dominated country charts but had only a modest run on the Hot 100. It looked for a moment as though Underwood was only going to find true success in country. Her trajectory changed at the start of 2007, when music lovers tuned into the Grammy Awards and saw Underwood's performing abilities firsthand.

Before the Grammys, "Before He Cheats" was threatening to fall off the charts entirely. Fueled by this new momentum, it surged back up and stayed on the charts until November 2007. In total, it spent an astounding 64 weeks in the Hot 100, making it one of the longest-charting singles in Billboard's history. When the single went multiplatinum, it became both the first country single and the first single by an *American Idol* winner to achieve such a feat.

This success was bolstered by the song's absolute bomb of a chorus, delivered with a gritty desperation by Underwood. Written by Nashville veterans Josh Kear and Chris Tompkins, the lyrics are a furious revenge fantasy from a woman scorned. Underwood imagines her partner flirting with another woman which culminates in a violent chorus that depicts Underwood trashing the would-be cheater's truck.

The fact that Underwood's ire is expressed in the destruction of a pickup truck puts the song in dialogue with the country scene at the time. By the 2000s, the country pop industry had begun to cash in with formulaic songs celebrating rural life, often sung by people who weren't rural themselves. The pickup truck had become an especially iconic symbol in these songs. It was used to represent virility, masculinity and freedom. Destroying the car is thus a metaphorical castration in the language of country pop, stripping a man of the object that he puts his own self-worth into. This destruction is made literal in the music video, which sees Underwood take a baseball bat to a shiny red truck.

"Before He Cheats" is an expression of a brewing female rage that had stewed for decades in country music. It's a moment of empowerment, but one that's closely tied up in many of the misogynistic tropes of its era. In the late 2000s, women's righteous anger was being directed not at patriarchal systems but rather at other women. Kear and Tomkins' lyrics play into the "not like other girls" trope that had women eschewing femininity and trying to take each other down.

The destruction also plays into a "scorned woman" trope that has pervaded for generations. For her part, Underwood acknowledged that the song was a performance, and that she wasn't the type to actually destroy someone's property. Even so, there's a truth to her performance. Much like the metal music that was in its last chart gasp at the time, Underwood's fury tapped into our wilder instincts to bring about musical catharsis.

Riding on the success of "Before He Cheats," Underwood spent the next decade as a queen of the country charts, while still maintaining mainstream pop relevance. Her crossover success predicted the decade to come, as artists like Taylor Swift would steer country into a head-on collision with mainstream pop.

Honorable Mention

"Crank That (Soulja Boy)" by Soulja Boy: The new millennium got is first big dance fad with Soulja Boy's pop-rap debut. Part of the success of his song and dance came from the still-young website YouTube, where the music video was an early viral hit. Soulja Boy would go down as a one-hit wonder, but his ride to success proved he was one of the first artists to see the true potential of the internet as a pop platform.

2008

"Time to Pretend"

MGMT

The digital revolution turned the music industry on its head in the 2000s. File-sharing threatened the decades-long hegemony of record labels and distributors; iPods and MP3 players completely transformed people's listening habits; and advances in personal computing gave more power than ever to creatives. The sands of the industry were shifting as music entered a chaotic and unpredictable era. One of the great unexpected benefactors of this strange new world was an experimental indie duo called MGMT.

MGMT were born in a dorm room at Wesleyan College in 2002, when two friends named Ben Goldwasser and Andrew VanWyngarden began to make music together. Neither really had any designs on stardom; they simply shared a love of experimental music and psychedelia. In another era that might have been the end of their story, but the digital age made recording and producing music easier than ever. Synthesizer sounds that once cost thousands of dollars and required an engineer's mind to create could now be produced on a laptop with a few clicks of the button. So,

Goldwasser and VanWyngarden started to mess around with creating their own music.

Their sound was inspired by a psychedelic revival happening in the underground at the time. Such groups as the Flaming Lips, Animal Collective and Of Montreal were reviving the dense soundscapes of the 1960s and mixing them with synthesizers, dance influences and a distinctly modern surrealism. Goldwasser and VanWyngarden decided to give themselves the ironic name "The Management," which was soon shortened to "MGMT." They started to play campus shows and, much to their surprise, developed a small following. When they graduated in 2005, they toured the country, opening for Of Montreal. That same year they released their debut EP, *Time to Pretend*.

The title track of *Time to Pretend* was a satire on rock star culture. MGMT put together a poppy little synth riff and filled their mix with layers of preset synthesizer tone. They wrote lyrics imagining themselves finding exorbitant wealth and fame, destroying their life in the process. Like with everything

> Neither really had any designs on stardom; they simply shared a love of experimental music and psychedelia.

about MGMT, the band never really meant it to be taken seriously. They were just twenty-somethings having a little bit of fun before adulthood. But the music industry had other plans for them.

Columbia Records saw the potential of "Time to Pretend" and offered MGMT a record deal. At first the band thought the offer was some sort of prank, but before they knew it, they were sitting in the studio with producer Dave Fridmann, who was responsible for the Flaming Lips albums that had inspired MGMT. Fridmann recognized the pop potential of MGMT's synth hooks, particularly "Time to Pretend." He convinced them to speed the tempo up a few notches, matching it to ABBA's superhit "Dancing Queen," and punched up the synth sounds to enrich the sound.

At the end of 2007, MGMT dropped their major label debut, *Oracular Spectacular*. On March 8, 2008, "Time to Pretend" was released as the lead single. As MGMT were drawing eyes in the indie world, the U.S. housing market was collapsing, and the economy was spiraling into the Great Recession. For a generation of college students watching their future erupt in flames, MGMT's fatalistic hedonism took on a new sort of resonance. "Time to Pretend" became a summer anthem for alternative youth looking to slip into a fantastical escape from harsh economic realities.

"Time to Pretend" never truly went mainstream, but it became a sensation in the alternative world, and MGMT became critical darlings. The magazines *NME, Rolling Stone* and *Time* all put the song in year-end lists, and MGMT found themselves playing with bigger and bigger acts, including Radiohead, and even Paul McCartney. They played late-night shows and headlined festivals, all while maintaining the detached irony that had birthed the band. They wore ridiculous costumes in parody of glam rock and seemed determined to resist their newfound fame at every turn.

In 2010, MGMT released their sophomore album, *Congratulations*. The catchy pop hooks that had brought them to unlikely success were completely absent on that album, replaced by dense experimental melodies more befitting of the band's true aspirations. Their moment in the sun faded, and they avoided turning the fatalism of "Time to Pretend" into prophecy. But the world was forever changed for their success. In the years that followed, the neo-psych revival would gain steam and become one of the most vibrant alternative scenes. Meanwhile, the record industry would also learn from MGMT's success. Across the late 2000s and early 2010s, indie acts of various persuasion, from Edward Sharpe and the Magnetic Zeros to Foster the People to Gotye, would leap from the alternative to the mainstream with enormous hit songs. Indie rock in all of its various shades would become the next great movement of millennial art.

Honorable Mentions

"Single Ladies (Put a Ring on It)" by Beyoncé: Beyoncé's reign as Queen Bee continued with a women's empowerment anthem decrying men who are unwilling to commit. The striking black-and-white video saw Beyoncé debut one of the greatest dances of the 2000s.

"I Kissed a Girl" by Katy Perry: Katy Perry added her name to the list of dance-pop stars hitting the scene at the end of the decade. Written with pop legend Max Martin, the bicurious lyrics of "I Kissed a Girl" spoke to a moment where conversations around sexuality were finally starting to break into mainstream America. In the coming decade, these early conversations would turn into a full-fledged social movement.

2009

"Empire State of Mind"

Jay-Z

The capital of American music is unquestionably New York City. It's the city where jazz found its voice, where singer-songwriter folk transformed music and where punk, disco and hip-hop were born. Across the twentieth century, the city has been home to such names as Frank Sinatra, Lou Reed, Joey Ramone and Biggie Smalls. But the longest reigning king of New York music is Jay-Z. Born and raised in a housing project in Brooklyn's Bedford-Stuyvesant neighborhood, he hustled his way from extreme poverty up to being one of the wealthiest and most successful men in the music industry.

Jay-Z came up from nothing. As a teenager, he sold drugs to make ends meet and then pivoted to selling self-produced CDs out of his car in his early 20s. When he couldn't find anybody to sign him in the early '90s, he cofounded his own independent record label called Roc-A-Fella, which he used to release his debut *Reasonable Doubt* in 1996. That album was the beginning of a run of critical acclaim

> "Empire State of Mind" has become one of the most celebrated tracks of Jay-Z's career, but it was a small miracle that it ended up in his hands in the first place.

and commercial success never before seen in hip-hop. Through the '90s, Jay-Z was one of New York's finest in the East-West rap wars. When the industry shifted at the end of the decade, many of his peers found themselves struggling for relevance, but he dropped seven consecutive multiplatinum records between 1998 and 2006. He was a prolific collaborator, working with a young Kanye West, R. Kelly, Linkin Park, Rick Rubin, Beyoncé and more.

By 2009, Jay-Z was sitting on the precipice of music history. His 2007 album *American Gangster* was his 10th consecutive album to top the Billboard 200, tying a record set by none other than Elvis Presley. He broke that record in September 2009 with the release of *The Blueprint 3*. Already 40 when the album was released, Jay-Z was starting to enter a new phase as hip-hop's designated elder statesman. This role is exemplified by "Empire State of Mind," the third single of *The Blueprint 3*, and a song that asserted his status as both a hip-hop titan and as the voice of New York City.

"Empire State of Mind" has become one of the most celebrated tracks of Jay-Z's career, but it was a small miracle that it ended up in his hands in the first place. The piece was written by Angela Hunte and Janet Sewell-Ulepic, two aspiring songwriters from Jay-Z's home borough of Brooklyn. Hunte had grown up in the very same building as Jay-Z in the Bed-Stuy projects. She and Sewell-Ulepic wrote the song while traveling in London and feeling homesick for New York. They sent the song to Jay-Z's Roc Nation talent agency but were turned down. Luckily, EMI executive Jon Platt heard the song and thought Jay-Z would like it. He sent it over and Jay-Z loved it so much that he recorded a demo that night.

Jay-Z's version of the song was a dramatic change from Hunte's original. She had written the song to be sung through, but he chose to cut the sung verses and replace them with his own raps. His verses are a love letter to his hometown, name-dropping the city's different neighborhoods and the artists who have made it such a historic place. Jay-Z's lyrics show a clear reverence for the history of New York, but also have a cockiness for his own place within it. As he brags, "I made the Yankee hat more famous than a Yankee can." Alongside its dense lyrical references to New York history, the song's title calls to mind a history of New York anthems. It serves as a reference to Billy Joel's classic "New York State of Mind," as well as "N.Y. State of Mind" by Nas,

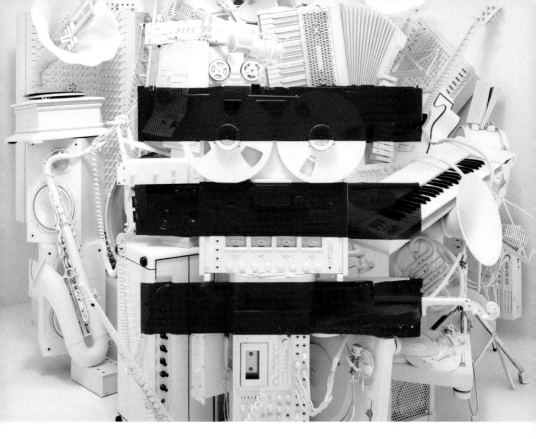

another hip-hop great who had a legendary beef with Jay-Z in the past.

Once he had rewritten the song to fit his own style, Jay-Z looped in another New York legend to sing Hunte's anthemic chorus. Alicia Keys was born in New York City's Hell's Kitchen neighborhood and rose to music stardom when she was just a teenager. Throughout the 2000s, she had established herself as one of rhythm and blues' premier divas, thanks to her piano talents and enormous voice. Her powerful emotional delivery contrasted Jay-Z's laid-back rap flows, milking a powerful emotion from the song. Jay-Z's verses hit with the boom-bap rhythm of the streets, sounding like walking through bustling streets, while Keys hook sounds

like standing atop the Empire State Building and taking in the breathtaking enormity of the Manhattan skyline. Overall, it's an anthem deserving of its audacious name. The song was destined to join "New York, New York" from the moment it was released, but its eternal status was cemented in the autumn of 2009, when the Yankees won the World Series just two weeks after the single was released.

"Empire State of Mind" was a final win for a decade that had seen Jay-Z continue to make his case as hip-hop's greatest. Its expansive production sound exemplified a hip-hop music that had climbed from one of New York's poorest neighborhoods all the way to the top of the mainstream. The mid-2000s had seen a dip in hip-hop's popularity, but by the end of the decade, Jay-Z was proving that was only a brief trend. "Empire State of Mind" represents the ambitious vision that he and his peers had for their music, and it served as a sneak peek for what was to come as the decade turned and hip-hop prepared itself for yet another reinvention.

Its expansive production sound exemplified a hip-hop music that had climbed from one of New York's poorest neighborhoods all the way to the top of the mainstream.

 # Honorable Mentions

"I Know You Want Me (Calle Ocho)" by Pitbull: Pitbull continued Latin pop's march toward the mainstream by embracing a South American dance music called reggaeton. "I Know You Want Me" is an homage to a street in Miami's Little Havana neighborhood. When it rose to number two on the Billboard Hot 100, it became one of the highest-charting Spanish-language songs in American history.

"I Gotta Feeling" by the Black Eyed Peas: The Black Eyed Peas wrote a party anthem that incorporated growing EDM (electronic dance music) influences from producer David Guetta. "I Gotta Feeling" spent 14 weeks on top of the Billboard charts and became one of the most successful pop songs of the entire decade, ushering in an era of upbeat party-pop.

idols
of the
internet
age

2010–19

Few inventions in human history have wrought such incredible change as the internet. By the time the 2010s began, it was already clear that the digital revolution was going to upset the world order, but when the new decade came, things kicked into overdrive. The advent of Wi-Fi and smartphones transformed the internet from an exciting digital escape into a ubiquitous force shaping daily life. Social media let people check in with friends at all times of the day and gave music fans unprecedented access to their favorite artists. Whereas fandom had once meant mailing fan letters and praying for a response, people could suddenly tweet at their favorite musicians and get actual responses. They could get voyeuristic peeks into musicians' lives through Instagram and dive through entire back catalogs at the click of a button on Spotify. Naturally, pop stars responded. The 2010s became an era of enormous personalities who used online discourse to seize control of cultural discourse.

That discourse often revolved around social justice. By giving voice to marginalized communities, the

2010

2011

2012

2013

2014

internet spawned a social revolution. Queer activists found places to organize and fought for marriage equality. The barbershop and beauty salon conversations that had driven Black cultural discourse for so long suddenly came into the open. Women from all walks of life spoke truth to power with the #MeToo movement and shone the light on a rampant culture of sexism and abuse. One by one, the skeletons were torn from America's closet and placed on display in front of a captive audience of millions. The audiences weren't the only ones driving this conversation. In the highly politicized world of the 2010s, the biggest pop stars were more vocal than ever. No longer being dissuaded by labels or misquoted by media, some of the biggest musicians of the era championed queer rights and women's rights, and stood as powerful allies for a movement of Black liberation.

As the old systems of consolidated power fell away, so too did the older forms of music. Rock fell almost entirely out of the mainstream, only appearing with occasional surprise indie rock hits. Metal was chased off the charts and relegated to its own corner of the internet. But they weren't gone forever. Hip-hop and pop music stretched further outward, incorporating other genres into their music. At the start of the decade, a new party culture sprung up, bringing electronic dance music into the mainstream. Dubstep had a brief moment in the sun and soon fused its way into pop. Latin pop started to knock on the door of the mainstream, fusing with hip-hop and Top 40 pop. Even the ever-stalwart country music scene started to adapt, pulling hints of hip-hop into its sound.

Drastic change never comes without a price. Midway through the decade, new groups of radicals rose up, platformed by the same social media connections building solidarity among the marginalized. A tide of homophobia and xenophobia swelled in the back half of the decade, bringing the most controversial politician in American history to power. People divided themselves into radically politicized bubbles, to the point that even truth itself was thrown into question. By the end of the decade, America was left confused and divided by a never-ending culture war that stretched its tendrils into all aspects of life.

From this darkness and chaos, the seeds of music's future were sprouting. Artists from Generation X were proving that the internet brought with it a new shot at relevancy, with many having enormous success even as they approached middle age. Millennial musicians flourished as they entered adulthood, opening up about their collective fears and struggles. And as the 2020s were rounding the corner, the first members of Generation Z started to hit the music scene, sure to transform it into their own image in the years to come.

2015

2016

2017

2018

2019

2010

"Runaway"

Kanye West

There's a similar pattern of evolution that most popular musical movements have gone through over the decades. The first generation innovates the music and brings it to the world's attention. The second generation builds on that momentum, expanding the sound enough that it starts to take over the mainstream and redefine what pop music is. By the time the third generation comes around, the music's aesthetic has solidified, and its place in the culture has been guaranteed. The only logical next step is to elevate the movement beyond pop and into high art. In jazz, such artists as Charlie Parker and Miles Davis stretched the limits of technical ability and stretched the genre to its limits. In rock, artists such as King Crimson, Genesis and Pink Floyd brought a high concept vision to their music. In soul, Curtis Mayfield, Marvin Gaye and Stevie Wonder got progressive with ambitious orchestral arrangements. For hip-hop, the third generation's coming-out party was on November 22, 2010, when Kanye West released *My Beautiful Dark Twisted Fantasy*.

> He and his enormous team meticulously pieced together an opulent showing of maximalism that West hoped might redeem him in the eyes of the public.

West was 33 years old when he released his magnum opus, but he already had more success than most artists could dream of. He got his start as one of the most sought-after beatmakers, producing timeless tracks for such artists as Jay-Z, Ludacris and Janet Jackson. Despite being one of the best producers in the game, West wasn't satisfied. He always dreamed of being a rapper, and he hustled to make that deal happen. Even as everybody in the industry was telling him he should stick behind the booth, he was hustling his way into *College Dropout*, an astounding debut album that shook the rap world with its "chipmunk soul" production style. West's profile rose from there with three more acclaimed records, and by the end of the decade, he was a bona fide A-lister.

It seemed that West had nowhere to go but up until the 2009 MTV Video Music Awards. He burst onstage in the middle of a young Taylor Swift accepting her award to announce that Beyoncé deserved the prize. Overnight, he went from one of the hottest names in hip-hop to music's latest villain. He canceled a planned world tour and dropped out

of the spotlight. He traveled the world, spending time in Japan and Rome before winding up in Honolulu, where he holed up and began to work on a new album.

West rented out a studio for 24 hours a day and flew in a murderers' row of collaborators that included Rihanna, Jay-Z, Nicki Minaj, Rick Ross, RZA, Bon Iver and even Elton John. Over the year that followed, he and his enormous team meticulously pieced together an opulent showing of maximalism that West hoped might redeem him in the eyes of the public. *My Beautiful Dark Twisted Fantasy* was sprawling and progressive. Most of the songs stretched well beyond five minutes, featuring an elaborate array of soundscapes and samples that pulled from classic rock, spoken-word poetry, electronica and more. The most audacious of these

tracks was a nine-minute ode to anti-heroism called "Runaway."

"Runaway" pairs a sparse, elegant piano line with a booming 808 beat and strange inhuman vocal samples that echo across the mix. It's a cold and eerie soundscape, putting the listener right inside West's lonely head. When the lyrics hit, they're an odd combination of ego and vulnerability. He toasts to the "douchebags" and the "assholes," presumably including himself in their number. It's a celebration of his relentless work ethic and singular vision of the world, an ethic that led him to a mental breakdown and the VMA incident in the first place. He isn't so much apologizing for his behavior as he is justifying it. But by the same measure, West criticizes himself, noting, "You've been puttin' up with my shit just way too long."

West's emotional verses give way to an incredible guest feature by Pusha T, who was encouraged by West to embody the biggest douchebag he could. Pusha T obliged with a materialistic verse playing a character who has screwed up a relationship but doesn't care, telling the partner that she can stay and enjoy the fruits of his wealth, or she can leave, and he can find somebody else. Pusha's verse underlines the unapologetic message of the song and displays one of West's greatest talents—knowing exactly where and how to feature his collaborators. Despite having a famously large ego himself, he was more than willing to step aside on *My Beautiful Dark Twisted Fantasy*. The album incorporates incredible features, including Pusha on "Runaway," and a

Nicki Minaj verse on "Monster" that remains one of the greatest of all time.

When Pusha is done, West comes in with his most vulnerable verse of all in which he admits that he couldn't deal with the intimacy of romance. "Runaway" is clearly inspired by a breakup, but he also hints that the romance is a metaphor for something larger—his ongoing, difficult relationship with the music press. With both his romantic life and his public persona, he is willing to acknowledge his own flaws, but ultimately, he won't apologize. In the song's extended outro, he displays that genius firsthand. A string orchestra adds an emotional depth to the song, while heavy, distorted vocals further the sense of loneliness and alienation, singing in mumbled, half-audible words. By the end of the song, the listener has been taken through a thoroughly unique aesthetic and emotional journey and is left breathless.

West paired this incredible piece of musicianship with a striking short film built around the song. That film makes his vision of hip-hop as high art clear. "Runaway" features a striking color palette and a stunningly beautiful ballet arrangement. It was an elaborate visual, underlining West's undeniable vision and egotism. On the whole, "Runaway" proved that, in his mind, he is a singular artistic genius, and any criticisms of his behavior necessarily must come second to that.

Whether West's behavior can be excused is still up for debate to this day, especially as he's gone on a shocking heel turn that's included overt antisemitism. But with *My Beautiful Dark Twisted Fantasy*, he made as good a case as anyone has made for his creative genius. The album succeeded in its ambitious goals and pushed hip-hop to new levels of artistic decadence. "Run-away" was just one of a half dozen songs that became instant classics on the album. All of them displayed West's unique lyricism, production genius and incredible knack at identifying and utilizing the talents of others. Together, it was enough for him to win back the respect of the music industry.

That respect would wax and wane throughout the next decade, as West became one of the defining figures of the 2010s. That year would see a cycle of controversy and artistic triumph as he publicly battled mental illness and overtly struggled with the pressures of fame. For better or worse, he's become a figure as important to the millennial generation as the Beatles or Michael Jackson have been to generations past.

Honorable Mentions

"Scary Monsters and Nice Sprites" by Skrillex: In the early 2000s, an electronic dance movement called dubstep started to ferment in the United Kingdom. When the decade turned, a group of American producers took this sound and combined it with influences from emo, metal and hip-hop to bring it into the mainstream. The biggest of these was Skrillex, who sampled a YouTube clip for the drop of "Scary Monsters and Nice Sprites," a song that became many Americans' introduction to a short-lived dubstep craze.

The Suburbs by Arcade Fire: Arcade Fire shocked the world at the 2011 Grammys when their 2010 concept album *The Suburbs* won Album of the Year. Although the band were critical darlings, many in the mainstream still had no idea who they were. *The Suburbs* changed that with a carefully produced art-rock sound and relatable lyrical themes about the alienation that came from growing up in the suburban sprawl of the '80s and '90s.

2011

"Born This Way"

Lady Gaga

Queer liberation and dance music have always gone hand in hand. Through the 1970s, disco provided a safe haven for queer organization and helped platform queer artists in the mainstream. When that movement ended in violent backlash, queer artists went underground and evolved disco into house music. Through the '80s, house influenced mainstream pop, but the queer community itself was reeling from the AIDS epidemic. This tragedy slowed progress for LGBTQ+ rights for two decades, but it could never truly be stopped. In the late 2000s, a new generation of LGBTQ+ youth born after the height of AIDS started to come of age and push for their rights. In 2011, this new generation got a dance anthem of their own when Lady Gaga released "Born This Way."

When she released the song, Gaga was already well on her way to becoming a queer icon. In 2008, she'd scored one of her first major hits with "Poker Face," a song about trying to conceal same-sex attraction, and a year later she publicly came out as bisexual. Her flamboyant, experimental fashion seemed to challenge the gender norms of the day, and her thumping electropop music was built on a long tradition of gay club music. "Born This Way" was a step beyond even that. It was an exuberant celebration of queer identity, and a utopian dream of a world without discrimination.

When she wrote "Born This Way," Gaga hoped to channel her pop diva foremothers. She was inspired by the self-love anthems of the late '80s and '90s sung by such acts as Madonna and TLC. Her influences stretched further back, too. The song's name came from a first wave disco song called "I Was Born This Way." That track was originally cut by Valentino in 1975, and then the openly gay singer and activist Carl Bean released a new version in 1977. Gaga meshed this empowering pop history with a more modern sound, powered by thick synth lines and a relentless dance beat.

Gaga had no desire to hide her anthem behind ambiguous poeticisms. The lyrics preach empowerment openly and honestly. Gaga name-drops a number of identities and ethnicities, including queer communities such as "gay," "bi," "lesbian" and "transgendered." Mentioning queer people so openly was rare enough at the time, but in 2011, almost nobody was speaking publicly about transgender issues, especially in the Top 40 pop world. Even with the tide of queer activism rising, Gaga was putting herself and her career at risk by so openly acknowledging these communities.

Her lyrics were an explicit refutation of the homophobic talking points of the era, which frequently described homosexuality as a choice and a sin. She refutes the religious right, declaring that she is beautiful in her own way, as God makes no mistakes. Gaga is happy to embrace all colors of the queer community, specifically shouting out drag culture with a chanted interlude of "Don't be a drag, just be a queen."

This lyricism drew backlash from homophobes, but Gaga also drew no shortage of criticism from the communities she was celebrating. The use of "transgendered" rather than "transgender" reflected a lack of knowledge on the community, and her lines about racial acceptance leave something to be desired, with lyrics like "No matter black, white or beige, chola or Orient made." Some accused Gaga of co-opting queer culture to further her own career, a complex accusation given her own bisexual orientation.

Even with all these criticisms factored in, by and large the queer community embraced Gaga just as she embraced them. "Born This Way" fed her rising stardom and elevated her to the pantheon of queer diva icons alongside Donna Summer and Cher. The song debuted at number one on Billboard's chart and became one of the defining pop tracks of the year. Gaga drew praise from such gay icons as Elton John, and her *Born This Way* album went 4x platinum in the United States. Gaga became one of the biggest and most controversial pop stars of the era, and her electro-pop sound helped define a new club scene emerging at the start of the decade.

The real influence of "Born This Way" stretches far beyond the music industry, though. Gaga's anthem became a staple song of pride parades across the country as the LGBTQ+ community made themselves louder and more visible. Four years after she dropped "Born This Way," that movement came to a climax. On June 26, 2015, the U.S. Supreme Court struck down all bans on same-sex marriage, ushering in a historic era of LGBTQ+ rights. But just like the end of the disco era, this new period of queer liberation has been met with fierce backlash from the American right wing. As homophobia and bigotry is on the rise once more, "Born This Way" remains an essential protest song. It is a bastion of bright-eyed idealism, forever encouraging the queer community to embrace their truth and fight for the place they deserve in the world.

 # Honorable Mentions

"Ni**as in Paris" by Kanye West + Jay-Z: Kanye West's imperial phase was in full swing as he teamed up with Jay-Z for *Watch the Throne*, an album that revels in commerciality even as it aspires to push hip-hop toward high art. The fourth single is a song that put Jay-Z and West—legally called "Ye" now—against the haute-couture backdrop of Paris, establishing them as international kings of rap.

"Pumped Up Kicks" by Foster the People: One of the strangest trends of the early 2010s was a surge of indie rock one-hit wonders that would explode onto the charts every summer only to fade back into the underground. Foster the People joined these ranks in 2011 when their sleeper hit "Pumped Up Kicks" shot up the mainstream charts, spending eight weeks at number three on the Billboard Hot 100. It paired a lighthearted melody with songs about a school shooting, tapping into the pulse of one of the biggest growing issues of the era.

2012

"We Are Young"

fun.

For the first time in a decade, optimism was starting to get its grip on a lot of Americans in 2012. The country was emerging from the Great Recession, the war on terror seemed to be near an end, and the rise of social media was making it easier than ever for marginalized voices to speak truth to power. This bright outlook for the future was reflected in a movement of open-hearted, earnest indie rock that was surging to the mainstream. Rock groups were finding success with big arrangements filled with chanted anthemic choruses. Indie outfits like Arcade Fire were enchanting music critics, and it seemed that for the first time in half a decade, rock was ready to return to mainstream relevance. In the spring of 2012, a months-old song from an upstart rock group started to climb the charts, reflecting the groundswell of hope from millennials who were entering college and the workforce. That song was "We Are Young" by fun.

On April 28, 2012, "We Are Young" topped the Billboard Hot 100. Once, this wouldn't have been a particularly remarkable feat for a rock song. But when fun. topped the charts, they became the first rock band to do so since Coldplay in 2008. This success was aided by a cover in the TV sensation *Glee*, as well as its use in a Super Bowl commercial, but it wasn't just a blip. "We Are Young" held the top spot on the chart for five weeks and stayed on the chart for a respectable 20-week run.

This success came from distilling the baroque pop sound that was dominating the indie world into a simpler, more accessible pop rock. fun. had some help in this process, teaming up with the producer Jeff Bhasker, who was riding high after playing a large part in the production of Kanye West's *My Beautiful Dark Twisted Fantasy* and *Watch the Throne*. Bhasker's production style was clearly influenced by West's vision of opulence and enormity. In fact, the beat he created for "We Are Young" was originally meant for *Watch the Throne* but when put under the sing-along shout of the chorus, it gave an undeniable sense of epic momentum and optimism.

This enormous chorus seemed to be a rousing call to arms for the millennial generation. It was a celebration of the energy and passion of youth, and all the potential that comes with it. It's a chorus that speaks beyond the song's lyrics, which depicts ex-lovers deciding to give it another shot at the end of a drunken night. Nate Ruess wrote the song remembering a particularly unflattering drunken night. It reflected the mistakes that come so easy with youth and the redemption that comes even easier.

"We Are Young" is a song that embodied so much promise, and yet almost none of it was fulfilled. There was no real rock revival that followed in its wake. The song was simply the pinnacle of a bubble that receded as the decade went on. The hopefulness of the millennials stuck around for a little longer, but before long they were met with a waning job market, an out-of-control housing market, a cultural backlash against progress and the threat of climate change made real. As time went by, the starry-eyed earnestness of fun. began to look more and more like naïveté.

As for the band themselves, they still have yet to make a third album. Riding the success of "We Are Young," both Jack Antonoff and Ruess put the band on hiatus to pursue other projects.

Antonoff would go on to become one of the biggest players in the music industry of the 2010s, but he'd do it from the other side of the booth. As a songwriter and producer, Antonoff has helped put out some of the biggest hits of the modern era, working with such artists as Taylor Swift, Lorde and Lana Del Rey.

In terms of mainstream success, the greatest victories from "We Are Young" come in the hands of Janelle Monáe, who features in the song's bridge. fun. recruited Monáe after hearing her Afrofuturist concept album *The Archandroid*. Her star was already on the rise before the collaboration, but having a chart topper certainly didn't hurt that momentum, as she went on to establish herself as one of the most distinct voices in pop music.

A decade on, the legacy of "We Are Young" is complicated. It captured the spirit of a moment, but in hindsight looks far more bittersweet than celebratory. In terms of broader cultural impact in the music world, it probably pales in comparison to songs by Arcade Fire or Vampire Weekend. Nevertheless, it stands as a perfect testament to a brief moment in time when the millennial generation truly did feel they could burn brighter than the sun.

 # Honorable Mentions

"I Knew You Were Trouble" by Taylor Swift: The dubstep craze reached its commercial pinnacle as country starlet Taylor Swift embraced EDM. "I Knew You Were Trouble" was created alongside Max Martin, and it represents Swift's early embrace of pop music. Already a country music heavyweight, Swift's crossing over was the beginning of a run of pop success that continues to this day.

"Starships" by Nicki Minaj: Nikki Minaj's Afrofuturist mega-hit combined techno pop with hip-hop to cement her status as hip-hop's leading woman. Minaj combined brilliant hip-hop lyricism with an ear for pop hooks to become one of the best-selling female rappers of all time.

"m.A.A.d city" by Kendrick Lamar: Kendrick Lamar's sophomore album, *Good Kid, m.A.A.d City* was like nothing hip-hop had ever seen. It's a narrative G. Funk concept album in which Lamar tells an autobiographical story about his own experience escaping the ghettos of Compton. "m.A.A.d city" embodies everything that makes the album excel, with Lamar delivering his stunning lyrics in a paranoid ramble, and an astounding beat switch midway through. The album was such a success that it launched him into the conversation of the greatest rapper even though he was just 25 years old.

"We Can't Stop"

Miley Cyrus

In the summer of 2013, Miley Cyrus completely transformed the world's perception of her in a matter of weeks. Up until that point, she was best known for her career as a child star, playing the lead role in the teen musical sitcom *Hannah Montana*. Throughout her teenage years, her wholesome persona, cherubic grin and golden hair made Cyrus white America's sweetheart. But as she aged into adulthood, she sought to break out of that box and establish herself as an adult artist. In 2010, at the age of 18, Cyrus released her third studio album, *Can't Be Tamed*. It came along with a slightly edgier more adult look, but the world didn't buy it. The album underperformed and received mixed reviews. She cut ties with her record label and took a break from music to pursue acting. When she returned to the pop world, she came back with a sound that nobody expected.

On June 9, 2013, Miley Cyrus began her musical comeback with the release of "We Can't Stop," the lead single to her fourth album, *Bangerz*. "We Can't Stop" was a far cry from the teen pop that had so endeared Cyrus to America. It was an explicit rhythm and blues party song that had originally been written with a completely different artist in mind. The songwriting and production team behind "We Can't Stop" was helmed by Mike Will Made

It, who was fresh off a string of hits for artists like Kanye West, 2 Chainz and Drake. He and his team originally planned for the song to go to Rihanna, an artist with a decidedly adult sound and a reputation for party songs full of sexuality and innuendo. When she opted for another Mike Will Made It song, "We Can't Stop" ended up in Cyrus' hands.

By this point, Cyrus was 20 years old and was starting to live a harder partying lifestyle like the one depicted in "We Can't Stop." The lyrics resonated with her experience, reminding her of the enormous drug-fueled parties that she had attended. The original lyrics of the song had even more explicit references to drugs—the line "Dancing with Molly" was originally written as "Getting high off mollies," a clear reference to MDMA (ecstasy), which was the party drug du jour in the 2010s.

This new Cyrus was far from the innocent girl who was singing "Party in the U.S.A." four years earlier. The change only became clearer when she dropped the video and premiered a new look. Gone were the long hair and modest outfits, replaced with a stylish androgynous cut and a series of tight, revealing outfits. These were paired with an array of surreal images interspersed between party shots. That video was a sensation when it hit YouTube. People watched it

more than 10 million times in the first 24 hours, and since then it's gone on to rack up nearly a billion views.

Part of the reason the video garnered such attention was because it was steeped in controversy. One of the first shots of the video sees Cyrus pop a golden grill into her teeth, and the rest of the video is full of imagery borrowed from Black hip-hop communities. Midway through, she twerks while surrounded by Black models, as the song shouts out her homegirls with big butts. Calls of cultural appropriation rained down on Cyrus, whose career had shown little disposition toward hip-hop up until this point. Alongside these accusations, an older generation who still saw her as a child wrung their hands over her overtly sexual imagery. They saw a young woman being objectified and exploited by the record industry.

But for the white millennials who had grown up alongside Cyrus, "We Can't Stop" was a coming-out party. They, too, were entering adulthood, partying far harder than their parents would approve of, and setting off to live their own life. "We Can't Stop" became a go-to club banger, and it climbed to number two on the Billboard Hot 100. It was proof that Cyrus had finally succeeded in escaping from the Hannah Montana image.

Child stars have never had it easy in the music industry. While many have had success as an adult, that almost always comes at a deep price. For Miley Cyrus, "We Can't Stop" marked the beginning of an adulthood that would see her break that trend. Over the rest of 2013, she would become one of the most controversial figures in pop culture thanks to appearances that saw her twerking onstage, debuting strange and sexual looks and advocating openly for drug use. The moral panics that surrounded Cyrus could have brought her down, but instead she struck forward and continued to forge a career of her own. Throughout the rest of the decade, she would prove to be a chameleon, changing her aesthetic and sound a number of times while constantly remaining in the spotlight. Along the way, she would come out as queer and become an outspoken advocate for queer rights and develop a cult following of loyal fans.

Cyrus' trajectory hasn't been perfect. There is legitimate basis to the accusations of cultural appropriation on "We Can't Stop," but in 2013 she proved that she was more than simply a child star. She used the tools and publicity available in the digital age to break free from a trajectory and establish herself as one of the most self-assured artists in the pop world.

The moral panics that surrounded Cyrus could have brought her down, but instead she struck forward and continued to forge a career of her own.

Honorable Mentions

"Harlem Shake" by Baauer: One of the biggest viral fads of the Web 2.0 era centered on Baauer's "Harlem Shake." People across the internet created videos in which the song's drop sees normal scenes smash cut to surreal dance numbers. The virality of this video trend carried Baauer's song all the way to the top of the pop charts.

"Flawless" by Beyoncé: Beyoncé's music had always embraced female empowerment, but in 2013 she took it to the next level. "Flawless" is her overt association with a new wave of feminism rising, thanks to the internet. The song samples a speech by the Nigerian writer Chimamanda Ngozie Adichie and channels it into an anthemic celebration of womanhood and beauty.

2014

"Style"

Taylor Swift

The 2010s saw the birth of an era of extreme aestheticization that has continued to this day. The rise of smartphones meant that suddenly everybody had a camera in their pocket, and social media meant that people had avenues to share these photos. People began to curate perfect images of their personality and life, creating a world of immaculate color palettes and stylized selfies. In this world of self-invention and constant digital gaze, a young country singer named Taylor Swift began to thrive. She broke free from the Nashville song factory, seized control of her career and, in 2014, established herself as the biggest pop star of her era and the undisputed queen of aesthetics.

In 2012, Swift signaled the beginning of her shift away from her country roots with *Red*. That album saw her teaming up with Max Martin, the pop genius who was instrumental in launching the careers of Britney Spears and Katy Perry. Together, they made pop songs that played into the dubstep craze sweeping the music scene. The pop world celebrated this collaboration and welcomed Swift into their fold. She responded two years later by giving pop fans one of the greatest pop albums ever made, *1989*.

Whereas *Red* mixed pop songs between more traditional Nashville country tunes, *1989* was pure pop

perfection from start to finish. Swift and Max Martin worked with a small team of superproducers that included Shellback, Jack Antonoff and Imogen Heap, to create a lush synth-pop dreamscape brimming with beautiful hooks. Swift's lyrics throughout the album show a step forward in maturity, as she claps back against a public that made fun of her confessional approach. She adds beautiful nuance into every turn of phrase and opens herself up to the world as a full, complex adult. The entire project is tied together with an aesthetic trend that was just starting to take off in the era: 1980s nostalgia. The album spawned an astounding seven singles, five of which cracked the Top 10 and went on to become pop radio staples. Among these, the track that best exemplifies this new era for both Taylor and pop culture was the third single, "Style."

"Style" is a moody piece of synth-pop, driven by a pulsing synthesizer and a crisp guitar tone. Martin and Shellback create an intricate soundscape that captures the feeling of driving through a sleepy city late at night. It's a dense, urban sound that reflects Swift's personal move from Nashville to New York, a move that embodies the shift from country to pop. The song is a slow build, painting a lyrical and musical mood before erupting into an enormous earworm of a chorus. The whole thing calls

daydream look in your eye." The song depicts a sort of timeless romance, but undercuts it in the second verse with the seeds of infidelity.

Swift's previous breakup songs were often full of accusation and heartbreak, but "Style" takes a different approach. It features an open admission of guilt and embodies the complications that come with adult relationships. While she has never openly admitted who the song is about, its title and lyrics seem to be a reference to a short-lived romance with fellow pop star Harry Styles. Swift gives further evidence for this theory in the video, which features a dramatic shot of a necklace that she and Styles gave to each other.

This sort of hinting is common across Swift's career. She was one of the first artists to truly understand the power of internet fan communities. As her career grew, her legions of so-called Swifties frequently flocked to web forums and social media to theorize about her life and songs. Rather than ignore or dispute the rumors they would come up with, Swift leaned in and turned these fans into a media empire. She would use social media to openly engage with her fans and welcome them into her life, creating a parasocial bond that makes her music resonate even deeper. It's a carefully crafted image of an imagined authenticity, planned to the finest detail and smattered with Easter eggs that keep Swift's fans speculating about her life and her career.

Swift's total control of her image and her fans' perception is clear in the packaging of *1989*. Rather than going with the typical glamour shots that had made up her album covers, Swift opted for a washed-out Polaroid that cut her face off at the nose. It's an image that creates a mystery and distance, representative

to mind the spacey, echo-soaked sound of the 1980s, but Swift's songwriting makes it indisputably modern. Swift fully embraces the world's growing obsession with nostalgia, both in the music and lyrics.

Like with so many of Swift's lyrics, "Style" is clearly a song inspired by one of her romantic dalliances. In the chorus, she paints this relationship in terms of aesthetics, calling back to an era that falls even earlier than the '80s with lyrics such as: "You've got that James Dean

of the more obscure lyrics contained within. The Polaroid look fits squarely within the nostalgic theme of the album, but also pairs well with the era of Instagram. Each copy of the album was paired with a random assortment of Polaroid printouts inside, encouraging Swifties to collect them all.

When Taylor Swift crossed over to pop with *1989*, she was following a rich country tradition that dates back to Dolly Parton. But while some country artists have pulled off the crossover, few have impacted pop music the way that Swift did. By seizing control of public perception and crafting a meticulous aesthetic for herself, she became one of the leaders in a new era of pop music. She embraced the nostalgia of the era and paired it with a decidedly modern approach to self-branding. In doing so, she endeared herself to both the public and the critical world. "Style" was celebrated as an artistic triumph in pop music, and *1989* became one of the best-selling records of the era. Swift would become the defining artist of the era for millions of twenty-something pop fans, along with many others.

# Honorable Mentions

"Chandelier" by Sia: One of the most eccentric pop stars of her era, Sia's music fit in with the club anthems that became hits in the 2010s, but offered an alternative view of the lifestyle. "Chandelier" portrays the party girl culture not as fun or empowerment, but rather as desperate escape from an existential fear that was gripping her generation.

"Transgender Dysphoria Blues" by Against Me!: Laura Jane Grace became one of music's most outspoken trans icons with "Transgender Dysphoria Blues," the title track on a concept album about her own experience transitioning. It was a key moment in an ongoing movement toward trans acceptance.

"Anaconda" by Nicki Minaj: Nicki Minaj proved she's worthy of her Queen of Rap title with a hilarious sex jam. "Anaconda" samples Sir Mix-A-Lot's big butt homage "Baby Got Back" and uses it to perform a gender inversion, telling stories about Minaj's sexual conquest. The jungle-themed video single-handedly brought the twerking dance into the mainstream.

2015

"Alright"

Kendrick Lamar

In 2015, the biggest protest movement in generations was gathering steam. A series of murders of Black youth over the past few years had spurred Black activists into motion. The phrase "Black Lives Matter" started to spread across social media as a defiant call for awareness and action about these killings. As more and more innocent Black people were murdered, often by the police, the Black Lives Matter movement spread out from the internet and into the real world, formalizing in protests in cities across America. These protests were met with police resistance, and protestors turned to art for motivation. While police were hosing down and tear-gassing protesters in Ferguson, Cleveland and across the country, protestors were responding with a defiant chant of joy and resilience: "We gon' be alright." The Black Lives Matter movement had adopted its unofficial anthem.

Kendrick Lamar's "Alright" was a perfect candidate for a protest anthem. It simmered with the same rage as the protestors—a rage made most clear in Lamar's controversial lyric "and we hate po-po / wanna kill us dead in the street fo sho'." But at the same time, the ultimate message was one of optimism and positivity for the Black community. In the chorus, producer Pharrell Williams chants the ultimate message that galvanized the Black Lives Matter community. It was a chant that gave the same sentiment as the age-old protest song "We Shall Overcome," which helped fuel the civil rights movement. And its origins go even further back than that. When Lamar was writing the song, he was thinking of the uplifting slave spirituals that helped his ancestors find hope through one of the most brutal experiences of human history.

If that was all there was to "Alright," it would still remain as one of the finest protest songs ever, but like all of Lamar's work, the song is filled with layer upon layer of meaning. Lamar wrote the song after taking a trip to South Africa in 2014. After the enormous success of his 2012 sophomore album *Good Kid, m.A.A.d City*, Lamar was already in the conversation for one of the greatest rappers of his era. He was able to tell elaborate, high concept stories in a catchy package. His rhyme schemes were sophisticated and complex, and he had a deep arsenal of voices and tones to pull from in his rapping. But above all else, he had a perspective and a self-awareness that is

> *To Pimp a Butterfly* was a living document of Black history, trauma and excellence.

rare for musicians of any persuasion. He had seen so many young rappers make it big only to flame out, get crucified by the media or, worst of all, succumb to addiction and violence and die. It was a pattern that he wasn't keen to repeat, so he took the money earned from his success and set off on a journey to find himself.

He toured around South Africa and learned about the history of colonialism and apartheid that had ravaged its Black communities. He was inspired to expand his political consciousness and started to write new material. Whereas his first two albums were about the cyclical trap of poverty and gang violence, South Africa made Lamar want to write something bigger and more comprehensive, something that captured all of the beautiful and terrible intricacies of the Black experience. He was particularly inspired by a visit to Robben Island, where he stood in the very jail cell that once held Nelson Mandela as a political prisoner. Humbled and inspired, Lamar put his feelings into words on his next project, *To Pimp a Butterfly*.

To Pimp a Butterfly was a living document of Black history, trauma and excellence. Many of the album's lyrics, as well as its title, were a comment on how the entertainment industry exploits Black talent for money only to toss artists by the wayside when they're no longer useful. Throughout the album, the white industry is characterized as "Lucy," a devilish figure who makes Faustian offers to Lamar. This temptation toward wealth and fame shows up in the second verse of "Alright," which ties the promises of fame and wealth to the unkept promises of reconstruction America, comparing modern material wealth to forty acres and a mule. Lamar's struggles with the temptation of fame play out in a poem that grows through-

out the album, in which he admits that he was abusing his power gained from fame, and recalls a moment in a hotel room where he was under so much pressure that he was tempted toward suicide.

One of Kendrick Lamar's greatest gifts is his ability to layer meaning and emotion into his songs. He's able to fit a thousand thoughts into three minutes, and still make the song catchy enough that people will chant and party to it. "Alright" is the embodiment of this. The Pharrell-made beat is eerie and haunted, with chanted voices and dissonant saxophones rolling around in the background. On top, Lamar's voice is full of determination and energy, hooking the listener on his every word. At the end of the second verse, he delivers his promise to his listeners. Even amid the paranoid pressures of fame, and the constant dread that comes from living under

systemic oppression, he is going to remain himself and stay true to his community.

Lamar finds this self-assuredness by looking to the history of Black creation and defiance. *To Pimp a Butterfly* uses jazz to connect him to American musical history. It's also an album loaded with rich references to the history of Black literature. The opening line of "Alright" is a quote of Alice Walker's *The Color Purple*: "Alls my life I has to fight." Lamar wants to embrace his cultural ancestors both known and unknown, and he wants to encourage his audience to do the same. As he sees it, to imagine a better future, the Black community must embrace its past.

When Black Lives Matter protesters chant "We gon' be alright" in the face of a brutal militarized police force, they are doing just that. They are embracing the rich protest history of a people that have had to fight for everything that they have in America. They are singing a song with inspirations that date all the way back to slavery, and with references to an international Black struggle that stretches far beyond the borders of the United States. Ever since Black Lives Matter adopted "Alright" as an anthem in 2015, the movement has only grown in power and relevance. Despite facing backlash after backlash, Black Lives Matter still goes strong today as one of the defining American social movements of the new millennium. And when you go to a Black Lives Matter protest in any city across the country to this very day, you will almost certainly hear hundreds of galvanized Black activists chanting "We gon' be alright."

 # Honorable Mentions

"Uptown Funk" by Mark Ronson (featuring Bruno Mars): Mark Ronson and Bruno Mars revived Prince's Minneapolis sound with a pitch-perfect dance-funk classic. "Uptown Funk" was one of the biggest hits of a new era of music streaming, with nearly five million streams in one week.

"Alexander Hamilton" by the cast of *Hamilton*: Lin Manuel Miranda announced himself as Broadway's new darling with *Hamilton*, a radical musical that uses old-school hip-hop to tell the story of one of America's founding fathers. *Hamilton* was an enormous hit, selling out night after night on Broadway and crossing over to the mainstream to become nothing short of a cultural sensation.

2016

"Formation"

Beyoncé

No artist in the history of pop music has achieved the sustained critical and commercial success of Beyoncé. Frankly, none have even come close. When Beyoncé first broke into the pop industry, it was as a teenage star in the girl group Destiny's Child. Over the course of five years, Destiny's Child sold more than 15 million records and racked up 14 Grammy nominations and three wins. When the '90s girl group era gave way to a new generation of pop divas, Beyoncé's profile only rose. She released a string of solo albums that sold even better than Destiny's Child and established herself as one of the most powerful women in pop music. When the 2010s came around and the digital era brought on an age of politicized pop auteurs, she was still on the cutting edge. Her 2013 self-titled album saw Beyoncé overtly embrace feminism to become a political icon and innovate an entirely new style of surprise album release along the way. Despite this unprecedented run of success, the greatest artistic triumph of Beyoncé's career was yet to come. In 2016, a full 18 years after Destiny's Child dropped their debut, she surprised the world by releasing a new video on YouTube, for a song called "Formation."

Released on the backdrop of rising racial tensions as Trump-mania was starting to sweep across America, "Formation" was an unapologetic celebration of Beyoncé's Blackness. The video is framed around imagery of New Orleans, the birthplace of American popular music, and a city famously abandoned by America's white majority after the catastrophe of Hurricane Katrina. Beyoncé is seen posing on a police car in a flooded city, a striking image that draws a direct line between the systemic failures of Katrina and the systemic racism prevalent in American police forces. But these images of pain and desolation are matched with striking shots of haute southern couture. She wears thick braids and dances in southern manors, subverting the aesthetics of the antebellum south. The entire video is a celebration of the rich cultural history of New Orleans, and an undeniable statement of Black power.

Beyoncé's lyrics are just as celebratory of Black culture as the video. In the opening of the song, she declares her

> . . . a full 18 years after Destiny's Child dropped their debut, [Beyoncé] suprised the world by releasing a new video . . .

southern credit through her parentage—an Alabama father, a Louisiana mother—and her own Texan upbringing. She follows that up with a celebration of Black beauty, which has been historically discriminated against by white society, saying she wants her baby with afros and her noses with Jackson Five nostrils. All of the verses were written by Beyoncé herself, though she got the chorus from Swae Lee of the rap duo Rae Sremmurd. Lee came up with the phrase "Ladies, let's get in formation" on the way to Coachella and thought that it might make a strong basis for a female empowerment song. Beyoncé proved him right. In the second half of the song, she flips gender roles on their head to make a statement about her own wealth and success, declaring herself a black Bill Gates in the making. This declaration is underlined by the video, which sees Beyoncé sporting haute couture and driving classic cars against the backdrop of ghettoized neighborhoods. "Formation" is a victory lap for an artist who more than proved her place in the pantheon of pop greats.

A day after dropping the video on YouTube, Beyoncé made a surprise appearance at the Super Bowl half-time show and performed the song in another striking outfit, black with a golden bandolier, a militaristic look of Black power that also paid homage to Michael

Jackson's outfit during his Super Bowl performance. Beyoncé's outfit is more than just a tribute—it was an audacious statement, a declaration that she belonged in the same conversation as the King of Pop himself.

With such an astounding résumé, it would have been easy for Beyoncé to rest on her laurels as she grew toward middle age. Instead, she took a dramatic risk with an experimental, political project. She used her platform to speak on the issues of her day. As the protests against police brutality were heating up, she became a powerful ally for the Black Lives Matter movement. The political manifesto that was "Formation" drew no shortage of criticism, but Beyoncé casually took it all in stride. She made her status as Queen Bee clear and let none of the backlash slow her momentum.

"Formation" was just the first video released in an ambitious project that she released later in the year. *Lemonade* was an hour-long visual album, filled with the sorts of stunning images of Black

history and empowerment that made "Formation" thrive. The concept of the film and the album are framed around an affair that her husband, Jay-Z, had. Beyoncé explores the hurt and pain of the affair but contextualizes it on a wider pain of Black trauma. *Lemonade* examines the ways that the generational trauma of slavery plays out in Black families and drives Black communities away from one another. The film quotes Malcolm X and pulls from such musicians as Sister Rosetta Tharpe and Bessie Smith. It references such Black writers as Toni Morrison, Octavia Butler and Zora Neale Hurston. It concludes on radical statements of love and acceptance, asserting that the only way Black communities can overcome their historic baggage is by trusting one another and building a better world together.

When Beyoncé surprised the world with the unannounced drop of "Formation," it marked the beginning of a new era of pop music. As America became more politicized and careened toward disaster, she made it clear that pop needed to deepen its social consciousness. There had been plenty of political songs in pop music history, but few had such depth and thoughtfulness. It was the sort of thing that could only come from the wisdom earned by nearly two decades in the institutionally racist American music industry. "Formation" is a revolutionary work of Black feminism created by a woman who had become thoroughly comfortable in her own skin, despite countless industry and cultural pressures encouraging her not to be. Its fierce politics predict the #MeToo movement that would explode over the next year as women of all backgrounds stood up to patriarchal systems of oppression. "Formation" is more than just a song that perfectly captured the tense political moment of 2017; it's one of the most stunning music videos in the history of the medium, and it's living proof that Beyoncé is an artist who sits in a league of her own.

Honorable Mentions

"Ultralight Beam" by Kanye West: Kanye West continued to revolutionize hip-hop with a brilliant gospel-rap tune about the struggles of fame. His reversed organ samples and gospel choir tie together a loose piece of music that lets his collaborators flourish. The highlight of the song is Chance the Rapper's guest verse, an earnest performance celebrating his unexpected ride to success.

"Sorry" by Justin Bieber: Justin Bieber teamed up with Skrillex to create a song embracing a new trend of tropical house that was bringing Caribbean sounds into American pop music. "Sorry" is a perfect summer jam, built on a thumping beat with lyrics that reference Bieber's public breakup with fellow pop star Selena Gomez.

"Despacito"

Luis Fonsi

Since the turn of millennium, America has been undergoing an enormous demographic shift. Between 2000 and 2020, the country's Latino population grew from 35 million to more than 62 million, a shift that's come with upward mobility for Latinos. More Latinos than ever are graduating from college, making up the labor force and buying property in America. This shift is reflected in all aspects of American culture, but perhaps nowhere more than in music. Latin music has always influenced American pop music. It helped shape jazz a century ago, and it was an essential ingredient to the disco music that swept across the nation in the '70s. By the '90s and 2000s, Latin pop artists were crossing over into mainstream pop and scoring hits with an English-speaking audience. Still, the only Spanish-language songs ever to top the American charts were Los Lobos' 1987 version of "La Bamba" and the '90s novelty dance craze "Macarena." That all changed in 2017, when a veteran Puerto Rican singer named Luis Fonsi dropped the surprise hit "Despacito."

Fonsi had worked in the Latin pop world since the late '90s, finding success in the Latin world but failing to cross over despite releasing an English language album in 2002. When he first started writing "Despacito" in late 2015, there were no signs that the song would be any different. Fonsi and cowriter Erika Ender wrote most of the song in just a few hours while playing around on an acoustic guitar in Fonsi's house. Fonsi had gained a reputation as a slow balladist, and he wanted to show that he could make a more upbeat dance song. He came up with a chorus that stretched out the word *despacito*, meaning "slowly," and built the song around that. It was a simple piece of genius, with form reflecting content in a slow-building earworm. Once the skeleton of the song was written, he looped in fellow Puerto Rican Daddy Yankee, who helped add a reggaeton edge to the song with a thumping beat and a guest rap verse.

The combination of a more romantic Spanish pop with the harder-hitting reggae worked wonders. "Despacito" was an instant hit in international markets, finding its way onto dance floors across the world, even in countries where Latin pop seldom got played. But

> Fonsi and cowriter Erika Ender wrote most of the song in just a few hours while playing around on an acoustic guitar . . .

as the song was rising, there was one barrier to true global dominance: the English markets of the United States and United Kingdom. "Despacito" entered the Billboard Hot 100 in February 2017, and climbed to number 44 on April 15, 2017. Then, Fonsi got a lucky break. Canadian pop star Justin Bieber heard "Despacito" while clubbing in Colombia and loved it. Bieber and Fonsi's management touched base, and within days, Bieber was recording a remix of the song. His version mixed English and Spanish, and he was even sure to hire a Spanish vocal coach to ensure that he got the pronunciations right.

On April 17, 2017, the Justin Bieber remix of "Despacito" dropped. His collaboration introduced the song to an English market, and within weeks, "Despacito" was on top of the Hot 100. Unlike the last two Spanish-language songs to hit the top, "Despacito" was not a passing fad. Its entire run at the top of the Billboard charts lasted 16 weeks, tying the record for longest run at the time. Meanwhile, the music video for Fonsi's original version shattered online streaming records. In August 2017 it became the most viewed YouTube video of all time, and it held that title for more than three years. Today, the video for Fonsi's original version of "Despacito" sits with an astounding 8.2 billion views, more views than the entire population of the earth.

The team-up success of Luis Fonsi, Daddy Yankee and Justin Bieber is representative of a positive vision for the future of America's music. Even as Donald Trump rode to the presidency on a wave of anti-Latino xenophobia, Fonsi and Bieber proved that cross-cultural collaborations could thrive and bring new, unique sounds to the American pop music scene. "Despacito" proved

that language doesn't need to be a barrier in pop music, as long as artists are making music that people can groove and dance to.

Luis Fonsi made history for Latin artists, and in his wake, Latin music has continued its upward rise. Such artists as Bad Bunny and J Balvin have since become some of the biggest names in American music, as the mainstream charts begin to shift to more accurately reflect the rich and diverse cultural makeup of America. Latin pop has always been an important piece of the American musical landscape, but thanks to "Despacito," it is finally getting a chance to shine in the spotlight that it's always deserved.

 # Honorable Mentions

"D.N.A." by Kendrick Lamar: After wowing the world with his ambitious jazz rap, Lamar turned to the most popular rap trend of the era, trap. This Atlanta-born sound used sparse instrumentation and complex drum-machine patterns to create heavy, paranoid beats. Lamar used this trap sound to lash back against a mainstream press vilifying him on "D.N.A.," going so far as to sample a fearmongering clip about him that aired on Fox News. "D.N.A." celebrates his Black heritage and furthers his argument for the title of GOAT.

"The Story of O.J." by Jay-Z: It looked like Jay-Z's prolific run of success might have finally been coming to an end with the flop of 2013's *Magna Carta Holy Grail*, but in 2017 he proved his doubters wrong with one of the best albums of his career. *4:44* is an introspective album apologizing for Jay-Z's public affair, while also establishing himself as rap's elder statesman. In "The Story of O.J.," he cautions younger rappers against getting caught up in the trappings of fame, reminding them that they're still part of an exploitive industry that will milk them for all they're worth. He paired it with one of the most striking videos of all time, coopting the history of racist cartoons to underscore his message of systemic racism.

2018

"This Is America"

Childish Gambino

Fifty-two seconds into the most celebrated music video of 2018, a topless Donald Glover pulls out a pistol, strikes a pose, shoots a man in the back of the head and turns to the camera to deliver the song's title: "This Is America." And that's just the beginning. Over the rest of the video, Glover, who released the song under his stage name Childish Gambino, dances around an enormous warehouse as surreal scenes play out in the background. Cars are looted and burned, Glover guns down a gospel choir, a hooded man on a horse runs by and onlookers use cell phones to film the chaos from the rafters. At the end of the video, the warehouse goes dark as Glover runs in terror from a crowd of pursuers. The whole effect is one of emotional whiplash. Dance moves collide with violence as a bright pop hook gives way to heavy trap beats. It's a disorienting and terrifying video devoid of any easy answers.

This absurdist abstraction invited a wave of analysis and speculation. From the moment "This Is America" first hit the internet, fans and media institutions alike were poring over it frame by frame

> From the moment "This Is America" first hit the internet, fans and media institutions alike were poring over it frame by frame to discover meaning.

to discover meaning. People pointed out that the sweatpants that Glover was wearing may have been taken from a Confederate Army uniform. They noted similarities between some of Glover's poses and the minstrel caricature Jim Crow. A false theory even sprang up stating that the man who Glover shoots in the opening sequence was portrayed by the father of Trayvon Martin.

Amid the many meanings buried in the video, the clearest is a condemnation of America's gun culture. Throughout the 2010s, the gun control debate turned into one of the biggest culture war issues gripping America, all while gun violence continued. By 2018, rates were so high that the United States saw 323 different mass shootings in a calendar year. Many of these shootings took place at schools, a fact that the video underlines by having teenage background dancers in school uniforms. The other culprit behind much of America's gun violence is the police, who are depicted in the song's video and its lyrics.

The heavy lyrics of the trap-beat section are juxtaposed with lighter lyrics about parties and money over a bright,

guitar-driven chorus. This sharp contrast creates an accusation of American culture that's backed up in the video—the country's industries of wealth and entertainment serve to distract from the deep trauma and violence that happen every day. This violence is especially prevalent against Black Americans, who are frequently denied access to the benefits of the country's wealth. In another bright break midway through the video, a gospel choir sings only to be gunned down by Glover holding a machine gun moments later.

The constant shifting of the song and video destabilize the viewer. There's no security to be found in the song. By creating a world of aesthetic and thematic juxtaposition, he captured the uneasy realities of being Black in America in 2018. The threat of violence, both individual and systemic, lingered around every corner, even as Black artists were enjoying unprecedented levels of mainstream success. Throughout most of the video, Glover seems immune to this vio-

lence as he dances and smiles. Black entertainers have a history of being treated better by white society up to a point. But at the end of the video, the turn comes. In the final shots, after dancing on top of old beat-up cars in parody of an age-old hip-hop trope, the video cuts to a tense, dark closing shot. Obscured near to the point of inhumanity by dramatic shadows, a sweaty Glover runs terrified away from a crowd chasing him. Nobody is truly immune from the brutal racialized violence of America.

Of course, this analysis is mere speculation. The whole time that fans were dissecting the video, Glover himself remained elusive. When a reporter asked whether he would explain the video, his answer was a simple but firm, "No." This isn't exactly surprising, as much of his work intentionally avoided simple answers. His TV show *Atlanta* frequently uses surreal sequences and emotional juxtaposition to pose the same sorts of questions about American society that he asks with "This Is

America." He is not an artist who preaches to his audience, but rather one who gives them art and trusts them to interpret it as they will.

The abstract nature of the video, along with its striking visuals and shock release made it one of the most discussed pop culture objects of the year. Countless parodies sprang up, with a half dozen international artists creating versions that criticized the harsh realities of their own country. The buzz around the song helped it rise to the top of the Billboard's charts in the spring, and it remained on the Hot 100 throughout the summer of 2018, giving America one of its darkest, strangest songs of the summer.

"This Is America" never appeared on any studio album, and while it saw millions of streams and got radio play, it will forever be remembered as a music video first and foremost. It's just one feather in the cap of one of the most versatile artists of the era, proving Glover's comprehensive artistic vision as more than just a musician, but a filmmaker, dancer, artist and all-around cultural provocateur. By creating a video full of wild abstraction, Glover and Hiro Murai ensured that "This Is America" wouldn't simply depict one moment but could remain an evergreen piece to be forever speculated by audiences trying to better understand their own experience of their complicated, violent country.

Honorable Mentions

"Sicko Mode" by Travis Scott: Travis Scott and Drake created a classic for the new millennium with the progressive rap epic "Sicko Mode." Building on a beat based on Jamaican dub, "Sicko Mode" earned a reputation as a hip-hop "Bohemian Rhapsody," thanks to its radical beat-switching structure. "Sicko Mode" becomes the first hip-hop song ever to spend 30 weeks in Billboard's Top 10.

"I Like It" by Cardi B: Cardi B teamed up with Puerto Rican rapper Bad Bunny and Colombian pop star J Balvin for a Latin trap song that fed the rising tide of Latin pop, following "Despacito" as another Spanish-language chart topper.

2019

"Bad Guy"

Billie Eilish

In 2019, the first Generation Z pop star arrived on the music scene with a splash. After drawing the attention of the music industry with a handful of independent releases when she was just 15, Billie Eilish made her major label debut at 18 years of age with *When We All Fall Sleep, Where Do We Go*. That album gave the world a peek into the mind of a new generation born into the paranoia of a post-9/11 world, raised under the constant gaze of social media and came of age into a world where the existential threat of climate change was becoming real. It was heavy and dark, full of ethereal electro-pop created by Eilish's brother, Finneas, in his bedroom studio. It was a sound palette that hadn't been heard in pop, with beats made of obscure found sound and a breathy vocal delivery by Eilish that oozed effortless stardom. But amid all the grim soundscapes, the album had a joyful sense of irony and self-awareness, something embodied in the biggest single, "Bad Guy."

Eilish wrote "Bad Guy" as a satire on people who pose tough on social media. In the opening line, she depicts a man posing as a tough badass then responds to these empty boasts with her own sarcastic retort, in which she boasts that she's the true bad one, even threatening that she might seduce his dad.

Eilish's message is paired with vivid production helmed by Finneas and Eilish herself. A heavy, pulsing bassline introduces the song in a place of tension, and Eilish's multitracked vocals are eerie and haunting, creating a powerful mockery of the target of her derision. When the verse gives way to a chorus, Eilish throws in a sarcastic "duh" before the hook comes in. That hook is a mock-spooky synth line, influenced by the *Wizards of Waverly Place* theme, as well as the video game *Plants vs. Zombies*. The beat beneath was actually sampled from the pinging sounds of a crosswalk in Australia, recorded by Eilish as a voice memo on her phone and adjusted to fit the song by Finneas. At the end of the song, this groovy rhythm gives way to a strange beat that was one of Eilish's first experiments on Logic. That beat is paired with an eerie sample of an Eilish laugh, and a quick, mechanical hi-hat pattern. It serves as a final statement in the last moments of the song—one that leaves the listener wondering whether Eilish might actually be the badass that she's sarcastically posing as.

> Eilish wrote "Bad Guy" as a satire on people who pose tough on social media.

The video for "Bad Guy" underlines the idea that Eilish might actually be as cool as her fake persona. In it, she displays herself as a Gen Z fashion icon, wearing bright colors and loose clothing, while sporting a green haircut that would be imitated by countless teens upon her success. These fashion choices complement the rich colors that populate the video's surreal vignettes. She dances carefree on a yellow backdrop, and spins around with childlike joy on a yellow-and-burgundy spiral rug. The video revels in irony, while simultaneously providing striking horror-inspired imagery, like Eilish's inhuman stare at the camera as her nose bleeds. The video is a carefully crafted piece of aesthetic, but at the same time, she staunchly refuses to take herself seriously in it. That's a big part of her appeal as an artist.

Raised in a world of constant observation, Generation Z developed an unprecedented self-awareness that manifested into layer upon layer of irony and detachment. And yet buried somewhere beneath layers of personality projection, cultural references and irreverent deflection is a radical generation that deeply cares about the world. Gen Z are more politically engaged than any of their immediate predecessors. Their aesthetic vision is reshaping the cultural world as their digital native status allows them to dismantle the old hierarchies of the analog world. While there was no overt political statement in "Bad Guy," it's a song with a clear feminist subtext, and it's happy to comment on the constructed identities of the modern world.

Just a month after its release, "Bad Guy" had soared to the top of Bill-

board's Hot 100 and turned Eilish into a teenage superstar. The critics were just as fond of "Bad Guy," too, naming her as an overnight icon. When the Grammys came around, "Bad Guy" won both Record of the Year and Song of the Year. Built in a bedroom by two siblings with a joyful, lighthearted approach to music, "Bad Guy" somehow managed to be one of the darkest, heaviest pop songs of the year. Its lyrics were an irreverent tease, but its music got at a creeping dread that the world was feeling in 2019. As climate change was accelerating and the far right was rising in America, an era of bright dance-pop gave way to darker songs with a cynical edge. "Bad Guy" captured the growing fears simmering beneath the surface of America. In doing so, it announced to the entire world that Gen Z were here and ready to reshape culture in their own image.

Honorable Mentions

"Old Town Road" by Lil Nas X: Lil Nas X showed a brilliant marketing savvy, gaming Billboard's chart system and taking advantage of TikTok to score a viral hit with his novelty country-rap song "Old Town Road." Its success signaled the beginning of a new era in which internet virality can be used to launch pop careers.

"Blinding Lights" by the Weeknd: The Weeknd perfected the '80s pop nostalgia sound that had gripped the 2010s in "Blinding Lights." Built around a catchy synth hook and elevated by a viral dance meme, "Blinding Lights" became the last true hit of the prepandemic era. But even a pandemic lockdown couldn't stop the momentum of the song, as it went on an incredible 90-week chart run, finally falling out of the Hot 100 in May 2021.

AN UNCERTAIN FUTURE

2020-23

The 2020s were only a few months old when it became clear that everything was about to change. The COVID-19 pandemic tore across the world in what might be the biggest historical happening since the Second World War. People locked themselves inside, and music had to adapt. Live music was temporarily replaced with awkward Zoom conversations. Pop musicians scrapped enormous world tours and retreated to cabins and bedrooms, writing introspective music about a complicated era. The turmoil from the pandemic accelerated a social destabilization half a decade in the making and resulted in waves of protests. The murder of George Floyd galvanized musicians to release a steady stream of protest music challenging police brutality and systemic racism. A growing movement of homophobia and transphobia inspired the queer community to stand up and fight loudly for their place in the world.

On the other side of the aisle, a rampant culture of conspiricism drew its own protests, with conservative musicians dropping antivax

2020

2021

2022

2023

songs and promoting a new authoritarian take on American patriotism. A year into the new decade, a violent mob stormed the U.S. Capitol in an attempt to overthrow a democratically elected government. And odds are, that's just the beginning.

It's impossible to know what the rest of the 2020s will bring, but one thing is clear: We are living in an era of instability not seen in generations. Recommendation algorithms are changing the way that we interact with all media in real time. The rise of artificial intelligence promises a democratization of art even as it threatens to annihilate creative labor markets. Streaming has made it easier than ever for people to listen to music, but harder than ever for musicians to make money.

And despite all this terrifying uncertainty, musicians are persisting. The 2020s have seen more marginalized artists take the stage than ever before. We live in a diverse pop world where, for the first time in history, people of all ethnicities, genders and sexualities are getting a chance to express themselves on a world stage. The arbitrary boundaries of genre that have divided music for generations are collapsing as technology makes it easier for people to expand their musical taste. The digital natives of Generation Z are rising to take over culture, bringing both a unique perspective on the world, and an inherent knowledge of the digital media systems that drive the world.

In times like these, it can sometimes be hard to see the light. But even against impossible odds, music will prevail. It will continue to give a platform for marginalized communities to protest and fight for their rights. It will continue to be an outlet for the myriad joys and pains of the human condition. It will continue to bring people together through rhythm and through groove. As humankind marches forward into an uncertain future, music will be right there next to us, supporting us and connecting us, elating us and inspiring us, just as it always has.

2020

"Walking in the Snow"

Run the Jewels

The year 2020 will forever be remembered as a turning point in world history. When the coronavirus pandemic swept across the world, killing millions, it brought with it turmoil and social upheaval not seen since the 1960s. A rampant culture of radicalism and conspiracism that had been growing online exploded with the pandemic. The global economy ground to a halt as people went into lockdown and the world was forced to question whether human lives or economic growth were more important. Simmering digital cultures and technologies were suddenly mainstream as the internet became the only place for social interaction. All of the tensions in American society that had been growing across the Trump era, and even earlier, threatened to come to a head as people grew lonely and desperate. Then, on May 25, 2020, the country experienced a flashpoint moment. A white police officer named Derek Chauvin stopped a Black man named George Floyd, believing that he had used a counterfeit $20 bill to buy cigarettes. During the process of the arrest, Chauvin and his fellow police officers held Floyd to the ground, and Chauvin knelt on Floyd's neck for nine minutes, all the while ignoring his pleas of "I can't breathe." After nine minutes of begging, George Floyd died. Horrified onlookers captured the incident on video and

posted it online. Overnight, America erupted into protest.

Floyd's death at the hands of the police was just one of countless similar incidents that had happened over the past decade. But the Black Lives Matter movement had grown to critical mass by 2020. Floyd's was the third overt murder of a Black person in just a few months in 2020. February saw Ahmaud Arbery murdered in a vicious hate crime while jogging, and March saw plainclothes police officers force entry into Breonna Taylor's home and murder her on-site. The racial tensions growing in the country were exacerbated by the pandemic, which had shut down the economy and left millions at home with nothing to occupy themselves. Sick of sitting in silence and watching innocents get murdered, American protestors took to the streets in the largest collective action the country had seen in decades. They were met with a violent, militarized police force and radical right-wing counterprotests. The protests erupted into a culture war, and the entire world watched with baited breath as America seemed to teeter on the verge of collapse.

A week into the George Floyd uprising, one of the most radical acts in hip-hop released a song that seemed to be written about that very moment: "Walkin' in the Snow." The song's pro-

duction is heavy and angry, with a relentless beat colored by electric guitar hits and crowd chants in the background. Its lyrics are a broad condemnation of systemic power in the United States and a prediction of where the country is headed if those in power are allowed to continue. In the opening verse, El-P characterizes the disenfranchised masses who became radicalized by a conspiratorial right-wing media machine. He explains the way that systemic power maintains its control of the hierarchy by turning one oppressed group, like poor whites, against groups that are lower down in the hierarchy, like Black people and queer people. El-P says that cages are never built for just one group, and predicts that once one community has been sufficiently marginalized, the eye of despots will turn to the next.

El-P's class-conscious protests are paired with an even more radical verse by Killer Mike, who describes the processes of systemic racism, which he has experienced firsthand as a Black man in America. Midway through his verse is a set of bars that seem to be directly addressing George Floyd's murder. Mike discusses the way that news media creates a culture of fear and desensitization that can culminate in people numbly watching police choke a man out as he cries "I can't breathe." In truth, "Walkin' in the Snow" had been written months before Floyd's murder. This seemingly prescient line was actually a reference to Eric Garner, yet another Black man who had been choked to death by a police officer in 2014. The moment the song was released, however, the meaning was forever changed. Killer Mike had already been a high-profile political activist, championing Black causes and even winning an endorsement from Bernie Sanders, but "Walkin' in the Snow" made him seem to some like a prophet. In the closing couplet of that verse, Killer Mike preaches a powerful statement to drive home the wider message, reminding everybody that even Jesus was killed by the state.

"Walkin' in the Snow" and the album that it came from, *RTJ4*, marked a new level of relevance for a duo who had a completely atypical career path. Both Killer Mike and El-P spent decades grinding in the underground until they teamed up to form Run the Jewels. Before long, they became some of hip-hop's most unexpected rising stars, and they used this newfound platform to preach a political message. As America began a slow descent toward fascism, that message became more and more relevant, and Run the Jewels became key figures in a new movement of musical resistance.

The radical politics championed in their lyrics are a big reason why Run the Jewels have become so successful, but their status as global icons is just as influenced by their ethic of playful irreverence. Run the Jewels frequently find ways to laugh at themselves and their world. *RTJ4* is full of raunchy bars and comedic turns of phrase that ground the band and make them relatable. It's not that Run the Jewels believe their political message needs to be undercut, but rather that they want to capture the true emotions of life. They understand that humor is one of the ways that we find meaning, and that joy is one of our most important tools against oppressive systems.

As 2020 saw a destabilized America careen toward authoritarianism, Run the Jewels stepped up as the latest in a rich lineage of rap activists. "Walkin' in the Snow" was a heated piece of rage against systemic racism and classism. It embodied the energy driving the Black Lives Matter protests and contextualized them within the wider systems of hierarchal power in America. The new decade brought with it a whole host of new issues for America, both seen and unseen. From the moment they dropped "Walkin' in the Snow," Run the Jewels made it clear that they intended to face these issues head on and do everything they could to help shepherd their country toward a brighter future.

Its lyrics are a broad condemnation of systemic power in the United States and a prediction of where the country is headed if those in power are allowed to continue.

Honorable Mentions

"WAP" by Cardi B (featuring Megan Thee Stallion): Cardi B and Megan Thee Stallion dropped a track that continued hip-hop's long legacy of explicit sex jams. The twist: This one sees two women taking sexuality to the kind of exclusive levels only allowed to men before. It's a piece of escapism from the pandemic, but also the center of one of the era's endless exhausting culture wars.

"Fetch the Bolt Cutters" by Fiona Apple: Just a few weeks after most of the world entered lockdown, Fiona Apple released a home-recorded album that captured the spirit of the time with heavy discussions of trauma and mental illness. Although it was written before the pandemic, the title track felt particularly poignant for the moment.

2021

"Montero (Call Me By Your Name)"

Lil Nas X

Six days into 2021, a violent mob of Donald Trump supporters stormed the U.S. Capitol as part of an effort to overturn the results of the 2020 election. It was the violent culmination of a culture of conspiracies and outrage that had been fostered by an enormous right-wing media engine. One of the most frequent targets of this outrage engine was America's LGBTQ+ community. After a decade of incredible progress that saw gay marriage legalized, queer culture enter the mainstream and transgender issues entering the public spotlight, the backlash came swift and hard. Right-wing provocateurs began to break out the same tropes that had been used to subjugate queer communities for decades—arguments about sin, declarations of sexual deviancy and mental illness and a continued air of vilification and dehumanization. But the queer community persisted. Amid this growing culture of homophobia, an openly gay pop star was able to co-opt the right-wing rage engine and use it as media fuel to dominate the discourse of the day and ride his way up to superstardom.

Nobody would have expected Lil Nas X to become a queer icon when he first hit the scene. His 2019 hit "Old Town Road" was a novelty song that found success through a combination of natural virality and gaming Billboard's chart system. By nearly anybody's reckoning, Lil Nas X and "Old Town Road" seemed destined to become one of the great one-hit wonders of all time. But Lil Nas X had different ideas. He leveraged the viral success of "Old Town Road" into a record deal with Columbia and began to piece together a debut studio album. On March 26, 2021, he dropped the lead single of his debut album, "Montero (Call Me By Your Name)."

"Montero" was a victory lap for Lil Nas X. It was a celebration of his ride to the top, but more importantly it was an overt embracing of his true identity. While "Old Town Road" was in the midst of its historic chart run, Lil Nas X publicly came out as gay, making him the first artist ever to do so while having a song on top of the charts. "Montero" is an overt exploration of Lil Nas X's experiences as a gay man. The song's chorus was inspired by *Call Me By Your Name*, a celebrated 2017 film that instantly became part of the queer canon. In that film, the act of calling a lover by your own name is used as a sign of deep intimacy between the two gay characters. It's a signal of a shared trust, understanding and experience of marginalization.

This romantic chorus is paired with overt celebrations of queer sexuality. In the verses, Lil Nas X pulls no punches. His overtly sexual lyrics have been seen in songs about heterosexual relationships since the early days of the blues, but few had ever talked so openly about gay sex in a pop song.

Just in case the sexual lyrics weren't enough to piss off the homophobes, Lil Nas X debuted "Montero" with a stunning music video full of biblical imagery. In that video, Lil Nas X depicts a utopian land called "Montero." It's a utopian Garden of Eden free from hate and discrimination. He runs through this garden while being tempted by a demonic figure before the video cuts to an elaborate stadium with a pink-clad Lil Nas X being put on trial by a crowd of stone-skinned clones. Finally, the most controversial image of the video sees Lil Nas X pole dance around a pole that descends all the way to hell before walking into Satan's castle to give him a lap dance. The whole piece revels in camp and blasphemy. It's a powerful subversion of the Christian conservatism that paints all queer people as sinners and demons, while celebrating queer culture.

Predictably, the video for "Montero" drew enormous criticism from the right-wing outrage machine and homophobic Black communities alike. But rather than run and hide, Lil Nas X faced these criticisms head on. He leaned into the satanic panic accusations by teaming with Nike to release a limited run shoe line complete with pentagrams and drops of human blood. It was an intentionally provocative act that kept Lil Nas X's name in the news cycle and kept his song rising up the charts. As conservative pundits were popping veins in their heads shouting about the blasphemy of "Montero," he was collecting paychecks and riding the media wave to the top of Billboard's charts.

Lil Nas X's arrival on the music scene heralded a new breed of pop star. As a member of Generation Z, he was raised on the internet. He understood the nature of the internet hype cycle better than anybody and took advantage of it to lift himself into stardom. Once he achieved that stardom, he turned his goals outward, using his platform to express his own sexuality and destigmatize queer love even as many in the world were trying to push people back in the closet. "Montero (Call Me By Your Name)" is more than just an anthem of queer love; it's Lil Nas X's declaration of his own relevance and continuing importance in a pop world undergoing immense transformation.

 # Honorable Mentions

"That Funny Feeling" by Bo Burnham: Bo Burnham's pandemic-themed musical comedy special *Inside* delivered an unexpected poignancy. He perfectly captured the existential dread that came with watching recommendation algorithms disintegrate the institutions of democracy while being stuck in a room with nothing to do about it.

"Good 4 U" by Olivia Rodrigo: A new teenage pop star arrived on the scene with a vicious breakup song that stands as the biggest hit of a new era of pop-punk revival. Olivia Rodrigo combined the confessional songwriting of Taylor Swift with the youthful rage of Paramore. She captured a TikTok audience and became one of the few promising new acts in a pop scene in turmoil.

2022

"About Damn Time"

Lizzo

After two long years of pandemic lockdowns, economic despair and political upheaval, the world finally started to return to some semblance of normal in 2022. While the coronavirus still raged, vaccines helped limit the effects to the point that people were able to go outside once more. Families that had been split apart reunited, businesses forced to shutter their windows finally reopened and people started to pour into venues and stadiums to see live music again for the first time in years. While the world remained irrevocably changed by the pandemic, and the societal cracks that appeared have yet to be patched up, 2022 still brought with it a shred of hope. New communities of solidarity and political action started to appear in response to the pandemic, a flood of brilliant art made during the lockdown hit the world, and voices that had been marginalized for generations were finally getting a chance to shape the world in their own image. It was on this backdrop in the spring of 2022 that Lizzo released a song that said what so many people were thinking: "About Damn Time."

Lizzo's celebratory post-COVID track was an ode to self-love and personal actualization, wrapped in the shell of a classic disco groove. It was just one track in a movement of nu-disco, embracing the tropes of a movement that was unjustly relegated to the underground for decades. Crisp chicken-scratch guitar grooves atop a funky slapped bassline revive a legacy of the disco greats like Chic and Donna Summer, providing a hopeful message for a new era. Lizzo sings of triumph over adversity in the chorus, asserting that she's going to come out of COVID stronger than she entered it. She embraces the change that has come with the world and encourages her audience to bring the same attitude into their lives.

Lizzo is a fitting artist to write the self-empowerment anthem of a new age. As a big Black woman in an industry that disproportionately valued thinness and whiteness, Lizzo's career looked to be floundering in the 2010s. Her first two studio albums failed to find much of an audience, and she found herself approaching age 30 without a hit to her name. Fortune changed for Lizzo when a viral TikTok trend began using her 2017 single "Truth Hurts." Suddenly, her messages of body positivity and female empowerment found an audience in a younger generation thirsty for representation. She had a second chance at becoming a pop star—and seized it, releasing a string of hits that proved to the world that she could perform and enchant as well as any thin diva.

Lizzo's brand of pop is openhearted and relentlessly optimistic. She challenges the toxic body image issues that have pervaded culture for generations, particularly in the world of pop. This body-positive approach has garnered her no shortage of hate, especially as she's displayed her body overtly in public appearances and music videos. Her response to this hatred has always been to deliver more radical self-love. "About Damn Time" is exactly that. The video sees Lizzo dancing around in a sparkling jumpsuit, unafraid to display her big body as a sexual object deserving of attention and love.

Such a message being delivered by a big woman is an anomaly in the modern pop world, but its lineage can actually be traced back to the very beginnings of American pop music. When the blues craze first caught on a century ago and created the American music industry, it was big Black women like Ma Rainey and Bessie Smith who became some of the country's first stars. It was only when the record industry started to take off that Black artists and women were pushed to the sidelines. Nevertheless, their creativity persisted. As mainstream American music platformed white artists, often performing Black art forms, the Black community continued to innovate, swimming against a tide of systemic racism to shape America's greatest cultural output.

In 2023, revelations about Lizzo's own treatment of her dancers shook the world. This undercuts much of the body positivity of her music, but also displays just how deeply ingrained these systems of hatred are. Many of her own disappointing actions are fueled by internalization of the very culture that she was trying to fight against. But as the world reevaluates its vision of Lizzo, the reality of her message remains relevant.

2023

"Paint the Town Red"

Doja Cat

The age of social media brought fans closer than ever to the musicians shaping the pop culture of the world. This platform allowed musicians to thrive and launch their careers to enormous height, but it has also become one of the phantoms plaguing today's pop stars. Fans in the modern age feel more ownership than ever over the musicians they adore, obsessing over their every move in some of the most rabidly created, toxic, one-sided relationships. This so-called "Stan" culture, named after Eminem's song about an obsessive fan, came to dominate internet discourse as the world moved into the mid-2020s. Some artists, such as Taylor Swift and Beyoncé, have capitalized on their obsessive fan bases to build global empires, but in 2023, Doja Cat took a different approach. In the middle of the summer, she dropped "Paint the Town Red," a searing hip-hop song that pivoted from Doja's light pop sound to a heavier hip-hop edge, and fired overt shots at the most obsessive of her fans.

"Paint the Town Red" came after an early career that had seen Doja Cat get wrapped up in controversy after controversy. In the early spring of 2023, she tweeted that her first two pop albums were "cash-grabs," a move that angered and alienated fans who adored those albums. She doubled down a few months later, when she rejected the "Kittenz" label that many of her most obsessive fans had adopted. These are just a few of the controversies that have followed Doja since her rise to fame. Some, like an attempted cancellation after discovering that she used to participate in alt-right chatrooms online, have real legs. Others, like an image surfacing of her vaping at the 2023 Met Gala, are reflections of a modern media world that thrives on outrage clicks. The most absurd of the supposed controversies came when Doja Cat shaved her head in the summer of 2022. Many of her fans took to Twitter to criticize this look, with people declaring that she was ugly, and some even saying she looked like a demon. These comments reflect the darkness of Stan culture, and the pervasive gaze that follows celebrities in the modern age.

"Paint the Town Red" is a scattershot response to all of Doja's controversies, big and small. She leaned into the "demonic" accusations, singing a hook of "Mm, she the devil / She a bad lil' bitch, she a rebel," and pairing with a stylized video full of demonic horror aesthetics. The song's verses are a triumphant call of self-actualization, with Doja declaring that she's not going to find success in new features or sidekicks, but rather by creating art that the people around her love. Doja Cat doubles down on her identity as an online

provocateur, teasing the fans and media alike, as a smooth sample of Dionne Warwick's "Walk on By" runs in the background, underlining the fact that Doja has no desire to engage with her haters anymore.

As it turns out, rejecting the temptation to play to the crowd only raised her profile. "Paint the Town Red" soared to the top of the Billboard Hot 100, giving Doja her second number one, and first as a solo artist.

Doja Cat is the quintessential artist of the digital age. Her career was launched by a surreal viral hit, and her entire ascent is filled with the markers of a digital native. She constantly trolls press and fans alike, using controversy as a tool to raise her own profile, while defying the traditional media training and road-mapped career path of the pop stars of old. "Paint the Town Red" was an assertion of Doja's status as one of the most singular artists of her era. It combined careful lyricism with a carefree

attitude to reshape her public image, and point a mirror back at the toxic fandoms developing in the modern age.

The mid-2020s are an era defined by controversy and collapse. Old institutions in politics, finance and the art industry are beginning to crumble under the sheer weight of modernity. Hard economic times have people throwing themselves deeper than ever into celebrity worship and online infighting as they search for escape and meaning. Rather than bow to this desire for an easy world, Doja Cat overtly toys with narrative and defies easy definition. As much as "Paint the Town Red" is a celebration of her own individuality, it also serves as a message to all those reeling from our strange age: Your salvation is not going to come from celebrity, and your war is not going to be won from behind a keyboard. The subtext of "Paint the Town Red" declares that the self-actualization that so many are desperate for can only come from within.

Closing Thoughts

I think that the natural inclination here at the end of our journey is to ask what comes next. As I write this book, popular music, like so many industries, is standing at a precipice. Platforms like Spotify and TikTok are radically changing the way that people interact with music as we speak, and generative A.I. is developing by leaps and bounds by the day, threatening to completely transform how music is made. Hip-hop's decades-long reign atop the charts seems to be slowly waning, but no new successor has risen up to challenge its throne. Nostalgia reigns supreme as old songs are made new again, and the cycle of virality has quickened to a relentless pace. It seems inevitable that something is going to give, but what that change will look like is anybody's guess.

If I've learned anything from this experiment, it's that nobody can truly know what's coming next. Time and time again, movements have risen from obscurity overnight to take over the musical world, challenge the mainstream and redefine our understandings of art. Almost without exception, these movements come from those on the margins. They come from people who have been left out of the power structures of society, from communities who have been forced to seek refuge and vitality in one another's shared experience. For all the brilliant individualism in the music industry, no great movement rises in a vacuum. Music is communal by its very nature, born from the love and joy that comes with sharing the human condition with another. Whatever collection of sounds coalesces to shock the world and transform the

industry next, it will come not from a single visionary, but from a commonwealth of expression, from communities standing on the shoulders of giants and imagining a better world.

Popular music is one of America's great gifts to the world. For over a century, it has provided comfort, joy and meaning to the lives of millions. It's been a tool used to fight oppression, and a soothing balm for anyone struggling with the sometimes suffocating weight of existence. It has brought communities together and created some of the greatest artistic triumphs in the history of our species. At the same time, the story of popular music is one rife with tragedy and exploitation. The music industry is one fraught with greed and systemic racism, legacies that still persist to this day. The tension between these twin legacies plays out in every new song you hear.

For all of the fears and uncertainties of modern music, it's important to remember that we live in unprecedented times. We live in an era where everyone with a song in their heart has easier access to the tools necessary to create music and the platforms that allow them to share it with the world. Never before have so many people had so much access to the brilliant creation that is American popular music. Right now, you have access to a century of human triumph at the click of a button. There is a river of song sprawling out in front of you, each a living marker of the complexities of American history, and each a reflection of brilliant diversity of humankind. So why not dive in?

References

Certifications

Any record certifications are taken from the Recording Industry Association of America. These certifications are based on record sales within the United States. The certifications are as follows:

Gold: 500,000 units

Platinum: 1,000,000 units

Diamond: 10,000,000 units

Charts

Any references to music chart numbers are drawn from the Billboard charts, which have historically based rankings on jukebox plays, radio plays and record sales, and has added streaming to its calculations in the modern era. Chart data can be found at https://www.billboard.com/charts.

Image Credits

1923: Bessie Smith on page 15 from the Carl Van Vechten Photographs collection at the Library of Congress, restored by Adam Cuerden/Wikimedia Commons

1924: George Gershwin on page 17 from the Carl Van Vechten Photographs collection at the Library of Congress

1925: Ma Rainey on page 19 from Wikimedia Commons

1926: Louis Armstrong on page 21 by from the New York World-Telegram and Sun collection at the Library of Congress/Wikimedia Commons

1927: Blind Willie Johnson on page 23 by Michael Ochs Archives/Getty

1928: Jimmie Rodgers on page 25 by the Victor Talking Machine Company, taken by Moss Photo, NYC/Wikimedia Commons

1929: Fats Waller on page 27 by Alan Fisher/Wikimedia Commons

1930: Duke Ellington on page 33 from the Library of Congress

1931: Florence Reece on page 35 from patrickhyde.com

1932: Cab Calloway on page 37 by William P. Gottlieb

1933: Ethel Waters on page 39 by William P. Gottlieb

1934: Lead Belly on page 41 from the Library of Congress

1935: Carter Family on page 43 by Eric Schaal/The LIFE Picture Collection/Shutterstock

1936: Fred Astaire (*Swing Time* movie poster) on page 45 by William Rose/Wikimedia Commons

1937: Robert Johnson on page 47 by Robert Johnson Estate/Getty

1938: Benny Goodman on page 49 from the Library of Congress

1939: Billie Holiday singing on page 52 by William P. Gottlieb; Billie Holiday by the piano on page 53 by United Artists/Kobal/Shutterstock

1940: Woody Guthrie on page 59 by New York World-Telegram and the Sun staff photographer: Al Aumuller/Wikimedia Commons

1941: Glenn Miller on page 61 from an ad on page 27 of May 16, 1942, *Billboard* magazine/Wikimedia Commons

1942: Bing Crosby on page 63 by CBS Radio/Wikimedia Commons

1943: *Oklahoma!* on page 65 from the Library of Congress

1944: Frank Sinatra on page 67 by William P. Gottlieb/Wikimedia Commons

1945: Sister Rosetta Tharpe on page 69 by James J. Kriegsmann; published by Tharpe's management/Wikimedia Commons

1946: Charlie Parker on page 71 by William P. Gottlieb/Wikimedia Commons

1947: Mahalia Jackson on page 73 from ETH Library

1948: Nat King Cole on page 75 from the Library of Congress

1949: Hank Williams on page 77 by WSM radio/Wikimedia Commons

1950: Muddy Waters on page 83 by Jean-Luc Ourlin from Toronto, Ontario, Canada/Wikimedia Commons

1951: Jackie Brenston on page 86 by Michael Ochs Archives/Getty

1952: Gene Kelly, *Singing in the Rain* poster on page 89 by Loew's Incorporated/Wikimedia Commons

1953: Big Mama Thorton on page 92 by Barbara Weinberg Barefield/Wikimedia Commons

1954: Elvis Presley on page 94 by Rossano aka Bud Care/Wikimedia Commons

1955: Little Richard on page 97 by Okeh Records/Wikimedia Commons

1956: Johnny Cash autographing on page 100 by Sun Records/Cash Box, September 7, 1957; cover page Johnny Cash poster on page 101 by Sun Records/Billboard, May 12, 1956

1957: Patsy Cline on page 104 by Decca Records/Wikimedia Commons

1958: Miles Davis on page 107 by Tom Palumbo from New York City, USA/Wikimedia Commons

1959: Ornette Coleman on page 110 by JPRoche/Wikimedia Commons

1960: Ray Charles on page 117 by William Morris Agency (management)/Photo by Maurice Seymour, New York/Wikimedia Commons

1961: Marvelettes on page 120 by Everett/Shutterstock

1962: The Beatles on page 123 by United Press International, photographer unknown/Wikimedia Commons

1963: John Coltrane on page 126 by Gelderen, Hugo van/Anefo/Wikimedia Commons

1964: Sam Cooke on page 129 by RCA Victor Records/Wikimedia Commons

1965: Bob Dylan on page 132 by unknown photographer/Wikimedia Commons; Bob Dylan on page 133 by Rowland Scherman/Wikimedia Commons

1966: The Beach Boys on page 136 by Capitol Records/Wikimedia Commons

1967: Aretha Franklin on page 140 by Atlantic Records/Wikimedia Commons

1968: Jimi Hendrix on page 143 by Hannu Lindroos/Lehtikuva/Wikimedia Commons

1969: Velvet Underground on page 146 by unknown photographer; published by Verve Records, at that time a subsidiary of MGM Records

1970: Cutis Mayfield on page 153 by Everett/Shutterstock

1971: Carole King on page 156 by Kingkong-photo & www.celebrity-photos.com from Laurel Maryland, USA/Wikimedia Commons

1972: Stevie Wonder on page 159 by UCLA digital library/Wikimedia Commons

1973: Dolly Parton on page 162 by Armando Pietrangeli/Shutterstock

1974: The Hues Corporation on page 165 by Michael Putland/Getty

1975: Bruce Springsteen on page 168 by Columbia Records/Wikimedia Commons

1976: The Ramones on page 171 by Danny Fields/Wikimedia Commons

1977: Donna Summer on page 174, photograph by Francesco Scavullo. Distributed by Casablanca Records/Wikimedia Commons

1978: Blondie on page 177 by Private Stock Records/Wikimedia Commons

1979: The Sugar Hill Gang on page 180 by Erik Pendzich/Shutterstock

1980: Talking Heads on page 187 by Steve Richards/Shutterstock

1981: Black Flag on page 190 by UCLA Library Special Collections/Wikimedia Commons

1982: Grandmaster Flash & the Furious Five on page 193 by ITV/Shutterstock

1983: Metallica on page 196 by MediaPunch/Shutterstock

1984: Prince on page 199 by Yves Lorson from Kapellen, Belgium/Wikimedia Commons

1985: Madonna on page 202 by Tom Lynn/Wikimedia Commons

1986: Run-DMC and Aerosmith on page 205, screenshot from "RUN DMC - Walk This Way (Official HD Video) ft. Aerosmith"

1987: Michael Jackson on page 208 by Eugene Adebari/Shutterstock

1988: N.W.A. on page 211 by Shutterstock

1989: Public Enemy on page 214 by Jack Barron/Shutterstock

1990: MC Hammer on page 221 by Eugene Adebari/Shutterstock

1991: Nirvana on page 224 by Stephen Sweet/Shutterstock

1992: Rage Against the Machine on page 227 by Herbert P Oczeret/EPA/Shutterstock

1993: Bikini Kill on page 230 by Paul Hudson/Wikimedia Commons

1994: TLC on page 233 by Dave Lewis/Shutterstock

1995: Alanis Morissette on page 236 by Swift/Mediapunch/Shutterstock

1996: 2Pac Shakur on page 239 by Eli Reed/Columbia/Kobal/Shutterstock

1997: Biggie Smalls (with Tupac Shakur) on page 242 by Film Four/Lafayette/Kobal/Shutterstock

1998: Britney Spears on page 245 and page 246, screenshots from "Britney Spears - ...Baby One More Time (Official Video)"

1999: Eminem on page 248 by Mika-photography/Wikimedia Commons

2000: Outkast on page 255 by Shutterstock

2001: Missy Elliot on page 258 by Nikola Spasenoski/Shutterstock

2002: Justin Timberlake on page 261, screenshot from "Justin Timberlake - Cry Me A River (Official Video)"

2003: The White Stripes on page 264 by Fabio Venni from London, UK; modified by anetode/Wikimedia Commons

2004: Green Day on page 267 by Greg Allen/Shutterstock

2005: System of a Down on page 270 by A.PAES/Shutterstock

2006: My Chemical Romance on page 273, screenshot from "My Chemical Romance - Welcome To The Black Parade [Official Music Video] [HD]"; on page 274 by Huw John/Shutterstock

2007: Carrie Underwood on page 277 by Debby Wong/Shutterstock

2008: MGMT on page 280 by Melanie Lemahieu/Shutterstock

2009: Jay-Z on page 283 by Debby Wong/Shutterstock; The Blueprint 3 album artwork on page 284 by Roc Nation

2010: Kanye West on page 291, screenshot from "Kanye West - Runaway (Video Version) ft. Pusha T"; Kanye West on page 292 by Everett Collection/Shutterstock

2011: Lady Gaga on page 295 by Brian Friedman/Shutterstock

2012: Fun. on page 298 by MPH Photos/Shutterstock

2013: Miley Cyrus on page 301, screenshot from "Miley Cyrus - We Can't Stop (Official Video)"

2014: Taylor Swift on page 304 by Matt Baron/BEI/Shutterstock

2015: Kendrick Lamar on page 307 by Batiste Safont/Wikimedia Commons; Kendrick Lamar on page 308 by Kobby Dagan/Shutterstock

2016: Beyoncé on pages 311 and 312, screenshots from "Beyoncé - Formation (Official Video)"

2017: Luis Fonsi on page 315 by Andrea Raffin/Shutterstock

2018: Childish Gambino on page 318, screenshot from "Childish Gambino - This Is America (Official Video)"

2019: Billie Eilish on page 321, screenshot from "Billie Eilish - bad guy (Official Music Video)"; Billie Eilish on page 322 by DNCC/EPA-EFE/Shutterstock

2020: Run the Jewels on page 329 by Christian Bertrand/Shutterstock

2021: Lil Nas X on page 333 by DFree/Shutterstock

2022: Lizzo on page 336 by Ben Houdijk/Shutterstock

2023: Doja Cat on page 338, screenshot from "Doja Cat - Paint The Town Red (Official Video)"

Acknowledgments

There are quite literally a million people to thank for this book's existence. Well, technically 1,043,521 (and counting) at the time of this writing. I could not have gotten here without my incredible subscribers on YouTube, who have supported my channel and helped make talking about music my job. I'd especially like to thank my brother Zak, who was the very first of those subscribers and who sparked my passion for music from a young age. Thank you to the rest of my siblings, who handed me down their music tastes and helped me turn this book into a reality. Thank you, Dad, for thousands of great conversations about jazz and rock and for instilling in me a love of Steely Dan. Thank you, Mom, for gifting me the Beatles' *1* album for Christmas and opening my mind up to the world of music. Thank you to my wife, Emma, for always supporting my passion, and for putting up with me spinning these 100 songs over and over again throughout the past few months.

Thank you to my dauntless research assistant and true friend Matt, who was instrumental in hammering out the shape of these stories. Thanks to Mitto, Elliot, Scott, Jenny and all of the other music friends whose ears I've talked off with musical hot takes over the years. Thank you to my podcasting partner Cory for countless conversational diversions that have enriched my musical perspective. A huge thank-you to my writing mentor Claudia Casper, and everyone in my writers' circle who helped hone my writing skills over the last few years. Thank you to the kind folks at Page Street Publishing, who thought I might be able to write a book and who helped develop this idea into a reality. Finally, I want to thank each and every one of the artists who I name in this book. Without your artistic vision, my world would be a far less colorful place.

About the Author

Noah Lefevre is a Canadian music journalist, podcaster and video essayist. He is the creator behind Polyphonic, a YouTube channel with over a million subscribers and more than 100 million views. Noah's work deals with the intersections between popular music and sociocultural history. He also tackles these topics on his monthly podcast *Ghost Notes*. Noah has also worked with the CBC, the *Ottawa Citizen* and *Alternative Press Magazine*. Beyond his musical obsessions, Noah is an avid skier, a tabletop roleplay aficionado and a long-suffering fan of the Toronto Maple Leafs.

Index